THE IRON KING

SPECIAL EDITION

Books by Julie Kagawa
available from Inkyard Press

**(Each series listed in reading order. Novellas complement
the full books but do not need to be read to enjoy the series.)**

The Iron Fey

The Iron King (special edition includes "Winter's Passage"* novella)
The Iron Daughter (special edition includes the "Guide to the Iron Fey"*)
The Iron Queen (special edition includes "Summer's Crossing"* novella)
The Iron Knight (special edition includes "Iron's Prophecy"* novella)
The Lost Prince
The Iron Traitor
The Iron Warrior

Shadow of the Fox

Shadow of the Fox
Soul of the Sword
Night of the Dragon

The Talon Saga

Talon
Rogue
Soldier
Legion
Inferno

Blood of Eden

Dawn of Eden (prequel novella)+
The Immortal Rules
The Eternity Cure
The Forever Song

*Also available in *The Iron Legends* anthology
+Available in the *'Til the World Ends* anthology by Julie Kagawa,
Ann Aguirre and Karen Duvall

THE IRON KING

SPECIAL EDITION

JULIE KAGAWA

inkyard
press

Recycling programs
for this product may
not exist in your area.

ISBN-13: 978-1-335-01603-4

The Iron King Special Edition

First published as The Iron King in 2010. This edition published in 2020 with revised text.

Copyright © 2010 by Julie Kagawa

Copyright © 2020 by Julie Kagawa, revised text edition

Winter's Passage
First published in 2010. This edition published in 2020 with revised text.
Copyright © 2010 by Julie Kagawa
Copyright © 2020 by Julie Kagawa, revised text edition

This edition published by arrangement with Harlequin Books S.A.

For questions and comments about the quality of this book, please contact us at CustomerService@Harlequin.com.

Inkyard Press
22 Adelaide St. West, 40th Floor
Toronto, Ontario M5H 4E3, Canada
www.InkyardPress.com

Printed in U.S.A.

CONTENTS

For Nick, Brandon and Villis.
May we continue to beat those dead horses into the ground.

AUTHOR'S FOREWORD

When my publisher told me that they would be releasing special editions of the first four books in The Iron Fey series for its ten-year anniversary, I was ecstatic. The Iron Fey remains near and dear to my heart as both the first series I ever published and the works for which I'm probably best known. The opportunity to update and release it into the wild once more is a true gift.

When the idea for a story about faeries first began tickling my brain, the first thing that came to mind was a character: an ordinary girl who knew nothing about the fey or their dangerous world. Plunking a wholly unprepared Meghan into the middle of the Nevernever and watching her struggle to survive allowed me to fully explore the beautiful lethality of Faery, and allowed readers to experience the wonders, dangers and surrealness of the Nevernever alongside her. As Meghan continued her journey into Faery, another idea began poking around my brain. A question. What do the fey fear? What could frighten these ancient beings who live off the fear, love and emotions of mortals? The answer in almost all faery lore is iron. The fey cannot abide the touch of iron; it burns and repels them and, in some cases, kills them. And then, I remembered that another common killer of faeries is mortal disbelief. Human imagination and belief in magic created the fey…and when humans stop believing in magic and faeries, the fey slowly fade away and die.

Enter the iron fey, faeries born of mankind's love of progress and technology. Brought to life by humans' dreams of the newest tech, gadgets, gizmos and everything electronic in between, these beings were the antithesis to the original fey, and so a conflict between them and the rest of the Nevernever was inevitable. And so began Meghan Chase's quest to bridge the gap between these destructive new fey and the traditional realm of Faery.

I've always loved the old fairy tales that put a darker spin on things, that were meant to caution and frighten instead of entertain. The faeries of this series are the fey of myth and legend; they are the fickle Good Neighbors that haunt thick forests and lure men and women to their deaths. They are creatures that switch human infants with faery offspring, hunt mortals through the woods like rabbits and think nothing about making a human fall in love with them only to discard, abandon or kill them later. They are old creatures, ancient creatures, who, in the general sense, see humans as playthings. And the games of the fey can be sinister indeed. These are traits that all fey possess to some degree, which is what makes them both alluring and deadly, though the heroes of our tale strive against their baser natures, as all heroes should.

So, if you ever find yourself wandering through the realms of Faery, be forewarned—it is a dangerous place, a place where the very landscape can poison you, and where an invitation to dinner might mean that you are the main course. And remember that the fey are old beings, set in their ways and, if you're not careful, may try to steal a kiss—or your very soul—beneath the pale rays of the moon.

The Iron Fey series has come a long way. I'm eternally grateful for my readers and fans who love the Iron Fey world, who started this journey with me and have followed this series through to the end. It is my hope that new readers will discover the magic of the Nevernever, and that old fans will fall in love with the world and the characters all over again, with Meghan, Ash, Puck and Grimalkin. For as long as Faery is remembered, it will never fade away.

Thank you for reading!

Julie Kagawa

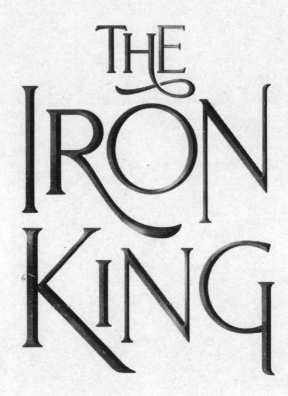

PART

I

THE GHOST IN THE COMPUTER

Ten years ago, on my sixth birthday, my father disappeared. No, he didn't leave. Leaving would imply suitcases and empty drawers, and late birthday cards with ten-dollar bills stuffed inside. Leaving would imply he was unhappy with Mom and me, or that he found a new love elsewhere. None of that was true. He also did not die, because we would've heard about it. There was no car crash, no body, no police mingling about the scene of a brutal murder. It all happened very quietly.

On my sixth birthday, my father took me to the park, one of my favorite places to go at that time. It was a lonely little park in the middle of nowhere, with a running trail and a misty green pond surrounded by pine trees. We were at the edge of the pond, feeding the ducks, when I heard the jingle of an ice cream truck in the parking lot over the hill. When I begged my dad to get me a Creamsicle, he laughed, handed me a few bills, and sent me after the truck.

That was the last time I saw him.

Later, when the police searched the area, they discovered

his shoes at the edge of the water, but nothing else. They sent divers into the pond, but it was barely ten feet down, and they found nothing but branches and mud at the bottom. My father had disappeared without a trace.

For months afterward, I had a recurring nightmare about standing at the top of that hill, looking down and seeing my father walk into the pond. As the water closed over his head, I could hear the ice cream truck singing in the background, a slow, eerie song with words I could almost understand. Every time I tried to listen to them, however, I'd wake up.

Not long after my father's disappearance, Mom moved us far away, to a tiny little hick town in the middle of the Louisiana bayou. Mom said she wanted to "start over," but I always knew, deep down, that she was running from something.

It would be another ten years before I discovered what.

My name is Meghan Chase.

In less than twenty-four hours, I'll be sixteen years old.

Sweet sixteen. It has a magical ring to it. Sixteen is supposed to be the age when girls become princesses and fall in love and go to dances and proms and such. Countless stories, songs, and poems have been written about this wonderful age, when a girl finds true love and the stars shine for her and the handsome prince carries her off into the sunset.

I didn't think it would be that way for me.

The morning before my birthday, I woke up, showered, and rummaged through my dresser for something to wear. Normally, I'd just grab whatever clean-ish thing is on the floor, but today was special. Today was the day Scott Waldron would finally notice me. I wanted to look perfect. Of course, my wardrobe is sadly lacking in the popular-attire department. While other girls spend hours in front of their closets crying, "What should I wear?" my drawers basically hold three things: clothes from Goodwill, hand-me-downs, and overalls.

I wish we weren't so poor. I know pig farming isn't the most glamorous of jobs, but you'd think Mom could afford to buy me at least one pair of nice jeans. I glared at my scanty wardrobe in disgust. *Oh, well, I guess Scott will have to be wowed with my natural grace and charm, if I don't make an idiot of myself in front of him.*

I finally slipped into cargo pants, a neutral green T-shirt, and my only pair of ratty sneakers, before dragging a brush through my white-blond hair. My hair is straight and very fine, and was doing that stupid floating thing again, where it looked like I'd jammed my finger up an electrical outlet. Yanking it into a ponytail, I went downstairs.

Luke, my stepfather, sat at the table, drinking coffee and leafing through the town's tiny newspaper, which reads more like our high school gossip column than a real news source. "Five-legged calf born on Patterson's farm," the front page screamed; you get the idea. Ethan, my four-year-old half brother, sat on his father's lap, eating a Pop-Tart and getting crumbs all over Luke's overalls. He clutched Floppy, his favorite stuffed rabbit, in one arm and occasionally tried to feed it his breakfast; the rabbit's face was full of crumbs and fruit filling.

Ethan is a good kid. He has his father's curly brown hair, but like me, inherited Mom's big blue eyes. He's the type of kid old ladies stop to coo at, and total strangers smile and wave at him from across the street. Mom and Luke dote on their baby, but it doesn't seem to spoil him, thank goodness.

"Where's Mom?" I asked as I entered the kitchen. Opening the cabinet doors, I scoured the boxes of cereal for the one I liked, wondering if Mom remembered to pick it up. Of course she hadn't. Nothing but fiber squares and disgusting marshmallow cereals for Ethan. Was it so hard to remember Cheerios?

Luke ignored me and sipped his coffee. Ethan chewed his Pop-Tart and sneezed on his father's arm. I slammed the cabinet doors with a satisfying bang.

"Where's Mom?" I asked, a bit louder this time. Luke jerked his head up and finally looked at me. His lazy brown eyes, like those of a cow, registered mild surprise.

"Oh, hello, Meg," he said calmly. "I didn't hear you come in. What did you say?"

I sighed and repeated my question for the third time.

"She had a meeting with some of the ladies at church," Luke murmured, turning back to his paper. "She won't be back for a few hours, so you'll have to take the bus."

I always took the bus. I just wanted to remind Mom that she was supposed to take me to get a learner's permit this weekend. With Luke, it was hopeless. I could tell him something fourteen different times, and he'd forget it the moment I left the room. It wasn't that Luke was mean or malicious, or even stupid. He adored Ethan, and Mom seemed truly happy with him. But, every time I spoke to my stepdad, he would look at me with genuine surprise, as if he'd forgotten I lived here, too.

I grabbed a bagel from the top of the fridge and chewed it sullenly, keeping an eye on the clock. Beau, our German shepherd, wandered in and put his big head on my knee. I scratched him behind the ears and he groaned. At least the *dog* appreciated me.

Luke stood, gently placing Ethan back in his seat. "All right, big guy," he said, kissing the top of Ethan's head. "Dad has to fix the bathroom sink, so you sit there and be good. When I'm done, we'll go feed the pigs, okay?"

"'Kay," Ethan chirped, swinging his chubby legs. "Floppy wants to see if Ms. Daisy had her babies yet."

Luke's smile was so disgustingly proud, I felt nauseous.

"Hey, Luke," I said as he turned to go, "bet you can't guess what tomorrow is."

"Mmm?" He didn't even turn around. "I don't know, Meg. If you have plans for tomorrow, talk to your mother." He snapped his fingers, and Beau immediately left me to follow him. Their footsteps faded up the stairs, and I was alone with my half brother.

Ethan kicked his feet, regarding me in that solemn way of his. "I know," he announced softly, putting his Pop-Tart on the table. "Tomorrow's your birthday, isn't it? Floppy told me, and I remembered."

"Yeah," I muttered, turning and lobbing the bagel into the trash can. It hit the wall with a thump and dropped inside, leaving a greasy smear on the paint. I smirked and decided to leave it.

"Floppy says to tell you happy early birthday."

"Tell Floppy thanks." I ruffled Ethan's hair as I left the kitchen, my mood completely soured. I knew it. Mom and Luke would completely forget my birthday tomorrow. I wouldn't get a card, or a cake, or even a "happy birthday" from anyone. Except my kid brother's stupid stuffed rabbit. How pathetic was that?

Back in my room, I grabbed books, homework, gym clothes, and the phone I'd spent a year saving for, despite Luke's disdain of those "useless, brain-numbing gadgets." My stepfather is stuck in the stone age; he dislikes and distrusts anything that could make life easier. Cell phones for the family? No way, we've got a perfectly good landline. Video games? They're the devil's tools, turning kids into delinquents and serial killers. I've begged Mom over and over to buy me a laptop for school, but Luke insists that if his ancient, clunky

PC is good enough for him, it's good enough for the family. Never mind that our wifi takes flipping *forever*.

I checked my watch and swore. The bus would arrive shortly, and I had a good ten-minute walk to the main road. Looking out the window, I saw the sky was gray and heavy with rain, so I grabbed a jacket, as well. And, not for the first time, I wished we lived closer to town.

I swear, when I get a license and a car, I am never coming back to this place.

"Meggie?" Ethan hovered in the doorway, clutching his rabbit under his chin. His blue eyes regarded me somberly. "Can I go with you today?"

"What?" Shrugging into my jacket, I gazed around for my backpack. "No, Ethan. I'm going to school now. Big-kids school, no rug rats allowed."

I turned away, only to feel two small arms wrap around my leg. Putting my hand against the wall to avoid falling, I glared down at my half brother. Ethan clung to me doggedly, his face tilted up to mine, his jaw set. "Please?" he begged. "I'll be good, I promise. Take me with you? Just for today?"

With a sigh, I bent down and picked him up.

"What's up, squirt?" I asked, brushing his hair out of his eyes. Mom would need to cut it soon; it was starting to look like a bird's nest. "You're awfully clingy this morning. What's going on?"

"Scared," Ethan muttered, burying his face in my neck.

"You're scared?"

He shook his head. "Floppy's scared."

"What's Floppy scared of?"

"The man in the closet."

I felt a small chill slide up my back. Sometimes, Ethan was so quiet and serious, it was hard to remember he was only four. He still had childish fears of monsters under his bed and bogeymen in his closet. In Ethan's world, stuffed animals spoke to him, invisible men waved to him from the bushes, and scary creatures tapped long nails against his bedroom window. He rarely went to Mom or Luke with stories of monsters and bogeymen; from the time he was old enough to walk, he always came to me.

I sighed, knowing he wanted me to go upstairs and check, to reassure him that nothing lurked in his closet or under his bed. I kept a flashlight on his dresser for that very reason.

Outside, lightning flickered, and thunder rumbled in the distance. I winced. My walk to the bus was not going to be pleasant.

Dammit, I don't have time for this.

Ethan pulled back and looked at me, eyes pleading. I sighed again. "Fine," I muttered, putting him down. "Let's go check for monsters."

He followed me silently up the stairs, watching anxiously as I grabbed the flashlight and got down on my knees, shining it under the bed. "No monsters there," I announced, standing up. I walked to the closet door and flung it open as Ethan peeked out from behind my legs. "No monsters here, either. Think you'll be all right now?"

He nodded and gave me a faint smile. I started to close the door when I noticed a strange gray hat in the corner. It was domed on top, with a circular rim and a red band around the base: a bowler hat.

Weird. Why would that be there?

As I straightened and started to turn around, something moved out of the corner of my eye. I caught a glimpse of a figure hiding behind Ethan's bedroom door, its pale eyes watching me through the crack. I jerked my head around, but of course there was nothing there.

Jeez, now Ethan's got me seeing imaginary monsters. I need to stop watching those late-night horror flicks.

A thunderous boom directly overhead made me jump, and fat drops plinked against the windowpanes. Rushing past Ethan, I burst out of the house and sprinted down the driveway.

I was soaked when I reached the bus stop. The late spring rain wasn't frigid, but it was cold enough to be uncomfortable. I crossed my arms and huddled under a mossy cypress, waiting for the bus to arrive.

Wonder where Robbie is? I mused, gazing down the road. *He's usually here by now. Maybe he didn't feel like getting drenched and stayed home.* I snorted and rolled my eyes. *Skipping class again, huh? Slacker. Wish I could do that.*

If only I had a car. I knew kids whose parents gave *them* cars for their sixteenth birthday. Me, I'd be lucky if I got a cake. Most of my classmates already had licenses and could drive themselves to clubs and parties and anywhere they wanted. I was always left behind, the backward hick girl nobody wanted to invite.

Except Robbie, I amended with a small mental shrug. *At least Robbie will remember. Wonder what kooky thing he has planned for my birthday tomorrow?* I could almost guarantee it would be something strange or crazy. Last year, he snuck me out of the house for a midnight picnic in the woods. It was weird; I remembered the glen and the little pond with the fireflies drifting over it, but though I explored the woods behind my house countless times since then, I never found it again.

Something rustled in the bushes behind me. A possum or a deer, or even a fox, seeking shelter from the rain. The wildlife out here was stupidly bold and had little fear of humans. If it wasn't for Beau, Mom's vegetable garden would be a buffet for rabbits and deer, and the local raccoon family would help themselves to everything in our cupboards.

A branch snapped in the trees, closer this time. I shifted uncomfortably, determined not to turn around for some stupid squirrel or raccoon. I'd lived in the woods nearly all my life. I'd pitched hay and killed rats and driven pigs through knee-deep mud. Wild animals didn't scare me.

Still, I stared down the road, hoping to see the bus turn the corner. Maybe it was the rain and my own sick imagination, but the woods felt like the set for *The Blair Witch Project*.

There are no wolves or serial killers out here, I told myself. *Stop being paranoid.*

The forest was suddenly very quiet. I leaned against the tree and shivered, trying to will the bus into appearing. A chill crawled up my back. I wasn't alone. Cautiously, I craned my neck up, peering through the leaves. An enormous black bird perched on a branch, feathers spiked out against the rain, sitting as motionless as a statue. As I watched, it turned its head and met my gaze, with eyes as green as colored glass.

And then, something reached around the tree and grabbed me.

I screamed and leaped away, my heart hammering in my ears. Whirling around, I tensed to run, my mind filled with rapists and murderers and Leatherface from *The Texas Chainsaw Massacre*.

Laughter exploded behind me.

Robbie Goodfell, my closest neighbor—meaning he lived nearly two miles away—slouched against the tree trunk, gasping with mirth. Lanky and tall, in tattered jeans and an old T-shirt, he paused to look at my pale face, before cracking up again. His spiky red hair lay plastered to his forehead and his clothes clung to his skin, emphasizing his lean, bony frame, as though his limbs didn't fit quite right. Being drenched and covered in twigs, leaves, and mud didn't seem to bother him. Few things did.

"Dammit, Robbie!" I raged, stomping up and aiming a kick at him. He dodged and staggered into the road, his face red from laughter. "That wasn't funny, you idiot. You nearly gave me a heart attack."

"S-sorry, princess," Robbie gasped, clutching his heart as he sucked in air. "It was just too perfect." He gave a final chortle and straightened, holding his ribs. "Man, that was impressive. You must've jumped three feet in the air. What, did you think I was, Leatherface or something?"

"Of course not, stupid." I turned away with a huff to hide my burning face. "And I told you to stop calling me that! I'm not ten anymore."

"Sure thing, princess."

I rolled my eyes. "Has anyone told you you have the maturity level of a four-year-old?"

He laughed cheerfully. "Look who's talking. I'm not the one who stayed up all night with the lights on after watching *The Texas Chainsaw Massacre.* I tried to warn you." He made a grotesque face and staggered toward me, arms outstretched. "Ooooh, look out, it's Leatherface."

I scowled and kicked water at him. He kicked some back, laughing. By the time the bus showed up a few minutes later, we were both covered in mud, dripping wet, and the bus driver told us to sit in the back.

"What are you doing after school?" Robbie asked as we huddled in the far backseat. Around us, students talked, joked, laughed, and generally paid us no attention. "Wanna grab a coffee later? Or we could sneak into the theater and see a movie."

"Not today, Rob," I replied, trying to wring water from my shirt. Now that it was over, I dearly regretted our little mud battle. I was going to look like the Creature from the Black Lagoon in front of Scott. "You'll have to do your sneaking without me this time. I'm tutoring someone after class."

Robbie's green eyes narrowed. "Tutoring someone? Who?"

My stomach fluttered, and I tried not to grin. "Scott Waldron."

"What?" Robbie's lip curled in a grimace of disgust. "The jockstrap? Why, does he need you to teach him how to read?"

I scowled at him. "Just because he's captain of the football team doesn't mean you can be a jerk. Or are you jealous?"

"Oh, of course, that's it," Robbie said with a sneer. "I've always wanted the IQ of a rock. No, wait. That would be an insult to the rock." He snorted. "I can't believe you're interested in that meathead. You can do so much better, princess."

"Don't call me that." I turned away to hide my burning face. "And it's just a tutoring session. He's not going to ask me to the prom. Jeez."

"Right." Robbie sounded unconvinced. "He's not, but you're *hoping* he will. Just admit it."

"So what if I am?" I snapped, spinning around. "It's none of your business, Rob. What do you care, anyway?"

He got very quiet, muttering something unintelligible under his breath. I turned my back on him and stared out the window. I didn't care what Robbie said. This afternoon, for one glorious hour, Scott Waldron would be mine alone, and no one would distract me from that.

School dragged. The teachers all spoke gibberish, and the clocks seemed to be moving backward. The afternoon crept by in a daze. Finally, finally, the last bell rang, freeing me from the endless torture of X equals Y problems.

Today is the day, I told myself as I maneuvered the crowded hallways, keeping to the edge of the teeming mass. Wet sneakers squeaked over tile, and a miasma of sweat, smoke, and body odor hung thick in the air. Nervousness fluttered inside me. *You can do this. Don't think about it. Just go in and get it over with.*

Dodging students, I wove my way down the hall and peeked into the computer room.

There he was, sitting at one of the desks with both feet up on another chair. Scott Waldron, captain of the football team. Gorgeous Scott. King-of-the-school Scott. He wore a red-and-white letterman jacket that showed off his broad chest, and his thick dark blond hair brushed the top of his collar.

My heart pounded. *A whole hour in the same room with Scott Waldron, with no one to get in the way.* Normally, I couldn't even get close to Scott; he was either surrounded by Angie and her cheerleader groupies, or his football buddies. There were other students in the computer lab with us, but they were nerds and academic types, beneath Scott Waldron's notice. The jocks and cheerleaders wouldn't be caught dead in here if they could help it. I took a deep breath and stepped into the room.

He didn't glance at me when I walked up beside him. He lounged in the chair with his feet up and his head back, tossing an invisible ball across the room. I cleared my throat. Nothing. I cleared it a little louder. Still nothing.

Gathering my courage, I stepped in front of him and waved. His coffee-brown eyes finally jerked up to mine. For a moment, he looked startled. Then an eyebrow rose in a lazy arc, as if he couldn't figure out why I wanted to talk to him.

Uh-oh. Say something, Meg. Something intelligent.

"Um…" I stammered. "Hi. I'm Meghan. I sit behind you. In computer class." He was still giving me that blank stare, and I felt my cheeks getting hot. "Uh… I really don't watch a lot of sports, but I think you're an awesome quarterback, not that I've seen many—well, just you, actually. But you really seem to know what you're doing. I go to all your games, you know. I'm usually in the very back, so you probably don't see me." *Oh, God. Shut up, Meg. Shut up now.* I clamped my mouth closed to stop the incessant babbling, wanting to crawl into a hole and die. What was I thinking, agreeing to this? Better to be invisible than to look like a complete and total moron, especially in front of Scott.

He blinked lazily, reached up, and pulled the earbuds from his ears. "Sorry," he drawled in that wonderful, deep voice of his. "I couldn't hear you." He gave me a once-over and smirked. "Are you supposed to be the tutor?"

"Um, yes." I straightened and smoothed out my remaining shreds of dignity. "I'm Meghan. Mr. Sanders asked me to help you out with your programming project."

He continued to smirk at me. "Aren't you that hick girl who lives out in the swamp? Do you even know what a computer is?"

My face flamed, and my stomach contracted into a tight little ball. Okay, so I didn't have a great computer at home. That was why I spent most of my after-school time here, in the lab, doing homework or just surfing online. In fact, I was hoping to make it into ITT Tech in a couple of years. Programming and Web design came easily to me. I knew how to work a computer, dammit.

But, in the face of Scott's criticism, I could only stammer: "Y-yes, I do. I mean, I know a lot." He gave me a dubious look, and I felt the sting of wounded pride. I had to prove to him that I wasn't the backward hillbilly he thought I was. "Here, I'll show you," I offered, and reached toward the keyboard on the table.

Then something weird happened.

I hadn't even touched the keys when the computer screen blipped on. When I paused, my fingers hovering over the board, words began to scroll across the blue screen.

Meghan Chase. We see you. We're coming for you.

I froze. The words continued, those three sentences, over and over. *Meghan Chase. We see you. We're coming for you. Meghan Chase we see you we're coming for you. MeghanChasewese eyouwe'recomingforyou...*over and over until it completely filled the screen.

Scott leaned back in his seat, glaring at me, then at the computer. "What is this?" he asked, scowling. "What the hell are you doing, freak?" Pushing him aside, I shook the mouse, punched Escape, and pressed Ctrl/Alt/Del to stop the endless string of words. Nothing worked.

Suddenly, without warning, the words stopped, and the screen went blank for a moment. Then, in giant letters, another message flashed into view.

SCOTT WALDRON PEEKS AT GUYS IN THE SHOWER ROOM, ROFL.

I gasped. The message began to scroll across all the computer screens, wending its way around the room, with me powerless to stop it. The other students at the desks paused, shocked for a moment, then began to point and laugh.

I could feel Scott's gaze like a knife in my back. Fearfully, I turned to find him glaring at me, chest heaving. His face was crimson, probably from rage or embarrassment, and he jabbed a finger in my direction.

"You think that's funny, swamp girl? Do you? Just wait. I'll show you funny. You just dug your own grave, bitch."

He stormed out of the room with the echo of laughter trailing behind him. A few of the students gave me grins, applause, and thumbs-up; one of them even winked at me.

My knees were shaking. I dropped into a chair and stared blankly at the computer screen, which suddenly flicked off, taking the offensive message with it, but the damage was already done. My stomach roiled, and there was a stinging sensation behind my eyes.

I buried my face in my hands. *I'm dead. I'm so dead. That's it, game over, Meghan. I wonder if Mom will let me move to a boarding school in Canada?*

A faint snicker cut through my bleak thoughts, and I raised my head.

Crouched atop the monitor, silhouetted black against the open window, was a tiny, misshapen *thing*. Spindly and emaciated, it had long, thin arms and huge batlike ears. Slitted green eyes regarded me across the table, gleaming with intelligence. It grinned, showing off a mouthful of pointed teeth that glowed with neon-blue light, before it vanished, like an image on the computer screen.

I sat there a moment, staring at the spot where the creature had been, my mind spinning in a dozen directions at once. *Okay. Great. Not only does Scott hate me, I'm starting to hallucinate, as well. Meghan Chase, victim of a nervous breakdown the day before she turned sixteen.*

Dragging myself upright, I shuffled, zombielike, into the hall.

Robbie waited for me by the lockers, a soda bottle in each hand. "Hey, princess," he greeted as I shambled past. "You're out early. How'd the tutoring session go?"

"Don't call me that," I muttered, banging my forehead into my locker. "And the tutoring session was fabulous. Please kill me now."

"That good, huh?" He tossed me a diet soda, which I barely caught, and twisted open his root beer in a hiss of foam. I could hear the grin in his voice. "Well, I suppose I could say 'I told you so—'"

I glared daggers at him, daring him to continue.

The smile vanished from his face. "—but... I won't." He

29

pursed his lips, trying not to grin. "'Cause...that would just be wrong."

"What are you doing here, anyway?" I demanded. "The buses have all left by now. Were you *lurking* by the computer lab, like some creepy stalker guy?"

Rob coughed loudly and took a long sip of his root beer. "Hey, I was wondering," he continued brightly, "what are you doing for your birthday tomorrow?"

Hiding in my room, with the covers over my head, I thought, but shrugged and yanked open my rusty locker. "I dunno. Whatever. I don't have anything planned." I grabbed my books, stuffed them in my bag, and slammed the locker door. "Why?"

Robbie gave me that smile that always makes me nervous, a grin that stretched his entire face so that his eyes narrowed to green slits. "I've got a bottle of champagne I managed to swipe from the wine cabinet," he said in a low voice, waggling his eyebrows. "How 'bout I come by your place tomorrow? We can celebrate your birthday in style."

I'd never had champagne. I did try a sip of Luke's beer once, and thought I was going to throw up. Mom sometimes brought home wine in a box, and that wasn't terrible, but I wasn't much of an alcohol drinker.

What the hell? You're only sixteen once, right? "Sure," I told Robbie, and gave a resigned shrug. "Sounds good. Might as well go out with a bang."

He cocked his head at me. "You okay, princess?"

What could I tell him? That the captain of the football team, whom I'd been crushing on for two years, was out to get me, that I was seeing monsters at every turn, and that the school computers were either hacked or possessed? Yeah, right. I'd get no sympathy from the school's greatest prankster. Knowing Robbie, he'd think it was a brilliant joke and congratulate me. If I didn't know him better, I might even think he set it up.

I just gave him a tired smile and nodded. "I'm fine. I'll see you tomorrow, Robbie."

"See you then, princess."

Mom was late picking me up, again. The tutoring session was only supposed to be an hour, but I sat on the curb, in the drizzling rain, for another good half hour, contemplating my miserable life and watching cars pull in and out of the parking lot. Finally, her blue station wagon turned the corner and pulled to a stop in front of me. The front seat was filled with grocery bags and newspapers, so I slid into the back.

"Meg, you're sopping wet," cried my mother, watching me from the rearview mirror. "Don't sit on the upholstery—get a towel or something. Didn't you bring an umbrella?"

Nice to see you, too, Mom, I thought, scowling as I grabbed a newspaper off the floor to put on the seat. No "how was your day?" or "sorry I'm late." I should've abandoned the stupid tutoring session with Scott and taken the bus home.

We drove in silence. People used to tell me I looked like her, that is, before Ethan came along and swallowed up the spotlight. To this day, I don't know where they saw the resemblance. Mom is one of those ladies who looks natural in a three-piece suit and heels; me, I like baggy cargo pants and sneakers. Mom's hair hangs in thick golden ringlets; mine is limp and fine, almost silver if it catches the light just right. She looks regal and graceful and slender; I just look skinny.

Mom could've married anyone in the world—a movie star, a rich business tycoon—but she chose Luke the pig farmer and a shabby little farm out in the sticks. Which reminded me…

"Hey, Mom. Don't forget, you have to take me to get a permit this weekend."

"Oh, Meg." Mom sighed. "I don't know. I've got a lot of

work this week, and your father wants me to help him fix the barn. Maybe next week."

"Mom, you promised!"

"Meghan, please. I've had a long day." Mom sighed again and looked back at me in the mirror. Her eyes were bloodshot and ringed with smeared mascara. I shifted uncomfortably. Had Mom been crying?

"What's up?" I asked cautiously.

She hesitated. "There was an...accident at home," she began, and her voice made my insides squirm. "Your father had to take Ethan to the hospital this afternoon." She paused again, blinking rapidly, and took a short breath. "Beau attacked him."

"What?" My outburst made her start. *Our* German shepherd? Attacking Ethan? "Is Ethan all right?" I demanded, feeling my stomach twist in fear.

"Yes." Mom gave me a tired smile. "Very shaken up, but nothing serious, thank God."

I breathed a sigh of relief. "What happened?" I asked, still unable to believe our dog actually attacked a family member. Beau adored Ethan; he got upset if anyone even scolded my half brother. I'd seen Ethan yanking on Beau's fur, ears, and tail, and the dog barely responded with a lick. I'd seen Beau take Ethan's sleeve and gently tug him back from the driveway. Our German shepherd might be a terror to squirrels and deer, but he'd never even shown teeth to anyone in the house. "Why did Beau go crazy like that?"

Mom shook her head. "I don't know. Luke saw Beau run up the stairs, then heard Ethan screaming. When he got to his room, he found the dog dragging Ethan across the floor. His face was badly scratched, and there were bite marks on his arm."

My blood ran cold. I saw Ethan being mauled, imagined

his absolute terror when our previously trustworthy shepherd turned on him. It was so hard to believe, like something out of a horror movie. I knew Mom was just as stunned as I was; she'd trusted Beau completely.

Still, Mom was holding back, I could tell by the way she pressed her lips together. There was something she wasn't telling me, and I was afraid I knew what it was.

"What will happen to Beau?"

Her eyes filled with tears, and my heart sank. "We can't have a dangerous dog running around, Meg," she said, and I heard the plea for understanding. "If Ethan asks, tell him that we found Beau another home." She took a deep breath and gripped the steering wheel tightly, not looking at me. "It's for the safety of the family, Meghan. Don't blame your father. But, after Luke brought Ethan home, he took Beau to the pound."

2

RINGTONE OF DOOM

Dinner was tense that night. I was furious at both my parents: Luke for doing the deed, and Mom for allowing him to do it. I refused to speak to either of them. Mom and Luke talked between themselves about useless, trivial stuff, and Ethan sat clutching Floppy in silence. It was weird not having Beau pacing round the table like he always did, looking for crumbs. I excused myself early and retreated to my room, slamming the door behind me.

I flopped back on my bed, remembering all the times Beau had curled up here with me, a solid, warm presence. He never asked anyone for anything, content just to be near, making sure his charges were safe. Now he was gone, and the house seemed emptier for it.

I wished I could talk to someone. I wanted to call Robbie and rant about the total unfairness of it all, but his parents—who were even more reclusive than mine, apparently—didn't have a phone, or even a computer. And neither did Robbie. Talk about living in the Dark Ages. Rob and I made our plans at school, or sometimes he would just show up outside my window, having walked the two miles to my house. It was a total pain in the ass, something I fully intended to fix once I got my own car. Mom and Luke couldn't keep me in this isolated bubble forever. Maybe my next big purchase would be cell phones for *both* of us, and screw what Luke thought about that. This whole "technology is evil" thing was getting really old.

There was a timid knock on the door, and Ethan's head peeked inside.

"Hey, squirt." I sat up on the bed, swiping at a few stray tears. A dinosaur Band-Aid covered his forehead, and his right arm was wrapped in gauze. "What's up?"

"Mommy and Daddy sent Beau away." His lower lip trembled, and he hiccuped, wiping his eyes on Floppy's fur. I sighed and patted the bed.

"They had to," I explained as he clambered up and snuggled into my lap, rabbit and all. "They didn't want Beau to bite you again. They were afraid you'd get hurt."

"Beau didn't bite me." Ethan gazed back at me with wide, teary eyes. I saw fear in them, and an understanding that went way beyond his years. "Beau didn't hurt me," he insisted. "Beau was trying to save me from the man in the closet."

Monsters again? I sighed, wanting to dismiss it, but a part of me hesitated. What if Ethan was right? I'd been seeing weird things, too, lately. What if...what if Beau really was protecting Ethan from something horrible and terrifying...?

No! I shook my head. This was ridiculous! I'd be turning sixteen in a few hours; that was way too old to believe in monsters. And it was high time Ethan grew up, as well. He was a smart kid, and I was getting tired of him blaming imaginary bogeymen whenever something went wrong.

"Ethan." I sighed again, trying not to appear cranky. If I was too harsh, he'd probably start bawling, and I didn't want to upset him after all he'd gone through today. Still, this had gone far enough. "There are no monsters in your closet, Ethan. There's no such thing as monsters, okay?"

"Yes, there are!" He scowled and kicked his feet into the covers. "I've seen them. They talk to me. They say the king wants to see me." He held out his arm, showing me the bandage. "The man in the closet grabbed me here. He was pulling me under the bed when Beau came in and scared him off."

Clearly, I wasn't going to change his mind. And I really didn't want a temper tantrum in my room right now. "Okay, fine," I relented, wrapping my arms around him. "Let's say something other than Beau grabbed you today. Why don't you tell Mom and Luke?"

"They're grown-ups," Ethan said, as if it was perfectly clear. "They won't believe me. They can't see the monsters." He sighed and looked at me with the gravest expression I'd ever seen on a kid. "But Floppy says *you* can see them. If you try hard enough. You can see through the Mist and the glamour, Floppy says so."

"The what and the what?"

"Ethan?" Mom's voice floated outside the door, and her silhouette appeared in the frame. "Are you in here?" Seeing us together, she blinked and offered a tentative smile. I glared back stonily.

Mom ignored me. "Ethan, honey, time to get ready for bed. It's been a long day." She held out her hand, and Ethan hopped down to pad across the room, dragging his rabbit behind him.

"Can I sleep with you and Daddy?" I heard him ask, his voice small and scared.

"Oh, I guess so. Just for tonight, okay?"

"'Kay." Their voices faded away down the hall, and I kicked my door shut.

That night, I had a strange dream about waking up and seeing Floppy, Ethan's stuffed rabbit, at the foot of my bed. In the dream, the rabbit was speaking to me, words that were grave and terrifying, filled with danger. It wanted to warn me, or it wanted me to help. I might have promised it something. The next morning, however, I couldn't remember much of the dream at all.

I woke to the sound of rain drumming on the roof. My birthday seemed destined to be cold, ugly, and wet. For a moment, a heavy weight pressed at the back of my mind, though I didn't know why I felt so depressed. Then everything from the previous day came back to me, and I groaned.

Happy birthday to me, I thought, burrowing under the covers. *I'll be spending the rest of the week in bed, thanks.*

"Meghan?" Mom's voice sounded outside my door, followed by a timid knock. "It's getting late. Are you up yet?"

I ignored her and curled up farther into the covers. Resentment simmered as I thought of poor Beau, carted off to the pound. Mom knew I was mad at her, but she could stew in her guilt for a while. I wasn't ready to pretend everything was fine just yet.

"Meghan, get up. You're going to miss the bus," said Mom, poking her head in the room. Her tone was matter-of-fact, and I snorted. So much for stewing in guilt.

"I'm not going to school," I muttered from beneath the covers. "I don't feel good. I think I've got the flu."

"Sick? On your birthday? That's unfortunate." Mom came into the room, and I peeked at her through a crack in the blankets. She remembered?

"Very sad," Mom continued, smiling at me and crossing her arms. "I was going to take you to get a learner's permit after school today, but if you're sick…"

I popped up. "Really? Um…well, I guess I don't feel all that bad. I'll just take some aspirin or something."

"I thought so." Mom shook her head as I bounced to my feet. "I'm helping your father fix the barn this afternoon, so I can't pick you up. But, as soon as you get home, we'll go to the license bureau together. That sound like a good birthday present?"

I barely heard her. I was too busy racing around the room, grabbing clothes and getting my stuff together. The sooner I got through the day, the better.

I was stuffing homework into my backpack when the door creaked open again. Ethan peeked in the doorway, his hands behind his back, a shy, expectant smile on his face.

I blinked at him and pushed back my hair. "What do you need, squirt?"

With a grin, he stepped forward and held out a folded piece of paper. Bright crayon drawings decorated the front; a smiley-faced sun hovered over a little house with smoke curling from the chimney.

"Happy birthday, Meggie," he said, quite pleased with himself. "See how I remembered?"

Smiling, I took the homemade card and opened it. Inside, a simple crayon drawing of our family smiled back: stick figures of Mom and Luke, me and Ethan holding hands, and a four-legged critter that had to be Beau. I felt a lump in my throat, and my eyes watered for just a moment.

"You like it?" Ethan asked, watching me anxiously.

"I love it," I said, ruffling his hair. "Thank you. Here, why don't you put it on the fridge, so everyone can see what a great artist you are."

He grinned and scampered off, clutching the card, and I felt my heart get a little bit lighter. Maybe today wouldn't be so terrible, after all.

★ ★ ★

"So, your mom is taking you to get a permit today?" Robbie asked as the bus pulled into the school parking lot. "That's cool. You can finally drive us downtown and to the movies. We won't have to depend on the bus, or spend another evening the same five channels on your twelve-inch screen."

"It's only a permit, Rob." I gathered my backpack as the bus lurched to a halt. "I won't have my license yet. Knowing Mom, it'll be another sixteen years before I can drive the car on my own. Ethan will probably get a license before I do."

The thought of my half brother sent an unexpected chill through me. I remembered his words from the night before: *You can see through the Mist and the glamour, Floppy says so.*

Stuffed rabbit aside, I had no idea what he was talking about.

As I walked down the bus steps, a familiar figure broke away from a large group and came striding toward me. Scott. My stomach twisted, and I gazed around for a suitable escape route, but before I could flee into the crowd, he was already in front of me.

"Hey." His voice, drawling and deep, made me shiver. Terrified as I was, he was still gorgeous, with his damp blond hair falling in unruly waves and curls on his forehead. For some reason, he seemed nervous today, running his hands through his bangs and gazing around. "Um..." He hesitated, narrowing his eyes. "What was your name again?"

"Meghan," I whispered.

"Oh, yeah." Stepping closer, he glanced back at his friends and lowered his voice. "Listen, I feel bad about the way I treated you yesterday. It was uncalled-for. I'm sorry."

For a moment, I didn't understand what he was saying. I'd been expecting threats, taunts, or accusations. Then a great balloon of relief swelled inside me as his words finally registered. "O-oh," I stammered, feeling my face heat, "that's okay. Forget about it."

"I can't," he muttered. "You've been on my mind since yesterday. I was a jerk, and I'd like to make it up to you. Do..." He stopped, chewing his lip, then got it all out in a rush. "Do you want to eat lunch with me this afternoon?"

My heart pounded. Butterflies swarmed madly in my stomach, and my feet felt like they were floating an inch off the ground. I barely had the voice to squeak a breathless "Sure." Scott grinned, showing blindingly white teeth, and gave me a wink.

"Hey, guys! Over here!" One of Scott's football buddies stood a few feet away, a camera-phone in hand, pointed at us. "Smile!"

Before I knew what was happening, Scott put a hand around my shoulders and pulled me close to his side. I blinked up at him, stunned, as my heart began racing around my chest. He flashed his dazzling grin at the camera, but I could only stare, stupefied, like a moron.

"Thanks, Meg," Scott said, breaking away from me. "See you at lunch." He smiled and trotted off toward the school with one final wink. The cameraman chuckled and sprinted after him, leaving me dazed and confused at the edge of the parking lot.

For a moment, I stood there, staring like an idiot as my classmates surged around me. Then a grin spread across my face and I had to stop myself from laughing like a maniac right there in the hall. Scott Waldron wanted to see me! He wanted to have lunch with me, just me, in the cafeteria. Maybe my luck was finally turning around. My best birthday ever might just be starting.

As a silvery curtain of rain crept over the parking lot, I felt eyes on me. Turning, I saw Robbie a few paces away, watching me through the crowd.

Through the rain, his eyes glittered, a too-bright green. As water pounded the concrete and students rushed toward the school, I saw a hint of something on his face: a long muzzle, slitted eyes, a tongue lolling out between pointed fangs. My stomach twisted, but I blinked and Robbie was himself again—normal, grinning, unconcerned that he was getting drenched.

And so was I.

With a little yelp, I sprinted beneath the overhang and ducked inside the school. Robbie followed, laughing, pulling at my limp strands of hair until I smacked him and he stopped.

All through the first class, I kept glancing at Robbie, looking for that eerie, predatory hint on his face, wondering if I was crazy. All it got me was a sore neck and a brusque comment from my English teacher to pay attention and stop staring at boys.

When the lunch bell rang, I leaped up, my heart fluttering a hundred miles a minute. Scott was waiting for me in the cafeteria. I grabbed my books, stuffed them into my backpack, whirled around—

And came face-to-face with Robbie, standing behind me.

I shrieked. "Rob, I'm going to smack you if you don't stop doing that! Now, move. I have to get somewhere."

"Don't go." His voice was quiet, serious. Surprised, I looked up at him. The perpetual goofy grin was gone, and his jaw was set. The look in his eyes was almost frightening. "This is bad, I can feel it. Something is about to happen, and you're going be right in the middle of it all. Promise me you won't go."

I recoiled. "Were you eavesdropping on us?" I demanded,

scowling. "What's wrong with you? Ever hear of a 'private conversation'?"

"Waldron doesn't care about you." Robbie crossed his arms, daring me to contradict him. "He'll break your heart, princess. Trust me, I've seen enough of his kind to know."

Anger flared, anger that he continuously stuck his nose into my affairs, anger that he could be right. "Again, it's none of your business, Rob!" I snapped, making his eyebrows arch. "And I can take care of myself, okay? Quit butting in where you're not wanted."

Hurt glimmered briefly, but then it was gone. "Fine, princess." He smirked, holding up his hands. "Don't get your royal pink panties in a twist. Forget I said anything."

"I will." Tossing my head, I stalked out of the room without looking back.

Guilt gnawed at me as I wove through the halls toward the cafeteria. I regretted snapping at Robbie, but sometimes his Big Brother act went too far. Still, Robbie had always been that way—jealous, overprotective, forever looking out for me, like it was his job. I couldn't remember when I first met him; it felt like he'd always been there.

The cafeteria was noisy and dim. I hovered just inside the door, looking for Scott, only to see him at a table in the middle of the floor, surrounded by cheerleaders and football jocks. I hesitated. I couldn't just march up to that table and sit down; Angie Whitmond and her cheerleading squad would rip me to shreds.

Scott glanced up and saw me, and a lazy smile spread over his face. Taking that as an invitation, I started toward him, weaving my way past the tables. He flipped out his iPhone, pressed a button, and looked at me with half-lidded eyes, still grinning.

A phone rang close by.

I jumped a bit, but continued walking. Behind me, there

were gasps, and then hysterical giggles. And then, the whispered conversation that always makes you think they're talking about you. I felt eyes on the back of my head. Trying to ignore it, I continued down the aisle.

Another phone rang.

And another.

And now, whispers and laughter were spreading like wildfire. For some reason, I felt horribly exposed, as if a spotlight shone right on me and I was on display. The laughter couldn't be directed at me, could it? I saw several people point in my direction, whispering among themselves, and tried my best to ignore them. Scott's table was only a few feet away.

"Hey, hot cheeks!" A hand smacked my ass and I shrieked. Spinning around, I glared at Dan Ottoman, a blond, pimply clarinet player from band. He leered back at me and winked. "Never took you for a player," he said, trying to ooze charm but reminding me of a dirty Kermit the Frog. "Come down to band sometime. I've got a flute you can play."

"What are you talking about?" I snarled, but he snickered and held up his phone.

At first, the screen was blank. But then a message flashed across it in bright yellow. *"How is Meghan Chase like a cold beer?"* it read. I gasped, and the words disappeared as a picture flashed into view.

Me. Me with Scott in the parking lot, his arm around my shoulders, a wide leer on his face. Only now—my mouth dropped open—I was butt naked, staring at him in wonder, my eyes blank and stupid. He'd obviously used Photoshop; my "body" was obscenely skinny and featureless, like a doll's, my chest as flat as a twelve-year-old's. I froze, and my heart stopped beating as the second part of the message scrolled over the screen.

"She's smooth and goes down easy!"

The bottom dropped out of my stomach, and my cheeks

flamed. Horrified, I looked up at Scott, to see his whole table roaring with laughter and pointing at me. Ringtones echoed through the cafeteria, and laughter pounded me like physical waves. I started trembling, and my eyes burned.

Covering my face, I turned and fled the cafeteria before I started wailing like a two-year-old. Shrieking laughter echoed around me, and tears stung my eyes like poison. I managed to cross the room without tripping over benches or my feet, bashed open the doors, and escaped into the hallway.

I spent nearly an hour in the corner stall of the girls' bathroom, sobbing my eyes out and planning my move to Canada, or possibly Fiji—somewhere far, far away. I didn't dare show my face to anyone in this state ever again. Finally, as the tears slowed and my gasping breaths returned to normal, I reflected on how miserable my life had become.

I guess I should feel honored, I thought bitterly, holding my breath as a group of girls flocked into the bathroom. *Scott took the time to personally ruin my life. I bet he's never done that to anyone else. Lucky me, I'm the world's biggest loser.* Tears threatened again, but I was tired of bawling and held them back.

At first, I planned to hole up in the bathroom until school ended. But, if anyone missed me from class, this would be the first place they'd look. So, I finally gathered the courage to tiptoe down to the nurse's office and fake a horrid stomachache so I could hide out there.

The nurse stood about four feet in thick-heeled loafers, but the look she gave me when I peered through the door suggested she wasn't going to take any teenage foolishness. Her skin looked like that of a shrunken walnut, her white hair was pulled into a severe bun, and she wore tiny gold glasses on the end of her nose.

"Well, now, Ms. Chase," she said in a gravelly, high-pitched voice, setting aside her clipboard. "What are you doing here?"

I blinked, wondering how she knew me. I'd only been to the nurse's office once before, when a stray soccer ball hit me in the nose. Back then, the nurse was bony and tall, with an overbite that made her look like a horse. This plump, shriveled little woman was new, and slightly unnerving, with the way she stared at me.

"I have a stomachache," I complained, holding my navel like it was about to burst. "I just need to lie down for a few minutes."

"Of course, Ms. Chase. There are some cots in the back. I'll bring you something to make you feel better."

I nodded and moved into a room divided by several huge sheets. Except for myself and the nurse, the room was empty. Perfect. I chose a corner cot and lay back on the paper-covered mattress.

Moments later, the nurse appeared, handing me a Dixie cup full of something that bubbled and steamed. "Take this, you'll feel better," she said, pressing the cup into my hand.

I stared at it. The fizzling white liquid smelled like chocolate and herbs, except stronger, somehow, a mix so potent it made my eyes water. "What is it?" I asked.

The nurse just smiled and left the room.

I took a cautious sip and felt warmth spread from my throat down to my stomach. The taste was incredible, like the richest chocolate in the world, with just a hint of bitter aftertaste. I quaffed the rest in two gulps, holding the cup upside down to get the last drops.

Almost immediately, I felt sleepy. Lying back on the crinkly mattress, I closed my eyes for just a moment, and everything faded away.

I awoke to low voices, talking in furtive tones, just beyond the curtains. I tried to move, but it felt like my body was wrapped in cotton, my head filled with gauze. I struggled to keep my eyes open. On the other side of the sheets, I saw two silhouettes.

"Don't do anything reckless," warned a low, gravelly voice. *The nurse,* I thought, wondering, in my delirium, if she would give me more of that chocolaty stuff. "Remember, your duty is to watch the girl. You must not do anything that will draw attention."

"Me?" asked a tantalizingly familiar voice. "Draw attention to myself? Would I do such a thing?"

The nurse snorted. "If the entire cheerleading squad turns into mice, Robin, I will be very upset with you. Mortal adolescents are blind and cruel. You know that. You mustn't take revenge, no matter how you feel about the girl. Especially now. There are more worrisome things on the move."

I'm dreaming, I decided. *That must be it. What was in that drink, anyway?* In the dim light, the silhouettes playing across the curtain looked confusing and strange. The nurse, it seemed, was even smaller, barely three feet in height. The other shadow was even more peculiar: normal-size, but with strange protrusions on the side of his head that looked like horns, or ears.

The taller shadow sighed and moved to sit in a chair, crossing his long legs. "I've heard the same," he muttered. "Dark rumors are stirring. The Courts are restless. Seems like something is out there that has both of them scared."

"Which is why you must continue to be both her shield and her guardian." The nurse turned, putting both hands on her hips, her voice chiding. "I'm surprised you haven't given her the mistwine yet. She is sixteen today. The veil is beginning to lift."

"I know, I know. I'm getting to it." The shadow sighed, putting his head in his hands. "I'll take care of that later this afternoon. How is she?"

"Resting," said the nurse. "Poor thing, she was traumatized. I gave her a mild sleep potion that will knock her out
until she goes home."

A chuckle. "The last kid who drank one of your 'mild'
sleep potions didn't wake up for two weeks. You're one to
talk about being inconspicuous."

The nurse's reply was garbled and broken, but I was almost
sure she said, "She's her father's daughter. She'll be fine." Or
maybe it was just me. The world went fuzzy, like an out-of-
focus camera, and I knew nothing for a time.

"Meghan!"

Someone was shaking me awake. I cursed and flailed, momentarily confused, and finally lifted my head. My eyes felt
like they had ten pounds of sand in them, and sleep gook
crusted the corners, making it impossible to focus. Groaning, I wiped my lids and stared blearily into Robbie's face.
For a moment, his brow was furrowed with concern. Then I
blinked and he was his normal, grinning self.

"Wakey wakey, sleeping beauty," he teased as I struggled
to a sitting position. "Lucky you, school is out. It's time to
go home."

"Huh?" I muttered intelligently, wiping the last traces of
sleep snot from my eyes. Robbie snorted and pulled me to
my feet.

"Here," he said, handing me my backpack, heavy with books.
"You're lucky I'm such a great friend. I got notes for all the
classes you missed after lunch. Oh, and you're forgiven, by the
way. I won't even say 'I told you so.'"

He was speaking too fast. My brain was still asleep, my
mind foggy and disconnected. "What are you talking about?"
I mumbled, shrugging into my pack.

And then I remembered.

"I need to call my mom," I said, dropping back on the cot. Robbie frowned and looked confused. "She has to come pick me up," I elaborated. "No way am I getting on the bus, ever again." Despair settled on me, and I hid my face in my hands.

"Look, Meghan," Robbie said, "I heard what happened. It's not a big deal."

"Are you insane?" I asked, glaring at him through my fingers. "The whole school is talking about me. This will probably go in the school paper. I'll be crucified if I show my face in public. And you say it's not a big deal?"

I drew my knees to my chest and buried my head in them. Everything was so horribly unfair. "It's my birthday," I moaned into my jeans. "This isn't supposed to happen to people on their birthdays."

Robbie sighed. Dropping his bag, he sat down and put his arms around me, pulling me to his chest. I sniffled and shed a few tears into his jacket, listening to his heartbeat through his shirt. It thudded rapidly against his chest, like he'd been sprinting several miles.

"Come on." Robbie stood, pulling me up with him. "You can do this. And I promise, no one will care what happened today. By tomorrow, everyone will have forgotten about it." He smiled, squeezing my arm. "Besides, don't you have a driver's permit to get?"

That one bright spark in the black misery of my life gave me hope. I nodded, steeling myself for what was to come. We left the nurse's office together, Robbie's hand clasped firmly around mine.

"Just stick close," he muttered as we neared the crowded part of the hallway. Angie and three of her groupies stood in front of the lockers, chattering away and snapping their gum. My stomach tensed and my heart began to pound. Robbie squeezed my hand. "It's okay. Don't let go of me, and don't say anything to anyone. They won't even notice we're here."

As we neared the cluster of girls, I prepared for them to turn on me with their laughter and their ugly remarks. But we swept by them without so much as a glance, though Angie was in the midst of describing my shameful retreat from the cafeteria.

"And then she, like, started bawling," Angie said, her nasal voice cutting through the hall. "And I was like, omygod she's *such* a loser. But what can you expect from a family of hillbillys?" Her voice dropped to a whisper and she leaned forward. "I heard her mom has an unnatural obsession with pigs, if you know what I mean."

The girls broke into a chorus of shocked giggles, and I almost snapped. Robbie, however, tightened his grip and pulled me away. I heard him mutter something under his breath, and felt a shudder go through the air, like thunder with no sound.

Behind us, Angie started to scream.

I tried to turn back, but Robbie yanked me onward, weaving through the crowd as the rest of the students jerked their heads toward the shrieking. But, for a split second, I saw Angie covering her nose with her hands, and her screams were sounding more and more like the squeals of a pig.

3

THE CHANGELING

The bus ride home was silent, at least between Robbie and me. Partly because I didn't want to draw attention to myself, but mainly because I had a lot on my mind. We sat in the back corner, with me crushed against the window, staring at the trees flashing by. I had my phone out and my headphones blasting my eardrums, but it was mostly an excuse not to talk to anyone.

Angie's piglike screams still echoed through my head. It was probably the most horrible sound I'd ever heard, and though she was a total bitch, I couldn't help but feel a little guilty. There was no doubt in my mind that Robbie had done something to her, though I couldn't prove it. I was actually afraid to bring it up. Robbie seemed like a different person now, quiet, brooding, watching the kids on the bus with predator-like intensity. He was acting weird—weird and creepy—and I wondered what was wrong with him.

Then there was that strange dream, which I was beginning to think hadn't really been a dream at all. The more I thought about it, the more I realized that the familiar voice talking to the nurse had been Robbie's.

Something was happening, something strange and creepy and terrifying, and the scariest part of all was that it wore a familiar, ordinary face. I snuck a glance at Robbie. How well did I know him, really know him? He'd been my friend for longer than I could remember, and yet I'd never been to his house, or met his parents. The few times I suggested meeting at his place, he'd always had some excuse not to; his folks were out of town, or they were remodeling the kitchen, a kitchen I'd never seen. That was strange, but what was weirder was the fact that I'd never wondered about it, never questioned it, until now. Robbie was simply *there,* like he'd been conjured out of nothing, with no background, no home, and no past. What was his favorite music? Did he have goals in life? Had he ever fallen in love?

Not at all, my mind whispered, disturbingly. *You don't know him at all.*

I shivered and looked out the window again.

The bus lurched to a halt at a four-way stop, and I saw we'd left the outskirts of town and were now heading into the boondocks. My neighborhood. Rain still spattered the windows, making the swampy marshlands blurry and indistinct, the trees fuzzy dark shapes through the glass.

I blinked and straightened up in my seat. Deep in the swamp, a horse and rider stood beneath the limbs of an enormous oak, as still as the trees themselves. The horse was a huge black animal with a mane and tail that rippled behind it, even drenched as it was. Its rider was tall and lean, garbed in silver and black. A dark cape fluttered from its shoulders. Through the rain, I caught the barest glimpse of a face: young, pale, strikingly handsome…staring right at me. My stomach lurched and I caught my breath.

"Rob," I murmured, pulling my headphones out, "look at tha—"

Robbie's face was inches from mine, staring out the window, his eyes narrowed to green slits, hard and dangerous. My stomach twisted and I leaned away from him, but he didn't notice me. His lips moved, and he whispered one word, so soft I barely caught it, even as close as we were.

"Ash."

"Ash?" I repeated. "Who's Ash?"

The bus coughed and lurched forward again. Robbie leaned back, his face so still it could've been carved from stone. Swallowing, I looked out the window, but the space beneath the oak was empty. Horse and rider were gone, like they'd never existed.

The weirdness kept getting weirder.

"Who's Ash?" I repeated, turning back to Robbie, who seemed to be in his own world. "Robbie? Hey!" I poked him in the shoulder. He twitched and finally looked at me. "Who is Ash?"

"Ash?" For a moment, his eyes were bright and feral, his face like that of a wild dog. Then he blinked and was normal again. "Oh, he's just an old buddy of mine, from long ago. Don't worry about it, princess."

His words slid over me strangely, like he was willing me to forget simply by requesting it. I felt a prickle of annoyance that he was hiding something, but it quickly faded, because I couldn't remember what we were talking about.

At our curb, Robbie leaped up as if the seat was on fire and rushed out the door. Blinking at his abrupt departure, I put my phone safely in my backpack before leaving the bus. The last thing I wanted was for the expensive thing to get wet.

"I have to go," Robbie announced when I joined him on the pavement. His green eyes swept through the trees, as if he expected something to come crashing out of the woods. I gazed around, but except for some bird trilling overhead, the forest was quiet and still. "I…um…forgot something at home." He turned to me then with an apologetic look. "See you tonight, princess? I'll bring that champagne over later, okay?"

"Oh." I'd forgotten about that. "Sure."

"Go straight home, okay?" Robbie narrowed his eyes, his face intense. "Don't stop, and don't talk to anyone you meet, got it?"

I laughed nervously. "What are you, my mom? Are you going to tell me not to run with scissors and to look both ways before crossing the street? Besides," I continued as Robbie smirked, looking more like his normal self, "who would I meet way out here in the boondocks?" The image of the boy on the horse suddenly came to mind, and my stomach did that strange little flop again. Who was he? And why couldn't I stop thinking about him, if he even existed at all? Things were getting really odd. If it wasn't for Robbie's weird reaction on the bus, I would think the boy was another of my crazy hallucinations.

"Fine." Robbie waved, flashing his mischievous grin. "See you later, princess. Don't let Leatherface catch you on your way home."

I kicked at him. He laughed, bounced away, and sprinted off down the road. Shouldering my backpack, I trudged up the driveway.

"Mom?" I called, opening the front door. "Mom, I'm home."

Silence greeted me, echoing off the walls and floor, hanging heavy in the air. The stillness was almost a living thing, crouched in the center of the room, watching me with cold eyes. My heart began a loud, irregular thud in my chest. Something was wrong.

"Mom?" I called again, venturing into the house. "Luke? Anybody home?" The door creaked as I crept in farther. The television blared and flickered, playing a rerun of an old black-and-white sitcom, though the couch in front of it was empty. I switched it off and continued down the hall, into the kitchen.

For a moment, everything looked normal, except for the refrigerator door, swinging on its hinges. A small object on the floor caught my attention. At first, I thought it was a dirty rag. But, looking closer, I saw it was Floppy, Ethan's rabbit. The stuffed animal's head had been torn off, and cotton spilled from the hole in the neck.

Straightening, I heard a small noise on the other side of the dining table. I walked around, and my stomach twisted so violently that bile rose to my throat.

My mother lay on her back on the checkered tile floor, arms and legs flung akimbo, one side of her face covered in glistening crimson. Her purse, its contents scattered everywhere, lay beside one limp white hand. Standing over her in the doorway, his head cocked to one side like a curious cat, was Ethan.

And he was smiling.

"Mom!" I screamed, flinging myself down beside her. "Mom, are you okay?" I grabbed one shoulder and shook her, but it was like shaking a dead fish. Her skin was still warm, though, so she couldn't be dead. Right?

Where the hell is Luke? I shook her again, watching her head flop limply. It made my stomach turn. "Mom, wake up! Can you hear me? It's Meghan." I looked around frantically, then snatched a washrag off the sink. As I dabbed it over her bloodied face, I became aware again of Ethan standing in the doorway, his blue eyes now wide and teary.

"Mommy slipped," he whispered, and I noticed a clear, slick puddle on the floor in front of the refrigerator. Hand trembling, I dipped a finger in the goo and sniffed. Vegetable oil? What the hell? I wiped more blood off her face and noticed a small gash on her temple, nearly invisible beneath blood and hair.

"Will she die?" Ethan asked, and I glanced at him sharply. Though his eyes were huge and round, and tears brimmed in the corners, he sounded more curious than anything.

I wrenched my gaze away from my half brother. I had to get help. Luke was gone, so the only thing left would be to call for an ambulance. But, just as I stood to get the phone, Mom groaned, stirred, and opened her eyes.

My heart leaped. "Mom," I said as she struggled into a sitting position, a dazed look on her face. "Don't move. I'll call 911."

"Meghan?" Mom looked around, blinking. A hand came up to touch her cheek, and she stared at the blood on her fingers. "What happened? I... I must've fallen..."

"You hit your head," I replied, standing up and looking around for the phone. "You might have a concussion. Hold on, I'm calling the ambulance."

"The ambulance? No, no." Mom sat up, looking a little clearer. "Don't do that, honey. I'm fine. I'll just clean up and put on a Band-Aid. There's no need to go to that trouble."

"But, Mom—"

"I'm fine, Meg." Mom snatched the forgotten washrag and began wiping the blood off her face. "I'm sorry if I frightened you, but I'll be fine. It's only blood, nothing serious. Besides, we can't afford a big doctor's bill." She abruptly straightened and looked around the room. "Where's your brother?"

Startled, I looked back to the doorway, but Ethan was gone.

Mom's protests were wasted when Luke got home. He took one look at her pale, bandaged face, threw a fit, and insisted they go to the hospital. Luke can be stubbornly persistent when he needs to be, and Mom eventually buckled under the pressure. She was still calling out instructions to me—take care of Ethan, don't let him stay up too late, there's frozen pizza in the fridge—as Luke bundled her into his battered Ford and roared off down the driveway.

As the truck turned a corner and vanished from sight, the chilly silence descended on the house once more. I shivered, rubbing my arms, feeling it creep into the room and breathe down my neck. The house where I'd lived most of my life seemed unfamiliar and frightening, as if things lurked in the cupboards and around corners, waiting to grab me as I walked past. My gaze lingered on the crumpled remains of Floppy, strewn across the floor, and for some reason, it made me very sad and scared. No one in this house would rip up Ethan's favorite stuffed animal. Something was very wrong.

Footsteps padded over the floor. I turned to find Ethan in the doorway, staring at me. He looked strange without the rabbit in his arms, and I wondered why he wasn't upset about it.

"I'm hungry," he announced, making me blink. "Cook me something, Meggie."

I scowled at the demanding tone.

"It's not dinnertime yet, squirt," I told him, crossing my arms. "You can wait a couple hours."

His eyes narrowed, and his lips curled back from his teeth. For just a moment, I imagined they were jagged and sharp. "I'm hungry *now*," he growled, taking a step forward. Dread shot through me and I recoiled.

Almost immediately, his face smoothed out again, his eyes enormous and pleading. "Please, Meggie?" he whined. "Please? I'm so hungry." He pouted, and his voice turned menacing. "Mommy didn't make me food, either."

"All right, fine! If it'll shut you up, fine." The angry words erupted from fear, and from a hot embarrassment because I was afraid. Of Ethan. Of my stupid, four-year-old half brother. I didn't know where these demonic mood swings of his were coming from, but I hoped they weren't the start of a trend. Maybe he was just upset because of Mom's accident. Maybe if I fed the brat, he'd fall asleep and leave me alone for the night. I stalked to the freezer, grabbed the pizza, and shoved it in the oven.

While the pizza cooked, I tried to clean up the puddle of vegetable oil in front of the refrigerator. I wondered how the stuff had ended up on the floor, especially when I found the empty bottle stuffed in the trash. I smelled like Crisco when I was done, and the floor still had a slick spot, but it was the best I could do.

The creak of the oven door startled me. I turned to see Ethan pulling it open and reaching inside.

"Ethan!" Grabbing his wrist, I yanked him back, ignoring his scream of protest. "What are you doing? You want to burn yourself?"

"Hungry!"

"Sit down!" I snapped, plunking him into a dining chair. He actually tried to hit me, the little ingrate. I resisted the urge to smack him. "God, you're being snotty today. Sit there and be quiet. I'll get your food in a second."

When the pizza came out, he fell on it like a wild thing, not waiting for it to cool. Astonished, I could only stare as he tore through the slices like a starved dog, barely stopping to chew as he gulped it down. Soon, his face and hands were smeared with sauce and cheese, and the pizza was rapidly diminished. In less than two minutes, he had consumed it all, down to the last crumb.

Ethan licked his hands, then raised his eyes to me and frowned. "Still hungry."

"You are not," I told him, snapping out of my daze. "If you eat anything else you'll get sick. Go play in your room or something."

He stared at me with a baleful expression, and it seemed that his skin grew darker, wrinkled, and shriveled beneath his baby fat. Without warning, he leaped off the chair, rushed me, and sank his teeth into my leg.

"*Ow!*" Pain lanced through my calf like an electrical shock. Grabbing his hair, I tried prying his teeth from my skin, but he clung to me like a leech and bit down harder. It felt like glass shards stabbing into my leg. Tears blurred my vision, and my knees almost buckled from the pain.

"Meghan!"

Robbie stood inside the front door, a backpack flung over his shoulder, his green eyes wide with shock.

Ethan released me, jerking his head toward the shout. Blood smeared his lips. Seeing Robbie, he hissed and—there's no other way to put it—*scuttled* away from us and up the stairs, vanishing from sight.

I shook so hard I had to sit down on the couch. My leg throbbed, and my breath came in short, uneven gasps. Blood, bright and vivid, seeped through my jeans like an unfurling blossom. Dazed, I stared at it, numbness deadening my limbs, freezing them in shock.

Robbie crossed the room in three strides and knelt beside me. Briskly, as if he'd done this kind of thing before, he began rolling up the cuff of one pant leg.

"Robbie," I whispered as he bent over his task, his long fingers surprisingly gentle. "What's happening? Everything's going crazy. Ethan just attacked me…like a wild dog."

"That wasn't your brother," Robbie muttered as he pushed back the material, revealing a bloody mess below my knee. An oval of jagged puncture wounds marred my leg, seeping blood, and the skin around them was already purpling. Rob whistled softly. "Nasty. Wait here. I'll be right back."

"Like I'm going anywhere," I replied automatically, and then his previous statement sank in. "Wait a minute. What do you mean, that wasn't Ethan? Who the hell else could it be?"

Rob ignored me. Walking to his backpack, he opened it and pulled out a long, green-tinted bottle and a tiny crystal cup. I frowned. Why was he going for champagne now? I was hurt, in pain, and my kid brother had turned into a monster. I was certainly not in the mood for celebrating.

With the utmost care, Robbie poured the champagne into the cup and walked back, being careful not to spill a single drop.

"Here," he said, giving it to me. The cup sparkled in his hand. "Drink this. Where do you keep the towels?"

I took it suspiciously. "In the bathroom. Just don't use Mom's good white ones." As Rob walked off, I peered into the tiny cup. There was barely enough for a swallow. It didn't look like champagne to me. I was expecting something fizzy white or pink, sparkling in the glass. The liquid in the cup was a deep, dark red, the color of blood. A fine mist writhed and danced on the surface.

"What is this?"

Robbie, returning from the bathroom with a white towel, rolled his eyes. "Do you have to question everything? It will help you forget the pain. Just drink it already."

I sniffed experimentally, expecting hints of roses or berries or some type of sweet scent mixed in with the alcohol.

It smelled of nothing. Nothing at all.

Oh, well. I raised the glass in a silent toast. "Happy birthday to me."

The wine filled my mouth, flooding my senses. It tasted of nothing, and everything. It tasted of twilight and mist, moonlight and frost, emptiness and longing. The room swayed, and I fell back against the couch, it was so strong. Reality blurred at the edges, wrapping me in a fuzzy haze. I felt sick and sleepy all at once.

By the time my senses cleared, Robbie was tying a bandage around my leg. I didn't remember him cleaning or dressing the wound. I felt numb and dazed, like a blanket had dropped over my thoughts, making it hard to concentrate.

"There," Robbie said, straightening up. "That's done. At least your leg won't fall off." His eyes swept up to mine, anxious and assessing. "How're you feeling, princess?"

"Un," I muttered, and tried to sweep the cobwebs from my brain. There was something I wasn't remembering, something important. Why was Robbie binding my leg? Had I hurt myself somehow?

I bolted upright.

"Ethan bit me!" I exclaimed, indignant and furious all over again. I turned on Robbie. "And you...you said that wasn't Ethan at all! What were you talking about? What's going on?"

"Relax, princess." Robbie tossed the bloody towel onto the floor and plopped onto a footstool. He sighed. "I was hoping it wouldn't come to this. My fault, I suppose. I shouldn't have left you alone today."

"What are you talking about?"

"You weren't supposed to see this, any of this," Robbie went on, to my utter confusion. He seemed to be talking more to himself than me. "Your Sight has always been strong, that was a given. Still, I didn't expect them to go after your family, too. This changes things."

"Rob, if you don't tell me what's going on—"

Robbie looked at me. His eyes gleamed, impish and feral. "Tell you? Are you sure?" His voice went soft and dangerous, and goose bumps crawled up my arms. "Once you start seeing things, you won't be able to stop. People have gone mad with too much knowledge." He sighed, and the menace dropped from his eyes. "I don't want that to happen to you, princess. It doesn't have to be this way, you know. I can make you forget all of this."

"Forget?"

He nodded and held up the wine bottle. "This is mistwine. You just had a swallow. A cup will make everything go back to normal." He balanced the bottle on two fingers, watching it sway back and forth. "One cup, and you'll be normal again. Your brother's behavior will not seem strange, and you won't remember anything weird or scary. You know what they say—ignorance is bliss, right?"

Despite my uneasiness, I felt a slow flame of anger burning my chest. "So, you want me to drink that... stuff, and just forget about Ethan. My only brother. That's what you're saying."

He raised an eyebrow. "Well, when you put it like that..."

The burning grew hotter, searing away the fear. I clenched my fists. "Of course I won't forget about Ethan. I'm his sister; I'm supposed to take care of him. I can't just close my eyes and ignore what's going on, especially if he's in danger." Robbie was still gazing at me, blank faced, and I frowned. "I know you don't have any siblings, Rob, but are you really that inhuman?"

To my surprise, a grin spread over his face. He dropped the bottle, caught it, and put it on the floor. "Yes," he said, very softly.

That threw me. "What?"

"Inhuman. I am." He was still grinning at me, the smile stretching his whole mouth so that his teeth gleamed in the fading light. "I warned you, princess. I'm not like you. And now, neither is your brother."

Despite the fear prickling my stomach, I leaned forward. "Ethan? What do you mean? What's wrong with him?"

"That wasn't Ethan." Robbie leaned back, crossing his arms. "The thing that attacked you today is a changeling."

I stared at Robbie, wondering if this was another one of his pranks. He sat there, observing me calmly, watching my reaction. Though he still wore a half grin, his eyes were hard and serious. He wasn't joking around.

"Ch-changeling?" I finally stammered. "Isn't that some kind of...of..."

"Faery," Robbie finished for me. "A changeling is a faery offspring that has been switched with a human child. Usually, a troll's or goblin's, though the sidhe—the faery nobility—have been known to make the switch, as well. Your brother has been replaced. That thing is not Ethan, any more than I am."

"You're crazy," I whispered. If I wasn't sitting, I'd be backing away from him toward the door. "Or this is a really bad practical joke. Time to cut back on the anime, Rob. There's no such thing as faeries."

Robbie sighed. "Really? That's what you're going with? How predictable." He leaned back and crossed his arms. "I thought better of you, princess."

"Thought better of *me*?" I cried, leaping off the couch.

"Listen to yourself! You really expect me to believe that my brother is some kind of pixie with glitter dust and butterfly wings?"

"Don't be stupid," Rob said mildly. "You have no idea what you're talking about. You're thinking 'Tinker Bell,' which is a typical human response to the word *faery*. The real fey aren't like that at all." He paused a moment. "Well, except for the piskies, of course, but that's a different story altogether."

I shook my head, my thoughts spinning in several directions at once. "I can't deal with this right now," I muttered and staggered away from him. "I have to check on Ethan."

Robbie only shrugged, leaned back against the wall, and put his hands behind his head. After one final glare at him, I rushed up the stairs and opened the door to Ethan's bedroom.

It was a mess, a war zone of broken toys, books, and scattered clothes. I looked around for Ethan, but the room appeared empty, until I heard a faint scratching noise under his bed.

"Ethan?" Kneeling down, pushing away broken action figures and snapped Tinkertoys, I peered into the space between the mattress and the floor. In the shadows, I could just make out a small lump huddled in the corner with his back to me. He was trembling.

"Ethan," I called softly. "Are you all right? Why don't you come out a second? I'm not mad." Well, that was a lie, but I was more shaken than angry. I wanted to drag Ethan downstairs and prove that he wasn't a troll or a changeling or whatever Robbie said he was.

The lump stirred a little, and Ethan's voice drifted out of the gap. "Is the scary man still here?" he asked in a small, frightened voice. I might've been sympathetic, if my calf wasn't throbbing so much.

"No," I lied. "He's gone now. You can come out." Ethan

didn't move, and my irritation sparked. "Ethan, this is ridiculous. Get out of there already, will you?" I stuck my head farther under the mattress and reached for him.

Ethan turned on me with a hiss, eyes burning yellow, and lunged at my arm. I jerked it back as his teeth, jaggedly pointed like a shark's, snapped together with a horrid clicking sound. Ethan snarled, his skin the ghastly blue of a drowned infant's, bared teeth shining in the darkness. I shrieked, scrabbling back, Lego blocks and Tinkertoys biting into my palms. Hitting the wall, I leaped to my feet, turned, and fled the room.

And ran smack into Robbie, standing outside the door.

He grabbed my shoulders as I screamed and started hitting him, barely conscious of what I was doing. He bore the attack wordlessly, simply holding me in place, until I collapsed against him and buried my head in his chest. And he held me as I sobbed out my fear and anger.

At last, the tears stopped, leaving me drained and utterly exhausted. I sniffed and backed away, wiping my eyes on my palm, shaking. Robbie still stood there quietly, his shirt damp with my tears. The door to Ethan's bedroom was shut, but I could hear faint thumps and cackling laughter beyond the door.

I shivered, looking up at Robbie. "Ethan is really gone?" I whispered. "He's not just hiding somewhere? He's really gone?"

Robbie nodded gravely. I looked at Ethan's bedroom door and bit my lip. "Where is he now?"

"Probably in Faeryland." Stated so simply, I almost laughed from the sheer ridiculousness of it all. Ethan had been stolen by faeries and replaced with an evil doppelgänger. *Faeries* kidnapped my brother. I was tempted to pinch myself to see if this was a twisted dream or hallucination. Maybe I had fallen into a drunken stupor on the couch. On impulse, I bit the inside of my cheek, hard. The sharp pain and taste of blood told me this was, indeed, real.

I looked to Robbie, and his grave expression banished the last of my doubts. A sick feeling rose to my stomach, making me nauseous and afraid.

"So…" I swallowed and forced myself to be calm. Okay, Ethan was kidnapped by faeries; I could deal with this. "What do we do now?"

Robbie raised one shoulder. "That's up to you, princess. There are human families that have raised changelings as their own, though they are usually unaware of the child's true nature. Generally speaking, if you feed it and leave it alone, it will settle into its new home without too much trouble. Changelings make a nuisance of themselves at first, but most families adapt." Robbie grinned, but it was an attempt at lightheartedness rather than humor. "Hopefully, your folks will think he's just going through a late terrible twos."

"Robbie, that thing bit me, and probably made Mom slip and fall in the kitchen. It's more than a nuisance, it's dangerous." I glared at Ethan's closed door and shuddered. "I want it gone. I want my brother back. How do we get rid of it?"

Robbie sobered. "Well, there are ways of getting rid of changelings," he began, looking uncomfortable. "One old method is to brew beer or cook stew in eggshells, and that will make the changeling comment on the weirdness of it. But that method was for infants who'd been switched—since the baby was too young to speak, the parents knew that the impostor was a changeling and the real parents had to take it back. I don't think it'll work for someone older, like your brother."

"Great. What's another way?"

"Er, the other way is to beat the changeling near to death, until the screams force the fey parents to return the real child.

Barring that, you could stick him in the oven and cook him alive—"

"Stop." I felt sick. "I can't do any of those things, Robbie. I just can't. There has to be another way."

"Well…" Rob looked hesitant and scratched the back of his neck. "The only other way is to travel into the faery lands and take him back. Bringing the real child into the home again will force the changeling to leave. But…" He paused, as if on the verge of saying something, only to think better of it.

"But what?"

"But…you don't know who took your brother. And without that knowledge, you'll just be walking in circles. And, if you're wondering, walking in circles in Faeryland is a very, very bad idea."

I narrowed my eyes. "I don't know who took him," I agreed, staring hard at Robbie, "but you do."

Robbie shuffled nervously. "I have a guess."

"Who?"

"It's just a guess, mind you. I could be wrong. Don't go jumping to conclusions."

"Robbie!"

He sighed. "The Unseelie Court."

"The what?"

"The Unseelie Court," Robbie repeated. "The Court of Mab, Queen of Air and Darkness. Sworn enemies of King Oberon and Queen Titania. Very powerful. Very nasty."

"Wait, wait, wait." I held up my hands. "Oberon? Titania? Like from *A Midsummer Night's Dream*? Aren't those just ancient myths?"

"Ancient, yes," Robbie said. "Myths, no. The faery lords are immortal. Those who have songs, ballads, and stories written about them never die. Belief, worship, imagination—we were born of the dreams and fears of mortals, and if we are remembered, even in some small way, we will always exist."

"You keep saying 'we,'" I pointed out. "As though you're one of those immortal faeries. As though you're one of them." Robbie smiled, a proud, impish smile, and I gulped. "Who are you, anyway?"

"Ah, well." Robbie shrugged, trying to look modest and failing entirely. "If you've read *A Midsummer Night's Dream,* you might remember me. There was this unfortunate incident, completely unplanned, where I gave someone a donkey's head and made Titania fall in love with him."

I ran through the play in my mind. I'd read it in the seventh grade, but had forgotten most of the plot. There were so many characters, so many names to sift through, people falling in and out of love so often it was ridiculous. I remembered a few human names: Hermia, Helena, Demetrius. On the faery side, there was Oberon and Titania and...

"Shit," I whispered, falling back against the wall. I stared at Robbie with new eyes. "Robbie Goodfell. Robin...you're Robin Goodfellow."

Robbie grinned. "Call me Puck."

Puck. *The* Puck was standing in my hallway.

"No way," I whispered, shaking my head. This was Robbie, my closest friend. I would've known if he was an ancient faery. Wouldn't I?

Frighteningly, the more I thought about it, the more likely it seemed. I'd never seen Robbie's house, or his parents. The teachers all loved him, though he never did a lick of school-work and slept through most of the classes. And strange things happened when he was around: mice and frogs ended up in desks, or names were switched around on term papers. Though

Robbie Goodfell thought these scenarios absolutely hilarious, no one ever suspected him.

"No," I muttered again, backing away toward my room. "That's impossible. Puck is a legend, a myth. I don't believe it."

Robbie gave me that eerie smile. "Then, princess, by all means, let me assure you."

His arms rose from his sides, as if he might levitate into the air. From downstairs, I heard the front door creak open, and I hoped Mom and Luke weren't home yet. *Yeah, Mom, Ethan's turned into a monster and my best friend thinks he's a faery. How was your day?*

An enormous black bird swooped into the hallway. I yelped and ducked as the raven, or crow or whatever it was, made a beeline straight for Robbie and perched on his arm. They watched me, the pair of them, with glittering eyes, and Robbie smiled.

A rush of wind, and suddenly, the air was filled with screaming black birds, swooping in from the open door. I gasped and ducked as the cloud of ravens filled the hallway, their raucous cries nearly deafening me. They swirled around Robbie, a tornado of beating wings and sharp claws, tearing at him with talons and beaks. Feathers flew everywhere, and Robbie disappeared within the swirling mass. Then, as one, the birds scattered, flying out the open door as swiftly as they had come. As the last bird swooped outside, the door slammed behind it, and silence descended once more. I caught my breath and glanced at Rob.

Robbie was gone. Only a swirl of black feathers and dust motes remained in the place where he'd stood.

It was too much. I felt my sanity unravel like frayed cloth. With a choked scream, I turned and fled into my room, slamming the door behind me. Flinging myself under my bedcovers, I put the pillow over my head and shook, hoping that when I woke up, things would be normal.

My door opened, and the sound of wings fluttered into my room. I didn't want to look and pulled the covers tighter around me, willing the nightmare to end. I heard a sigh, and footsteps padded over the floor.

"Well, I tried to warn you, princess."

I peeked out. Robbie stood there, looking down at me, a pained smile on his face. Seeing him, I felt relieved, angry, and terrified at the same time. I threw off the covers and sat up, narrowing my eyes as I stared at him. Robbie waited, hands in the pockets of his jeans, as if daring me to contradict him some more.

"You really are Puck?" I said finally. "*The* Puck? Like in the stories?"

Robbie/Puck gave a little bow. "The one and only."

My heart was still pounding. I took a deep breath to calm it and glared at the stranger in my room. My emotions churned; I didn't know what to feel. I settled on anger; Robbie had been my best friend for years, and he never saw fit to share his secret with me. "You could have told me sooner," I said, trying not to sound hurt. "I would have kept your secret." He only smirked and raised an eyebrow, infuriating me even more. "Fine. Go back to Faeryland, or wherever you come from. Aren't you supposed to be Oberon's jester or something? Why were you hanging around *me* so long?"

"You wound me, princess." Robbie sounded anything but hurt. "And after I made up my mind to help you get your brother back."

My anger vanished instantly, replaced with fear. With all the talk of fey and faery lords, I'd nearly forgotten about Ethan.

I shivered as my stomach twisted into a tight little ball. This still felt like something out of a nightmare. But Ethan was gone, and faeries were real. I had to accept that now. Robbie stood there, gazing at me expectantly. A black feather dropped from his hair, spiraling down to the bed. Gingerly, I picked it up, twirling it in my fingers.

"You'll help me?" I whispered.

He gave me a shrewd look, one corner of his mouth turning up. "Do you know a way into Faery by yourself?"

"No."

"Then you need my help." Robbie smiled and rubbed his hands together. "Besides, it's been a while since I've gone home, and nothing ever happens here. Storming the Unseelie Court sounds like fun."

I didn't share his enthusiasm. "When do we leave?" I asked.

"Now," Robbie replied. "The sooner the better. Do you have anything you want to take, princess? You might not be back for a while."

I nodded, trying to stay calm. "Just give me a minute."

Robbie nodded and walked into the hallway. I snatched my bright orange backpack and tossed it on the bed, wondering what to take. What did one need for an overnight trip to Faeryland? I grabbed jeans and an extra shirt, a flashlight, and a bottle of aspirin, stuffing them into the pack. Walking down to the kitchen, I tossed in a Coke and a couple of bags of chips, hoping Robbie would know where to find food on the journey. Finally, I grabbed my phone, slipping it into my front pocket.

Mom was supposed to take me to the DMV today. I hesitated, biting my lip. What would Mom and Luke think when they found me gone? I'd always followed the rules, never sneaking out—except that one time with Robbie—never staying up past curfew. I wondered what Rob meant when he said we'd be gone "awhile." Luke might not even notice I'd left, but Mom would worry. Grabbing an old homework sheet, I started to write her a quick note, but stopped, my pen hovering over the paper.

What are you going to tell her? "Dear Mom, Ethan's been kidnapped by faeries. Gone to get him back. Oh, and don't trust the Ethan that's here—he's really a faery changeling." It sounded insane even to me. I hesitated, thinking, then scrawled a quick:

Mom, there's something I have to take care of. I'll be back soon, I promise. Don't worry about me. Meghan

I stuck the note on the refrigerator door, trying not to think that I might never see home again. Shouldering the pack, feeling my insides squirm like a nest of snakes, I climbed the stairs.

Robbie waited on the landing, arms crossed over his chest, wearing a lazy grin. "Ready?"

Apprehension tickled my stomach. "Will it be very dangerous?"

"Oh, extremely," Robbie said, walking up to Ethan's bedroom door. "That's what makes it fun. You can die in so many interesting ways—skewered on a glass sword, dragged underwater and eaten by a kelpie, turned into a spider or a rosebush for all time." He looked back at me. "Well, are you coming or not?"

I noticed my hands were shaking and held them to my chest. "Why are you saying these things?" I whispered. "Are you trying to scare me?"

"Yes," Robbie replied, unabashed. He paused at Ethan's door, one hand on the knob, and stared at me. "These are the things you're going to face, princess. I'm giving you fair warning now. Still think you want to go? My previous offer still stands."

I remembered the taste of the mistwine, the desperate longing for more, and shivered. "No," I said quickly. "I won't leave

Ethan with a bunch of monsters. I've lost a father already—I won't lose a brother, as well."

And then, something occurred to me, something that left me breathless, wondering why I didn't think of it before. *Dad.* My heart pounded, recalling half-remembered dreams, where my father vanished beneath a pond and never resurfaced. What if he'd been kidnapped by faeries, as well? I could find Ethan *and* my dad, and bring them *both* home.

"Let's go," I demanded, looking Robbie in the eyes. "Come on, we've wasted enough time here. If we're gonna do this, let's get it over with."

Rob blinked, and a strange look passed over his face. For a moment, it seemed like he wanted to say something. But then he shook himself, like he was coming out of a trance, and the moment was gone.

"All right, then. Don't say I didn't warn you." He grinned, and the gleam in his eyes grew brighter. "First things first. We have to find an entrance to the Nevernever. That's Faeryland to you. It's not a place you can just walk to, and the doors are usually very well hidden. Fortunately, I have a good idea of where one is lurking." He grinned, turned away, and pounded on Ethan's bedroom door. "Knock, knock!" he called in a high, singsong voice.

For a moment, silence. Then came a thud and a crash, as if something heavy had been hurled at the door. "Go away!" snarled the voice from within.

"Ah, no. That's not how the joke goes," called Rob. "I say 'knock, knock,' and you're supposed to answer with 'who's there?'"

"Fuck off!"

"Nope, that's still wrong." Robbie seemed unperturbed. I, however, was horrified at Ethan's language, though I knew it wasn't him. "Here," continued Rob in an amiable voice,

"I'll go through the whole thing, so you'll know how to answer next time." He cleared his throat and pounded the door again. "Knock, knock!" he bellowed. "Who's there? Puck! Puck who? Puck, who will turn you into a squealing pig and stuff you in the oven if you don't get out of our way!" And with that, he banged open the door.

The thing that looked like Ethan stood on the bed, a book in each hand. With a hiss, he hurled them at the doorway. Robbie dodged, but one paperback hit me in the stomach and I grunted.

"Please," I heard Rob mutter, and a ripple went through the air. Suddenly, all the books in the room flapped their covers, rose off the floor and shelves, and began dive-bombing Ethan like a flock of enraged seagulls. I could only stare, feeling my life get more surreal by the second. The fake Ethan hissed and snarled, swatting at the books as they buzzed around him, until one hit him smack in the face and tumbled him off the mattress. Spitting in fury, he darted under the bed. I heard claws scrabbling against the wood as his feet vanished into the crawl space. Curses and growls drifted out from the darkness.

Robbie shook his head. "Amateurs." He sighed as the books swooping around the room froze midflight and rained to the floor with echoing thuds. "Let's go, princess."

I shook myself and picked my way over fallen books, joining Robbie in the middle of the room. "So," I ventured, trying to sound casual, as if flying books and faeries were something I encountered every day. "Where's this entrance to Faeryland? Will you have to make a magic ring or cast a spell or something?"

Rob snickered. "Not exactly, princess. You're making it too complicated. Doorways to the Nevernever tend to appear in places where there is a lot of belief, creativity, or imagination. Often you can find one in a child's bedroom closet, or under his bed."

Floppy's afraid of the man in the closet. I shivered, mentally apologizing to my half brother. When I found him again, I'd be sure to tell him I believed in the monsters, too.

"The closet, then," I murmured, stepping over books and toys to reach it. My hand shook a bit as I grabbed the door-knob. *No turning back now,* I told myself, and pulled it open.

A tall, emaciated figure with a narrow face and sunken eyes stared at me as the door swung open. A black suit clung to its rail-thin body, and a bowler hat perched atop its pointed head. It blinked wide, staring at me, and bloodless lips pulled back in a grimace, revealing thin, pointed teeth. I leaped back with a shriek.

"My closet!" hissed the figure. A spiderlike hand darted out and grabbed the doorknob. "My closet! Mine!" And it slammed the door with a bang.

Robbie gave an exasperated sigh as I skittered behind him, my heart careening around my rib cage like a bat. "Bogeys," he muttered, shaking his head. He strode to the door, tapped on it three times, and flung it open.

This time, the space stood empty, except for hanging shirts, stacked boxes, and normal closet things. Robbie shoved aside the clothes, maneuvered around the boxes, and put a hand to the back wall, tracing his fingers along the wood. Curious, I edged closer.

"Where are you?" he muttered, feeling along the wall. I crept to the doorway and peered over his shoulder. "I know you're here. Where is… Aha."

Crouching down, he took a breath and blew against the wall. Instantly, a cloud of dust arose, billowing around him and sparkling like orange glitter.

When he straightened, I saw a gold handle on the back wall,

and the faint outline of a door, pale light shining through the bottom crack.

"Come on, princess." Rob turned and beckoned me forward. His eyes glowed green in the darkness. "This is our ride. Your one-way ticket to the Nevernever."

I hesitated, waiting for my pulse to slow to something resembling normal. It didn't. *This is insane,* a small, scared part of me whispered. Who knew what waited through that doorway, what horrors lurked in the shadows? I might never come home again. This was my last chance to turn back.

No, I told myself. *I can't turn back. Ethan is out there, somewhere. Ethan is counting on me.* I took a deep breath and one step forward.

A wrinkled hand shot from beneath the bed, latching on to my ankle. It yanked savagely and I nearly fell, as a snarl echoed from the dark space beneath. With a shriek, I kicked free of the flailing claw, charged blindly into the closet, and slammed the door behind me.

5

THE NEVERNEVER

In the musty darkness of Ethan's closet, I pressed a hand to my chest and waited once more for my heartbeat to return to normal. Blackness surrounded me, except for the thin rectangle of light outlined against the far wall. I couldn't see Robbie, but I felt his presence close by, heard his quiet breathing in my ear.

"Ready?" he whispered, his breath warm on my skin. And before I could answer, he pushed the door back with a creak, revealing the Nevernever.

Pale silver light flooded the room. The clearing beyond the door frame was surrounded by enormous trees, so thick and tangled I couldn't see the sky through the branches. A curling mist crept along the ground, and the woods were dark and still, as if the forest was trapped in perpetual twilight. Here and there, brilliant splashes of color stood out among the gray. A patch of flowers, their petals a shocking electric-blue, waved gently in the mist. A creeper vine snaked around the trunk of a dying oak, long red thorns a stark contrast to the tree it was killing.

A warm breeze blew into the closet, carrying with it a shocking assortment of smells—smells that should not be together in one place. Crushed leaves and cinnamon, smoke and apples, fresh earth, lavender, and the faint, cloying scent of rot and decay. For a moment, I caught a tang of something metallic and coppery, wrapped around the smell of rot, but it was gone in the next breath. Clouds of insects swarmed overhead, and if I listened hard I could almost imagine I heard singing. The forest was still at first, but I then caught movement deep in the shadows, and heard leaves rustle all around us. Invisible eyes seemed to watch me from every angle, boring into my skin.

Robbie, his hair a bright flame atop his head, stepped through the doorway, gazed around, and laughed. "Home." He sighed, flinging his arms wide, as if to embrace it all. "I'm finally home." He spun in place and, with another laugh, fell backward into the mist, like he was making a snow angel, and vanished.

I gulped and took a cautious step forward. Mist swirled around my ankles like a living thing, caressing my skin with damp fingers. "Rob?"

The silence mocked me. Out of the corner of my eye, something big and white darted into the trees like quicksilver. "Rob?" I called again, edging to the place he had fallen. "Where are you? Robbie?"

"Boo." Rob appeared behind me, rising out of the mist like a vampire from its coffin. To say I screamed was a bit of an understatement.

"A little jumpy today, aren't we?" Robbie laughed and darted out of reach before I could kill him. "Time to switch to decaf, princess. If you're going to shriek at every bogey that jumps out and says 'boo,' you'll be exhausted before we reach the edge of the woods."

He had changed. Dark brown pants and a thick green hoodie replaced his jeans and ratty T-shirt. I couldn't see his feet very well in the mist, but it looked like he'd traded his sneakers for soft leather boots. His face was leaner, harsher, with sharp angles and pointed features. Combined with his bright auburn hair and green eyes, he reminded me of a grinning fox.

But the most noticeable difference was his ears. Slender and pointed, they jutted out from the sides of his head, like... well, like an elf's. And, in that moment, all traces of Robbie Goodfell disappeared. The boy I'd known for most of my life was gone, like he never existed, and only Puck remained.

"What's the matter, princess?" Puck yawned, stretching his long limbs. Was it my imagination, or had he gotten taller, too? "You look like you lost your best friend."

I ignored the question, not wanting to dwell on it. "How did you do that?" I asked, to steer the conversation elsewhere. "Your clothes, I mean. They're different. And the way you made the books fly around the room. Was it magic?"

Puck grinned. "Glamour," he said, as if that meant anything to me at all. I frowned at him, and he sighed. "I didn't have time to change before we came here, and my lord King Oberon frowns on wearing mortal clothes to court. So I used glamour to make myself presentable. Just like I used glamour to make myself look human."

"Wait a minute." I thought back to the dream conversation between Robbie and the nurse. "Are there others like you... you faery-types, walking around back home? Right under everyone's noses?"

Puck gave me a very eerie smile. "We're everywhere, princess," he said firmly. "Under your bed, in your attic, walking past you on the street." His smile grew wider, more wolfish. "Glamour is fueled by the dreams and imagination of mortals.

Writers, artists, little boys pretending to be knights—the fey are drawn to them like moths to a flame. Why do you think so many children have imaginary friends? Even your brother had one. Floppy, I think he called it, though that wasn't its true name. A pity the changeling managed to kill it."

My stomach felt tight. "And…no one can see you?"

"We're invisible, or we use glamour to hide our true nature." Puck leaned against a tree, lacing his hands behind his head in a very Robbie-like fashion. "Don't look so shocked, princess. Mortals have perfected the art of not seeing what they don't expect to be there. Though, there are a few rare humans who can see through the mist and the glamour. Usually, these are very special individuals—innocent, naive dreamers—and the fey are even more attracted to them."

"Like Ethan," I murmured.

Puck gave me a strange look, one corner of his mouth quirked up. "Like you, princess." He seemed about to say something else, but then a branch snapped somewhere in the tangled darkness.

He straightened quickly. "Whoops, time to go. It's dangerous to linger in any one place. We'll attract unwanted attention."

"What?" I exclaimed as he strode across the clearing, moving as gracefully as a deer. "I thought you said this was home."

"The Nevernever is home to all fey," Puck said without looking back. "It's divided into territories, or more technically, Courts. The Seelie Court is Oberon's domain, while Mab rules the Unseelie territories. While in the Courts, it is usually forbidden to torment, maim, or kill another fey without permission from its rulers.

"However," he continued, looking back at me, "right now, we are in neutral territory, home of the wild fey. Here, as you humans put it, all bets are off. The things coming at us now could be a herd of satyrs who will make you dance until you're exhausted, then rape you one by one, or it could be a pack of hedge wolves that will tear us both apart. Either way, I don't think you want to hang around."

My stomach twisted, and I swallowed hard. "You're scaring me, Rob."

"Good. I meant to."

I was afraid again. It seemed I was always afraid. I didn't want to be here, in this eerie forest, with this person I only thought I knew. I wanted to go home. Only, home had become a frightening place as well, almost as much as the Nevernever. I felt lost and betrayed, out of place in a world that wished me harm.

Ethan, I reminded myself. *You're doing this for Ethan. Once you get him, you can go home and everything will go back to normal.*

The rustling grew louder, and twigs snapped as whatever was out there drew closer. "Princess," Puck snapped, right next to me. I jumped and bit down a shriek as he grabbed my wrist. "The aforementioned nasties have picked up our scent and are coming for us." Though his voice was casual, I could see the strain in his eyes. "If you don't want your first day in the Nevernever to be your last, I suggest we move."

I looked back and saw the door we came through standing upright in the middle of the clearing. "Will we be able to get back home this way?" I asked as Puck pulled me along.

"Nope." When I stared at him in horror, he shrugged. "Well, you can't expect the doors to stand around in one place, princess. Don't worry, though. You have me, remember? When the time comes, we'll find the way home."

We ran for the far side of the clearing, straight for a tangle of bushes with hooked yellow thorns as long as my thumb. I held back, sure we'd be sliced to ribbons, but as we neared, the branches shivered and peeled away from us, revealing a narrow path cutting through the trees. As we stepped through, the bushes knitted together again, hiding the trail and protecting our retreat.

We walked for hours, or at least it felt that way to me. Puck kept up a steady pace, neither hurrying nor slowing down, and in time the sounds of pursuit faded away. Sometimes the trail split, wending off in different directions, but Puck always chose a path without hesitation. Many times, I'd catch movement from the corner of my eye—a flash of color in the brush, a figure silhouetted between the trees—but when I turned, there'd be nothing. Sometimes, I almost swore I heard singing or music, but, of course, it would fade when I tried to focus on it. The sickly luminescence of the forest never dimmed or brightened, and when I asked Puck what time night would fall, he cocked an eyebrow at me and said night would come when it was ready.

Annoyed, I checked my watch, wondering how long we'd been traveling. I received an unpleasant shock. The slender hands were frozen in place. Either the watch's battery was dead, or something else was interfering.

Or maybe time doesn't exist in this place. I don't know why I found that immensely disturbing, but I did.

My feet were aching, my stomach hurt, and my legs were burning with exhaustion when the eternal twilight finally began to dim. Puck stopped, gazing up at the sky, where an enormous moon glimmered over the treetops, so close you could see pits and craters marring the surface.

"I suppose we should rest for the night." Puck sounded reluctant. He gave me a sideways grin as I collapsed on a moldy log. "We wouldn't want you stumbling onto a dancing mound, or following a white bunny down a dark hole. Come on, I know a place not far from here where we can sleep undisturbed."

He took my hand and pulled me to my feet. My limbs screamed in protest, and I almost sat down again. I was tired, cranky, and the last thing I wanted was more hiking. Gazing around, I saw a lovely little pond through a stand of trees. The water shimmered in the moonlight, and I paused, gazing out over the mirrored surface. "Why not stop there?" I asked.

Puck took one look at the pond, grimaced, and pulled me onward. "Ah, no," he said quickly. "Too many nasties lurking underwater—kelpies and glaistigs and mermaids and such. Best not to risk it."

I looked back and saw a dark shape breach the perfect surface of the pond, sending ripples across the still water. The top of a horse's head, coal-black and slick like a seal, watched me with baleful white eyes. With a gasp, I hurried on.

A few minutes later, we came to the trunk of a huge, gnarled tree. The bark was so knobby and rough that I could almost see faces peering out of the trunk. It reminded me of wrinkled old men, stacked atop each other and waving their crooked arms indignantly.

Puck knelt among the roots and knocked on the wood. I peered over his shoulder and, with a start, saw a tiny door, barely a foot tall, near the base of the tree. As I watched, wide-eyed, the door creaked open, and a head peered out suspiciously.

"Eh? Who's there?" a rough, squeaky voice asked as I stared in wonder. The little man's skin was the color of walnuts; his hair looked like a bundle of twigs sticking out of his scalp. He wore a brown tunic and brown leggings, and looked like a stick come to life, except for the eyes peering out of his face, black and shiny like a beetle's.

"Good evening, Twiggs," Puck greeted politely.

The little man blinked, squinting up at the figure towering over him. "Robin Goodfellow?" he squeaked at last. "Haven't seen you round these parts in a while. What brings you to my humble tree?"

"Escort duty" Puck replied, shifting to the side so that Twiggs could get a clear view of me. Those beady eyes fixed on me, blinking in confusion. Then, suddenly, they got huge and round, as Twiggs looked back at Puck.

"Is…is that…?"

"It is."

"Does she…?"

"No."

"Oh, my." Twiggs opened the door wide, beckoning with a sticklike arm. "Come in, come in. Quickly, now. Before the dryads catch sight of you, the irritating gossips." He vanished inside, and Puck turned to me.

"I'll never be able to fit in there," I told him before he could say a word. "There's no way I'm going to squeeze through, unless you've got a magic toadstool that'll shrink me to the size of a wasp. And I'm not eating anything like that. I've seen *Alice in Wonderland,* you know."

Puck grinned and took my hand.

"Close your eyes," he told me, "and just walk."

I did, half expecting to walk nose first into the tree, courtesy of a great Robbie-prank. When nothing happened, I almost peeked but thought better of it. The air turned warm, and I heard a door slam behind me, when Puck said I could open my eyes again.

I stood in a cozy, round room, the walls made of smooth red wood, the floor covered with mossy carpet. A flat rock on three stumps served as a table in the center of the room, displaying berries the size of soccer balls. A rope ladder hung on the far wall, and when my gaze followed it up, I nearly fainted. Dozens of insects crawled on the walls or hovered in the air high above us, for the trunk extended farther than I could see. Each bug was the size of a cocker spaniel, and their rear ends glowed a luminescent yellow-green.

"You've been renovating, Twiggs," Puck said, sitting on a bundle of furs that passed for a couch. I looked closer and saw the head of a squirrel still attached to the skin, and had to look away. "This place was barely a hole in the tree when I saw it last."

Twiggs looked pleased. He was our height now—actually, I guess we were more *his* height—and up close he smelled of cedar and moss.

"Yes, I've grown quite fond of it," Twiggs said, walking over to the table. He picked up a knife and split a berry into thirds, arranging the pieces on wooden plates. "Still, I might have to move soon. The dryads whisper to me, tell me dark things. They say parts of the wyldwood are dying, vanishing more every day. No one knows what is causing it."

"You know what's causing it," Puck said, draping the squirrel tail over his lap. "We all do. This is nothing new."

"No." Twiggs shook his head. "Mortal disbelief has always taken a bit of the Nevernever, but not like this. This is…different. It's hard to explain. You'll see what I mean if you go any farther."

He handed us each a plate with a huge slab of red berry, half an acorn, and a pile of what looked like steamed white grubs. Despite the weirdness of the day, I was ravenous after hours of hiking. The berry wedge tasted tart and sweet, but I wasn't about to touch the maggoty-looking things and gave them all to Puck. After dinner, Twiggs made me a bed of squirrel hides and chipmunk fur, and though I was mildly grossed out, I fell asleep immediately.

That night, I dreamed.

In my dream, my house was dark and still, the living room cloaked in shadow. A brief glimpse of the wall clock pronounced it 3:19 a.m. I floated through the living room past the kitchen and made my way up the stairs. The door to my room was closed, and I heard Luke's grizzly-bear snores coming from the master bedroom, but at the end of the hall, Ethan's door stood slightly ajar. I padded down the hallway and peeked in through the crack.

A stranger stood in Ethan's bedroom, a tall, lean figure dressed in silver and black. A boy, perhaps a little older than me, though it was impossible to tell his exact age. His body was youthful, but there was a stillness to him that hinted at something far older, something incredibly dangerous. With a shock, I recognized him as the boy on the horse, who had watched me through the forest that day. Why was he here now, in my house? How did he even get in? I toyed with the idea of confronting him, knowing this was all a dream, when I noticed something else, something that made my blood run cold. Thick, raven-wing hair tumbled to his shoulders, not quite covering the delicate, pointed ears.

He wasn't human. He was one of *them,* one of the fey. Standing in my house, in my brother's bedroom. I shuddered and began to ease back down the hall.

He turned then, looking right through me, and I would've gasped if I had the breath. He was gorgeous. More than gorgeous, he was beautiful. Regal beautiful, prince-of-a-foreign-nation beautiful. If he walked into my classroom during finals, students and teachers alike would be throwing themselves at his feet. Still, it was a cold, hard beauty, like that of a marble statue, inhuman and otherworldly. His slanted eyes, beneath long, jagged bangs, glimmered like chips of steel.

The changeling was nowhere to be seen, but I could hear faint noises coming from beneath the bed, the thud of a rapidly beating heart. The fey boy didn't seem to notice. He turned and placed one pale hand on the closet door, running his fingers down the faded wood. A ghost of a smile touched his lips.

In one smooth motion, he pushed the door open and walked through. The door shut behind him with a soft click, and he was gone.

Warily, I edged toward the closet door, keeping a careful eye on the space beneath the bed. I still heard muffled heartbeats, but nothing reached out to grab at me. I crossed the room without incident. As quietly as I could, I grasped the closet doorknob, turned it, and pulled the door open.

"My closet!" shrieked the bowler hat man, leaping out at me. "Mine!"

I gasped and jerked myself awake.

For a moment, I glared wildly around the room, not knowing where I was. My heart pounded, and a cold sweat made my forehead clammy and slick. Scenes from a vivid nightmare danced across my mind: Ethan attacking me, Robbie making books fly around the room, a portal opening to an eerie new world.

A loud snore caught my attention, and I turned. Puck was sprawled out on the couch across from me, one arm flung over his eyes, his torso wrapped in a squirrel blanket.

My heart sank as the memories came flooding back. This wasn't a nightmare. I hadn't been dreaming this. Ethan was gone; a monster had replaced him. Robbie was a faery. And I was in the middle of the Nevernever searching for my brother, though I had no idea where to look, and no real hope of finding him.

I lay back, shivering. It was dark in Twiggs's home; the fireflies or whatever they were had stopped blinking and were now clinging to the walls, apparently asleep. The only light came from a flickering orange glow outside the window. Maybe Twiggs had the porch light on or something.

I bolted upright. That glow was actually candlelight, and above it, a face was peering into the room from outside. I opened my mouth to yell for Puck, when those blue eyes turned to me, and a face I knew all too well backed away into the night.

Ethan.

I scrambled out of bed and sprinted across the floor, not bothering to put on my shoes. Puck snorted and shifted under his mound of furs, but I ignored him. Ethan was out there! If I could get to him, we could go home and forget this mess ever existed.

I yanked on the door and stepped out, scanning the woods for my brother. Only later did it occur to me that I was normal-size again, and that the door was still only a foot tall. All I could think about was Ethan and getting him home, getting us both home.

Darkness greeted me, but up ahead, I saw a flickering orange glow bouncing along, getting steadily farther away. "Ethan!" I called, my voice echoing into the stillness. "Ethan, wait!"

I started to run, my bare feet slapping against leaves and branches, slipping on rocks and mud. My toe hit something sharp, and it should've hurt, but my mind didn't register the pain. I could see him up ahead, a small figure making his way through the trees, holding a candle out before him. I ran as fast as I could, branches scraping my skin and tearing at my hair and clothes, but it seemed he was always the same distance away.

Then he stopped and looked back over his shoulder, smiling. The flickering candlelight cast his features in an eerie glow. I put on a burst of speed, and was just a few feet away when the ground suddenly dropped away from me. With a shriek, I plummeted like a stone, landing with a splash in icy water that closed over my head, flooding my nose and mouth.

Gasping, I floundered to the surface, my face stinging and my limbs already numb. Above me, a giggle rang out, and a glowing ball of light hovered overhead. It dangled there a moment, as if enjoying my predicament, then sped away into the trees, high-pitched laughter echoing behind it.

Treading water, I gazed around. A muddy bank rose above me, slick and treacherous. There were several old trees growing out over the water, but their branches were too high for me to reach. I tried finding handholds in the bank to pull myself out, but my feet slipped in the mud, and the plants I grabbed came loose from the soil, dumping me into the lake with a noisy splash. I'd have to find another way out.

And then I heard another splash, farther out, and knew I wasn't alone.

Moonlight shone upon the water, painting everything in a relief of silver and black. Except for the buzzing of insects, the night was very still. On the far side of the lake, fireflies danced and whirled above the surface, some glowing pink and blue instead of yellow. Maybe I'd only imagined I'd heard a noise. Nothing seemed to be moving except for an old log drifting toward me.

I blinked and looked again. That log suddenly looked a lot like the top half of a horse's head, if a horse could swim like an alligator. And then I saw the dead white eyes, the thin shiny teeth, and panic rose up in me like a black tide.

"Puck!" I screamed, scrabbling at the bank. Mud tore loose in clumps; I'd find a handhold only to slip back again. I could feel the thing draw closer. "Puck, help me!"

I looked over my shoulder. The horse thing was only a few feet away, raising its neck out of the water to expose a mouthful of needlelike teeth. *Oh, God, I'm going to die! That thing is going to eat me! Somebody, help!* I clawed frantically at the bank—and felt a solid branch under my fingers. Grasping it, I yanked with all my strength, and felt the branch lift me out of the water, just as the horse monster lunged with a roar. Its wet, rubbery nose hit the bottom of my foot, jaws snapping with an evil *snick*. Then the branch flung me, gasping and coughing, to the bank, and the horse thing sank below the surface once more.

Puck found me minutes later, curled into a ball several yards from the bank, wet to the skin and shaking like a leaf. His eyes were a mix of sympathy and exasperation as he pulled me upright.

"Are you all right?" He ran his hands up my arms, making sure I was still in one piece. "Still in there, princess? Talk to me."

I nodded, shivering. "I saw... Ethan," I stammered, trying to make sense of it all. "I followed him, but he turned into a light and flew away, and then this horse thing tried to *eat* me...." I trailed off. "That wasn't Ethan, was it? That was just another faery, playing with my emotions. And I fell for it."

Puck sighed and led me back down the trail. "Yeah," he muttered, glancing back at me. "Wisps are like that, making you see what you want to see, before leading you off the path. Though, that one seemed particularly spiteful, leading you right to a kelpie's pond. I suppose I could tell you never to go off alone, but I think it'd be a waste of breath. Oh, what the hell." He stopped and whirled around, stopping me in my tracks. "*Don't go off alone, princess.* Under any circumstances, understand? In this world, you're viewed as either a plaything or a light snack. Don't forget that."

"Yeah," I muttered. "Yeah, I get that now."

We continued down the trail. The door in the knobby tree

was gone, but my sneakers and backpack lay outside, a clear sign our welcome was over. Shivering, I slipped the shoes over my bloody feet, hating this world and everything in it, wanting only to go home.

"Well," Puck said too cheerfully, "if you're done playing with will-o'-the-wisps and kelpies, I think we should continue. Oh, but do tell me the next time you want to have tea with an ogre. I'll be sure to bring my club."

I shot him a poisonous glare. He only grinned. Above us, the sky was lightening into that eerie gray twilight, silent and still as death, as we ventured deeper into the Nevernever.

6

THE WILD HUNT

W e hadn't gone far when we came upon the patch of death in the middle of the forest.

The wyldwood was an eerie, quiet place, but it was still alive. Trees stood ancient and tall, plants bloomed, and splashes of vibrant color pierced the grayness, indicating life. Animals slipped through the trees, and strange creatures moved about in the shadows; you never got a clear view of them, but you knew they were there. You could feel them watching you.

Then, all of a sudden, the trees dropped away, and we stood at the edge of a barren clearing.

What little grass remained was yellow and dying, sparse patches of vegetation in the rocky ground. A few trees were scattered here and there, but they were withered, twisted things, empty of leaves and blackened. From a distance, the branches glinted, jagged and sharp, like weird metal sculptures. The hot wind smelled of copper and dust.

Puck stared at the dead forest for a long time. "Twiggs was right," he muttered, staring at a withered tree. He made as if to touch one of the branches, but withdrew his hand with a shudder. "This isn't natural. Something is poisoning the wyldwood."

I reached up to touch one of the glittering branches, and jerked back with a gasp. "Ouch!"

Puck whirled on me. "What?"

I showed him my hand. Blood welled from a slice in my finger, thin as a paper cut. "The tree. It cut me."

Puck examined my finger and frowned. "Metallic trees," he mused, pulling a hankie from his pocket and wrapping it around my finger. "That's new. If you see any steel dryads, be sure to tell me so I can run away screaming."

I scowled and looked back at the tree. A single drop of blood glistened on the offending branch before dropping to the cracked earth. The twigs gleamed along their edges, as if honed to fine blades.

"Oberon must know about this," Puck muttered, crouching to examine a circle of dry grass. "Twiggs said it was spreading, but where is it coming from?" He rose quickly and swayed on his feet, putting out a hand to steady himself. I grabbed his arm.

"Are you all right?" I asked.

"I'm fine, princess." He nodded and gave me a pained smile. "A little perturbed about the state of my home, but what can you do?" He coughed and waved a hand in front of his face, as if he smelled something foul. "But this air is making me sick. Let's get out of here."

I sniffed, but smelled nothing bad, just dirt and the sharp tang of something metallic, like rust. But Puck was already leaving, his brow furrowed in anger or pain, and I hurried to catch up.

The howling began a few hours later.

Puck stopped in the middle of the trail, so abruptly that I

nearly ran into him. He held up a hand, silencing me, before I could ask what was going on.

I heard it then, drifting over the breeze, a chorus of chilling bays and howls echoing behind us. My heart revved up, and I inched closer to my companion.

"What is that?"

"A hunt," Puck replied, looking off into the distance. He grimaced. "You know, I was just thinking we needed to be run down like rabbits and torn apart. My day just isn't complete without something trying to kill me."

I grew cold. "Something's after us?"

"You've never seen a wild hunt, have you." Puck groaned, running his fingers through his hair. "Damn. Well, this will complicate things. I was hoping to give you the grand tour of the Nevernever, princess, but I guess I'll have to put it on hold."

The baying grew closer, deep, throaty howls. Whatever was coming at us, it was big. "Shouldn't we run?" I whispered.

"You'll never be able to outrun them," Puck said, backing away. "They've got our scent now, and no mortal has ever escaped a wild hunt." He sighed and dramatically flung his arm over his eyes. "I guess the sacrifice of my dignity is the only thing that will save us now. The things I endure for love. The Fates laugh at my torment."

"What are you talking about?"

Puck smiled his eerie little grin and began to change.

His face stretched out, becoming longer and narrower, as his neck began to grow. His arms spasmed, fingers turning black and fusing into hooves. He arched his back, spine expanding, as his legs became hindquarters bunched with muscle. Fur covered his skin as he dropped to all fours, no longer a boy but a sleek gray horse with a shaggy mane and tail. The transformation had taken less than ten seconds.

I backed up, remembering my encounter with the thing

in the water, but the dappled horse stamped its foreleg and swished its tail impatiently. I saw its eyes, shining like emeralds through the dangling forelocks, and my fear abated somewhat.

The howling was very close now, growing more and more frenzied. I ran to horse-Puck and threw myself on his back, grabbing his mane to heave myself up. Despite living on a farm, I'd only been on horseback once or twice, and it took me a couple of tries to get up. Puck snorted and tossed his head, annoyed with my lack of equestrian skills.

Struggling upright, I grasped the mane and saw Puck's eyes roll back at me. Then, with a half rear, we plunged into the bushes and were off.

Riding bareback is not fun, especially when you have no control over your mount or where it's going. I can honestly say this was the most terrifying ride of my life. The trees flashed by in a blur, branches slapped at me, and my legs burned from gripping the horse's sides with my knees. My fingers were locked around his mane in a death grip, but that didn't keep me from sliding halfway off whenever Puck changed direction. The wind shrieked in my ears, but I could still hear the terrifying bays of our pursuers, seemingly right on our heels. I didn't dare look back.

I lost track of time. Puck never slowed or grew winded, but sweat darkened his body and made my seating slick and even more terrifying. My legs grew numb, and my hands seemed to belong to somebody else.

And then a huge black creature burst from the ferns to our right and lunged at the horse, snapping its jaws. It was a hound, bigger than any I'd seen, with eyes of blue fire. Puck leaped aside to avoid it and reared, nearly spilling me to the forest floor. As I screamed, one foreleg slashed out, striking the hound in the chest midleap, and the dog yelped as it was hurled away.

The bushes exploded, and five more monstrous dogs spilled into the road. Surrounding us, they snarled and howled, snapping at the horse's legs and leaping back as he kicked at them. I was frozen, clinging to Puck's back, watching as those massive jaws clicked shut inches from my dangling feet.

Then, through the trees, I saw him, a lean figure on a huge black horse. The boy from my dream, the one I saw from the bus that day. His cruel, angelic face wore a smile as he drew back a large bow, an arrow glistening at the tip.

"Puck!" I screeched, knowing it was already too late. "Look out!"

The leaves above the hunter rustled, and then a large branch swept down, striking the boy in the arm just as he released the string. I felt the hum as the arrow zipped past my head and lodged into a pine tree. A spiderweb of frost spread out from where the arrow hit, and Puck's equine head whipped toward the source. The hunter fit another arrow to the string, and with a shrill whinny, Puck reared and leaped over the dogs, somehow avoiding their snapping teeth. When his hooves struck dirt again, he fled, the hounds barking and snapping at his heels.

An arrow whistled past, and I looked back to see the other horse pursuing us through the trees, its rider reaching back for another shot. Puck snorted and switched directions, nearly unseating me, plunging into a deeper part of the forest.

The trees here were monsters, and grew so close together that Puck had to swerve and weave around them. The hounds fell back, but I still heard their bays and occasionally caught a glimpse of their lean black bodies, hurtling through the undergrowth. The rider had disappeared, but I knew he still followed, his deadly arrows ready to pierce our hearts.

As we passed under the boughs of an enormous oak, Puck skidded to a halt, then bucked so violently that I flew off his back, my hands torn from his mane. I soared over his head, my stomach in my throat, and landed with a jarring impact in a crossbeam of connecting branches. My breath exploded from my lungs, and a stab of pain shot through my ribs, bringing tears to my eyes. With a snort, Puck galloped on, the dogs following him into the shadows.

Moments later, the black horse and rider passed under the tree.

He slowed for a chilling heartbeat, and I held my breath, sure he would look up and see me. Then the excited howl of one of the dogs rang through the air, and he spurred his horse onward, following the hunt into the trees. In a moment, the sounds had faded. Silence fell through the branches, and I was alone.

"Well," someone said, very close by. "That was interesting."

7

OF GOBLINS AND GRIMALKIN

I didn't scream this time, but came very close. As it was, I nearly fell out of the tree. Hugging a branch, I looked around wildly, trying to determine the owner of the voice, but I glimpsed nothing but leaves and sickly gray light shining through the branches.

"Where are you?" I gasped. "Show yourself."

"I am not hiding, little girl." The voice sounded amused. "Perhaps…if you open your eyes a bit wider. Like this."

Directly in front of me, not five feet away, a pair of saucerlike eyes opened up out of nowhere, and I stared into the face of an enormous gray cat.

"There," it purred, regarding me with a lazy yellow gaze. Its fur was long and wispy, blending perfectly into the tree and the entire landscape. "See me now?"

"You're a cat," I blurted stupidly, and I swore it arched a brow at me.

"In the crudest sense of the word, I suppose you could call me that." The feline rose, arching its back, before sitting and curling its plumed tail around its legs. Now that my shock was fading, I realized the cat was a *he,* not an it. "Others have called me Cait Sith, Grimalkin, and Devil's Cat, but since they all mean the same, I suppose you would be correct."

I gaped at him, but the sharp throb of my ribs returned my mind to other things. Namely, that Puck had left me alone in this world that viewed me as a snack, and I had no idea how to survive.

Shock and anger came first—Puck had really *left* me—and after that came a fear so real and terrifying it was all I could do not to hug the branch and sob. How could Puck do this to me? I'd never make it out on my own. I'd end up as dessert for a carnivorous horse monster, torn apart by a pack of wolves, or hopelessly lost for decades, because I was sure time had ceased to exist and I'd be stuck here forever.

I took a deep breath, forcing myself to be calm. *No, Robbie wouldn't do that to me. I'm sure of it.* Perhaps he ditched me to lead the hunt away, to make sure the hunt followed him and left me alone. Maybe he thought he was saving my life. Maybe he *had* saved my life. If that was the case, I hoped he came back soon, I didn't think I would get out of the Nevernever without him.

Grimalkin, or whatever his name was, continued to observe me as if I was a particularly interesting insect. I eyed him with new feelings of suspicion. Sure, he looked like an enormous, slightly plump house cat, but horses weren't generally meat-eaters and normal trees did not have little men living inside. This feline could be sizing me up for its next meal. I gulped and met his eerie, intelligent gaze head-on.

"W-what do you want?" I asked, thankful that my voice only trembled a little bit.

The cat didn't blink. "Human," he said, and if a cat could sound patronizing, this one nailed it, "think about the absurdity of that question. I am resting in my tree, minding my own business and wondering if I should hunt today, when you come flying in like a bean sidhe and scare off every bird for miles around. Then, you have the audacity to ask what *I* want." He sniffed and gave me a very catlike stare of disdain. "I am aware that mortals are rude and barbaric, but still."

"I'm sorry," I muttered automatically. "I didn't mean to offend you."

Grimalkin twitched his tail, and then turned to groom his hindquarters.

"Um," I continued after a moment of silence, "I was wondering if, maybe…you could help me."

Grimalkin paused midlick, then continued without looking up. "And why would I want to do that?" he asked, weaving words and grooming together without missing a beat. He still didn't look at me.

"I'm trying to find my brother," I replied, stung by Grimalkin's casual refusal. "He's been stolen by the Unseelie Court."

"Mmm. How terribly uninteresting."

"Please," I begged. "Help me. Give me a hint, or just point me in the right direction. Anything. I'll make it up to you, I swear."

Grimalkin yawned, showing off long canines and a bright pink tongue, and finally looked at me.

"Are you suggesting I do you a favor?"

"Yes. Look, I'll pay you back somehow, I promise."

He twitched an ear, looking amused. "Be careful throwing those words around so casually," he warned. "Doing this will put you in my debt. Are you sure you wish to continue?"

I didn't think about it. I was so desperate for help, I'd agree to anything. "Yes! Please, I need to find Puck. The horse I was riding when he bucked me off. He's not really a horse, you know. He's a—"

"I know what he is," Grimalkin said quietly.

"Really? Oh, that's good. Do you know where he could've gone?"

He fixed me with an unblinking stare, and then lashed his tail, once. Without a word, he rose, leaped gracefully onto a lower limb, and dropped to the ground. He stretched, arching his bushy tail over his spine, and vanished into the bushes without looking back.

I yelped, scrambling to untangle myself from the branches, wincing at the shard of pain between my ribs. I more or less fell out of the tree, landing with a thump on my backside that sparked a word Mom would ground me for. Dusting off my rear, I looked around for Grimalkin.

"Human." He appeared like a gray ghost sliding out of the bushes, big glowing eyes the only evidence he was there. "This is our agreement. I will lead you to your Puck, and you will owe me a small favor in return, yes?"

Something about the way he said *agreement* caused my skin to prickle, but I nodded.

"Very well, then. Follow me. And do try to keep up."

Easier said than done.

If you've ever tried following a cat through a dense forest filled with briars, bushes, and tangled undergrowth, you'll know how impossible it is. I lost track of the times Grimalkin vanished from sight, and I'd spend a few heart-pounding minutes searching for him, hoping I was going the right way. I always felt a desperate relief when I'd finally catch a glimpse of him slinking through the trees ahead, only to go through the same thing minutes later.

It didn't help that my mind was occupied with what could've happened to Puck. Was he dead, shot down by the dark fey boy and ripped apart by the hounds? Or had he really fled, already resolved that he wasn't coming back for me, and I could take my chances on my own?

Fear and anger welled, and my thoughts shifted to my present guide. Grimalkin seemed to know the path we should take, but how did he know where Puck would be? Why should I trust him? What if the devious feline was leading me into some sort of trap?

As I was entertaining these bleak thoughts, Grimalkin disappeared again.

Dammit, I'm going to tie a bell around the stupid thing's neck if it doesn't stop that. The light was fading, and the forest was even more gray. I stopped and squinted at the bushes, searching for the elusive feline. Up ahead, the bushes rustled, which surprised me. Grimalkin had been completely silent up until now.

"Human!" whispered a familiar voice, somewhere above me. "Hide!"

"What?" I said, but it was too late. Twigs snapped, bushes parted, and a slew of creatures spilled into view.

They were short, ugly things, standing two to three feet high, with knobby yellow-green skin and bulbous noses. Their ears were large and pointed. They wore tattered clothing and carried bone-tipped spears in yellow claws. Their faces were mean and cruel, with beady eyes and mouths full of broken, jagged teeth.

For a moment, they stopped, blinking in surprise. Then the whole pack of them screeched and swarmed forward, jabbing at me with their spears.

"What is it? What is it?" snarled one, as I cringed away from the stabbing points. Laughter and jeers filled the air as they surrounded me.

"It's an elf," hissed another, giving me a toothy leer. "An elf what lost its ears, maybe."

"No, a goat-girl," cried yet a third. "Good eatin', them."

"She ain't no goat, cretin! Lookit, she ain't got no 'ooves!"

I trembled and looked around for an escape route, but wherever I turned, those sharp bony points were thrust at me.

"Take 'er to the chief," someone suggested at last. "The chief'll know what she is, and if she's safe to eat."

"Right! The chief'll know!"

A couple of them rushed me from behind, and I felt a blow to the backs of my knees. With a shriek, I collapsed, and the whole pack of them swarmed me, hooting and hollering. I screamed and kicked, flailing my arms, thrashing under the weight of the creatures. A few went flying into the bushes, but they bounced up with shrill cries and pounced on me again. Blows rained down on me.

Then something struck me behind the head, making lights explode behind my eyes, and I knew nothing for a time.

I woke with the mother of all headaches doing a jig inside my skull. I was in a sitting position, and something that felt like broom handles pressed uncomfortably into my back. Groaning, I probed around my skull, searching for anything cracked or broken. Except for a massive lump just above my hairline, everything seemed to be intact.

When I was sure I was still in one piece, I opened my eyes.

And regretted it immediately.

I was in a cage. A very small cage, made of branches lashed together with leather bindings. There was barely enough room for me to raise my head, and when I moved, something sharp poked me in the arm, drawing blood. I looked closer and saw that many of the branches were covered in thorns about an inch long.

Beyond the bars, several mud huts sat in no particular arrangement around a large fire pit. The squat, ugly little creatures scampered to and fro around the camp, fighting, arguing, or gnawing on bones. A group of them sat around my backpack, pulling things out one by one. My extra clothes they just tossed in the dirt, but the chips and bottle of aspirin they immediately ripped open, tasted, and squabbled over. One managed to open the soda can and spray fizzy liquid everywhere, to the angry shrieks of his companions.

One of them, shorter than its fellows and wearing a muddy red vest, saw that I was awake. With a hiss, it scuttled up to the cage and thrust its spear through the bars. I cringed back, but there was nowhere to go; the thorns stung my flesh as the spear jabbed me in the thigh.

"Ouch, stop it!" I cried, which only encouraged it further. Cackling, it poked and prodded me, until I reached down and grabbed the head of the spear. Snarling and cursing, the creature tried yanking it back, and we held a ridiculous tug-of-war until another goblin saw what we were doing. It rushed up and stabbed me through the bars on the opposite side, and I released the spear with a yelp.

"Greertig, stop pokin' the meat," snapped the second, taller creature. "Ain't no good if all the blood runs out."

"Pah, I was just makin' sure it was tender, is all." The other snorted and spit on the ground, then glared at me with greedy red eyes. "Why we waitin' about? Let's just eat it already."

"The chief ain't back yet." The taller creature looked at me, and to my horror, a long string of drool dripped down its chin. "He 'as to make sure this thing is safe to eat."

They gave me a last longing glare, then stomped back to the fire pit, arguing and spitting at each other. I drew my knees to my chest and tried to control my shaking.

"If you are going to cry, please do it quietly," murmured a familiar voice at my back. "Goblins can smell fear. They will only torment you more if you give them a reason."

"Grimalkin?" Squirming in my cage, I glanced around to

see the nearly invisible gray cat crouched by one corner. His eyes were narrowed in concentration, and his strong, sharp teeth were chewing at one of the leather bindings.

"Idiot human, do not look at me!" he spat, and I quickly glanced away. The cat growled, tugging on one of the bars. "Goblins are not very smart, but even they will notice if you start talking to nobody. Just sit tight and I will have you out of here in a minute."

"Thank you for coming back," I whispered, watching two goblins fight over some unfortunate beast's rib cage. The quarrel ended when one goblin bashed the other over the head with a club and scampered off with its trophy. The other goblin lay stunned for a moment, then leaped to its feet in pursuit.

Grimalkin sniffed and began chewing the bindings again. "Do not put yourself even more in debt," he said around a mouthful of leather. "We have already made a contract. I agreed to take you to Puck, and I always keep my end of the bargain. Now, shut up so I can work."

I nodded and fell silent, but suddenly there was a great cry in the goblin camp. Goblins leaped to their feet, hissing and scuttling about, as a large creature sauntered out of the forest into the middle of the encampment.

It was another goblin, only bigger, broader, and meaner-looking than its fellows. It wore a crimson uniform with brass buttons, the sleeves rolled up and the tails dragging along the ground. It also carried a curved blade, rusty bronze and jagged along the edge. It snarled and swaggered into the camp, the other goblins cringing away from it, and I knew this must be the chief.

"Shut up, ya pack of jabberin' dogs," the chief roared, aiming a blow at a couple of goblins who didn't get out of his way quick enough. "Worthless, the lot of ya! I been hard at work, raidin' the borderlands, an' what have you lot got to show me, eh? Nothin'! Not even a rabbit fer the stewpot. Ya make me sick."

"Chief, chief!" cried several goblins at once, dancing around and pointing. "Lookit, lookit! We caught something! We brought it back for you!"

"Eh?" The chief's gaze flashed across the camp, his evil eyes fastening on me. "What's this? Did you miserable louts actually manage to catch a high an' mighty elf?"

He sauntered toward the cage. I couldn't help myself and snuck a quick glance at Grimalkin, hoping the cat would flee. But Grimalkin was nowhere to be seen.

Swallowing hard, I looked up and met the chief's beady red eyes.

"What in Pan's privates is this?" the goblin chief snorted. "This ain't no elf, you cretins. Not unless she bartered away her ears! Besides—" he sniffed the air, wrinkling his snotty nose "—it smells different. Ey, funny elf-thing." He smacked the cage with the flat of his sword, making me jump. "What are ya?"

I took a deep breath as the rest of the goblin tribe crowded around the cage, watching me, some curious, most hungry-looking. "I'm a…an otaku faery," I said, drawing a confused scowl from the chief and bewildered looks from the rest of the camp. Whispers began to erupt from the crowd, gaining strength like wildfire.

"A what?"

"Ain't never 'erd of that before."

"Is it tasty?"

"Can we eat it?"

The chief frowned. "I admit, I ain't never come across no otaku faery before," he growled, scratching his head. "Ah, but that ain't important. Ya look young an' juicy enough, I figure you'll feed me crew fer several nights. So, what's yer preference, otaku?" He grinned and raised his sword. "Boiled alive, or skewered over the fire?"

I clenched my hands to stop them from shaking. "Either way is fine with me," I said, trying to sound casual. "Tomorrow it won't matter at all. There's a deadly poison running through my veins. If you swallow one bite of me, your blood will boil, your insides will melt, and you'll dissolve into a steaming pile of muck." Hisses went around the tribe; several goblins bared their teeth at me and snarled. I crossed my arms and raised my chin, staring down the goblin chief. "So, go ahead and eat me. Tomorrow you'll be a big puddle of goo, sinking into the ground."

Many of the goblins were backing away now, but the chief stood firm. "Shut up, you sniveling lot!" he snarled at the nervous goblins. Giving me a sour look, he spat on the ground. "So, we can't eat ya." He sounded unimpressed. "Pity, that is. But don't think that'll save ya, girl. If yer so deadly, I'll just kill ya now, except I'll bleed ya slow, so yer poison blood won't hurt me. Then I'll skin ya and hang yer hide on me door, and use yer bones for arrowheads. As me grandmother always said, waste not."

"Wait!" I cried as he stepped forward, raising his sword. "It—it would be a shame for me to go to waste like that," I stammered as he glared at me with suspicious eyes. "There *is* a way to purify the poison from my blood so that I'm safe to eat. If I'm going to die anyway, I'd rather be eaten than tortured."

The goblin chief smiled. "I knew you'd see it my way," he gloated. Turning to his minions, he puffed out his chest. "See there, dogs? Yer chief is still lookin' out fer ya! We feast tonight!"

A raucous cheer went up, and the chief turned to me again, leveling his sword at my face. "So then, otaku girl. What's yer secret?"

I thought quickly. "To cleanse the poison from my blood, you have to boil me in a big pot with several purifying ingredients. Spring water from a waterfall, an acorn from the tallest oak tree, blue mushrooms, and…um…"

"Don't tell me ya forgot," the chief said in a menacing tone, and poked the sword tip through the bars of the cage. "Maybe I can help ya remember."

"Pixie dust!" I blurted desperately, making him blink. "From a live pixie," I added. "Not dead. If it dies, the recipe won't work." I prayed that there were pixies in this world. If not, I was as good as dead.

"Huh," the chief grunted, and turned to the waiting tribe. "All right, louts, you heard it! I want those ingredients back here before dawn! Anyone who don't work, don't eat! Now, get movin'."

The tribe scattered. Hissing, jabbering, and cursing at one another, they vanished into the forest until only one guard remained, leaning on a crooked spear.

The chief eyed me warily and pointed his sword through the bars.

"Don't think ya can trick me by givin' false ingredients," he threatened. "I plan to cut off yer finger, toss it in the stew, an' have one of me mates taste it. If he dies, or melts into a puddle, it be a long, slow death fer you. Understand?"

Chilled, I nodded. I knew none of the goblins would die, because my claim of poison and the recipe for the stew was, of course, completely bogus. Still, I wasn't thrilled about losing one of my fingers. *Terrified* would be a better word.

The chief spat and looked around the near-deserted campsite. "Bah, none of them dogs will know how to catch a piskie," he muttered, scratching his ear. "They'd probably eat the damn thing if they caught it. Arg, I'd better find one myself. Bugrat!"

A few yards away, the lone guard snapped to attention. "Chief?"

"Keep an eye on our dinner," the chief ordered, sheathing his sword. "If it tries to escape, cut off its feet."

"You got it, chief."

"I'm goin' huntin'." The chief shot me one last warning glare, then bounded off into the undergrowth.

"That was clever," Grimalkin murmured, sounding reluctantly impressed.

I nodded, too breathless to answer. After a moment, the sound of chewing recommenced.

It took a while, during which time I gnawed my lip, wrung my hands, and tried not to ask how Grimalkin was doing every twenty seconds. As the minutes stretched, I cast anxious glances at the trees and the forest, expecting the chief or the goblin horde to come bursting through. The lone guard stalked the perimeter of the camp, shooting me an evil look as it walked by and triggering Grimalkin's vanishing act. Finally, on the eighth or ninth circle, Grimalkin's voice floated up after the guard had passed.

"There. I think you can get through now."

I wiggled around as best I could. Peering at the bars, I saw that several of the bindings were chewed in half, testament to Grim's strong jaws and sharp teeth.

"Come on, come on, let us go," Grimalkin hissed, lashing its tail. "You can gawk later—they are coming back."

Bushes rustled around me, and harsh laughter filled the air, getting closer. Heart pounding, I grasped the bars, being careful to avoid the thorns, and pushed. They resisted me, held in place by interlocking branches, and I shoved harder. It was like trying to push through a heavy briar patch; the bars shifted a bit, teasing me with freedom, but stubbornly gave little ground.

The goblin chief stepped out of the trees, followed by three more goblins. He clutched something small and wriggling in one fist, and his followers' arms were filled with pale blue toadstools.

"Mushrooms were the easy part," the chief snorted, casting a derisive glance back at the others. "Any idiot can collect plants. If I'd left these dogs ta catch a piskie, we'd be nothin' but bones before—"

He stopped, and his gaze snapped to me. For a moment, he stood there, blinking, then his eyes narrowed and he clenched his fists. The creature in his grasp gave a high-pitched squeal as the goblin crushed the life from it and flung it to the ground. With a roar of outrage, the chief drew his sword. I screamed and shoved on the cage as hard as I could.

With a great snapping of twigs and thorns, the back of the cage came loose, and I was free.

"Run!" Grimalkin snapped, and I didn't need encouragement. We bolted into the forest, the enraged cries of the goblins on our heels.

8

MOONLIT GROVE

I tore through the forest, branches and leaves slapping at my face, following Grimalkin's shadowy form as best I could. Behind me, twigs snapped, snarls echoed, and the angry cursing of the goblin chief grew louder in my ears. My breath rasped in my chest, my lungs burned, but I forced my legs to keep moving, knowing that if I stumbled or fell, I would die.

"This way!" I heard Grimalkin shout, darting into a patch of bramble. "If we can get to the river, we will be safe! Goblins cannot swim!"

I followed him into the briars, bracing myself for thorns tearing at my flesh and ripping at my clothes. But the branches parted easily for me, as they had when I was with Puck, and I slipped through with minimal scrapes. As I exited the bramble patch, a great crashing noise echoed behind me, followed by loud yelps and swearing. It seemed the goblins weren't finding the path as easy to navigate, and I thanked whatever forces were at work as I continued on.

Over the roaring in my ears and my own ragged breaths,

I heard the sound of rushing water. When I staggered out of the trees, the ground abruptly dropped away into a rocky embankment. A great river loomed before me, nearly a hundred yards across, with no bridges or rafts in sight. I couldn't see the other side because a coiling wall of mist hovered over the water, stretching as far as I could see. Grimalkin stood at the edge, almost invisible in the fog, lashing his tail impatiently.

"Hurry!" he ordered as I stumbled down the bank, exhaustion burning my legs. "The Erlking's territory is on the other side. You must swim, quickly!"

I hesitated. If monster horses lurked in quiet ponds, what would great black rivers hold? Images of giant fish and sea monsters flashed across my mind.

Something flew past my arm, startling me, bouncing off the rocks with a clatter. It was a goblin spear, the bone-white tip gleaming against the stones. The blood drained from my face. I could either stay put and be skewered, or take my chances with the river.

Scrambling down the bank, I flung myself into the water.

The cold shocked me, and I gasped, struggling against the current as it pulled me downstream. I was a fairly strong swimmer, but my limbs felt like jelly, and my lungs were gasping to suck in enough oxygen. I floundered and went under, snorting water up my nose and making my lungs scream. The current pulled me farther away, and I fought down panic.

Another lance zipped over my head. I looked back and saw the goblins following me along the bank, scrambling over the rocks and hurling spears. Terror shot through me, giving me new strength. I struck out for the opposite shore, arms and legs churning madly, fighting the current for all I was worth. More spears splashed around me, but thankfully, the goblins' aim seemed to match their intelligence.

As I drew close to the wall of mist, something struck my

shoulder with jarring force, sending a flare of agony across my back. I gasped and went under. Pain paralyzed my arm, and as the undertow dragged me down, I was sure I was going to die.

Something grabbed my waist, and I felt myself pulled upward. My head broke water and I gasped air into my starving lungs, fighting the blackness on the edge of my vision. As my senses returned, I realized someone was pulling me through the water, but I could see nothing around me because of the mist. Then my feet touched solid ground, and the next thing I knew, I was lying in the grass, the sun shining warmly on my face. My eyes were closed, and I cracked them open cautiously.

A girl's face hovered over mine, blond hair brushing my cheeks, wide green eyes both anxious and curious. Her skin was the color of summer grass, and tiny scales gleamed silver around her neck. She grinned, and her teeth flashed as sharp and pointed as an eel's.

A scream welled in my throat, but I swallowed it down. This…girl?…had just saved my life, even if it meant she wanted to eat me herself. It would be rude if I just shrieked in her face, plus any sudden moves might spark an aggressive feeding frenzy. I couldn't show any fear. With a deep breath, I sat up, wincing as a bolt of pain lanced through my shoulder.

"Um…hello," I stammered, watching her sit back and blink. I was surprised that she had legs instead of a fishtail, though webbing spanned her fingers and toes, and her claws were very, very sharp. A small white dress clung to her body, the hem of it dripping wet. "I'm Meghan. What's your name?"

She cocked her head, reminding me of a cat that couldn't decide whether to eat the mouse or play with it. "You're funny-looking," she stated, her voice rippling like water over rocks. "What are you?"

"Me? I'm human." The moment I said it, I wished I hadn't. In the old fairy tales, which I was remembering more and more of, humans were always food, playthings, or the tragic love interest. And as I was quickly discovering, the inhabitants here had no qualms about eating a speaking, sentient creature. I held the same rung on the food chain as a rabbit or squirrel. It was a scary, rather humbling thought.

"Human?" The girl cocked her head the other way. I caught a glimpse of pink gills under her chin. "My sisters told me stories of humans. They said they sometimes sing to them to lure them underwater." She grinned, showing off her sharp needle-teeth. "I've been practicing. Want to hear?"

"No, she certainly does not." Grimalkin came stalking through the grass, bottlebrush tail held high in the air. The feline was soaked, water dripping off his fur in rivulets, and he did not look pleased.

"Shoo," he growled at the girl, and she drew back, hissing and baring her teeth. Grimalkin seemed unimpressed. "Go away. I am in no mood to play games with nixies. Now, get!"

The girl hissed once more and fled, sliding into the water like a seal. She glared at us from the middle of the river, then vanished in a spray of mist.

"Irritating sirens," Grimalkin fumed, turning to glare at me, eyes narrowed. "You did not promise her anything, did you, human?"

"No." I bristled. I was happy to see the cat, of course, but didn't like the weary resignation in his eyes. As if I was already beyond hope. "You didn't have to scare her off, Grim. She did save my life."

The cat flicked his tail, spraying me with drops. "The only reason she pulled you out of the river was curiosity. If I had not come along, she would have either sung you underwater to drown, or she would have eaten you. Fortunately, nixies are not very brave. They would much prefer a fight beneath the water where they have all the advantages. Now, I suggest we find somewhere to rest. You are wounded, and the swim took a lot out of me. If you can walk, I encourage you to do so."

Grimacing, I pulled myself to my feet. My shoulder felt like it was on fire, but if I held my arm close to my chest, the pain receded to a dull throb. Biting my lip, I followed Grimalkin, away from the river and into the lands of the Erlking.

Even wet, tired, and in pain, I still had the energy to gawk. Pretty soon, my eyes felt huge and swollen from staring so long without blinking. The land on this side of the river was a far cry from the eerie gray forest of the wild fey. Rather than colors being faded and washed out, everything was overly vibrant and vivid. The trees were too green, the flowers screamingly colorful. Leaves glittered, razor sharp in the light, and petals flashed like jewels as they caught the sun. It was all very beautiful, but I couldn't shake the feeling of apprehension as I took it in. Everything seemed...fake somehow, as if this was a fancy coating over reality, as if I wasn't looking at the real world at all.

My shoulder burned, and the skin around it felt puffy and hot. As the sun rose higher in the sky, the throbbing heat leeched down my arm and spread through my back. Sweat ran down my face, making my eyes sting, and my legs trembled.

I finally collapsed under a pine tree, gasping, my body hot and cold at the same time. Grimalkin circled around and trotted back, his tail held high in the air. For a moment, there were two Grimalkins, but then I blinked sweat out of my eyes and there was only one.

"There's something wrong with me," I panted as the cat regarded me coolly. His eyes abruptly floated off his face and hovered in the air between us. I blinked, hard, and they were normal again.

Grimalkin nodded. "Dreamlace venom," he said, to my

confusion. "Goblins poison their spears and arrows. When the hallucinations start coming, you do not have long."

I took a ragged breath. "Isn't there a cure?" I whispered, ignoring the fern that started crawling toward me like a leafy spider. "Someone who can help?"

"That is where we are going." Grimalkin stood, looking back at me. "Not far now, human. Keep your eyes on me, and try to ignore everything else, no matter what comes at you."

It took three tries to get back on my feet, but at last I managed to pull myself up and hold my balance long enough to take a step. And then another. And another. I followed Grimalkin for miles, or at least it seemed that way. After the first tree lunged at me, rattling its branches, it became difficult to concentrate. I nearly lost Grimalkin several times, as the landscape twisted into terrifying versions of itself, reaching for me with twiggy fingers. Distant shapes beckoned from the shadows, calling my name. The ground turned into a writhing mass of spiders and centipedes, crawling up my legs. A deer stepped into the middle of the path, cocked its head, and asked me for the time.

Grimalkin paused. Jumping onto a rock, ignoring the boulder's indignant shouts for him to get off, he turned to face me. "You are on your own from here, human," he said, or at least that's what I heard over the rock's bellowing. "Just keep walking until *he* shows himself. He owes me a favor, but also tends to distrust humans, so the chances that he will help you are about fifty-fifty. Unfortunately, he is the only one who can cure you now."

I frowned, trying to follow his words, but they buzzed around like flies and I couldn't follow. "What are you talking about?" I asked.

"You will know what I mean when you find him, if you

find him." The cat cocked his head and gave me a scrutinizing look. "You are still a virgin, right?"

I decided that last part was a figment of my delirium. Grimalkin slipped away before I could ask him anything else, leaving me confused and disoriented. Waving away a swarm of wasps that circled my head, I stumbled after him.

A vine reached up and snagged my foot. I fell, bursting through the ground, to land on a bed of yellow flowers. They turned their tiny faces to me and screamed, filling the air with pollen. I sat up and found myself in a moonlit grove, the ground carpeted with flowers. Trees danced, rocks laughed at me, and tiny lights zipped through the air.

My limbs were numb, and I was suddenly very tired. Blackness crawled on the edge of my vision. I lay back against a tree and watched the lights swarm through the air. Vaguely, some part of me realized I'd stopped breathing, but the rest of me didn't really care.

A strand of moonlight broke away from the trees and glided toward me. I watched without interest, knowing it was a hallucination. As it got closer, it shimmered and changed shape, sometimes resembling a deer, sometimes a goat or a pony. A horn of light grew from its head, as it regarded me with ancient golden eyes.

"Hello, Meghan Chase."

"Hello," I replied, though my lips didn't move and I had no breath to speak. "Am I dead?"

"Not quite." The moonlight creature laughed softly, shaking its mane. "It is not your destiny to die here, princess."

"Oh." I pondered that, my thoughts swirling muzzily in my head. "How do you know who I am?"

The creature snorted, swishing a lionlike tail. "Those of us who watch the sky have seen your coming for a long time, Meghan Chase. Catalysts always burn brightly, and your light shines unlike any I've seen before. Now, the only question remaining is, what path will you take, and how will you choose to rule?"

"I don't understand."

"You aren't supposed to." The moonlight creature stepped forward and breathed. Silver air washed over me, and my eyelids fluttered shut. "Now, sleep, my princess. Your father awaits you. And tell Grimalkin that I choose to help, not as a favor, but for reasons of my own. The next time he calls on me will be the last."

I didn't want to sleep. Questions swirled to mind, buzzing and insistent. I opened my mouth to ask about my father, but the creature's horn touched my chest, sending a rush of heat through my body. I gasped and opened my eyes.

The moonlit grove had disappeared. A meadow surrounded me, tall grasses waving in the wind, a faint pink glow lighting the horizon. The last traces of a weird dream fluttered across my mind: moving trees, talking deer, a creature made of frost and moonlight. I wondered what was real, and what had just been the effects of the delirium. I felt fine now—better than fine. Some of it must have been real.

Then the grass rustled, as if something crept up behind me.

I whipped around and saw my backpack sitting a few feet away, bright orange against the green. Snatching it up, I pulled it open. The food was gone, of course, as were the flashlight and the aspirin, but my extra clothes were there, crumpled into a ball and sopping wet.

Confused, I stared at the pack. What could have brought it here all the way from the goblins' camp? I didn't think Grimalkin would have gone back for it, especially since that would have meant crossing the river again. But, here was my pack—moldy and wet, but still here. At least the clothes would dry.

And then I remembered something else. Something that made me wince.

Unzipping the side pouch, I pulled out my dripping, waterlogged phone.

"Dammit." I sighed, looking it over. The screen was blurry and warped, totally ruined, a year's savings down the drain. I shook it and heard water sloshing inside. Not good. Just to be sure, I plugged in the headphones and turned it on. Nothing. Not even a buzz. It was well and truly dead.

Sadly, I replaced it in the pocket and zipped it back up. So much for listening to music in Faeryland. I was about to go looking for Grimalkin when a giggle overhead made me glance up.

Something crouched in the branches. Something small and misshapen, watching me with glowing green eyes. I saw the outline of a sinewy body, long thin arms, and goblinlike ears. Only it wasn't a goblin. It was too small for that, and more disturbing, it seemed intelligent.

The monster saw me watching it and offered a slow smile. Its teeth, pointed and razor sharp, glimmered with neon-blue fire, just before it vanished. And I don't mean it scuttled off or faded away like a ghost. It *blipped* out of sight, like the image on a computer screen.

Like that thing I saw in the computer lab.

Definitely time to go.

I found Grimalkin sunning himself on a rock, eyes shut, purring deep in his throat. He cracked open a lazy eye as I came rushing up.

"We're leaving," I told him, shrugging into my backpack. "You're going to take me to Puck, I'm going to rescue Ethan, and we're going home. And if I never see another goblin, nixie, cait sith or whatever, it'll be too soon."

Grimalkin yawned. Infuriatingly, he took his sweet time

getting up, stretching, yawning, scratching his ears, making sure every hair was in place. I stood, nearly dancing with impatience, wanting to grab him by the scruff of the neck, though I knew I'd probably be shredded for it.

"Arcadia, the Summer Court, is close," Grimalkin said as he finally deemed himself ready to start. "Remember, you owe me a small debt when we find your Puck." He leaped from the rock to the ground, looking back at me solemnly. "I will claim my price as soon as we find him. Don't forget."

We walked for hours, through a forest that seemed to be constantly closing in on us. In the corners of my eyes, branches, leaves, even tree trunks moved and shifted, reaching out for me. Sometimes I'd pass a tree or bush, only to see the same one farther down the path. Laughter echoed from the canopy overhead, and strange lights winked and bobbed in the distance. Once, a fox peeked at us from beneath a fallen log, a human skull perched on its head. None of this bothered Grimalkin, who trotted down the forest trail with his tail up, never looking back to see if I followed.

Night had descended, and the enormous blue moon was high overhead, when Grimalkin stopped, flattening his ears. With a hiss, he slipped off the trail and vanished into a patch of ferns. Startled, I looked up to see a pair of riders approaching, glowing bright in the darkness. Their mounts were gray and silver, and the hooves didn't touch the ground as they broke into a canter, straight for me.

I stood my ground as they approached. There was no use trying to outrun hunters on horseback. As they got closer, I saw the riders: tall and elegant, with sharp features and coppery hair tied into a tail. They wore silver mail that flashed in the moonlight, and carried long, thin blades at their sides.

The horses surrounded me, snorting steam, their breath hanging in the air like clouds. Atop their mounts, the knights glared down with unnatural beauty, their features too fine and delicate to be real. "Are you Meghan Chase?" one of them asked, his voice high and clear like a flute. His eyes flashed, the color of the summer sky.

I swallowed. "Yes."

"You will come with us. His Majesty King Oberon, Lord of the Summer Court, has sent for you."

9

IN THE SEELIE COURT

I rode in front of an elven knight, who had one arm wrapped securely around my waist while the other held the reins. Grimalkin dozed in my lap, a warm, heavy weight, and refused to talk to me. The knights wouldn't answer any of my questions, either: where we were going, if they knew Puck, or why King Oberon wanted me. I didn't even know if I was a prisoner or a guest of these people, though I supposed I would find out soon enough. The horses flew over the forest floor, and I saw up ahead that the trees were beginning to thin.

We broke through the tree line, and ahead of us rose an enormous mound. It towered above us in ancient, grassy splendor, the pinnacle seeming to brush the sky. Thorny trees and brambles grew everywhere, especially near the top, so the whole thing resembled a large bearded head. Around it grew a hedge bristling with thorns, some longer than my arm. The knights spurred their horses toward the thickest part of the hedge. I wasn't surprised when the brambles parted for them, forming an arch that they rode beneath, before settling back with a loud crunching sound.

I *was* surprised when the horses rode straight at the side of the hill without slowing, and I clutched Grimalkin tightly, making him growl in protest. The mound neither opened up nor moved aside in any way; we rode *into* the hill and through, sending a shiver all the way down my spine to my toes.

Blinking, I gazed around at total chaos.

A massive courtyard stretched before me, a great circular platform of ivory pillars, marble statues, and flowering trees. Fountains hurled geysers of water into the air, multicolored lights danced over the pools, and flowers in the full spectrum of the rainbow bloomed everywhere. Strains of music reached my ears, a combination of harps and drums, strings and flutes, bells and whistles, somehow lively and melancholy at the same time. It brought tears to my eyes, and suddenly all I wanted to do was slide off the horse and dance until the music consumed me and I was lost in it. Thankfully, Grimalkin muttered something like "Get hold of yourself" and dug his claws into my wrist, snapping me out of it.

Faeries were everywhere, sitting on the marble steps or benches, dancing together in small groups, or just wandering around. My eyes could not take it in fast enough. A boy with a bare chest and shaggy legs ending in hooves winked at me from the shade of a bush. A willowy girl with green-tinted skin stepped out of a tree, scolding a child hanging from the branches. The boy stuck out his tongue, flicked his squirrel tail, and darted higher into the foliage.

I felt a sharp tug on my hair. A tiny figure hovered near my shoulder, gossamer wings buzzing like a humming-bird's. I gasped, but the knight holding me didn't so much as glance at it. She grinned and held out what looked like a plump grape, except the skin of the fruit was bright blue and speckled with orange. I smiled politely and nodded, but she frowned and pointed at my hand. Confused, I held up my palm. She dropped the fruit into it, gave a delighted giggle, and sped away.

"Be careful," Grimalkin rumbled, as a heady aroma rose from the little fruit, making my mouth water. "Eating or drinking certain things in Faery could have unpleasant consequences for someone like you. Do not eat anything. In fact, until we find your Puck, I would not talk to anyone. And whatever you do, do not accept gifts of any sort. This is going to be a long night."

I swallowed and dropped the fruit into one of the fountains as we rode by, watching huge green-and-gold fish swarm around it, mouths gaping. The knights scattered faeries as we rode through the courtyard toward a high stone wall with a pair of silver gates in front. Two massive creatures, each ten feet tall, blue-skinned and tusked, guarded the doors. Their eyes glimmered yellow beneath ropey black hair and heavy brows. Even dressed up, their arms and chests bulging through the fabric of their red uniforms, popping the brass buttons, they were still terrifying. "Trolls," muttered Grimalkin, as I shrank against the unyielding frame of the elven knight. "Be thankful we're in Oberon's land. The Winter Court employs ogres."

The knights stopped and let me down a few feet from the gate. "Be courteous when you speak to the Erlking, child," the knight I'd ridden with told me, and wheeled his mount away. I was left facing two giant trolls with nothing but a cat and my backpack.

Grimalkin squirmed in my arms, and I let him drop to the stones. "Come on." The cat sighed, lashing his tail. "Let us meet Lord Pointy Ears and get this over with."

The two trolls blinked as the cat fearlessly approached the gate, looking like a gray bug scuttling around their clawed feet. One of them moved, and I braced myself, expecting him to stomp Grimalkin into kitty pudding. But the troll only reached over and pulled the gate open as the other did the same on his side. Grimalkin shot me a backward glance, twitched his tail, and slipped through the archway. I took a deep breath, smoothed down my tangled hair, and followed.

The forest grew thick on the other side of the gates, as if the wall had been built to keep it in check. A tunnel of flowering trees and branches stretched away from me, fully in bloom, the scent so overpowering I felt light-headed.

The tunnel ended with a curtain of vines, opening up into a vast clearing surrounded by giant trees. The ancient trunks and interlocking branches made a sort of cathedral, a living palace of giant columns and a leafy vaulted ceiling. Even though I knew we were underground, and it was night outside, sunlight dappled the forest floor, slanting in through tiny cracks in the canopy. Glowing balls of light danced in the air, and a waterfall cascaded gently into a nearby pool. The colors here were dazzling.

A hundred faeries clustered around the middle of the clearing, dressed in brilliant, alien finery. By the look of it, I guessed these were the nobles of the court. Their hair hung long and flowing, or was styled in impossible fashions atop their heads. Satyrs, easily recognized by their shaggy goat legs, and furry little men padded back and forth, serving drinks and trays of food. Slender hounds with moss-green fur milled about, hoping for dropped crumbs. Elven knights in silvery chain armor stood stiffly around the room; a few held hawks or even tiny dragons.

In the center of this gathering sat a pair of thrones, seemingly grown out of the forest floor and flanked by two liveried centaurs. One of the thrones stood empty, except for a caged raven on one of the arms. The great black bird cawed and beat its wings against its prison, its beady eyes bright and green. However, in the throne on the left…

King Oberon, for I could only assume this was him, sat with his fingers steepled together, gazing out at the crowd.

Like the rest of the fey nobles, he was tall and slender, with silver hair that fell to his waist and eyes like green ice. An antlered crown rested on his brow, casting a long shadow over the court, like grasping talons. Power radiated from him, as subtle as a thunderstorm.

Over the colorful sea of nobles, our gazes met. Oberon raised one eyebrow, graceful as the curve of a hawk's wing, but no expression showed on his face. And at that moment, every faery in the room stopped what it was doing and turned to stare at me.

"Great," muttered Grimalkin, forgotten beside me. "Now they all know we are here. Well, come on, human. The Seelie Court is waiting."

My legs felt weak, my mouth dry, but I forced myself to walk. Fey lords and ladies parted for me, but whether out of respect or disdain, I couldn't tell. Their eyes, cold and amused, gave nothing away. A green faery hound sniffed me and growled as I passed, but other than that, the place was silent.

What was I doing here? I didn't even know. Grimalkin was supposed to be leading me to Puck, but now Oberon wanted to see me. It seemed I was getting further and further from my goal of rescuing Ethan. Unless, of course, Oberon knew where Ethan was.

Unless Oberon was holding him hostage.

I reached the foot of the throne. Heart pounding, not knowing what else to do, I dropped to one knee and bowed. I felt the Erlking's eyes on the back of my neck, as ancient as the forest surrounding us. Finally, he spoke.

"Rise, Meghan Chase."

His voice was soft, yet the lilting undertone made me think of roaring oceans and savage storms. The ground trembled beneath my fingers. Controlling my fear, I stood and looked at him and saw something flicker across his masklike face. Pride? Amusement? It was gone before I could tell.

"You have trespassed in our lands," he told me, sending a murmur down the faery court. "You were never meant to see the Nevernever, and yet you tricked a member of this court into bringing you across the barrier. Why?"

Not knowing what else to do, I told him the truth. "I'm searching for my brother, sir. Ethan Chase."

"And you have reason to believe he is here?"

"I don't know." I cast a desperate look at Grimalkin, who was grooming a back leg and paying no attention to me. "My friend Robbie... Puck...he told me that Ethan was kidnapped by faeries. That they left a changeling in his place."

"I see." Oberon turned his head slightly, regarding the caged bird on his throne. "And that is yet another transgression, Robin."

I gaped, my mouth dropping open. "Puck?"

The raven looked at me with bright green eyes, cawed softly, and seemed to shrug. I glared back at Oberon. "What are you doing to him?"

"He was commanded never to bring you to our land." Oberon's voice was calm but pitiless. "He was ordered to keep you blind to our ways, our life, our very existence. I punished him for his disobedience. Perhaps I will turn him back in a few centuries, after he has had time to think on his transgressions."

"He was trying to help me!"

Oberon smiled, but it was cold, empty. "We immortals do not think of life in the same way as humans. Puck should have had no interest in rescuing a human child, especially if it conflicted with my direct orders. That he caved to your demands suggests he may be spending too much time with mortals, learning their ways and their capricious emotions. It is time he remembers how to be fey."

I swallowed. "But what about Ethan?"

"I know not." Oberon leaned back, shrugging his lean

shoulders. "He is not here, within my territories. That much I can tell you."

Despair crushed me like a ten-ton weight. Oberon didn't know where Ethan was, and worse, didn't care. Now I'd lost Puck as a guide, as well. It was back to square one. I'd have to find the other court—the Unseelie one—sneak in and rescue my brother, all by myself. That is, if I could get there in one piece. Maybe Grimalkin would agree to help me. I looked down at the cat, who was completely absorbed in washing his tail, and my heart sank. Probably not. Well, then. I was on my own.

The enormity of my task loomed ahead, and I fought back tears. Where would I go now? How would I even survive?

"Fine." I didn't mean to sound surly, but I wasn't feeling very positive at the moment. "I'll be leaving now, I guess. If you won't help me, I'll just have to keep looking."

"I'm afraid," said Oberon, "that I can't let you go just yet."

"What?" I recoiled. "Why?"

"Much of the land knows you are here," the Erlking continued. "Outside this court, I have many enemies. Now that you are here, now that you are *aware,* they would use you to get to me. I'm afraid I cannot allow that."

"I don't get it." I looked around at the fey nobles; many of them looked grim, unfriendly. The stares they leveled at me now glittered with dislike. I turned back to Oberon, pleading. "Why would they want me? I'm just a human. I don't have anything to do with you people. I just want my brother back."

"On the contrary." Oberon sighed, and for the first time, age seemed to weigh him down. He looked old; still deadly and extremely powerful, but ancient and tired. "You are more connected to our world than you know, Meghan Chase. You see, you are my daughter."

10

THE ERLKING'S DAUGHTER

I stared at Oberon as the world fell away beneath me. The Erlking gazed back, his expression cool and unruffled, his eyes blank once more. The silence around us was absolute. I didn't see anyone except Oberon; the rest of the court faded into the background, until we were the only two in the whole world.

Puck gave an indignant *caw* and flapped his wings against the cage.

That broke the spell. *"What?"* I choked out. The Erlking didn't so much as blink, which somehow infuriated me even more. "That's not true! Mom was married to my dad. She stayed with him until he disappeared, and she remarried Luke."

"That is true," Oberon nodded. "But that man is not your father, Meghan. I am." He stood, his courtly robes billowing around him. "You are half-fey, half my blood. Why do you think I had Puck guard you, keep you from seeing our world? Because it comes naturally to you. Most mortals are blind, but you could see through the Mist from the beginning."

I thought back to all those times I almost saw something, out of the corner of my eye, or silhouetted in the trees. Glimpses of things not quite there. I shook my head. "No, I don't believe you. My mom loved my dad. She wouldn't—" I broke off, not wanting to think about the implications.

"Your mother was a beautiful woman," Oberon continued softly. "And quite extraordinary, for a mortal. Artistic people can always see a bit of the fey world around them. She would often go to the park to paint and draw. It was there, beside the pond, that we first met."

"Stop it," I gritted out. "You're lying. I'm not one of you. I can't be."

"Only half," Oberon said, and from the corner of my eye I caught looks of disgust and contempt from the rest of the court. "Still, that is enough for my enemies to attempt to control me through you. Or, perhaps, to turn you against me. You are more dangerous than you know, daughter. Because of the threat you represent, you must remain here."

My world seemed to be collapsing around me. "For how long?" I whispered, thinking of Mom, Luke, school, everything I left behind in my world. Had I been missed already? Would I return to find a hundred years had passed while I was gone, and everyone I knew was long dead?

"Until I deem otherwise," Oberon said, in the tone my mother often used when she settled the matter. *Because I said so.* "At the very least, until Elysium is through. The Winter Court will be arriving in a few days, and I will have you where I can see you." He clapped, and a female satyr broke away from the crowd to bow before him. "Take my daughter to her room," he ordered, sitting back on his throne. "See that she is made comfortable."

"Yes, my lord," murmured the satyr, and began to clop

away, glancing back to see if I was coming. Oberon leaned back, not looking at me, his face blank and stony.

My audience with the Erlking was over.

I had stumbled back, prepared to follow the goat-girl out of the court, when Grimalkin's voice floated up from the ground. I'd completely forgotten about the cat. "Begging your pardon, Erlking," Grimalkin said, sitting up and curling his tail around himself, "but our business is not yet complete. You see, the girl is in my debt. She promised me a favor for bringing her safely here, and that obligation has yet to be paid."

I glared at the feline, wondering why it was bringing that up now. Oberon, however, looked at me with a grim expression. "Is this true?"

I nodded, wondering why the nobles were giving me looks of horror and pity. "Grim helped me escape the goblins," I explained. "He saved my life. I wouldn't be here if it weren't for…" My voice trailed off as I saw the look in Oberon's eyes.

"A life debt, then." He sighed. "Very well, Cait Sith. What would you have of me?"

Grimalkin lowered his eyelids. It was easy to see that the cat was purring. "A small favor, great lord," he rumbled, "to be called in at a later time."

"Granted." The Erlking nodded, and yet he seemed to grow bigger in his chair. His shadow loomed over the cat, who blinked and flattened his ears. Thunder growled overhead, the light in the forest dimmed, and a cold wind rattled the branches in the trees, showering us with petals. The rest of the court shrank away; some vanished from sight completely. In the sudden darkness, Oberon's eyes glowed amber. "But be warned, feline," he boomed, his voice making the ground quiver. "I am not to be trifled with. Do not think to make a fool out of me, for I can grant your request in insurmountably unpleasant ways."

"Of course, Erlking," Grimalkin soothed, his fur whipping about in the gale. "I am always your servant."

"I would be foolish indeed to trust the flattering words of a cait sith." Oberon leaned back, his face an expressionless mask once more. The wind died down, the sun returned, and things were normal again. "You have your favor. Now go."

Grimalkin bowed his head, turned, and trotted back to me, bottlebrush tail held high.

"What was that about, Grim?" I demanded, scowling at the feline. "I thought you wanted a favor from me. What was all that with Oberon?"

Grimalkin didn't so much as pause. Tail up, he passed me without comment, slipped into the tunnel of trees, and vanished from sight.

The satyr touched my arm. "This way," she murmured, and led me away from the court. I felt the eyes of the nobles and the hounds on my back as we left the presence of the Erlking.

"I don't understand," I said miserably, following the satyr girl across the clearing. My brain had gone numb; I felt awash in a sea of confusion, moments away from drowning. I just wanted to find my brother. How had it come to this?

The satyr gave me a sympathetic glance. She was shorter than me by a foot, with large hazel eyes that matched her curly hair. I tried to keep my eyes away from her furry lower half, but it was difficult, especially when she smelled faintly like a petting zoo.

"It is not so bad," she said, leading me not through the tunnel, but to a far side of the clearing. The trees here were so thick the sunlight didn't permeate the branches, shadowing everything in emerald darkness. "You might enjoy it here. Your father does you a great honor."

"He's not my father," I snapped. She blinked wide, liquid brown eyes, and her lower lip quivered. I sighed, regretting my harsh tone. "Sorry. It's just a lot to take in. Two days ago, I was home, sleeping in my own bed. I didn't believe in goblins or elves or talking cats, and I certainly didn't ask for any of this."

"King Oberon took a great chance for you," the satyr said, her voice a bit firmer. "The cait sith held a life debt over you, which meant it could've asked for anything. Lord Oberon took it and made it his, so Grimalkin can't request you to poison anyone or to give up your first child."

I recoiled in horror. "He would have?"

"Who knows what goes on in the mind of a cat?" The satyr shrugged, picking her way over a tangle of roots. "Just… be careful what you say around here. If you make a promise, you're bound to it, and wars have been fought over 'small favors.' Be especially careful around the high lords and ladies— they are all adept at the game of politics and pawn-making." She suddenly paled and put a hand to her mouth. "I've said too much. Please forgive me. If that gets back to King Oberon…"

"I won't say anything," I promised.

She looked relieved. "I am grateful, Meghan Chase. Others might have used that against me. I am still learning the ways of the court."

"What's your name?"

"Tansy."

"Well, you're the only one who has treated me nicely without expecting anything in return," I told her. "Thank you."

She looked embarrassed. "Truly, you do not need to put yourself in my debt, Meghan Chase. Here, let me show you your room."

We were standing at the edge of the trees. A wall of flowering bramble, so thick I couldn't see to the other side, loomed above us. Between the pink-and-purple flowers, thorns bristled menacingly.

Tansy reached out and brushed one of the petals. The hedge shuddered, then curled in and rearranged itself, forming a tunnel not unlike the one leading into the court. At the end of the prickly tube stood a small red door.

In a daze, I followed Tansy into the briar tunnel and through the door as she opened it for me. Inside, a dazzling bedroom greeted my senses. The floor was white marble, inlaid with patterns of flowers, birds, and animals. Under my disbelieving stare, some of them moved. A fountain bubbled in the middle of the room, and a small table stood nearby, covered with cakes, tea, and bottles of wine. A massive, silk-covered bed dominated one wall, while a fireplace stood at the other. The flames crackling in the hearth changed color, from green to blue to pink and back again.

"This is the guest-of-honor suite," Tansy announced, gazing around enviously. "Only important guests of the Seelie Court are allowed here. Your father really is giving you a great honor."

"Tansy, please stop calling him that." I sighed, looking around the massive room. "My dad was an insurance salesman from Brooklyn. I'd know if I wasn't fully human, wouldn't I? Wouldn't there be some sort of sign, pointed ears or wings or something like that?"

Tansy blinked, and the look she gave me sent chills up my back. Hooves clopping, she crossed the room to stand beside a large dresser with a mirror overhead. Looking back, she beckoned me with a finger.

Anxiously, I moved to stand beside her. Somewhere deep inside, a voice began screaming that I didn't want to see what would be revealed next. I didn't listen in time. With a solemn look, Tansy pointed to the mirror, and for the second time that day, my world turned upside down.

I hadn't seen myself since the day I stepped through the

closet with Puck. I knew my clothes were filthy, sweat-stained, and ripped to shreds by branches, thorns, and claws. From the neck down, I looked how I expected to look: like a bum that had been tramping through the wilderness for two days without a bath.

I didn't recognize my face.

I mean, I knew it was me. The reflection moved its lips when I did, and blinked when I blinked. But my skin was paler, the bones of my face sharper, and my eyes seemed enormous, those of a deer caught in headlights. And through my matted, tangled hair, where nothing had been yesterday, two long pointed ears jutted up from both sides of my head.

I gaped at the reflection, feeling dizzy, unable to comprehend the meaning. *No!* my brain screamed, violently rejecting the image before it, *that isn't you! It isn't!*

The floor swayed under my feet. I couldn't catch my breath. And then, all the shock, adrenaline, fear, and horror of the past two days descended on me at once. The world spun, tilted on its axis, and I fell away into oblivion.

PART
II

"Meghan," Mom called from the other side of the door. "Get up. You're going to be late for school."

I groaned and peeked out from under the covers. Was it morning already? Apparently so. A hazy gray light filtered in my bedroom window, shining on my alarm clock, which read 6:48 a.m.

"Meghan!" Mom called, and this time a sharp rapping accompanied her voice. "Are you up?"

"Ye-es!" I hollered from the bed, wishing she'd go away.

"Well, hurry up! You're going to miss the bus."

I shambled to my feet, threw on clothes from the cleanest pile on the floor, and grabbed my backpack. My phone tumbled out, landing with a splat on my bed. I frowned. Why was it wet?

"Meghan!" came Mom's voice yet again, and I rolled my eyes. "It's almost seven! If I have to drive you to school because you missed the bus, you're grounded for a month!"

"All right, all right! I'm coming, dammit!" Stomping to the door, I threw it open.

Ethan stood there, his face blue and wrinkled, his lips pulled into a rictus grin. In one hand, he clutched a butcher knife. Blood spattered his hands and face.

"Mommy slipped," he whispered, and plunged the knife into my leg.

I woke up screaming.

Green flames sputtered in the hearth, casting the room in an eerie glow. Panting, I lay back against cool silk pillows, the nightmare ebbing away into reality.

I was in the Seelie king's court, as much a prisoner here as poor Puck, trapped in his cage. Ethan, the real Ethan, was still out there somewhere, waiting to be rescued. I wondered if he was all right, if he was as terrified as I was. I wondered if Mom and Luke were okay with that demon changeling in the house. I prayed Mom's injury wasn't serious, and that the changeling wouldn't cause harm to anyone else.

And then, lying in a strange bed in the faery kingdom, another thought came to me. A thought sparked by something Oberon said. *That man is not your father, Meghan. I am.*

Is your father, not *was*. As if Oberon knew where he was. As if he was still alive. The thought made my heart pound in excitement. I knew it. My dad must be in Faeryland, somewhere. Maybe somewhere close. If only I could reach him.

First things first, though. I had to get out of here.

I sat up...and met the impassive green eyes of the Erlking.

He stood by the hearth, the shifting light of the flames washing over his face, making him even more eerie and spectral. His long shadow crept over the room, the horned crown branching over the bedcovers like grasping fingers. In the darkness, his eyes glowed green like a cat's. Seeing I was awake, he nodded and beckoned to me with an elegant, long-fingered hand.

"Come." His voice, though soft, was steely with authority. "Approach me. Let us talk, my daughter."

I'm not your daughter, I wanted to say, but the words stuck in my throat. Out of the corner of my eye, I saw the mirror atop the dresser, and my long-eared reflection within. I shuddered and turned away.

Throwing off the bedcovers, I saw that my clothes had changed. Instead of the ripped, disgusting shirt and pants I'd worn for the past two days, I was clean and draped in a lacy white nightgown. Not only that, but there was an outfit laid out for me at the foot of the bed: a ridiculously fancy gown encrusted with emeralds and sapphires, as well as a cloak and long, elbow-length gloves. I wrinkled my nose at the whole ensemble.

"Where are my clothes?" I asked, turning to Oberon. "My real ones."

The Erlking sniffed. "I dislike mortal clothes within my court," he stated quietly. "I believe you should wear something suited for your heritage, as you are to stay here awhile. I had your mortal rags burned."

"You *what?*"

Oberon narrowed his eyes, and I realized I might've gone too far. I figured the King of the Seelie Court wasn't used to being questioned. "Um…sorry," I murmured, sliding out of bed. I'd worry about clothes later. "So, what did you want to talk about?"

The Erlking sighed and studied me uncomfortably. "You put me in a difficult position, daughter," he murmured at last, turning back to the hearth. "You are the only one of my offspring to venture into our world. I must say, I was a bit surprised that you managed to survive this long, even with Robin looking after you."

"Offspring?" I blinked. "You mean, I have other brothers and sisters? Half siblings?"

"None that are alive." Oberon made a dismissive gesture. "And none within this century, I assure you. Your mother was the only human to catch my eye in nearly two hundred years."

My mouth was suddenly dry. I stared at Oberon in growing anger. "Why?" I demanded, making him arch a slender eyebrow. "Why her? Wasn't she already married to my dad? Did you even care about that?"

"I did not." Oberon's look was pitiless, unrepentant. "What do I care for human rituals? I need no permission to take what I want. Besides, had she been truly happy, I would not have been able to sway her."

Bastard. I bit my tongue to keep the angry word from coming out. Furious as I might be, I wasn't suicidal. But Oberon's gaze sharpened, as if he knew what I was thinking. He gave me a long, level stare, challenging me to defy him. We glared at each other for several heartbeats, the shadows curling around us, as I struggled to keep my gaze steady. It was no use; staring at Oberon was like facing down an approaching tornado. I shivered and dropped my eyes first.

After a moment, Oberon's face softened, and a faint smile curled his lips. "You are a lot like her, daughter," he continued, his voice split between pride and resignation. "Your mother was a remarkable mortal. If she had been fey, her paintings would have come to life, so much care was put into them. When I watched her at the park, I sensed her longing, her loneliness and isolation. She wanted more from her life than what she was getting. She wanted something extraordinary to happen."

I didn't want to hear this. I didn't want anything ruining my perfect memory of our life before. I wanted to keep believing that my mom loved my dad, that we were happy and content, and she was his whole life. I didn't want to hear about a mother who was lonely, who fell prey to faery tricks and glamour. With one casual statement, my past had shattered into an unfamiliar mess, and I felt I didn't know my mother at all.

"I waited a month before I made myself known to her," Oberon went on, oblivious to my torment. I slumped against the bed as he continued. "I grew to know her habits, her emotions, every inch of her. And when I did reveal myself, I showed her only a glimpse of my true nature, curious to see if she would approach the extraordinary, or if she would cling to her mortal disbelief. She accepted me eagerly, with unrestrained joy, as if she had been waiting for me all along."

"Stop," I choked. My stomach churned; I closed my eyes to avoid being sick. "I don't want to hear this. Where was my dad when all this was happening?"

"Your *mother's husband* was away most nights," Oberon replied, putting emphasis on those two words, to remind me that man was not my father. "Perhaps that was why your mother yearned for something more. I gave her that; one night of magic, of the passion she was missing. Just one, before I returned to Arcadia, and the memory of us faded from her mind."

"She doesn't remember you?" I looked up at him. "Is that why she never told me?"

Oberon nodded. "Mortals tend to forget their encounters with our kind," he said softly. "At best, it seems like a vivid dream. Most times, we fade from memory completely. Surely you've noticed this. How even the people you live with, who see you every day, cannot seem to remember you. Though, I always suspected your mother knew more, remembered more, than she let on. Especially after you were born." A dark tone crept into his voice; his slanted eyes turned black and pupilless. I trembled as the shadow crept over the floor, reaching for me with pointed fingers. "She tried to take you away," he said in a terrible voice. "She wanted to hide you from us. From me." Oberon paused, looking utterly inhuman, though he hadn't moved. The fire leaped in the hearth, dancing madly in the eyes of the Erlking.

"And yet, here you are." Oberon blinked, his tone softening, and the fire flickered low again. "Standing before me, your human mien faded at last. The moment you set foot in the Nevernever, it was only a matter of time before your heritage began to show itself. But now I must be very cautious." He drew himself up, gathering his robes around him, as if to leave. "I cannot be too wary, Meghan Chase," he warned. "There are many who would use you against me, some within this very court. Be careful, daughter. Even I cannot protect you from everything."

I sagged on the bed, my thoughts spinning crazily. Oberon watched me a moment longer, his mouth set in a grim line, then crossed the room without looking back. When I looked up, the Erlking was gone. I hadn't even heard the door close.

A knock on the door startled me upright. I didn't know how much time had passed since Oberon's visit. I still lay on the bed. The colored flames burned low, flickering erratically in the hearth. Everything seemed surreal and foggy and dreamlike, as if I'd imagined the whole encounter.

The knock came again, and I roused myself. "Come in!"

The door creaked open, and Tansy entered, smiling. "Good evening, Meghan Chase. How do you feel today?"

I slipped to the floor, realizing I was still in the nightgown. "Fine, I guess," I muttered, looking around the room. "Where are my clothes?"

"King Oberon has given you a gown." Tansy smiled and

pointed to the gown on the bed. "He had it designed especially for you."

I scowled. "No. No way. I want my real clothes."

The little satyr blinked. She clopped over and picked up the hem of the dress, running it between her fingers. "But…lord Oberon wishes you to wear this." She seemed bewildered that I would defy Oberon's wishes. "Does this not please you?"

"Tansy, I am *not* wearing that."

"Why not?"

I recoiled at the thought of parading around in such finery. My whole life, I had worn ratty jeans and T-shirts. My family was poor and couldn't afford designer clothes and name brands. Rather than bemoan the fact that I never got nice things, I flaunted my grunginess and told myself I'd rather be comfortable than spend hours in front of a mirror perfecting my outfit. The only dress I'd ever worn was to someone's wedding.

Besides, if I wore the fancy outfit Oberon picked for me, it would be like admitting to being his daughter. And I wasn't about to do that.

"I—I just don't want to," I stammered lamely. "I'd rather wear my own clothes."

"Your clothing was burned."

"Where's my backpack?" I suddenly remembered the change of clothes I'd shoved inside. They'd be damp, moldy, and disgusting, but better that than wearing faery finery.

I found my backpack, stuffed carelessly behind the dresser, and unzipped it. A sour, dank smell rose from within as I dumped the contents onto the floor. The wadded ball of clothes rolled out, wrinkled and smelly, but mine. The broken phone also tumbled free, skidded across the marble floor, and came to a stop a few feet from Tansy.

The satyr girl yelped, and in one fantastic bound, leaped

onto the bed. Clutching the bedpost, she stared wide-eyed at the device on the floor.

"What is *that?*"

"What? This? It's just a phone." Blinking, I retrieved the device and held it up. "It's used to call people in the real world, but it's broken now, so I can't show you how it works. Sorry."

"It stinks of iron!"

I didn't know what to say to that, so I opted for a confused frown.

Tansy stared at me with huge brown eyes, very slowly coming down from her perch. "You…you can hold it?" she whispered. "Without burning your flesh? Without poisoning your blood?"

"Um." I glanced at the phone, lying harmlessly in my palm. "Yes?"

She shuddered. "Please, put it away." I shrugged, grabbed my backpack, and stuffed it into a side pocket. Tansy sighed and relaxed. "Forgive me, I did not wish to upset you. King Oberon has bid me keep you company until Elysium. Would you care to see more of the court?"

Not really, but it was better than being cooped up in here with nothing to do. *And maybe I'll find a way out of this place.*

"All right," I told the satyr girl. "But I want to change first."

She cast a glance at my mortal clothes, lying wrinkled on the floor, and her nostrils flared. I could tell she wanted to say something but was polite enough not to comment on it. "As you wish. I will wait outside."

I slipped into the baggy jeans and the wrinkled, smelly T-shirt, feeling a nasty glow of satisfaction as they slid comfortably over my skin. *Burn my things, will he?* I thought, dragging my sneakers out and shoving my feet into them. *I'm not part of his court, and I'm certainly not claiming to be his daughter. No matter what he says.*

There was a brush lying on the dresser, and I grabbed it to run through my hair. As I looked in the mirror, my stomach twisted. I seemed less recognizable than before, in ways that I couldn't even put a finger on. I knew only that the longer I stayed here, the more I was fading away.

Shivering, I grabbed my backpack, happy for the familiar, comfortable weight, and slung it over my shoulders. Even though it carried nothing but a broken iPod, it was still mine. Refusing to glance at the mirror, feeling eyes on the back of my neck, I opened the door and slipped into the briar tunnel.

Moonlight filtered through the branches, dappling the path with silver shadows. I wondered how long I'd been asleep. The night was warm, and faint strings of music drifted on the breeze. Tansy approached, and in the darkness, her face looked less human and more staring-black-goat. A strand of moonlight fell over her, and she was normal again. Smiling, she took my hand and led me forward.

The bramble tunnel seemed longer this time, filled with twists and turns I didn't remember. I looked back once and saw the thorns closing behind us, the tunnel vanishing from sight.

"Um…"

"It's all right," said Tansy, pulling me forward. "The Hedge can take you wherever you want to go within the court. You just have to know the right paths."

"Where are we going?"

"You'll see."

The tunnel opened into a moonlit grove. Music drifted on the breeze, played by a willowy green girl on an elegant golden harp. A small group of elven girls clustered around a tall, vine-backed chair with white roses growing out of the arms.

Sitting at the foot of the chair was a human. I blinked, rubbing my eyes to make sure they weren't playing tricks on me. No, it was a human, a young man with curly blond hair, his eyes blank and bemused. He was shirtless, and a golden collar encircled his neck, attached to a thin silver chain. The group of fey girls swarmed around him, kissing his bare shoulders, rubbing their hands over his chest, whispering things in his ear. One of them ran a pink tongue up his neck, her fingernails drawing bloody gouges down his back, making him arch with ecstasy. My stomach turned and I looked away. A moment later, I forgot all about them.

On the throne was a woman of such otherworldly beauty, I was instantly mortified by my ratty clothes and casual appearance. Her long hair shifted colors in the moonlight, sometimes silver, sometimes brightest gold. Arrogance warred with the aura of power surrounding her. As Tansy pulled me forward and bowed, the woman narrowed glittering blue eyes and regarded me as though examining a slug found beneath a log.

"So," she said at last, her voice dripping poisoned icicles, "this is Oberon's little bastard."

Oh, crap. I knew who this was. She sat the second, empty throne in Oberon's court. She was the other driving force in *A Midsummer Night's Dream*. She was nearly as powerful as Oberon himself.

"Queen Titania," I gulped, bowing.

"It speaks," the lady went on, feigning surprise, "as if it knows me. As if being Oberon's throwback will protect it from my wrath." Her eyes glittered like chips of diamond, and she smiled, making her even more beautiful and terrifying. "But I am feeling merciful tonight. Perhaps I will not cut out its tongue and feed it to the hounds. Perhaps." Titania looked past me to Tansy, still bowed low, and crooked one elegant finger. "Come forward, goat-child."

Keeping her head bowed, Tansy edged forward until she

stood at the faery queen's arm. Queen Titania leaned forward, as though whispering to the satyr, but spoke loud enough for me to hear. "I will allow you to be the voice for this conversation," she explained, as if to a small child. "I will direct all questions to you, and you will speak for the bastard over there. If, at any point, it attempts to speak to me directly, I will turn it into a hart and set my hounds after it until it collapses from exhaustion or is torn apart. Is this perfectly clear?"

"Yes, my lady," Tansy whispered.

Perfectly clear, bitch-queen, I echoed in my thoughts.

"Excellent." Titania leaned back, looking pleased. She shot me a brittle smile, as hostile as a snarling dog, then turned to Tansy. "Now, goat-girl, why is the bastard here?"

"Why are you here?" Tansy repeated, directing the question to me.

"I'm looking for my brother," I replied, being careful to keep my gaze on Tansy and not the vindictive ice-hag next to her.

"She's looking for her brother," Tansy confirmed, turning again to the faery queen. Good God, this was going to take forever.

"He was stolen and brought into the Nevernever," I said, plunging on before Titania could ask another question. "Puck led me here through the closet. I came to get my brother and take him home, and be rid of the changeling left in his place. That's all I want. I'll leave as soon as I find him."

"Puck?" mused the lady. "Aah, that is where he has been all this time. How very clever of Oberon, hiding you like that. And then you have to ruin his little deception by coming here." She *tsked* and shook her head. "Goat-girl," she said, looking at Tansy once more, "ask the bastard this—would she prefer being a rabbit or a hart?"

"M-my lady?" Tansy stammered as I felt the shadows closing in on me. My heart pounded and I looked around for an escape route. Thorny briars surrounded us; there was nowhere to run.

"It is a simple question," Titania went on, her tone perfectly conversational. "What would she prefer I change her into—a rabbit or a hart?"

Looking like a trapped rabbit herself, Tansy turned and met my eyes. "M-my lady would like to know if you—"

"Yes, I heard," I interrupted. "A rabbit or a hart. How about neither?" I dared look up and meet the faery queen's eyes. "Look, I know you hate me, but just let me rescue my brother and go home. He's only four, and he must be terrified. Please, I know he's waiting for me. Once I find him, we'll leave and you'll never see us again, I swear."

Titania's face glowed with angry triumph. "The creature dares to speak to me! Very well. She has chosen her fate." The faery queen raised a gloved hand, and lightning flashed overhead. "A hart it is, then. Set free the hounds. We will have a merry hunt!"

Her hand swept down, pointing at me, and spasms rocked my body. I screamed and arched my back, feeling my spine lengthen and pop. Invisible pliers grabbed my face and pulled, stretching my lips into a muzzle. I felt my legs getting longer, thinner, my fingers turning into cloven hooves. I screamed again, but what left my throat was the agonized bleat of a deer.

Then, suddenly, it stopped. My body snapped into the proper shape, like a taut rubber band, and I collapsed, gasping, to the forest floor.

Through my blurry vision, I saw Oberon standing at the mouth of the tunnel, a pair of faery knights behind him, his arm outstretched. For a moment, I was sure I saw Grimalkin standing by his feet, but I blinked and the shadows were empty. With his appearance, the lilting harp music ground to a halt. The fey girls surrounding the collared human flung themselves to the floor and bowed their heads.

"Wife," Oberon said calmly, stepping into the clearing. "You will not do this."

Titania rose, her face a mask of fury. "You dare speak to me that way," she spat, and wind rattled the branches of the trees. "You dare, after you hid her from me, after you sent your little pet to protect her!" Titania sneered, and lightning crackled overhead. "You deny me a consort, and yet you flaunt your half-breed abomination in the court for all to see. You are a disgrace. The court mocks you in secret, and you still protect her."

"Nonetheless." Somehow, Oberon's composed voice rose above the howling of the wind. "She is my blood, and you will not touch her. If you have any grievances, my lady, cast them on me, not on the girl. It is not her fault."

"Perhaps I shall turn her into a cabbage," the queen mused, shooting me a look of black hatred, "and plant her in my garden for the rabbits to enjoy. Then she would be useful and wanted."

"You will *not* touch her," Oberon said again, his voice rising in authority. His cloak billowed out, and he grew taller, his shadow lengthening on the ground. "I command it, wife. I have given my word that she shall not come to harm within my court, and you will follow me on this. Do I make myself clear?"

Lightning sizzled, and the ground shook under the intensity of the rulers' gazes. The girls at the foot of the throne cringed, and Oberon's guards grasped the hilts of their swords. A branch snapped nearby, barely missing the harp girl, who cowered under the trunk. I pressed myself to the earth and tried to make myself as small as possible.

"Very well, husband." Titania's voice was as cold as ice,

but the wind gradually died and the earth stopped moving. "As you command. I will not harm the half-breed while she is within the court."

Oberon gave a curt nod. "And your servants will not do her ill, either."

The queen pursed her lips as if she'd swallowed a lemon. "No, husband."

The Erlking sighed. "Very well. We will speak on this later. I bid you good-night, my lady." He turned, his cloak billowing behind him, and left the clearing, the guards trailing in his wake. I wanted to call after him, but I didn't want it to look like I was running after Daddy's protection, especially after he put the smackdown on Titania.

Speaking of which…

I swallowed and turned to face the faery queen, who glared at me as if hoping the blood would boil in my veins. "Well, you heard His Majesty, half-breed," she cooed, her voice laced with poison. "Get out of my sight before I forget my promise and change you into a snail."

I was only too happy to leave. However, no sooner did I stand up and prepare to flee than Titania snapped her fingers.

"Wait!" she ordered. "I've a better idea. Goat-girl, come here."

Tansy appeared at her side. The satyr looked terrified; her eyes were bulging out of her head and her furry legs trembled. The queen flicked a finger at me. "Take Oberon's bastard to the kitchens. Tell Sarah we've found her a new serving girl. If the bastard must stay, she might as well work."

"B-but, my lady," Tansy stammered, and I marveled that she had the courage to contradict the queen, "King Oberon said—"

"Ah, but King Oberon is no longer here, is he?" Titania's eyes gleamed, and she smiled. "And what Oberon does not know will not hurt him. Now, go, before I truly lose my patience."

We went, trying not to trip over each other as we fled the queen's presence and went back into the tunnel.

As we reached the edge of the brambles, a ripple of power shook the air, and the girls behind us gave cries of dismay. A moment later, a fox darted into the tunnel with a flash of red fur. It stopped a few yards away and looked at us, amber eyes wide with confusion and fear. I saw the gleam of a golden collar around its throat, before it gave a frightened bark and vanished into the thorns.

In silence, I followed Tansy through the twisting maze of briars, trying to process all that had happened. Okay, so Titania had a serious grudge against me; that was really, really bad. As the record of "Enemies-I-did-not-want" went, the Queen of the Faeries would probably top the list. I would have to be really careful from now on, or risk ending up a mushroom in somebody's soup.

Tansy didn't say a word until we came to a pair of large stone doors in the hedge. Tendrils of steam curled out beneath the cracks, and the air was hot and greasy.

Pushing the doors open released a blast of hot, smoky air. Blinking tears from my eyes, I stared into an enormous kitchen. Brick ovens roared, copper kettles bubbled over fires, and a dozen aromas flooded my senses. Furry little men in aprons scuttled back and forth between several long counters, cooking, baking, testing the contents of the kettles. A bloody boar carcass lay on a table, and hacking into it was a huge, green-skinned woman with thick tusks and brown hair pulled into a braid.

She saw us in the doorway and came stomping over, blood and bits of meat clinging to her apron.

"No loafers in my kitchen," she growled, waving a large

bronze butcher knife at me. "I got no scraps for the likes of you. Take your sneaky, thieving fingers elsewhere."

"S-Sarah Skinflayer, this is Meghan Chase." As Tansy introduced us, I gave the troll woman a sickly, please-don't-kill-me smile. "She's to help you in the kitchen by order of the queen."

"I don't need help from a skinny half-human whelp," Sarah Skinflayer growled, eyeing me disdainfully. "She'd only slow us down, and we're running ourselves into the ground, getting ready for Elysium." Looking me over, she sighed and scratched her head with the blunt end of the knife. "I guess I could find a place for her. But tell Her Majesty that if she wants to torture someone else, try the stables or the kennel runs. I've got all the help I need here."

Tansy nodded and scampered off, leaving me alone with the giantess. I felt sweat dripping down my back, and it wasn't from the fires. "All right, whelp," Sarah Skinflayer barked, pointing at me with her knife. "I don't care if you are His Majesty's by-blow, you're in my kitchen now. Rules here are simple—you don't work, you don't eat. And I have a little fun with the horsewhip in the corner. They don't call me Sarah Skinflayer for nothing."

The rest of the night passed in a blur of scrubbing and cleaning. I mopped blood and bits of flesh from the stone floor. I swept ashes from the brick ovens. I washed mountains of plates, goblets, pots, and pans. Every time I paused to rub my aching limbs, the troll woman would be there, barking orders and pushing me to my next chore. Toward the end of the night, after catching me sitting on a stool, she growled something about "lazy humans," snatched the broom from my hands, and gave me the one she was carrying. As soon as my hands closed around the handle, the broom leaped to life and began sweeping vigorously, brisk, hard strokes, while my feet carried me around the room. I tried letting go of the thing, but my fingers seemed glued to the handle, and I couldn't open my hands. I swept the floor until my legs ached and my arms burned, until I couldn't see for the sweat in my eyes. Finally, the troll woman snapped her fingers and the broom stopped its mad sweeping. I collapsed, my knees buckling underneath me, tempted to hurl the sadistic broom into the nearest oven.

"Did you enjoy that, half-breed?" Sarah Skinflayer asked, and I was too winded to answer. "There will be more of the same tomorrow, I guarantee it. Here." Two pieces of bread and a lump of cheese hit the ground. "That's the dinner you earned tonight. It should be safe for you to eat. Maybe tomorrow you'll get something better."

"Fine," I muttered, ready to crawl back to my room, thinking there was no way I was ever coming back here. I planned to conveniently "forget" about my forced servitude tomorrow, maybe even find a way out of the Seelie Court. "See you tomorrow."

The troll blocked my path. "Where do you think you're going, half-breed? You're part of my workforce now, so that means you're *mine*." She pointed to a wooden door in the corner. "The servants' quarters are full. You can take the pantry closet there." She smiled at me, fierce and terrible, showing blunt yellow teeth and tusks. "We start work at dawn. See you tomorrow, whelp."

I ate my measly dinner and crawled beneath shelves of onions, turnips, and strange blue vegetables to sleep. I had no blanket, but the kitchens were uncomfortably warm. I was trying to turn a sack of grain into a pillow, when I remembered my backpack, tossed onto a shelf, and crawled out to retrieve it. There was nothing in the orange pack now but a broken phone, but still, it was mine, the only reminder of my old life.

I snatched the backpack off the shelf and was walking back

toward my tiny room when I felt something wriggle inside the pack. Startled, I nearly dropped it, and heard a soft snicker coming from inside. Edging over to the counter, I put the bag down, grabbed a knife, and unzipped it, ready to plunge the blade into whatever jumped out.

My phone lay there, dead and silent. With a sigh, I zipped the pack up and carried it into the pantry with me. Tossing it into a corner, I curled up on the floor, put my head on the bag of grain, and let my thoughts drift. I thought of Ethan, and Mom, and school. Was anyone missing me back home? Were there search parties being sent out for me, police and dogs sniffing around the last places I was seen? Or had Mom forgotten me, as I was sure Luke had? Would I even have a home to go back to, if I did manage to find Ethan?

I started to shake, and my eyes grew misty. Soon, tears flowed down my cheeks, staining the sack under my head and making my hair sticky. I turned my face into the rough fabric and sobbed. I'd hit rock bottom. Lying in a dark pantry, with no hope of rescuing Ethan and nothing to look forward to but fear, pain, and exhaustion, I was ready to give up.

Gradually, as my sobs stilled and my breathing grew calmer, I realized I was not alone.

Raising my head, I first saw my backpack, where I'd flung it in the corner. It was unzipped, lying open like a gaping maw. I saw the glint of the phone inside.

Then, I saw the eyes.

My heart stopped, and I sat up quickly, banging my head against the shelf. Dust showered me as I scooted to the far corner, gasping. I'd seen those eyes before, glowing green and intelligent. The creature was small, smaller than the goblins, with oily black skin and long, spindly arms. Except for the large, goblinlike ears, it looked like a horrible cross between a monkey and a spider.

The creature smiled, and its teeth lit the corner with pale blue light.

Then it spoke.

Its voice echoed flatly in the gloom, like a radio speaker hissing static. I couldn't understand it at first. Then, as if it were changing the station, the static cleared away and I heard words.

"—are waiting," it crackled, its voice still buzzing with static. "Come to...iron...your brother...held in..."

"Ethan?" I bolted upright, banging my head again. "Where is he? What do you know about him?"

"... Iron Court...we...waiting for..." The creature flickered in the darkness, going fuzzy like a weak signal. It hissed and blipped out of sight, plunging the room into blackness again.

I lay there in the gloom, my heart pounding, thinking about what the creature had said. I couldn't glean much from the eerie conversation, except that my brother was alive, and something called the Iron Court was waiting for something.

All right, I told myself, taking a deep breath. *They're still out there, Meghan. Ethan and your dad. You can't give up now. Time to stop being a crybaby and get your act together.*

I snatched up the phone and stuffed it into my back pocket. If that monster-thing came to me with any more news of Ethan, I wanted to be ready. Lying back on the cold floor, I closed my eyes and started to plan.

The next two days passed in a blur. I did everything the troll woman told me to do: washed dishes, scrubbed floors, sliced meat off animal carcasses until my hands were stained red. No more spells were cast on me, and Sarah Skinflayer began to eye me with grudging respect. The food they offered was simple fare: bread and cheese and water. The troll woman informed me anything more exotic might wreak havoc with my delicate half-human system. At night, I would crawl, exhausted, into my bed in the pantry and fall asleep immediately. The spindly creature visited me no more after that first night, and my sleep was blissfully free of nightmares.

All the while, I kept my eyes and ears open, gleaning information that would help me when I finally made my escape. In the kitchen, under the hawk eye of Sarah Skinflayer, escape was impossible. The troll woman had a habit of appearing whenever I thought about taking a break, or striding into a room just as I finished a task. I did try to sneak out of the kitchen one night, but when I pulled open the front door, a small storage room greeted me instead of the tunnel of thorns. I almost despaired at that point, but forced myself to be patient. The time would come, I told myself; I would just have to be ready when it did.

I spoke with the other kitchen workers when I could, creatures called brownies and house gnomes, but they were so busy I gained little information from them. I did discover something that made my heart pound excitedly. Elysium, the event that had everyone in the kitchen running around like mad things, would be held in a few days. As tradition dictated, the Seelie and Unseelie courts would meet on neutral ground, to discuss politics, sign new accords, and maintain their very uneasy truce. Since it was spring, the Unseelie Court would be traveling to Oberon's territory for Elysium; in winter, the Unseelie would play host. Everyone in the court was invited, and as kitchen staff, we were required to be there.

I continued working hard, my own plans for Elysium running around in my head.

Then, three days after my sentence to the kitchens, we had visitors.

I was standing over a basket of tiny dead quail, plucking them after Sarah Skinflayer broke their necks and passed them to me. I tried to ignore the troll as she reached into a cage, grabbed a flapping, bright-eyed bird, and twisted its neck with a faint popping sound. She then tossed the lifeless body into the basket like a plucked fruit and reached for another.

The doors swung open abruptly, streaming light into the room, and three faery knights walked in. Long silver hair, pulled into simple ponytails, glimmered in the dimness of the room, and their faces were haughty and arrogant.

"We have come for the half-breed," one of them announced, his voice ringing through the kitchen. "By order of King Oberon, she will come with us."

Sarah Skinflayer glanced my way, snorted, and picked up another quail. "That's fine with me. The brat's been nothing but deadweight since she came here. Take her out of my kitchens, and good riddance to her." She punctured the statement with the sharp crack of the bird's neck, and a brownie left the oven to take my place, shooing me away as it hopped onto a stool.

I started to follow them, but remembered my backpack, lying on the floor of the pantry closet. Muttering an apology, I hurried to grab it, slinging it over my back as I returned. None of the brownies looked up at me as I left, though Sarah Skinflayer glowered as she wrung a bird's neck. Battling relief and an odd sense of guilt, I followed the knights out of the room.

They led me through the twisting brambles to yet another door, opening it without preamble. I walked into a small bedroom, not nearly as fancy as my first, but nice enough. I glimpsed a round, steaming pool through a side-room door, and thought longingly of a bath.

I heard muffled clops on the carpeted floor, and turned to see a pair of satyr girls enter behind a tall, willowy woman with pure white skin and straight raven hair. She wore a dress so black it sucked in the light, and her fingers were long and spiderlike.

One of the satyr girls peeked at me from behind the woman's dress. I recognized Tansy, who gave me a timid smile, as if she feared I was mad about the encounter with Titania. I wasn't; she had been a pawn in the faery queen's game, just like me. But before I could say anything, the tall woman swept up and grabbed me, holding my chin in her bony fingers. Black eyes, with no iris or pupil, scanned my face.

"Filthy," she rasped, her voice like silk over a steel blade. "What a plain, dirty little specimen. What does Oberon expect me to do with this? I'm not a miracle worker."

I wrenched my face from her grasp, and the satyr girls squeaked. The lady, however, seemed amused. "Well, I suppose we shall have to try. Half-breed—"

"My name is not 'half-breed,'" I snapped, tired of hearing the word. "It's Meghan. Meghan Chase."

The woman didn't blink. "You give out your full name so easily, child," she stated, making me frown in confusion. "You are lucky that it is not your True Name, else you might find yourself in a dire situation. Very well, Meghan Chase. I am Lady Weaver, and you will listen to me carefully. King Oberon has asked me to make you presentable for Elysium tonight. He will not have his half-breed daughter parading around in peasant rags, or worse, mortal clothes, in front of the Unseelie Court. I told him I would do my best and not to expect miracles, but we shall try. Now—" she gestured to the side room "—first things first. You reek of human, troll, and blood. Go take a bath." She clapped once, and the two satyrs trotted around to face me. "Tansy and Clarissa will attend you. Now I must design something for you to wear that will not make a laughingstock of your father."

I glanced at Tansy, who wasn't meeting my eyes. Silently, I

followed them to the pool, stripped off my disgusting clothes, and sank into the hot water.

Bliss. I floated for several minutes, letting the heat soak into my bones, easing the aches and pains from the past three days. I wondered if faeries ever got dirty or sweaty; I'd never seen any of the nobles look anything less than elegant.

The heat was making me sleepy. I must've dozed, for I had disturbing dreams of spiders crawling over my body in great black swarms, covering me with webs as if I were a giant fly. When I awoke, shuddering and itchy, I was lying on the bed and Lady Weaver stood over me.

"Well." She sighed as I struggled to my feet. "It's not my greatest work, but I suppose it will have to do. Come here, girl. Stand before the mirror a moment."

I did as she asked, and gaped at the reflection it showed me. A shimmering silver dress covered me, the material lighter than silk. It rippled like water with the slightest movement, lacy sleeves billowing out from my arms, barely touching my skin. My hair had been elegantly curled and twisted into a graceful swirl atop my head, held in place by sparkling pins. A sapphire the size of a baby's fist flashed blue fire at my throat.

"Well?" Lady Weaver gently touched one of my sleeves, admiring it like an artist would a favorite painting. "What do you think?"

"It's beautiful," I managed to say, staring at the elven prin-cess in the glass. "I don't even recognize myself." An image flashed through my head and I giggled with slight hysteria. "I won't turn into a pumpkin when midnight comes, will I?"

"If you annoy the wrong people, you might." Lady Weaver turned away, clapping her hands. Like clockwork, Tansy and Clarissa appeared wearing simple white dresses, their curly hair brushed out. I caught a glimpse of horns beneath Tansy's hazel bangs. She held my orange backpack in two fingers, as if afraid it would bite her.

"I had the girls wash your mortal clothes," Lady Weaver said, turning away from the mirror. "Oberon would have them destroyed, but then that would mean more work for me, so I put them in your bag. Once Elysium is over, I'll be taking that dress back, so you'll want to hang on to your own clothes."

"Um, okay," I said, taking the backpack from Tansy. A quick inspection showed my jeans and shirt folded inside, and the phone still hidden in a side pocket. For a moment, I thought to leave the pack behind, but decided against it. Oberon might find it offensive and have someone burn it without my knowledge. It was still mine, and held everything I owned in this world. Feeling slightly embarrassed, I swung it over one shoulder, the hillbilly princess with a bright orange pack.

"Let us go," Lady Weaver rasped, wrapping a gauzy black shawl around her throat. "Elysium awaits. And, half-breed, I worked hard on that dress. Do try not to get yourself killed."

12

ELYSIUM

We walked through the briar tunnels into the courtyard. As before, it was packed with fey, but the mood had changed into something dark. Music played, haunting and feral, and faeries danced, leaped, and cavorted in wild abandon. A satyr knelt behind a smiling girl with red skin, running his hands up her ribs and kissing her neck. Two women with fox ears circled a dazed-looking brownie, their golden eyes bright with hunger. A group of fey nobles danced in hypnotic patterns, their movements erotic, sensual, lost in music and passion.

I felt the wild urge to join them, to throw back my head and spin into the music, not caring where it took me. I closed my eyes for a moment, feeling the lilting strains lift my soul and make it soar toward the heavens. My throat tightened, and my body began to sway in tune with the music. I opened my eyes with a start. Without meaning to, I'd begun walking toward the circle of dancers.

I bit my lip hard, tasting blood, and the sharp pain brought me back to my senses. *Get it together, Meghan. You can't let down your guard. That means no eating, dancing, or talking to strangers. Focus on what you have to do.*

I saw Oberon and Titania sitting at a long table, surrounded by Seelie knights and trolls. The king and queen sat side by side, but were actively ignoring each other. Oberon's chin rested on his hands as he gazed out over his court; Titania sat like she had an icy pole shoved up her backside.

Puck was nowhere to be seen. I wondered if Oberon had freed him yet.

"Enjoying the festivities?" asked a familiar voice.

"Grimalkin!" I cried, spotting the gray cat perched on the edge of a raised pool, tail curled around his legs. His golden eyes regarded me with the same lazy disinterest. "What are you doing here?"

He yawned. "I was taking a nap, but it appears things might get interesting soon, so I think I will stick around." Rising, the cat stretched, arching his back, and gave me a sideways look. "So, human, how is life in Oberon's court?"

"You knew," I accused him as he sat down and licked a paw. "You knew who I was all along. That's why you agreed to take me to Puck—you were hoping to blackmail Oberon."

"*Blackmail,*" said Grimalkin, blinking languid yellow eyes, "is a barbaric word. And you have much to learn about the fey, Meghan Chase. You think others would not have done the same? Everything here has a price. Ask Oberon. For that matter, ask your Puck."

I wanted to ask what he meant, but at that moment, a shadow fell over my back and I turned to see Lady Weaver looming over me.

"The Winter Court will arrive soon," she rasped, pencil-thin fingers closing on my shoulder. "You must take your place at the table, beside King Oberon. He has requested your presence. Go, go."

Her grip tightened, and she steered me to the table where Oberon and the lords of the Summer Court waited. Oberon's gaze was carefully neutral, but Titania's glare of utter hatred made me want to run and hide. Between scary spider lady and the Queen of the Seelie Court, I was pretty sure I would end the night as a mouse or cockroach.

"Pay your respects to your father," Lady Weaver hissed in my ear, before giving me a small push toward the Erlking. I swallowed and, under the stark gazes of the nobles, approached the table.

I didn't know what to say. I didn't know what to do. I felt like I was giving a speech before the school auditorium and had forgotten my notes. Pleading silently for a clue, I met Oberon's empty green eyes and dropped into a clumsy curtsy.

The Erlking shifted in his seat. I saw his eyes flicker to the bright orange backpack and narrow slightly. My cheeks flamed, but I couldn't take it off now. "The Court welcomes Meghan Chase," Oberon said in a stiff, formal voice. He paused, as if waiting for me to say something, but my voice caught in my throat. Silence stretched between us, and someone in the crowd snickered. Finally, Oberon gestured toward an empty chair near the end of the table, and I sat, red and blushing under the eyes of the entire court.

"That was impressive," mused a voice near my feet. Grimalkin leaped into the chair beside me, just as I was about to put my backpack where he stood. "You definitely inherited your father's rapier wit. Lady Weaver must be so proud."

"Shut up, Grim," I muttered, and shoved the pack under my seat. I would've said more, but at that moment the music stopped and a loud trumpeting began.

"They've arrived," Grimalkin stated, eyes narrowing to golden slits. The cat almost seemed to smile. "This should be very interesting."

The trumpeting grew louder, and at one end of the court, the ever-present wall of thorns shifted, curled back, and formed a grand archway, much taller and more elegant than any I'd seen before. Black roses burst into bloom among the thorns, and an icy wind hissed through the gate, coating nearby trees with frost.

A creature padded through the arch, and I shuddered from more than the cold. It was a goblin, green and warty, dressed in a fancy black coat with gold buttons. It cast a sly look around the waiting court, puffed out its chest, and cried in a clear yet gravelly voice:

"Her Majesty, Queen Mab, Lady of the Winter Court, Sovereign of the Autumn Territories, and Queen of Air and Darkness!"

And the Unseelie came.

At first glance, they looked very similar to the Seelie fey. The little men carrying the Unseelie banner looked like gnomes in fancy cloaks and red caps. Then I noticed their jagged, sharklike grins and the bright madness in their eyes, and knew these were not friendly garden gnomes, not in any sense of the word.

"Redcaps," Grimalkin mused, wrinkling his nose. "You will want to stay away from them, human. Last time they came, a not-to-bright phouka challenged one to a rigged shell game and won. It did not go well."

"What happened?" I asked, wondering what a phouka was.

"They ate him."

He pointed out the ogres next, great hulking beasts with thick, ponderous faces and tusks slick with drool. Manacles bound their wrists, and silver chains were wrapped about their huge necks. They shambled into court like drugged gorillas, knuckles dragging on the ground, oblivious to the murderous glares they were receiving from the trolls.

More Unseelie spilled into the clearing. Thin, skulking bogeys like the one in Ethan's closet, creeping along the ground like spindly spiders. Snarling, hissing goblins. A man with the head and chest of a shaggy black goat, his horns sweeping into wicked points that caught the light. And more creatures, each one more nightmarish than the first. They leered when they caught sight of me, licking their lips and teeth. Thankfully, under the stern glares of Oberon and Titania, none of them approached the table.

Finally, as the court swelled to nearly twice its number, Queen Mab made her appearance.

The first hint I received was that the temperature in the clearing dropped about ten degrees. Goose bumps rose along my arms, and I shivered, wishing I had something heavier than a dress made of spider silk and gauze. I was about to move my chair a few feet down the table, out of the wind, when a cloud of snow burst from the mouth of the tunnel, and in walked the kind of woman that made ladies weep in envy and men launch wars.

She wasn't tall, like Oberon, or willowy-thin like Titania, but her presence drew every eye in the courtyard. Her hair was so black it appeared blue in places, and it spilled down her back like a waterfall of ink. Her eyes were of the void, of a night without stars, a sharp contrast to her marble skin and pale mulberry lips. She wore a dress that writhed around her like shadow incarnate. And, like Oberon and Titania, she radiated power.

The amount of fey in the courtyard, both Seelie and Unseelie, was making me very, very nervous. But just as I thought things couldn't get any eerier, Mab's entourage walked in.

The first two were tall and beautiful like the rest of their kind, all sharp angles and graceful limbs. They wore their black-and-silver suits with the easy confidence of nobles, raven hair pulled back to highlight their proud, cruel features. Like dark princes, they marched behind Mab with all the arrogance of the queen, thin hands resting on their swords, their capes flapping behind them.

The third noble, walking behind them, was also dressed in black and silver. Like the other two, he carried a sword, resting comfortably on his hip, and his face bore the fine lines of an aristocrat. But, unlike the others, he looked disinterested, almost bored, with the entire event. His eyes caught the moonlight and glittered like silver coins.

My heart turned to ice, and my stomach threatened to crawl up my throat. It was him, the boy from my dreams, the one who had chased Puck and me through the forest. I glanced around wildly, wondering if I could hide before he saw me. Grimalkin gave me a bemused stare and twitched his tail.

"It's him!" I whispered, cutting my gaze to the nobles approaching behind the queen. "That boy! He was hunting me that day in the forest, when I landed in your tree. He tried to kill me!"

Grimalkin blinked. "That is Prince Ash, youngest son of Queen Mab. They say he is quite the hunter, and spends much of his time in the wyldwood, instead of at court with his brothers."

"I don't care who he is," I hissed, ducking down in my seat. "I can't let him see me. How do I get out of here?"

Grimalkin's snort sounded suspiciously like laughter. "I would not worry about that, human. Ash would not risk Oberon's fury by attacking you in his own court. The rules of Elysium prevent violence of any kind. Besides—" the cat sniffed "—that hunt was days ago. It is likely he has forgotten all about you."

I scowled at Grimalkin and kept the fey boy in my sights as he bowed to Oberon and Titania, murmuring something I couldn't hear. Oberon nodded, and the prince stepped back, still bowing. When he straightened and turned around, his gaze swept over the table—

—to rest solely on me. His eyes narrowed, and he smiled, giving me a small nod. My heart sped up and I shivered.

Ash hadn't forgotten me, not by a long shot.

As the night wore on, I thought longingly of my days in the kitchens.

Not just because of Prince Ash, though that was the main reason I tried to avoid notice. The minions of the Unseelie Court made me jumpy and uncomfortable, and I wasn't the only one. Tension ran high among the ranks of Seelie and Unseelie; it was plain that these were ancient enemies. Only the fey's devotion to rules and proper etiquette—and the power of their sidhe masters—kept things from erupting into a bloodbath.

Or so Grimalkin told me. I took his word for it and remained very still in my seat, trying not to attract attention.

Oberon, Titania, and Mab stayed at the table all night. The three princes sat to Mab's left, with Ash farthest down the table, much to my relief. Food was served, wine was poured, and the sidhe rulers spoke among themselves. Grimalkin yawned, bored with it all, and left my side, vanishing into the crowds. After what seemed like hours, the entertainment began.

Three brightly dressed boys with monkey tails swung onto the stage set before the table. They performed amazing leaps and tumbles over, onto, and through one another. A satyr played his pipes, and a human danced to the tune until her feet bled, her face a mixture of terror and ecstasy. A stunning woman with goat hooves and piranha teeth sang a ballad about a man who followed his lover beneath the waters of the lake, never to be seen again. At the end of the song, I gasped air into my burning lungs and sat up, unaware that I'd been unable to breathe.

Sometime during the course of the festivities, Ash disappeared.

Frowning, I scanned the courtyard for him, searching for a pale face and dark hair among the chaotic sea of fey. He wasn't in the courtyard, as far as I could see, and he wasn't at the table with Mab and Oberon....

There was a soft chuckle beside me, and my heart stopped.

"So this is Oberon's famous half-blood," Ash mused as I whirled around. His eyes, cold and inhuman, glimmered with amusement. Up close, he was even more beautiful, with high cheekbones and dark tousled hair falling into his eyes. My traitor hands itched, longing to run my fingers through those bangs. Horrified, I clenched them in my lap, trying to concentrate on what Ash was saying. "And to think," the prince continued, smiling, "I lost you that day in the forest and didn't even know what I was chasing."

I shrank back, eyeing Oberon and Queen Mab. They were deep in conversation and did not notice me. I didn't want to interrupt them simply because a prince of the Unseelie Court was talking to me.

Besides, I was a faery princess now. Even if I didn't quite believe it, Ash certainly did. I took a deep breath, raised my chin, and looked him straight in the eye.

"I warn you," I said, pleased that my voice didn't tremble, "that if you try anything, my father will remove your head and stick it to a plaque on his wall."

He shrugged one lean shoulder. "There are worse things." At my horrified look, he offered a faint, self-derogatory smile. "Don't worry, princess, I won't break the rules of Elysium. I have no intention of facing Mab's wrath should I embarrass her. That's not why I'm here."

"Then what do you want?"

He bowed. "A dance."

What! I stared at him in disbelief. "You tried to kill me!"

"Technically, I was trying to kill Puck. You just happened to be there. But yes, if I'd had the shot, I would have taken it."

"Then why the hell would you think I'd dance with you?"

"That was then." He regarded me blandly. "This is now. And it's tradition in Elysium that a son and daughter of opposite territories dance with each other, to demonstrate the goodwill between the courts."

"Well, I just got here." I crossed my arms and glared. "I don't know anything about faery traditions. So, you can forget it. I am not going anywhere with you."

He raised an eyebrow. "Would you insult my monarch, Queen Mab, by refusing? She would take it very personally, and blame Oberon for the offense. And Mab can hold a grudge for a very, very long time."

Oh, damn. I was stuck. If I said no, I would insult the faery queen of the Unseelie Court. I'd also be on the shit lists of both Mab *and* Titania, and between them, my chances of survival were easily and completely nil.

"So, you're saying you're not giving me a choice."

"There is always a choice." Ash held out his hand. "I will not force you. I only follow the orders of my queen. But know that the rest of the court is expecting us." He smiled then, bitter and self-mocking. "And I promise to be a perfect gentleman until the night is done. You have my word."

"Dammit." I hugged my arms, trying to think of something to get me out of this. "I'll just embarrass you, anyway," I told him defiantly. "I can't dance."

"You're Oberon's blood." A cool note of amusement colored his voice. "Of course you can dance."

I struggled with myself a moment longer. *This is the prince of the Unseelie Court,* I thought, my mind racing. *Maybe he'll know something about Ethan. Or your dad! The least you can do is ask.*

I took a deep breath. Ash waited patiently with his hand outstretched, and when I finally put my fingers into his palm, he offered a faint smile. His skin was cold as he smoothly moved my hand to his arm, and I shivered at the nearness of him. He smelled sharply of frost and something alien—not unpleasant, but strange.

We left the table together, and my stomach twisted as I saw hundreds of glowing fey eyes watching us. Seelie and Unseelie alike parted for us, bowing, as we approached the open stage.

My knees trembled. "I can't do this," I whispered, clutching Ash's arm for support. "Let me go. I think I'm going to be sick."

"You'll be fine." Ash didn't look at me as we stepped onto the dance floor. He faced the trio of fey rulers with his head up and his expression blank. I looked over the sea of faces and shook in terror.

Ash tightened his grip on my hand. "Just follow my lead."

He bowed to Oberon's table, and I curtsied. The Erlking gave a solemn nod, and Ash turned to face me, taking one of my hands and guiding the other to his shoulder.

The music started.

Ash stepped forward, and I almost tripped, biting my lip as I tried to match his steps. We more or less minced around the stage, me concentrating on not falling or stepping on toes, Ash moving with tigerlike grace. Thankfully, no one booed or threw things, but I stumbled forward and back in a daze, only wanting the humiliation to end.

Somewhere in this waking nightmare, I heard a chuckle.

"Stop thinking," Ash muttered, pulling me into a spin that ended with me against his chest. "The audience doesn't matter. The steps don't matter. Just close your eyes and listen to the music."

"Easy for you to say," I growled, but he spun me again, so quickly that the stage whirled and I closed my eyes. *Remember why you're doing this,* my mind hissed. *This is for Ethan.*

Right. I opened my eyes and faced the dark prince. "So," I muttered, trying to sound conversational, "you're Queen Mab's son, right?"

"I think we've established that, yes."

"Does she like to...collect things?" Ash looked at me strangely, and I hurried on. "Humans, I mean? Does she have a lot of humans in her court?"

"A few." Ash spun me again, and this time I went with it. His eyes were bright as I came back to his arms. "Mab usually gets bored with mortals after a few years. She either releases them or turns them into something more interesting, depending on her mood. Why?"

My heart pounded. "Does she have a little boy in her court?" I asked as we swirled around the stage. "Four years old, curly brown hair, blue eyes? Quiet most of the time?"

Ash regarded me strangely. "I don't know," he said, to my disappointment. "I haven't been to court lately. Even if I had, I cannot keep track of all the mortals the queen acquires and releases over the years."

"Oh," I muttered, lowering my eyes. Well, that idea was shot. "But if you're not in court, where are you, then?"

Ash gave me a chilling smile. "The wyldwood," he replied, spinning me away. "Hunting. I rarely let my prey escape, so be grateful Puck is such a coward." Before I could answer, he pulled me close again, his mouth against my ear. "Although,

I am happy I didn't kill you then. I told you a daughter of Oberon could dance."

I'd forgotten about the music, and realized my body was acting on autopilot, sweeping over the dance floor as if I'd done it a thousand times. For a long moment, we said nothing, lost in the music and the dance. My emotions soared as the crescendo rose into the night, and there was no one except us, spinning around and around.

The music ceased as Ash pulled me into a final spin. I ended up pressed against him, his face inches from mine, his gray eyes bright and intense. We stood there a moment, frozen in time, our hearts thrumming wildly between us. The rest of the world had disappeared. Ash blinked and offered a tiny smile. It would take only a half step to meet his lips.

A scream shattered the night, jerking us back to our senses. The prince released me and stepped away, his face shutting into that blank mask once more.

The scream came again, followed by a thunderous roar that rattled the tables and sent fine crystal goblets crashing to the floor. Over the crowd of spectators, I saw the bramble wall shaking wildly as something large tore its way through. Fey began shouting and pushing one another, and Oberon stood, his ringing voice calling for order. For just a moment, everyone froze.

The brambles parted with deafening snaps, and something huge clawed its way free. Blood streaked the tawny hide of a monster—not a shadowy, under-your-bed bogey that jumped out at you, but a real monster that would rip open your stomach and eat your entrails. It had three horrible heads: a lion with a bloody satyr in its jaws, a goat with mad white eyes, and a hissing dragon with molten flame dripping from its teeth. *A chimera?*

For a heartbeat, it paused, staring at the party it had just interrupted, the heads blinking in unison. The dead satyr, now a chewed, mangled mess, dropped to the ground, and someone in the crowd screamed.

The chimera roared, three voices rising to a deafening shriek. The crowd scattered as the monster gathered its hindquarters under it and leaped into the fray. It came down beside a fleeing redcap and lashed out with a claw-tipped paw, catching the faery in the stomach and disemboweling it instantly. As the redcap staggered and fell, holding its intestines, the chimera turned and pounced on a troll, bearing it to the ground. The troll snarled and grabbed the lion's throat, holding it away, but then the dragon head came down, clamping its jaws around the troll's neck and twisting. Dark blood exploded in a fine spray, filling the air with a sickening coppery smell. The troll shuddered and went limp.

Gore dripping from its snout, the chimera looked up and saw me, still frozen on the stage. With a roar, it sprang, landing on the edge of the dance floor. My brain screamed at me to run, but I couldn't move. I could only stare in detached fascination as it crouched, muscles rippling under its bloody fur. Its hot breath washed over me, stinking of blood and rotten meat, and I saw a scrap of red clothing on the lion's tooth.

With a shriek, the chimera pounced, and I closed my eyes, hoping it'd be quick.

13

ESCAPE FROM THE SEELIE COURT

Something slammed into me, pushing me away. Pain shot up my arm as I landed on my shoulder, and I opened my eyes with a gasp.

Ash stood between me and the chimera, his sword unsheathed. The blade glowed an icy-blue, wreathed in frost and mist. The monster roared and swatted at him, but he leaped aside, slashing with his blade. The frozen edge bit into the chimera's paw, drawing a humanlike scream from the monster. It pounced, and Ash rolled away. On his feet again, he raised an arm, bluish light sparkling from his fingers. As the monster whirled on him, he flung his hand out, and the chimera shrieked as a flurry of glistening ice shards ripped into its hide.

"To arms!" Oberon's booming voice rose above the roars of the chimera. "Knights, hold the beast back! Protect the envoys! Quickly!"

Mab's voice joined the chaos, ordering her subjects to attack. Now more fey were arriving, leaping onto the stage with weapons and battle cries, fangs and teeth bared. Less warrior-type fey scurried off the stage, fleeing for their lives as the others attacked. Trolls and ogres slammed great spiked clubs onto the beast's hide, redcaps sliced at it with tarnished bronze knives, and Seelie knights brandishing swords of flame cut at its flanks. I saw Ash's brothers join the fray, their ice blades stabbing at the monster's back. The chimera roared again, badly wounded, momentarily cowed by its attackers.

Then the dragon's head came up, steam billowing from its jaws, and blasted a stream of liquid fire at the fey surrounding it. The molten spittle covered several of its attackers, who screamed and fell to the ground, thrashing wildly as the flesh melted from their bones. The monster tried to leave the dance floor, but the fey pressed closer, jabbing at it with their weapons, keeping it in place.

As the last of the civilian fey left the stage, the Seelie King stood, his face alien and terrifying, long silver hair whipping behind him. He raised his hands, and a great rumbling shook the ground. Plates clattered and smashed to the ground, trees trembled, and the fey backed away from the snarling monster. The chimera growled and snapped at the air, its eyes wary and confused, as if it were unable to understand what was happening.

The stage—four feet of solid marble—splintered with a deafening crack, and huge roots unfurled through the surface. Thick and ancient, covered in gleaming thorns, they wrapped around the chimera like giant snakes, digging into its hide. The monster roared, raking the living wood with its claws, but the coils continued to tighten.

The fey swarmed the monster again, hacking and cutting. The chimera fought on, lashing out with deadly claws and fangs, catching those who ventured too close. An ogre smashed his club into the beast's side, but took a savage blow from the monster's paw that tore his shoulder open. A Seelie knight cut at the dragon's head, but the jaws opened and it blasted the faery with molten fire. Screaming, the knight wheeled back, and the dragon raised its head to glare at the Erlking standing at the table, his eyes half closed in concentration. Its lips curled, and it took a breath. I yelled at Oberon, but my voice was lost in the cacophony, and I knew my warning would come too late.

And then Ash was there, dodging the beast's claws, his sword streaking down in an icy blur. It sliced clean through the dragon's neck, severing it, and the head struck the marble with a revolting splat. Ash danced away as the neck continued to writhe, spraying blood and liquid fire from the stump. Fey howled in pain. As Ash retreated from the lava spray, a troll rammed his spear through the lion's open maw and out the back of its head, and a trio of redcaps managed to dodge the flailing claws to swarm the goat's head, biting and stabbing. The chimera jerked, thrashed, and finally slumped in the web of branches, twitching sporadically. Even as it died, the redcaps continued to rip out its flesh.

The battle was over, but the carnage remained. Charred, mangled, mutilated bodies lay like broken toys around the fractured stage. Gravely wounded fey clutched at their injuries, their faces twisted in agony. The smell of blood and burning flesh was overwhelming.

My stomach heaved. Twisting my head from the gruesome sight, I crawled to the edge of the stage and vomited into the rose bushes.

"Oberon!"

The shriek sent chills through me. Queen Mab was on her feet, eyes blazing, pointing a gloved finger at the Erlking.

"How dare you!" she rasped, and I shivered as the temperature dropped to freezing. Frost coated the branches and crept along the ground. "How dare you set this monster on us during Elysium, when we come to you under the banner of trust! You've broken the covenant, and I will not forgive this heresy!"

Oberon looked pained, but Queen Titania leaped to her feet. "You dare?" she cried, as lightning crackled overhead. "You dare accuse us of summoning this creature? This is obviously the work of the Unseelie Court to weaken us in our own home!"

Fey began to mutter among themselves, casting suspicious glances at those from another court, though seconds ago they'd fought side by side. A redcap, its mouth dripping black chimera blood, hopped down from the stage to leer at me, beady eyes bright with hunger.

"I smell a human," it cackled, running a purple tongue over its fangs. "I smell young girl blood, and sweeter flesh than a monster's." I hurried away, walking around the stage, but it followed. "Come to me, little girl," it crooned. "Monster flesh is bitter, not like sweet young humans. I just want a nibble. Maybe just a finger."

"Back off." Ash appeared out of nowhere, looking dangerous with dark blood speckling his face. "We're in enough trouble without you eating Oberon's daughter. Get out of here."

The redcap sneered and scurried off. The fey boy sighed and turned to me, his gaze scanning the length of my dress. "Are you hurt?"

I shook my head. "You saved my life," I murmured. I was about to say "thank you," but caught myself, since those words seemed to indebt you in Faery. A thought came, unbidden and disturbing. "I... I'm not bound to you or anything like that, am I?" I asked fearfully. He raised an eyebrow, and I swallowed. "No life debt, or having to become your wife, right?"

"Not unless our sires made a deal without our knowledge." Ash glanced back at the arguing rulers. Oberon was trying to silence Titania, but she would have none of it, turning her anger on him as well as Mab. "And I'd say any contracts they made are officially broken now. This will probably mean war."

"War?" Something cold touched my cheek, and I glanced up to see snowflakes swirling in a lightning-riddled sky. It was eerily beautiful, and I shivered. "What will happen then?"

Ash stepped closer. His fingers came up to brush the hair from my face, sending an electric shock through me from my spine to my toes. His cool breath tickled my ear as he leaned in.

"I'll kill you," he whispered, and walked away, joining his brothers at the table. He did not look back.

I touched the place where his fingers had brushed my skin, giddy and terrified at the same time.

"Careful, human." Grimalkin appeared on the corner of the stage, overshadowed by the dead chimera. "Do not lose your heart to a faery prince. It never ends well."

"Who asked you?" I glared at him. "And why do you always pop up when you're not wanted? You got your payment. Why are you still following me?"

"You are amusing," purred Grimalkin. Golden eyes flicked to the bickering rulers and back again. "And of great interest to the king and queens. That makes you a valuable pawn, indeed. I wonder what you will do next, now that your brother is not in Oberon's territory?"

I looked at Ash, standing beside his brothers, stone-faced as the argument between Mab and Titania raged on. Oberon was trying to calm them both, but with little success.

"I have to go to the Unseelie Court," I whispered as Grimalkin smiled. "I'll have to look for Ethan in Queen Mab's territory."

"I would imagine so," Grimalkin purred, slitting his eyes at me. "Only, you don't know where the Unseelie Court is, do you? Mab's entourage came here in flying carriages. How will you find it?"

"I could sneak into one of the carriages, maybe. Disguise myself."

Grimalkin snorted with laughter. "If the redcaps do not smell you out, the ogres will. There would be nothing left but bones by the time you reached Tir Na Nog." The cat yawned and licked a forepaw. "Unfortunate that you lack a guide. Someone who knows the way."

I stared at the cat, a slow anger building as I realized what it was saying. "You know the way to the Unseelie Court," I said quietly.

Grimalkin scrubbed a paw over his ears. "Perhaps."

"And you'll take me there," I continued, "for a small favor."

"No," Grimalkin said, looking up at me. "There is nothing small about going into Unseelie territory. My price will be steep, human, make no mistake about that. So, you must ask yourself, how much is your brother worth to you?"

I fell silent, staring at the table, where the queens were still going at it.

"Why would I summon the beast?" Mab questioned with a sneer in Titania's direction. "I've lost loyal subjects, as well. Why would I set the creature against my own?"

Titania matched the other queen's disdain. "You don't care who you murder," she said with a sniff, "as long as you get what you want in the end. This is a clever ploy to weaken our court without casting suspicion on yourself."

Mab swelled in fury, and the snow turned to sleet. "Now you accuse me of murdering my own subjects! I will not listen to this a moment longer! Oberon!" She turned to the Erlking with her teeth bared. "Find the one who did this!" she hissed, her hair writhing around her like snakes. "Find them and give them to me, or face the wrath of the Unseelie Court."

"Lady Mab," Oberon said, holding up his hand, "do not be hasty. Surely you realize what this will mean for both of us."

Mab's face didn't change. "I will wait until Midsummer's Eve," she announced, her expression stony. "If the Seelie Court does not turn over those responsible for this atrocity to me, then you will prepare yourselves for war." She turned to her sons, who awaited her orders silently. "Send for our healers," she told them. "Gather our wounded and dead. We will return to Tir Na Nog tonight."

"If you are going to decide," Grimalkin said softly, "decide quickly. Once they leave, Oberon will not let you go. You are too valuable a pawn to lose to the Unseelie Court. He will keep you here against your will, under lock and key if he has to, to keep you out of Mab's clutches. After tonight, you may not get another chance to escape, and you will never find your brother."

I watched Ash and his brothers disappear into the crowd of dark fey, saw the grim, terrifying look on the Erlking's face, and made my decision.

I took a deep breath. "All right, then. Let's get out of here."

Grimalkin stood. "Good," he said. "We leave now. Before the chaos dies down and Oberon remembers you." He looked over my elegant gown and sniffed, wrinkling his nose. "I will fetch your clothes and belongings. Wait here, and try not to draw attention to yourself." He twitched his tail, slipped into the shadows, and vanished.

I stood by the dead chimera, looking around nervously and trying to keep out of Oberon's sight.

Something small dropped from the lion's mane, glimmering briefly as it caught the light, hitting the marble with a faint clink. Curious, I approached warily, keeping my eye on the huge carcass and the few redcaps still gnawing on it. The object on the ground winked metallically as I knelt and picked it up, turning it over in my palm.

It looked like a tiny metal bug, round and ticklike, about the size of my pinkie nail. Its spindly metal legs were curled up over its belly, the way insects' legs do when they die. It was covered in black ooze, which I realized with horror was chimera blood.

As I stared at it, the legs wiggled, and it flipped over in my hand. I yelped and hurled the bug to the ground, where it scuttled over the marble stage, squeezed into a crack, and vanished from sight.

I was wiping the chimera blood from my hands, discovering it stained flesh, when Grimalkin appeared, materializing from nowhere with my bright orange backpack. "This way," the cat muttered, and led me from the courtyard into a cluster of trees. "Hurry and change," he ordered as we ducked beneath the shadowy limbs. "We don't have much time."

I unzipped the pack and dumped my clothes to the ground. I started to wriggle out of the dress, when I noticed Grimalkin still watching me, eyes glowing in the dark. "Could I get a little privacy?" I asked. The cat hissed.

"You have nothing I'd be interested in, human. Hurry up."

Scowling, I shed the gown and changed into my old, comfortable clothes. As I jammed my feet into my sneakers, I noticed Grimalkin staring back at the courtyard. A trio of Seelie knights wandered toward us across the lawn, and it appeared they were looking for someone.

Grimalkin flattened his ears. "You have already been missed. This way!"

I followed the cat through the shadows toward the hedge wall surrounding the courtyard. The brambles peeled back as we approached, revealing a narrow hole in the hedge, just big enough for me to squeeze into on my hands and knees. Grimalkin slipped through without looking back. I grimaced, knelt down, and crawled in after the cat, dragging my backpack behind me.

The tunnel was dark and winding. I pricked myself a dozen times as I maneuvered my way through the twisting maze of thorns. Squeezing through a particularly narrow stretch, I cursed as the thorns kept snagging my hair, clothes, and skin. Grimalkin looked over his shoulder, blinking luminous glowing eyes as I struggled.

"Try not to bleed so much on the thorns," he said as I jabbed myself in the palm and hissed in pain. "Right now, anyone could follow us, and you are leaving a very easy trail."

"Right, 'cause I'm bleeding all over the place for shits and giggles." A bramble caught my hair, and I yanked it free with a painful tearing sound. "How much farther till we're out?"

"Not far. We are taking a shortcut."

"This is a shortcut? What, does it lead into Mab's garden or something?"

"Not really." Grimalkin sat down and scratched his ear. "This path actually leads us back to your world."

I jerked my head up, jabbing myself in the skull and bringing tears to my eyes. "What? Are you serious?" Relief and excitement flared; I could go home! I could see my mom; she must be worried sick about me. I could go to my own room and—

I stopped, the balloon of happiness deflating as suddenly as it had come. "No. I can't go home yet," I said, feeling my throat tighten. "Not without Ethan." I bit my lip, resolved, then glared at the cat. "I thought you were taking me to the Unseelie Court, Grim."

Grimalkin yawned, sounding bored with it all. "I am. The Unseelie Court sits much closer to your world than the Seelie territories. It is faster to enter the mortal lands and slip into Tir Na Nog from there."

"Oh." I thought about that for a moment. "Well, then, why did Puck take me through the wyldwood? If it's easier to reach the Unseelie Court from my world, why didn't he use that way?"

"Who knows? Trods—the paths into the Nevernever—are difficult to find. Some are constantly shifting. Most lead directly into the wyldwood. Only a very few will take you to the Seelie or Unseelie territories, and they have powerful guardians protecting them. The trod we are using now is a one-way trip. Once we are through, we will not be able to find it again."

"Isn't there another way in?"

Grimalkin sighed. "There are other paths to Tir Na Nog from the wyldwood, but you would have to deal with the creatures that live there, as you found out with the goblins, and they are not the worst things you could meet. Also, Oberon's guards will be hunting for you, and the wyldwood will be the first place they'll look. The fastest way to the Unseelie Court is the way I am taking you now. So, decide, human. Do you still want to go?"

"Doesn't look like I have a choice, does it?"

"You keep saying that," Grimalkin observed, "but there is always a choice. And I suggest we stop talking and keep moving. We are being followed."

We kept going, wending our way through the briar tunnel, picking through the thorns until I lost all sense of time and direction. At first, I tried avoiding the brambles scratching at me, but continued to be pricked and poked, until I finally gave in and stopped bothering about it. Strangely, once I did, I was scratched a lot less. Once I stopped moving like a snail, Grimalkin set a steady pace through the brambles, and I followed as best I could. Occasionally, I saw side tunnels spin off in other directions, and caught glimpses of shapes moving through the brush, though I never got a clear look.

We turned a corner, and suddenly found a large cement tube in our path. It was a drainage pipe; I could see open air and blue sky through the hole. Oddly, it was sunny on the other side.

"The mortal world is through here," Grimalkin informed me. "Remember, once we are through, we will not be able to return to the Nevernever this way. We will have to find another trod to go back."

"I know," I said.

Grimalkin gave me a long, uncomfortable stare. "Also, remember, human—you have been to the Nevernever. The glamour over your eyes is gone. Though other mortals will not see anything strange about you, you will see things a little...differently. So, try not to overreact."

"Differently? Like how?"

Grimalkin smiled. "You will see."

We emerged from the drainage pipe to the sounds of car engines and street traffic, a shock after being in the wilderness for so long. We were in a downtown area, with buildings looming over us on either side. A sidewalk extended over the drainage pipe; beyond that, rush-hour traffic clogged the roads, and people shuffled down the walkway, absorbed in their own small worlds. No one seemed to notice a cat and a scruffy, slightly bloodied teenager crawl out of a drainage ditch.

"Okay." Despite my worry, I was thrilled to be back in my own familiar world, and astounded by the huge glass-and-metal buildings towering above me. The air here was cold, uncomfortably so, and dirty slush clogged the sidewalks and drains. Craning my neck, I gazed up at the looming skyscrapers, feeling slightly dizzy as they seemed to sway against the sky. There was nothing like this in my tiny Louisiana town. "Where are we?"

"Detroit." Grimalkin half closed his eyes, peering around the town and the people rushing by us. "One moment. It has been a while since I have been here. Let me think."

"Detroit, *Michigan?*"

"Hush."

As he was thinking, a large figure in a tattered red hoodie lurched out of the crowd and came toward us, clutching a bottle in a sack. Though I tensed, I wasn't *too* worried; we were on a well-traveled street, with a lot of witnesses to hear me scream should he try anything. He would probably ask me for change or a cigarette, and keep going.

However, as he got close, he raised his head, and I saw a wrinkled, bearded face with fangs jutting crookedly from its jaw. In the shadows of the hood, his eyes were yellow and slitted like a cat's. I jumped as the stranger leered and stepped closer. His stench nearly knocked me down; he smelled of roadkill and bad eggs and fish rotting in the sun. I gagged and nearly lost my breakfast.

"Pretty girl," the stranger growled, reaching out with a claw. "You came from *there,* didn't you? Send me back, now. Send me back!"

I backed away, but Grimalkin leaped between us, fluffed out to twice his size. His yowling screech jerked the man to a halt, and the bum's eyes widened in terror. With a gurgling cry, he turned and ran, knocking people aside as he fled. People cursed and looked around, glaring at one another, but none seemed to notice the fleeing bum.

"What was that?" I asked Grimalkin.

"A norrgen." The cat sighed. "Disgusting things. Terrified

of cats, if you can believe it. He was probably banished from the Nevernever at some point. That would explain his words to you, wanting you to send him back."

I looked for the norrgen, but it had vanished into the crowd. "Are all the fey walking around the human world outcasts?" I wondered.

"Of course not." Grimalkin's look was scornful, and no one does scornful better than a cat. "Many choose to be here, going back and forth between this world and the Nevernever at will, so long as they can find a trod. Some, like brownies or bogarts, haunt a house forever. Others blend in to human society, posing as mortals, feeding off dreams, emotions, and talent. Some have even been known to marry a particularly exceptional mortal, though their children are shunned by faery society, and the fey parent usually leaves if things get too tough.

"Of course, there are those who *have* been banished to the mortal world. They make their way as best they can, but spending too much time in the human world does strange things to them. Perhaps it is the amount of iron and technology that is so fatal to their existence. They start to lose themselves, a little at a time, until they are only shadows of their former selves, empty husks covered in glamour to make them look real. Eventually, they simply cease to exist."

I looked at Grimalkin in alarm. "Could that happen to you? To me?" I thought of my phone, remembering the way Tansy leaped away from it in terror. I suddenly recalled the way Robbie was mysteriously absent from all of his computer classes. I'd simply thought he hated typing. I had no idea it was deadly to him.

Grimalkin seemed unconcerned. "If I stay here long enough, perhaps. Maybe in two or three decades, though I certainly do not plan to stay that long. As for you, you are half-human. Your mortal blood protects you from iron and the banal effects of your science and technology. I would not worry too much if I were you."

"What's wrong with science and technology?"

Grimalkin actually rolled his eyes. "If I thought this would turn into a history lesson, I would have picked a better classroom than a city street." His tail lashed, and he sat down. "You will never find a faery at a science fair. Why? Because science is all about proving theories and understanding the universe. Science folds everything into neat, logical, well-explained packages. The fey are magical, capricious, illogical, and unexplainable. Science cannot prove the existence of faeries, so naturally, we do not exist. That type of nonbelief is fatal to faeries."

"What about Robbie...er... Puck?" I asked, not knowing why he suddenly popped into my head. "How did he stay so close to me, going to school and everything, with all the iron around?"

Grimalkin yawned. "Robin Goodfellow is a very old faerie," he said, and I squirmed to think of him like that. "Not only that, he has ballads, poems, and stories written about him, so he is very near immortal, as long as humans remember them. Not to say he is immune to iron and technology—far from it. Puck is strong, but even he cannot resist the effects."

"It would kill him?"

"Slowly, over time." Grimalkin stared at me with solemn eyes. "The Nevernever is dying, human. It grows smaller and smaller every decade. Too much progress, too much technology. Mortals are losing their faith in anything but science. Even the children of man are consumed by progress. They sneer at the old stories and are drawn to the newest gadgets, computers, or video games. They no longer believe in monsters or magic. As cities grow and technology takes over the world, belief and imagination fade away, and so do we."

"What can we do to stop it?" I whispered.

"Nothing." Grimalkin raised a hind leg and scratched an ear. "Maybe the Nevernever will hold out till the end of the world. Maybe it will disappear in a few centuries. Everything dies eventually, human. Now, if you are quite done with the questions, we should keep moving."

"But if the Nevernever dies, won't you disappear, as well?"

"I am a cat," Grimalkin replied, as if that explained anything.

I followed Grimalkin down the sidewalk as the sun set over the horizon and the streetlamps flickered to life.

I caught glimpses of fey everywhere, walking past us, hanging out in dark alleys, stealing over the rooftops or skipping along the power lines. I wondered how I could've been so blind before. And I remembered a conversation with Robbie, in my living room so long ago, a lifetime ago. *Once you start seeing things, you won't be able to stop. You know what they say—ignorance is bliss, right?*

If only I'd listened to him then.

Grimalkin led me down several more streets and suddenly stopped. Across the street a two-story dance club, lit with pink-and-blue neon lights, radiated in the darkness. The sign proclaimed it Blue Chaos. Young men and women lined up outside the club, the lights sparkling off earrings, metal studs, and bleached hair. Music pounded the walls outside.

"Here we are," Grimalkin said, sounding pleased with himself. "The energy around a trod never changes, though when I was here last this place was different."

"The trod thingy is the dance club?"

"*Inside* the dance club," Grimalkin said with a great show of patience.

"I'll never get in there," I told the feline, looking at the club. "The line is, like, a mile long, and I don't think this is a minor-friendly place. I won't make it past the front door."

"I would think your Puck taught you better than this." Grimalkin sighed and slipped into a nearby alley. Confused, I followed, wondering if we were going in another way.

But Grimalkin leaped atop an overflowing Dumpster and faced me, his eyes floating yellow orbs in the dark. "Now," he began, lashing his tail, "listen closely, human. You are half fey. More important, you are Oberon's daughter, and it is high time you learned to access some of that power everyone is so worried about."

"I don't have any—"

"Of course you do." Grimalkin's eyes narrowed. "You stink of power, which is why fey react to you so strongly. You just do not know how to use it. Well, I shall teach you, because it will be easier than having to sneak you into the club myself. Are you ready?"

"I don't know."

"Good enough. First—" and Grimalkin's eyes disappeared "—close your eyes."

Feeling not a little apprehensive, I did so.

"Now, reach out and feel the glamour around you. We are very close to the dance club, so glamour is in ready supply from the emotions inside. Glamour is what fuels our power. It is how we change shape, sing someone to their death, and appear invisible to mortal eyes. Can you feel it?"

"I don't—"

"Stop talking and just *feel*."

I tried, though I didn't know what I was supposed to experience, sensing nothing but my own discomfort and fear.

And then, like an explosion of light on the inside of my eyes, I *felt* it.

It was like color given emotion: orange passion, vermillion

lust, crimson anger, blue sorrow, a swirling, hypnotic play of sensations in my mind. I gasped, and heard Grimalkin's approving purr.

"Yes, that is glamour. The dreams and emotions of mortals. Now open your eyes. We are going to start with the simplest of faery glamour, the power to fade from human sight, to become invisible."

Still groggy from the torrent of swirling emotions, I nodded. "All right, becoming invisible. Sounds easy."

Grimalkin glared at me. "Your disbelief will cripple you if you think like that, human. Do not believe this impossible, or it *will* be."

"All right, all right, I'm sorry." I held up my hands. "So, how will I do this?"

"Picture the glamour in your mind." The cat half slitted its eyes again. "Imagine it is a cloak that covers you completely. You can shape the glamour to resemble anything you wish, including an empty space in the air, a spot where no one is standing. As you drape the glamour over yourself, you must believe that no one can see you. Just, so."

The eyes vanished, along with the rest of the cat. Even knowing Grimalkin was capable of it, it was still eerie seeing him fade from sight right before my eyes.

"Now." The eyes opened again, and the cat's body followed. "Your turn. When you believe you are invisible, we will go."

"What? Don't I get a practice run or something?"

"All it takes is belief, human. If you do not believe you are invisible on the first try, it only gets more difficult. Let us go. And remember, no doubts."

"Right. No doubts." I took a breath and closed my eyes, willing the glamour to come. I pictured myself fading from sight, swirling a cloak of light and air around my shoulders and pulling up the hood. *No one can see me,* I thought, trying not to feel foolish. *I'm invisible now.*

I opened my eyes and looked down at my hands.

They were still there.

Grimalkin shook his head as I looked up in disappointment. "I will never understand humans," he muttered. "With everything you have seen, magic, fey, monsters, and miracles, you still could not believe you could become invisible." He sighed heavily, leaping off the Dumpster. "Very well. I suppose *I* will have to get us in."

14

BLUE CHAOS

We stood in line for nearly an hour.

"All this could have been avoided if you just did what I told you," Grimalkin muttered for about the hundredth time. His claws dug into my arm, and I resisted the urge to drop-kick him over the fence like a football.

"Give me a break, Grim. I tried, okay? Just drop it already." I ignored the odd stares I was getting from the people around me, listening to the crazy girl muttering to herself. I didn't know what they saw when they looked at Grim, but it certainly wasn't a live, talking cat. And a heavy one at that.

"A simple invisibility spell. There is nothing easier. Kittens can do it before they walk."

I would've said something, but we were approaching the bouncer, who guarded the front doors to Blue Chaos. Dark, muscular, and massive, he checked the ID of the couple in front of us before waving them through. Grim pricked my arm with his claws, and I stepped up.

Cold black eyes raked me up and down. "I don't think so,

honey," the bouncer said, flexing a muscle in his arm. "Why don't you turn around and leave? You have school tomorrow."

My mouth was dry, but Grim spoke up, his voice low and soothing. "You are not looking at me right," he purred, though the bouncer didn't glance at him at all. "I am actually much older than I look."

"Yeah?" He didn't seem convinced, but at least he wasn't throwing me out by the scruff of my neck. "Let's see some ID, then."

"Of course." Grim poked me, and I shifted his weight to one hand so I could hand my student ID card to the bouncer. He snatched it, peering at it suspiciously, while my stomach roiled and cold sweat dripped down my neck. But Grimalkin continued to purr in my arms, completely undisturbed, and the bouncer handed the card back with a grudging look.

"Yeah, fine. Go on, then." He waved a huge hand at me, and we were through.

Inside *was* chaos. I'd never been to a club before, and was momentarily stupefied by the lights and the noise. Dry-ice smoke writhed along the floor, reminding me of the mist that crept through the wyldwood. Colored lights turned the dance floor into an electric fantasyland of pink, blue, and gold. Music rattled my ears; I could feel the vibrations in my chest, and wondered how anyone could communicate in such a cacophony.

Dancers spun, twisted, and swayed on the stage, bouncing in time to the music, sweat and energy pouring off them as they danced. Some danced alone, some in pairs that could not keep their hands off each other, their energy turning to passion.

Among them, writhing and twisting in near frenzies, feeding off the outpouring of glamour, danced the fey.

I saw faeries in leather pants and outfits that sparkled, slinked, and were half-torn, far different from the medieval finery of the Summer Court. A girl with birdlike talons and feathers for hair fluttered through the crowd, slashing young skin and licking the blood. A stick-thin boy with triple-jointed arms wrapped them around a dancing couple, long fingers entwined in their hair. Two fox-eared girls danced together, a mortal between them, their bodies pressed against his. The human's face was flung back in ecstasy, unaware of the girls' true forms.

Grimalkin squirmed and jumped out of my arms. He trotted toward the back of the club, his tail looking like a fuzzy periscope navigating the ocean of mist. I followed, trying not to stare at the unearthly dancers spinning among the mass of humanity.

Near the bar, a small door with the words Staff Only stood near the back of the club. I could see the shimmer of glamour around it, making the door difficult to look at; my gaze wanted to slide past. Casually, I approached the door, but before I got too close, the bartender rose up from behind the counter and narrowed his eyes.

"You don't wanna do that, love," he warned. His dark hair was pulled back in a tail, and horns curled up from his brow. He moved to the edge of the bar, and I heard hooves clopping over the wood. "Why don't you come over here and I'll fix you something nice? On the house, what'd you say?"

Grimalkin leaped onto a bar stool and put his front paws on the counter. A human on the stool next to him sipped his drink like nothing was happening. "We're looking for Shard," Grim said as the bartender shot him an irritated look, turning away from me.

"Shard is busy," the satyr replied, but he didn't meet Grim's eyes as he said it, and a moment later he began wiping down the bar. Grim continued to stare at him, until the satyr looked up. His eyes slitted dangerously. "I said, she's busy. Now, why don't you beat it, before I get the redcaps to stuff you into a bottle?"

"David, that's no way to treat customers," a cool female voice breathed from behind me, and I jumped. "Especially if one is an old friend."

The woman behind us was small and slight, with pale skin and neon-blue lips that curled sardonically at the edges. Her spiky hair stuck out at every angle, its dyed shades of blue, green, and white resembling ice crystals growing out of her scalp. She wore tight leather pants, a midriff tee that barely covered her breasts, and a dagger on one thigh. Her face glittered from countless piercings: eyebrows, nose, lips, and cheeks, all silver or gold. Her long ears sparkled with rings, studs, and bars, looking like gem encrusted daggers in the shifting lights. A silver needle lanced through her belly button, and a tiny dragon pendant dangled from it.

"Hello, Grimalkin," the woman said, sounding resigned. "It's been a while, hasn't it? What brings you to my humble club? And with the Summer whelp in tow?" Her eyes, scintillating blue and green, looked me over curiously.

"We need passage into Tir Na Nog," Grimalkin said without hesitation. "Tonight, if you can."

"Don't ask for much, do you?" Shard grinned, motioning us into a corner booth. Once seated, she leaned back and snapped her fingers. A human, lean and gangly, melted out of the shadows to stand beside her, his face slack with adoration.

"Appletini," she told him. "Spill it, and spend the rest of your days as a roach. Do you two want anything?"

"No," Grimalkin said firmly. I shook my head.

The human scurried off, and Shard leaned forward. Her blue lips curved in a smile.

"So. Passage to Winter's territory. You want to use my trod, is that correct?"

"It is not your trod," Grimalkin said, thumping his tail against the booth cushions.

"But it is under *my* dance club," Shard replied. "And the Winter Queen won't be pleased if I let the Summer whelp into her territory unannounced. Don't look at me like that, Grim. I'm not stupid. I know the daughter of the Erlking when I see her. So, the question is, what do I get out of this?"

"A favor repaid." Grimalkin narrowed his eyes at her. "Your debt to me canceled."

"That's fine for you," Shard said, and turned her leer on me, "but what about this one? What can she offer?"

I swallowed. "What do you want?" I asked before Grimalkin could say anything. The cat shot me an exasperated glare, but I ignored him. If anyone would barter away my fate, it would be me. I didn't want Grimalkin promising this woman my firstborn child without my consent.

Shard leaned back again, crossing her legs with a smile. The gangly boy appeared with her drink, a green concoction with a tiny umbrella, and she sipped it slowly, her eyes never leaving mine.

"Hmm, that's a good question," Shard murmured, swirling her 'tini thoughtfully. "What do I want of you? It must be awfully important for you to get into Mab's territory. What would that be worth?"

She took another sip, appearing deep in thought. "How about…your name?" she offered at last. I blinked.

"My…my name?"

"That's right." Shard smiled disarmingly. "Nothing much. Just promise me the use of your name, your True Name, and we'll call it even, yes?"

"The girl is young, Shard," Grimalkin said, watching us both with slitted eyes. "She might not even know her true calling yet."

"That's all right." Shard smiled at me. "Just give me the name you call yourself now, and we'll make do, yes? I'm sure I can find *some* use for it."

"No," I told her. "No deal. You're not getting my name."

"Oh, well." Shard shrugged and raised the glass to her lips. "I guess you'll have to find another way into Mab's territory, then." She shifted toward the end of the booth. "It has been a pleasure. Now, if you'll excuse me, I've a club to run."

"Wait!" I blurted out.

Shard paused, watching me expectantly.

"All right," I whispered. "All right, I'll give you a name. After that, you'll open the trod, right?"

The faery smiled, showing her teeth. "Of course."

"Are you sure you want to do this?" Grimalkin asked softly. "Do you know what happens when you give a faery your name?"

I ignored him. "Swear it," I told Shard. "Promise that you'll open the trod once I give you the name. Say the words."

The faery's smile turned vicious. "Not as stupid as she first appears," she muttered, and shrugged. "Very well. I, Shard, keeper of the Chaos trod, do swear to open the path once I have received payment in the form of a single name, spoken by the requesting party." She broke off and smirked at me. "Good enough?"

I nodded.

"Fine." Shard licked her lips, looking inhumanly eager, as her eyes gleamed. "Now, give me the name."

"All right." I took a deep breath as my stomach twisted wildly. "Buffy Summers."

Shard's face went blank. "What?" For one glorious moment, she looked utterly bewildered. "That is not your name, half-blood. That's not what we agreed on."

My heart pounded. "Yes, it is," I told her, keeping my voice firm. "I promised to give you *a* name, not *my* name. I've upheld my end of the contract. You have your name. Now, show us the trod."

Beside me, Grimalkin started sneezing, a sudden explosion of feline laughter. Shard's face remained blank a moment longer, then cold rage crept into her features and her eyes turned black. Her quills bristled, and ice coated the glass in her hand before it shattered into a million sparkling pieces.

"You." Her gaze stabbed into me, cold and terrifying. I fought the urge to run screaming out of the club. "You will regret this insolence, half-breed. I will not forget this, and will make you beg for mercy until your throat is raw from it."

My legs trembled, but I stood and faced her. "Not before you show us the trod."

Grimalkin stopped laughing and jumped onto the table. "You have been out-negotiated, Shard," he said, his voice still thick with amusement. "Cut your losses and try again some other time. Right now, we need to be going."

The faery's eyes still glimmered black, but she made a visible effort to control herself. "Very well," she said with great dignity. "I will uphold my end of the bargain. Wait here a moment. I need to inform David that I'll be gone for a bit."

She stalked away with her chin in the air, her spines quivering like icicles.

"Very clever," Grimalkin said softly as the faery marched toward the bar. "Shard has always been too rash, never pausing to listen for important details. She thinks she is too smart for that. Still, it is never wise to anger a Winter sidhe. You might regret your little battle of wits before this is over. The fey never forget an insult."

I remained silent, watching Shard lean over and whisper something to the satyr. David looked up at me, eyes narrowing, before jerking his head once and turning to wipe the counter.

Shard returned. Her eyes were normal again, though they still glared at me with cold dislike. "This way," she announced frostily, and led us across the room, toward the Staff Only door on the far wall.

We followed her down five or six flights of stairs, pausing at another door with the words *Danger! Keep Out!* painted on the surface in bright red. Shard looked back at me with an evil little smile.

"Don't mind Grumly. He's our last deterrent against those who poke their noses where they don't belong. Occasionally, some phouka or redcap will think themselves clever, and sneak past David to see what's down here. Obviously, I can't have that. So, I use Grumly to dissuade them." She chuckled. "Sometimes, a mortal will find his way down here, as well. That's the best entertainment. It cuts down on his food bill, too."

She gave me a razor-sharp grin and pushed the door open. The stench hit me like a giant hammer, a revolting mix of rot and sweat and excrement. I recoiled, and my stomach heaved. Bones littered the stone floor, some animal, some decidedly not. A pile of dirty straw lay in one corner, next to a door on the far wall. I knew that was the entrance to the Unseelie territory, but reaching it would be a real challenge.

Chained to a ring in the floor, manacled by one tree-stump leg, was the biggest ogre I'd ever seen. His skin was bruise purple, and four yellow tusks curled from his lower jaw. His torso was massive, muscles and tendons rippling under his mottled hide, and his thick fingers ended in curved black claws.

He also wore a heavy collar around his throat, the skin underneath red and raw, showing old scars where he'd clawed at it. A moment later, I realized both the collar and the manacles were made of iron. The ogre limped across the room, favoring the chained leg as he moved, his ankle festering with blisters and open sores. Grimalkin gave a small hiss.

"Interesting," he said. "Is the ogre really that strong, to be bound that way?"

"He's escaped a few times in the past, before we started using the iron," Shard replied, looking pleased with herself. "Smashed the club to bits, and ate a few patrons before we stopped him. I thought drastic measures were called for. Now he behaves himself."

"It is killing him." Grimalkin's voice was flat. "You must realize this will considerably shorten his life span."

"Don't lecture me, Grimalkin." Shard gave the cat a disgusted look and stepped through the door. "If I didn't keep him here, he'd only be rampaging somewhere else. The iron won't kill him right away. Ogres heal so fast."

She sauntered up to the ogre, who glared at her with pain-filled yellow eyes. "Move," she ordered it, pointing toward the pile of straw in the corner. "Go to your bed, Grumly. Now."

The ogre stared at her, snarled feebly, and shuffled to his bed, the chain clinking behind him. I couldn't help but feel a little sorry for him.

Shard opened the door. A long hallway stretched beyond the door, and mist flowed through the opening into the room. "Well?" she called back to us. "Here's your trod to the Winter territory. Are you going to stand there or what?"

Keeping a wary eye on Grumly, I started forward.

"Wait," Grimalkin muttered.

"What's the matter?" I turned and found him scanning the room, eyes narrowed to slits. "Afraid of the ogre? Shard will keep him off us, right?"

"Not at all," the cat replied. "Her bargain is done. She just opened the path to Tir Na Nog for us. She never promised us protection."

I looked into the room again and found Grumly staring at us, drool dripping to the floor from his teeth. On the other side, Shard was smirking at me.

There was a sudden clatter on the stairs, the sound of many feet skipping down the steps. Over the railing, a wrinkled, evil face peered down at me, shark-teeth gleaming. A red bandanna fell off its head to land at my feet.

"Redcaps," I gasped, stepping into the room without thinking.

Grumly roared, surging to the end of his chain, raking the ground with his claws. I yelped and flattened myself against the wall as the ogre snarled and slashed at the air, straining to reach me. His huge fists pounded the floor not ten feet away, and he bellowed in frustration. I couldn't move. Grimalkin had disappeared. Shard's laughter rang in the air as a dozen redcaps swarmed into the room.

"Now," she said, leaning against the door frame, "this is entertainment."

15

PUCK'S RETURN

The redcaps crowded through the doorway, teeth flashing in the dim light. They wore biker jackets and leather pants, and sported crimson bandannas instead of their trademark caps. Snarling and gnashing their teeth, they spotted Grumly at the same time the ogre noticed them, and leaped back as a huge fist pounded the pavement.

Snarls and curses rose in the air. The redcaps danced madly out of the ogre's reach, brandishing bronze knives and wooden baseball bats. "What is this?" I heard one of them screech. "Goat-man promised us young flesh if we followed the stairs. Where's our meat?"

"There!" snarled another, pointing at me with what looked like a tarnished shiv. "In the corner. Don't let the monster get our meat!"

They slid toward me, hugging the wall as I had done, keeping out of the ogre's grasp. Grumly roared and slashed the ground, raking deep trenches into the cement floor, but the redcaps were small and quick, and he couldn't reach them. I watched in horror as the hideous fey swarmed toward me, laughing and waving their weapons, and I couldn't move. I was about to be eaten alive, but if I ventured any farther into the room, Grumly would tear me apart.

Through it all, I was aware of Shard, lounging in the other doorway, a self-satisfied smirk on her face. "Do you like where our contract has gone, little bitch?" she called over the bellows of Grumly and the clattering teeth of the redcaps. "Throw me your real name, and I might call them off."

One of the redcaps leaped at me, jaws gaping, springing right for my face. I threw up my arm, and the jagged teeth sank into my flesh, clamping down like a steel trap. With a scream, I flailed wildly, dislodging the repulsive weight and flinging it at the ogre. The redcap hit the ground and leaped to his feet snarling, just as Grumly's fist smashed him into bloody paste.

Time seemed to slow. I guess that happens when you're about to die. The redcaps surged forward, shark teeth grinning and clacking, Grumly bellowed at the end of his chain, and Shard leaned against the door frame and laughed.

A huge black bird flapped through the open door.

The redcaps leaped.

The bird dove, sinking its talons into a redcap's face, shrieking and flapping its wings. Startled and confused, the redcaps hesitated as the bird thrashed about, beating its wings and stabbing at the faery's eyes with its beak. The pack hooted and slugged at it with their bats, but the bird darted up at the last second, and the redcap howled as the weapons slammed into him instead.

In the confusion, the bird exploded, changing shape in mid-air. A body dropped between me and the redcaps, shedding black feathers and giving me a familiar grin.

"Hi, princess. Sorry I'm late. Traffic was a bitch."

"Puck!"

He winked at me, then shot a glance at the Winter sidhe, standing in the doorway. "Hey, Shard." He waved. "Nice place you've got here. I'll have to remember it, so I can give it the special 'Puck touch.'"

"It's an honor to have you, Robin Goodfellow," Shard answered, grinning evilly. "If the redcaps leave your head intact, I'll mount it over the bar so everyone can see it when they come in." She turned to the redcaps and jabbed a ring-studded finger at Puck. "Kill him!"

Snarling, the redcaps leaped, teeth flashing like piranhas swarming a drowning bird. Puck pulled something out of his pocket and tossed it. It exploded into a thick log, and the redcaps clamped their jaws around the wood, teeth sinking into the bark. With muffled yelps, they clattered to the floor.

"Fetch," Puck called.

Shrieking with rage, the redcaps splintered the log, shredding it like buzz saws. Teeth chattering, they spit wood chips and glared at us murderously. Puck turned to me with an apologetic look. "Excuse me a moment, princess. I have to go play with the puppies."

He stepped toward them, grinning, and the redcaps lunged, brandishing knives and baseball bats. Puck waited until the last second before he dodged, *into* the room and away from the wall. The pack followed. I gasped as Grumly's fist hammered down, but Puck leaped aside just in time, and a redcap was smashed flatter than a pancake.

"Whoops," Puck exclaimed, putting both hands to his mouth, even as he sidestepped Grumly's second swing. "Clumsy of me."

The redcaps snarled curses and lunged at him again.

They continued this deadly dance around the room, Puck leading the redcaps on with taunts, laughter, and cheers. Grumly roared and smashed his fists at the little men scurrying around his feet, but the redcaps were quick, and now wary to the danger. This didn't stop them from launching an all-out attack on Puck, who danced, dodged, and pirouetted his way around the ogre, almost seeming to enjoy himself. My heart stayed lodged in my throat the whole time; one wrong move, one miscalculation, and Puck would be a bloody smear on the floor.

The air around me chilled. I'd been so focused on Puck, I didn't realize Shard had slipped away from the door frame and was now a few feet away. Her eyes glimmered black, and her lips curled in a smile as she raised a hand. A long spear of ice formed overhead, angled at me.

There was a yowl, and an invisible weight must have thumped onto her back, for she staggered and nearly fell. Something flashed golden on her chest: a key, attached to a thin silver chain. With a curse, Shard flung the invisible assailant into the wall; there was a thud and a hiss of pain as Grimalkin materialized for a split second and winked out of sight again.

In that moment of distraction, I lunged, grabbing the key around her neck. She turned with blinding speed, and a pale white hand clamped around my throat. I gasped, clawing at her arm with my free hand, but it seemed to be made of stone. Her skin burned with cold; ice crystals formed on my neck as Shard slowly tightened her grip, smiling. I sank to my knees as the room began to dim.

With a fierce screech, Grimalkin landed on her back, sinking claws and teeth into her neck. Shard screamed, and the pressure on my throat disappeared. Lurching upright, I shoved the sidhe with all my might, pushing her away. There was a jerk and a tinny snap, and the key came loose in my hand.

Coughing, I staggered away from the wall, looking up at the

ogre. "Grumly!" I yelled, my voice raw and hoarse. "Grumly, look at me! Listen to me!"

The ogre stopped pounding the floor and swung his tormented gaze to me. Behind me, a feline yowl cut through the air, and Grimalkin's body tumbled to the floor.

"Help us!" I cried, holding up the key. It winked golden in the light. "Help us, Grumly, and we'll free you! We'll set you free!"

"Free...me?"

Something smashed into the back of my head, nearly knocking me out. I collapsed, clutching the key, as pain raged across my senses. Something kicked me in the ribs, flipping me to my back. Shard loomed overhead, her dagger in one raised hand.

"No!"

Grumly's bellow filled the room. Startled, Shard looked up, just realizing she was within the ogre's reach. Too late. Grumly's backhand smashed into her chest, hurling her into the wall with a nasty thud. Even the redcaps stopped chasing Puck around and looked back.

I scrambled to my feet, ignoring the way my muscles screamed in protest. I staggered toward Grumly, hoping the ogre wouldn't forget and smash me into pudding. He didn't move as I reached the chains, the cruel iron manacle digging into his flesh. Shoving the key into the hole, I turned it until it clicked. The iron band loosened and dropped away.

Grumly roared, a roar filled with triumph and rage. He spun, surprisingly quick for his bulk, and kicked a redcap into the wall. Puck scrambled out of the way as the ogre raised a foot and stomped two more like roaches. The redcaps went berserk. Snarling and screeching, they swarmed Grumly's feet, pounding them with bats and sinking teeth into his ankles. Grumly stomped and kicked, barely missing me, and the ground shook with his blows, but I didn't have the strength to move.

Dodging the carnage, Puck grabbed me and pulled me away from the battle. "Let's go," he muttered, looking back over his shoulder. "While they're distracted. Head for the trod."

"What about Grimalkin?"

"I am here," the cat said, appearing beside me. His voice sounded strained, and he favored his left forepaw, but otherwise seemed fine. "It is definitely time to leave."

We staggered toward the open door, but found our path blocked by Shard. "No," the sidhe growled. Her left arm hung limp, but she raised an ice spear and angled it at my chest. "You will not pass. You will die here, and I will nail you to the wall for everyone to see."

A rumbling growl echoed behind us, and heavy footsteps shook the ground.

"Grumly," Shard said without taking her eyes from me, "kill them. All is forgiven. Rip them apart, slowly. Do it, now."

Grumly growled again, and a thick leg landed next to me. "Frrriends," the ogre rumbled, standing over us. "Free Grumly. Grumly's friends." He took another step, the raw, chafed wound on his leg smelling of gangrene and rot. "Kill mistress," he growled.

"What?" Shard backed away, her eyes widening. Grumly shuffled forward, raising his huge fists. "What are you doing? Get back, you stupid thing. I command you! No, no!"

"Let's go," Puck whispered, tugging my arm. We ducked under Grumly's legs and sprinted for the open door. The last thing I saw, as the door closed behind us, was Grumly looming over his former master, and Shard bringing up her spear as she backed away.

★ ★ ★

The corridor stretched away before us, filled with mist and flickering lights. I slumped against the wall, shaking as the adrenaline wore off.

"You all right, princess?" Puck asked, green eyes bright with concern. I staggered forward and threw my arms around him, hugging him tightly. He wrapped his arms around me and pulled me close. I felt his warmth and the rapid beat of his heart, his breath against my ear. Finally, I pulled away and sank back against the wall, drawing him down with me.

"I thought Oberon changed you into a bird," I whispered.

"He did," Puck answered with a shrug. "But when he discovered you had run away, he sent me find you."

"So, it was you I heard following us," Grimalkin said, nearly invisible in the mist.

Puck nodded. "I figured you were heading for the Unseelie Court. Who do you think created that shortcut? Anyway, once I was out, I sniffed around and a piskie told me he saw you heading for this part of town. I knew Shard owned a club here, and the rest, as the mortals say, is history."

"I'm glad you came," I said, standing up. My legs felt a bit stronger now, and the shaking had almost stopped. "You saved my life. Again. I know you might not want to hear it, but thanks."

Puck gave me a sidelong glance that I didn't like at all. "Don't thank me just yet, princess. Oberon was quite upset that you had left the safety of the Seelie territories." He rubbed his hands and looked uncomfortable. "I'm supposed to bring you back to Court."

I stared at him, feeling as though he'd just kicked me in the stomach. "But...you won't, right?" I stammered. He looked away, and my desperation grew. "Puck, you can't. I have to find Ethan. I have to go to the Unseelie Court and bring him home."

Puck scrubbed a hand through his hair, a strangely human gesture. "You don't understand," he said, sounding uncharacteristically unsure. "I'm Oberon's favorite lackey, but I can only push him so far. If I fail him again, I might end up a lot worse than a raven for two centuries. He could banish me from the Nevernever for all time. I'd never be able to go home."

"Please," I begged, taking his hand. He still didn't look at me. "Help us. Puck, I've known you forever. Don't do this." I dropped his hand and stared at him, narrowing my eyes. "You realize you'll have to drag me back kicking and screaming, and I'll never speak to you again."

"Don't be like that." Puck finally looked up. "You don't realize what you're doing. If Mab finds you…you don't know what she's capable of."

"I don't care. All I know is, my brother is still out there, in trouble. I have to find him. And I'm going to do it with or without your help."

Puck's eyes glittered. "I could cast a charm spell over you," he mused, one corner of his lip quirking up. "That would solve a lot of problems."

"No," Grimalkin spoke up before I could explode, "you will not. And you know you will not, so stop posturing. Besides, I have something that might solve this little problem."

"Oh?"

"A favor." Grimalkin waved his tail languidly. "From the king."

"That won't stop Oberon from banishing me."

"No," Grimalkin agreed. "But I could request that you be banished for a limited time only. A few decades or so. It is better than nothing."

"Uh-huh." Puck sounded unconvinced. "And this would just cost me a small favor in return, is that right?"

"You pulled me into this conflict the moment you dropped this girl into my tree," Grimalkin said, blinking lazily. "I cannot believe that was an act of coincidence, not from the infamous Robin Goodfellow. You should have known it might come to this."

"I know better than to make deals with a cait sith," Puck shot back, then sighed, scrubbing a hand over his eyes. "Fine," he said at last. "You win, princess. Freedom is highly overrated, anyway. If I'm going to do anything, I might as well do it big."

My heart lifted. "So, you'll help us?"

"Sure, why not?" Puck gave me a resigned smile. "You'd get eaten alive without me. Besides, storming the Unseelie Court?" His grin widened. "Can't pass that up for anything."

"Then let us go," Grimalkin said as Puck pulled me to my feet. "The longer we tarry, the farther word will spread about our intentions. Tir Na Nog is not far now." He turned and trotted down the corridor, his tail held upright in the fog.

We followed the hallway for several minutes. After a while, the air turned cold and sharp; frost coated the walls of the corridor, and icicles dangled from the ceiling.

"We are getting close," came Grimalkin's disembodied voice in the mist.

The hallway ended with a simple wooden door. A thin powder of snow lined the bottom crack, and the door trembled and creaked in the wind howling just outside.

Puck stepped forward. "Ladies and felines," he stated grandly, grasping the doorknob, "welcome to Tir Na Nog. Land of endless winter and shitloads of snow."

A billow of freezing powder caressed my face as he pulled the door open. Blinking away ice crystals, I stepped forward.

I stood in a frozen garden, the thornbushes on the fence coated with ice, a cherub fountain in the center of the yard spouting frozen water. In the distance, beyond the barren trees and thorny scrub, I saw the pointed roof of a huge Victorian estate. I glanced back for Grim and Puck and saw them standing under a trellis hung with purple vines and crystal blue flowers. As they stepped through, the corridor vanished behind them.

"Charming," Puck commented, gazing around in distaste. "I love the barren, dead feel they're going for. Who's the gardener, I wonder? I'd love to get some tips."

I was already shivering. "H-how far are we from Queen Mab's court?" I asked, my teeth chattering.

"The Winter Court is maybe two days' walk from here," Grimalkin said, leaping onto a tree stump. He shook his paws, one by one, and sat down carefully. "We should find shelter soon. I am uncomfortable in this weather, and the girl will certainly freeze to death."

A dark chuckle echoed across the garden. "I wouldn't worry about that now."

A figure stepped out from behind a tree, sword held loosely in one hand. My heart skipped a beat, and then picked up again, louder and more irregular than before. The breeze ruffled the figure's black hair as he moved toward us, graceful and silent as a shadow. Grimalkin hissed and disappeared, and Puck shoved me behind him.

"I've been waiting for you," Ash murmured into the silence.

16

THE IRON FEY

"Ash," I whispered as the lean, stealthy figure glided toward us, his boots making no sound in the snow. He was devastatingly gorgeous, dressed all in black, his pale face seeming to float over the ground. I remembered the way he smiled, the look in his silver eyes as we danced. He wasn't smiling now, and his eyes were cold. This wasn't the prince I'd danced with Elysium night; this wasn't anything but a predator.

"Ash," Puck repeated in a conversational tone, though his face had gone hard and feral. "What a surprise to see you here. How did you find us?"

"It wasn't difficult." Ash sounded bored. "The princess mentioned that she was looking for someone within Mab's court. There are only so many ways into Tir Na Nog from the mortal world, and Shard doesn't exactly make it a secret that she guards the trod. I figured it was only a matter of time before you came here."

"Very clever," Puck said, smirking. "But then, you were always the strategist, weren't you? What do you want, Ash?"

"Your head," Ash answered softly. "On a pike. But what I

want doesn't matter this time." He pointed his sword at me. "I've come for her."

I gasped as my heart and stomach began careening around my chest. *He's here for me, to kill me, like he promised at Elysium.*

"Over my dead body." Puck smiled, as if this was a friendly conversation on the street, but I felt muscles coiling under his skin.

"That was part of the plan." The prince raised his sword, the icy blade wreathed in mist. "I will avenge her today, and put her memory to rest." For a moment, a shadow of anguish flitted across his face, and he closed his eyes. When he opened them, they were cold and glittered with malice. "Prepare yourself."

"Stay back, princess," Puck warned, pushing me out of the way. He reached into his boot and pulled out a dagger, the curved blade clear as glass. "This might get a little rough."

"Puck, no." I clutched at his sleeve. "Don't fight him. Someone could die."

"Duels to the death tend to end that way." Puck grinned, but it was a savage thing, grim and frightening. "But I'm touched that you care. One moment, princeling," he called to Ash, who inclined his head. Taking my wrist, Puck steered me behind the fountain and bent close, his breath warm on my face.

"I have to do this, princess," he said firmly. "Ash won't let us go without a fight, and this has been coming for a long time now." For a moment, a shadow of regret flickered across his face, but then it was gone.

"So," he murmured, grinning as he tilted my chin up, "before I march off to battle, how 'bout a kiss for luck?"

I hesitated, wondering why now, of all times, he would ask for a kiss. He certainly didn't think of me in that way… did he? I shook myself. There was no time to wonder about that. Leaning forward, I kissed him on the cheek. His skin was warm, and bristly with stubble. "Don't die," I whispered, pulling back.

Puck looked disappointed, but only for a second. "Me? Die? Didn't they tell you, princess? I'm Robin Goodfellow."

With a whoop, he flourished his knife and charged the waiting prince.

Ash lunged, a dark blur across the snow, his sword hissing down in a vicious arc. Puck leaped out of the way, and the blow sent a miniature blizzard arching toward me. I gasped, the freezing spray stinging like needles, and rubbed at my burning eyes. When I could open them again, Ash and Puck were deep in battle, and it looked like each was intent on killing the other.

Puck ducked a vicious blow and tossed Ash something from his pocket. It erupted into a large boar, squealing madly as it charged the prince, tusks gleaming. The ice sword hammered into it, and the boar exploded in a swirl of dry leaves. Ash flung out his arm, and a spray of glittering ice shards flew toward Puck like daggers. I cried out, but Puck inhaled and blew in their direction, like he was blowing out a birthday candle. The shards shimmered into daisies, raining harmlessly around him, and he grinned.

Ash attacked viciously, his blade singing as he bore down on his opponent. Puck dodged and parried with his dagger, retreating before the onslaught of the Winter prince. Diving away, Puck snatched a handful of twigs from the base of the tree, blew on them, and tossed them into the air—

—and now there were *four* Pucks, three grinning wickedly as they set upon their opponent. Three knives flashed, three bodies surrounded the dark prince, as the real Puck leaned against the tree and watched Ash struggle.

But Ash was far from beaten. He spun away from the Pucks,

his sword a blur as he dodged and parried, whirling from one attack to the next. He ducked beneath an opponent's guard, ripped his blade up, and sliced cleanly through a Puck's stomach. The doppelgänger split in two, changing into a severed stick that dropped away. Ash spun to meet the Puck rushing up from the side. His sword whirled, and Puck's head dropped from his shoulders before reverting to a twig. The last Puck charged the prince from behind, dagger raised high. Ash didn't even turn, but rammed his blade backward, point up. Puck's lunge carried him onto the blade and drove it through his stomach, the point erupting out his back. The prince yanked the sword free without turning, and a shattered twig dropped to the snow.

Ash lowered his sword, gazing around warily. Following his gaze, I gave a start. Puck had disappeared, pulling a Grimalkin while we were distracted. Instantly wary, the Winter prince scanned the garden, edging forward with his sword raised. His gaze flicked to me, and I tensed, but he dismissed me almost as quickly, stepping beneath the boughs of a frozen pine.

As Ash stepped under the branches, something leaped out of the snow, howling. The prince dodged, the knife barely missing him, and Puck overbalanced, stumbling forward. With a snarl, Ash drove the point of the sword through Puck's back and out his chest, pinning him to the ground.

I screamed, but as I did, the body vanished. For a split second, Ash stared at the pierced leaf on his sword tip, then threw himself to the side as something dropped from the tree, dagger flashing in the light.

Puck's laughter rang out as Ash rolled to his feet, clutching his arm. Blood seeped between pale fingers. "Almost too slow that time, prince," Puck mocked, balancing the dagger on two fingers. "Really, that's the oldest trick in the book. I know, 'cause I *wrote* the book. I've got a million more, if you want to keep playing."

"I'm getting tired of sparring with copies." Ash straightened, dropping his hand. "I guess honor isn't as prevalent in the Seelie Court as I thought. Are you the real Puck, or is he too cowardly to face me himself?"

Puck regarded him disdainfully, before shimmering into nothingness. Another Puck stepped out from behind a tree, a nasty grin on his face.

"All right, then, prince," he said, smirking as he approached, "if that's what you want, I'll kill you the old-fashioned way." And they flew at each other again.

I watched the battle, my heart in my throat, wishing I could do something. I didn't want either of them to die, but I had no idea how to stop this. Shouting or rushing between them seemed like a really bad idea; one could be distracted, and the other would waste no time finishing him off. A sick despair churned in my stomach. I hadn't realized Puck was so bloodthirsty, but the mad gleam in his eyes told me he would kill the Winter prince if he could.

They have a history, I realized, watching Ash cut viciously at Puck's face, barely missing as his opponent ducked. *Something happened between them, to make them hate each other. I wonder if they were ever friends.*

My skin prickled, an uneasy shiver from more than the cold. Over the clang and screech of metal, I heard something else, a faint rustling, as if a thousand insects were scuttling toward us.

"Human!" Grimalkin's voice made me jump. Tracks appeared in the snow, rushing toward me, and invisible claws scrabbled against bark as the feline fled up a tree. "Something is coming! Hide, quickly!"

I glanced at Puck and Ash, still locked in combat. The rustling grew louder, accompanied by static and faint, high-pitched laughter. Suddenly, through the trees, hundreds of eyes glowed electric-green in the darkness, surrounding us. Puck and Ash stopped fighting and broke apart, finally aware that something was wrong, but it was too late.

They poured over the ground like a living carpet, appearing from everywhere: small, black-skinned creatures with spindly arms, huge ears, and razor grins that shone blue-white in the darkness. I heard the boys' cries of shock, and Grimalkin's yowl of horror as he fled farther up the tree. The creatures spotted me, and I had no time to react. They swarmed me like angry wasps, crawling up my legs, hurling themselves onto my back. I felt claws dig into my skin, my ears filled with loud buzzing and shrieking laughter, and I screamed, thrashing wildly. I couldn't see, didn't know which way was up. The weight of their bodies bore me down, and I fell onto a grasping, wriggling mass. Hundreds of hands lifted me up, like ants carrying a grasshopper, and began to cart me away.

"Puck!" I cried, struggling to free myself. But whenever I rolled away from one group, a dozen more slid in to take their place, bearing me up. I never touched the ground. "Grimalkin! Help!"

Their voices seemed distant and far away. Carried on a buzzing, living mattress, I glided rapidly over the ground and into the waiting darkness.

I don't know how long they carried me. When I struggled, the claws gripping me would dig into my skin, turning the mattress into a bed of needles. I soon ceased thrashing about, and tried to concentrate on where they were taking me. But it was difficult; being carried on my back, the only thing I saw clearly was the sky. I tried to turn my head, but the creatures had their claws sunk into my hair and would yank on it until tears formed in my eyes. I resigned myself to lying still, shivering with cold, waiting to see what would happen. The cold and the gnawing worry drained me…. I allowed my eyes to slip closed, and found solace in the darkness.

When I opened my eyes again, the night sky had disappeared, replaced by a ceiling of solid ice. I realized we were traveling underground. The air grew even colder as the tunnel opened up into a magnificent ice cavern, glistening with a jagged, alien beauty. Huge icicles dripped from the ceiling, some longer than I was tall and wickedly sharp. It was a tad disturbing passing under those bristling spikes, watching them sparkle like crystal chandeliers, praying they wouldn't fall.

My teeth chattered, and my lips were numb with cold. However, as we traveled deeper into the cave, the air gradually warmed. A faint noise echoed through the lower caverns: a roaring, hissing sound, like steam escaping a cracked pipe. Water dripped from the ceiling in rivulets now, soaking my clothes, and some of the ice shards looked dangerously unstable.

The hissing grew louder, punctuated with great roaring coughs and the acrid smell of smoke. Now I saw that some of the icicles had indeed fallen, smashed to pieces on the ground and glittering like broken glass.

My abductors brought me into a large cavern littered with shattered shards of ice. Puddles saturated the floor, and water fell like rain from the ceiling. The creatures dropped me to the icy ground and scuttled off. I rubbed my numb, aching limbs and looked around, wondering where I was. The cave was mostly empty, save for a wooden box filled with black rocks—coal?—in one corner. More were stacked along the far wall, next to a wooden archway that led off into the darkness.

A piercing whistle, like a steam engine roaring into the station, erupted from the tunnel, and black smoke churned from the opening. I smelled ashes and brimstone, and then a deep voice echoed throughout the cavern. "HAVE YOU BROUGHT HER?"

The scuttling creatures scattered, and several icicles smashed to the floor with an almost musical chime. I ducked behind an ice column as heavy footsteps clanked down the tunnel. Through the smoke, I saw something huge and grossly distorted, something definitely not human, and shook in terror.

A massive black horse emerged from the writhing smoke, eyes glowing like hot coals, flared nostrils blowing steam. It was as big as the horses that pulled the Budweiser wagon, but there the resemblance ended. At first, I thought it was covered in iron plates; its hide was bulky with metal, rusted and black, and it moved awkwardly with the weight. Then I realized its body was *made* of iron. Pistons and gears jutted out from its ribs. Its mane and tail were steel cables, and a great fire burned in its belly, visible through the chinks in its hide. Its face was a terrifying mask as it turned to me, blasting flame from its nostrils.

I fell back, certain I was going to die.

"ARE YOU MEGHAN CHASE?" The horse's voice shook the room. More icicles fell like glass knives, but they were the least of my worries. I cringed back as the iron monster loomed over me, tossing its head and snorting flame. "ANSWER ME, HUMAN. ARE YOU MEGHAN CHASE, DAUGHTER OF THE SUMMER KING?"

"Yes," I whispered as the horse moved closer, iron hooves pounding the ice. "Who are you? What do you want with me?"

"I AM IRONHORSE," the beast replied, "ONE OF KING MACHINA'S LIEUTENANTS. I HAVE BROUGHT YOU HERE BECAUSE MY LORD HAS REQUESTED IT. YOU WILL COME WITH ME TO SEE THE IRON KING."

The booming voice was giving me a headache. I tried to focus through the pounding in my skull. "The Iron King?" I asked stupidly. "Who—?"

"KING MACHINA," Ironhorse confirmed. "SOVER- EIGN LORD OF THE IRON COURT, AND RULER OF THE IRON FEY."

Iron fey?

A chill slid up my spine. I looked around, at the count- less eyes of the gremlinlike monsters, to the massive bulk of Ironhorse, and felt dizzy at the implications. Iron fey? Could there be such a thing? In all the stories, poems, and plays, I'd never encountered anything like this. Where did they come from? And who was this Machina, ruler of the Iron Fey? More important…

"What does he want with me?"

"IT IS NOT MINE TO KNOW." Ironhorse snorted, swishing its tail with a clanking sound. "I ONLY OBEY. HOWEVER, YOU WOULD BE WISE TO COME WITH US, IF YOU WISH TO SEE YOUR BROTHER AGAIN."

"Ethan?" I jerked my head up, glaring at Ironhorse's expres- sionless mask. "How do you know about him?" I demanded. "Is he all right? Where is he?"

"COME WITH ME, AND ALL YOUR QUESTIONS WILL BE ANSWERED. THE IRON COURT AND MY LORD MACHINA AWAIT."

I stood as Ironhorse turned, clanking back toward the tun- nel. Its pistons creaked and the gears complained loudly as it shuffled forward. It was old, I realized, watching a bolt come loose and fall to the ground. A relic of days gone by. I won- dered if there were newer, sleeker models out there, and what they looked like. Faster, better, more superior iron fey. After a moment, I decided I didn't want to find out.

Ironhorse stood at the mouth of the tunnel, stamping impatiently. Sparks flew from its hooves as it glowered at me. "COME," it ordered, with a blast of steam from its nostrils. "FOLLOW THE TROD TO THE IRON COURT. IF YOU WILL NOT WALK, THE GREMLINS WILL CARRY YOU." It tossed its head and reared, flames shooting out its muzzle. "OR PERHAPS I WILL RUN BEHIND YOU, BREATHING FIRE—"

An ice spear flew through the air, striking Ironhorse between the ribs, bursting into steam as the fire engulfed it. The horse screamed, a high-pitched whistle, and whirled, hooves sparking as they struck the ice. The gremlins skittered forward, gazing wildly about, searching for intruders.

"Hey, ugly!" called a familiar voice. "Nice place you got here! Here's a thought, though. Next time, try a hideout a little more resistant to fire than an ice cave!"

"Puck!" I cried, and the red-haired elf waved at me, grinning from the far side of the cavern. Ironhorse screamed and charged, scattering gremlins like birds as he bore down on Puck. Puck didn't move, and the great iron beast knocked him flat in the ice, trampling him with his steel hooves.

"Oh, that looked painful," called another Puck, a little farther down. "We really need to talk about your anger-management issues."

With a roar, Ironhorse charged the second Puck, moving farther away from me and the trod. The gremlins followed, laughing and hissing, but kept a fair distance from the raging beast and its hooves.

A cool hand clamped over my mouth, muffling my startled yelp. I turned to gaze into glittering silver eyes.

"Ash?"

"This way," he said in a low voice, tugging on my hand, "while the idiot has them distracted."

"No, wait," I whispered, pulling back. "He knows about Ethan. I have to find my brother—"

Ash narrowed his eyes. "Hesitate now, and Goodfellow will die. Besides…" He reached out and took my hand again. "I'm not giving you a choice."

Dazed, I followed the Winter prince along the wall of the cavern, too stunned to ask why he was helping me. Didn't he want to kill me? Was this rescue just to get me alone to finish the job in peace? But that didn't make any sense; he could have just killed me while Puck was distracted with Ironhorse.

"Hellooooooooo." Puck's voice echoed farther down the cavern. "Sorry, ugly, wrong me! Keep going, I'm sure you'll get it right next time!"

Ironhorse looked up from stomping a fake Puck into the ground, crimson eyes blazing with hate. Seeing yet another Puck, it tensed iron muscles to charge, when one of the gremlins spotted us sneaking along the wall and gave a yelp of alarm.

Ironhorse whirled, eyes flaring as they settled on us. Ash muttered a curse. With a bellow and a blast of flame from its nostrils, it charged, bearing down on us like the steam engine it was named for. Ash drew his sword and flung a shower of ice shards at the monster. They shattered harmlessly on its armored hide, doing nothing but enraging it further. As the roaring, flaming bulk of metal descended, Ash shoved me out of the way and dove forward, the flailing hooves missing him by inches. Rolling to his feet behind the monster, he cut at its flank, but Ironhorse plunged its head down and kicked him in the ribs. There was a sickening crack, and Ash was hurled away, crumpling to the floor in a heap.

A screaming flock of ravens descended on Ironhorse before it could stomp Ash into the ground. They swirled around its head, pecking and clawing, and Ironhorse roared as it lashed out at the flock, blasting them to cindery bits. Ash staggered to his feet as Puck appeared beside us, grabbing my hand.

"Time to go," he announced cheerfully. "Prince, either keep up or get left behind. We're leaving."

We ran through the caverns, slipping on ice and slush, the insane roars of Ironhorse and the hissing of the gremlins on our heels. I didn't dare look back. The cavern shook, and icicles smashed to the ground all around us, spraying me with stinging shards, but we kept going.

A fuzzy gray shape bounded toward us, tail held high. "You found her," Grimalkin said, stopping to glare at Puck. "Idiot. I told you not to fight the horse thing."

"Can't talk now, little busy at the moment!" Puck gasped as we tore past the feline, continuing down the tunnel. Grimalkin flattened his ears and joined us as the shrieks of the gremlins ricocheted off the walls. I could see the mouth of the cave, dripping with icicles, and put on a burst of speed.

Ironhorse bellowed, and an ice shard smashed down inches from my face.

"Collapse the cave!" Grimalkin shouted, bounding along beside us. "Bring the ceiling down on their heads! Do it!" He zipped away, through the cave entrance, and was gone.

We burst out of the cave moments later, gasping, stumbling in the snow. Looking back, I saw dozens of green eyes skittering forward, heard the pounding hooves of Ironhorse as he followed close behind.

"Keep going!" Ash ordered, and whirled around. Closing his eyes, he brought a fist to his face and bowed his head. The gremlins swarmed toward him, and the red glow of Ironhorse appeared, flames streaming in the darkness.

Ash opened his eyes and flung out a hand.

A low rumble shook the ground, and the cave trembled. Huge clumps of icicles shivered, wobbling back and forth. As the gremlins reached the mouth of the cave, the entire ceiling collapsed with a roar and a sound like breaking glass. Gremlins shrieked as they were crushed under several tons of ice and rock, and the dismayed bellow of Ironhorse rose above the cacophony.

The noise died away, and silence fell. Ash, standing two feet from the solid wall of ice sealing the cave, collapsed into the snow.

Puck grabbed my arm as I rushed forward. "Whoa, whoa, princess," he said as I tried yanking free. "What do you think you're doing? In case you forgot, princeling there is the enemy. We don't help the enemy."

"He's hurt."

"All the more reason to leave now."

"He just saved our lives!"

"Technically, he was saving his own life," Puck replied, still not letting go. I shoved him, hard, and he finally released me. "Look, princess." He sighed as I glared at him. "Do you think Ash will play nice now? The only reason he helped—the only reason he agreed to a truce—was so he could bring you to Mab. She wants you alive, to use as leverage against Oberon. That's the *only* reason he came along. If he wasn't hurt, he'd be trying to kill me now."

I looked at Ash, lying motionless in the snow. Flakes speckled his body—soon they would hide him completely. "We can't just leave him to die."

"He's a Winter prince, Meghan. He won't freeze to death, trust me."

I scowled at him. "You're just as bad as they are." He blinked, startled, and I turned away from him. "I'm going to see if he's all right, at least. Either come along or get out of my way."

Puck threw up his hands. "Fine, princess. I'll help the son

of Mab, eternal enemy of our court. Even though he'll probably stick a sword in my back the second my guard is down."

"I wouldn't worry about that," Ash muttered, rising slowly
to his feet. One hand gripped his sword; the other arm was
wrapped around his ribs. He shook the snow from his hair
and raised his weapon. "We can continue now, if you like."

Grinning, Puck pulled his dagger. "I'd be thrilled," he
muttered, taking a step forward. "This won't take long at all."

I threw myself between them.

"Stop it!" I cried, glaring at both in turn. "Stop it right
now! Put your weapons up, both of you! Ash, you're in no
condition to fight, and, Puck, shame on you, agreeing to duel
him when he's obviously hurt. Sit down and shut up."

They blinked at me, astounded, but slowly lowered their
weapons. A sneezing laugh rang out in the branches of a tree,
and Grimalkin peered down, swishing his tail in mirth.

"A daughter of Oberon after all," he called, baring his teeth
in a feline grin. "Queen Titania would be proud."

Puck shrugged and flopped down on a log, crossing his arms
and legs. Ash continued to stand, watching me with an unreadable expression. Ignoring Puck, I walked up to him. His
eyes narrowed, and he tensed, raising his sword, but I wasn't
afraid. For the first time since I came here, I wasn't afraid at all.

"Prince Ash," I murmured, drawing closer, "I propose we
make a deal."

Surprise flickered across his face.

"We need your help," I continued, gazing straight into his
eyes. "I don't know what those things were, but they called
themselves iron fey. They also mentioned someone called
Machina, the Iron King. Do you know who that is?"

"The Iron King?" Ash shook his head. "There is no one
by that name in the courts. If this King Machina exists, he

is a danger to all of us. Both courts will want to know about him and these…iron fey."

"I need to find him," I said, forcing as much determination into my voice as I could. "He's got my brother. I need you to help us escape the Unseelie territory and find the court of the Iron King."

Ash raised an eyebrow. "And why would I do that?" he asked softly. Not mocking, but dead serious.

I swallowed. "You're injured," I pointed out, holding his gaze. "You won't be able to take me by force, not with Puck so eager to stick a knife in your ribs." I glanced back at Puck, sulking on the log, and lowered my voice. "Here's my bargain. If you help me find my brother and get him safely home, then I'll go with you to the Unseelie Court. Without a fight, from me or Puck."

Ash's eyes gleamed. "He means that much to you? You would exchange your freedom for his safety?"

I took a deep breath and nodded. "Yes." The word hung in the air between us, and I hurried on before I could take it back. "So, do we have a deal?"

He inclined his head, as if still trying to puzzle me out. "No, daughter of Oberon. We have a contract."

"Good." My legs trembled. I backed away from him, needing to sit before I fell over. "And no trying to kill Puck, either."

"That wasn't part of the bargain," Ash said, before he grimaced and sank to his knees, arms around his middle. Dark blood trickled between his lips.

"Puck!" I called, turning to glare at the faery on the log. "Get over here and help."

"Oh, we're playing nice now?" Puck remained seated, looking anything but compliant. "Shall we have tea first? Brew up a nice pot of kiss-my-ass?"

"Puck!" I shouted in exasperation, but Ash raised his head and stared at his enemy.

"Truce, Goodfellow," he grated out. "The Chillsorrow manor is a few miles east of here. Right now, the lady of the house is away at court, so we'll be safe there. I suggest we postpone our duel until we arrive and the princess is out of the cold. Unless you'd like to kill me now."

"No, no. We can kill each other later." Puck hopped off the stump and padded up, shoving his dagger into his boot. Putting the prince's arm over his shoulders, he jerked him to his feet. Ash grunted and pursed his lips but didn't cry out. I glared at Puck. He ignored me.

"Off we go." Puck sighed. "You coming, Grimalkin?"

"Oh, definitely." Grimalkin landed with a soft thump in the snow. His golden eyes, bright with amusement, regarded me knowingly. "I would not miss this for the world."

17

THE ORACLE

The Chillsorrow manor lived up to its name. The outside of the sprawling estate was blanketed in ice, the lawn was frozen, the numerous thorn trees were encased in crystallized water. Inside wasn't much better. The stairways were slick, the floors resembled ice rinks, and my breath hung in the air as we made our way through the frigid, narrow halls. At least the servants were helpful, if extremely creepy; skeleton-thin gnomes with pure white skin and long, long fingers glided silently around the house, not saying a word. Their pupil-less black eyes seemed too big for their faces, and they had the unnerving habit of staring at you mournfully, as if you had a fatal disease and were not long for the world.

Still, they welcomed us into the house, bowing respectfully to Ash, making him comfortable in one of the rooms. The biting chill didn't affect the Winter prince, though I was shaking, teeth chattering, until one of the servants offered me a heavy quilt and padded off without a word.

Clutching the quilt gratefully, I peeked into the room where Ash sat on a bed surrounded by ice gnomes. His shirt was off, showing his lean, muscular arms and chest. He was built more like a dancer or martial artist than a bodybuilder, the elegant frame hinting at a grace a human simply could not match. His tousled black hair fell into his eyes, and he absently raked it out of his face.

My stomach fluttered weirdly, and I backed out into the hall. *What are you doing?* I asked myself, appalled. *That is Ash, prince of the Unseelie Court. He tried to kill Puck, and he might try to kill you, as well. He is not sexy. He's not.*

But he was, extremely, and it was useless to deny it. My heart and my brain were at odds, and I knew I'd better come to terms with this quickly. *Okay, fine,* I told myself, *he's gorgeous, I'll admit it. I'm just reacting to his good looks, that's all. All the sidhe are stunning and beautiful. It doesn't mean anything.*

With that thought to buoy me, I stepped back into the room.

Ash glanced up as I approached, the quilt wrapped around my shoulders. A pair of gnomes were wrapping his torso in bandages, but above his stomach, I could see an angry black welt.

"Is that where—?"

Ash nodded, once. I continued to stare at it, noting how the flesh was blackened and crusted with scabs. I shuddered and looked away.

"It looks almost burned."

"The creature's hooves were made of iron," Ash replied. "Iron tends to burn, when it doesn't kill outright. I was lucky the blow wasn't over my heart." The gnomes tugged the bandages tight, and he winced.

"How badly are you hurt?"

He gave me an appraising look. "The fey heal faster than you mortals," he answered, and rose gracefully to his feet, scattering gnomes. "Especially if we're within our own territories. Except for this—" he lightly touched the iron burn on his ribs "—I should be fine by tomorrow."

"Oh." I was a bit breathless, suddenly unable to take my eyes from him. "That's...good, then."

He smiled then, a cold, humorless gesture, and stepped closer.

"Good?" His voice was mocking. "You shouldn't wish for my good health, princess. It would've been easier for you if Puck had killed me when he had the chance."

I resisted the urge to back away from him. "No, it wouldn't." His shadow loomed over me, prickling my skin, but I stood my ground. "I need your help, both to get out of Unseelie territory, and to find my brother. Besides, I couldn't let him kill you in cold blood."

"Why not?" He was very close now, so close I could see the pale scars on his chest. "He seems very devoted to you. Perhaps you'll wait until we leave Tir Na Nog to have him stab me in the back? What would happen if we fought again, and I killed him?"

"Stop it." I glared at him, meeting his eyes. "Why are you doing this? I gave you my word. Why are you pulling this crap now?"

"Just want to see where you stand, princess." Ash backed up a step, no longer smiling. "I like to get a feel for my enemies before we engage in combat. See what their strengths and weaknesses are."

"We aren't in combat—"

"Combat doesn't have to be with swords." Ash walked back to the bed, drawing his blade and examining the gleaming length. "Emotions can be deadly, and knowing your enemy's breaking point can be key to winning a battle. For example..." He turned and pointed the sword, staring at me down the polished edge. "You would do anything to find your brother—

put yourself in danger, bargain with the enemy, give up your own freedom—if it means saving him. You'd likely do the same for your friends, or anyone else you care about. Your personal loyalty is your breaking point, and your enemies will certainly use it against you. *That* is your weakness, princess. That is the most dangerous aspect in your life."

"So what?" I challenged, pulling the quilt tighter around myself. "All you're telling me is I won't betray my friends or family. If that's a weakness, I'm okay with it."

He regarded me with glittering eyes, the expression on his face unreadable. "And, if the choice was between saving your brother and letting me die, which would you choose? The answer should be obvious, but could you do it?"

I chewed my lip and remained silent. Ash nodded slowly and turned away. "I'm tired," he said, sitting down on the bed. "You should find Puck and decide where we go from here. Unless, of course, you know where this Machina's court is. I do not. If I'm going to help you, I need to rest."

"It isn't obvious," I said quietly.

Ash glanced at me with a puzzled frown. "The answer," I went on. "If it came to choosing between who lives or dies. I couldn't do it. I would try to save you both."

"Don't be a fool." The Winter prince narrowed his eyes to silver slits. "I'm your enemy. Thoughts like that will only get you killed. The right choice, the logical choice, would be to abandon me and save the one you came to find."

"And let you die."

"It's what I would do."

I bit my lip, feeling a lump in my throat. "I'm not you," I whispered. "I'm not a Winter faery—I'm human. I couldn't… Of course I would try to save Ethan, but I don't want to see you die, either."

"Why not?" The Winter prince seemed genuinely puzzled,

his features lowered into a slight frown. "You know nothing about me. I'm the enemy of your father and the Seelie fey. If I'm killed, our contract is broken. You won't have to come with me to the Winter Court." One corner of his lip curled up in a wry, humorless smile. "Not that I plan on dying, princess, but it's foolish and illogical to hope I will survive this mission."

"Well, I guess I'm going to be foolish and illogical," I said firmly, "and hope that everyone comes through this alive and well. Even you, Ash. We might be enemies, but I'm not going to hate you just because the Summer Court says I should."

The prince shook his head, but I thought I saw a flicker of…something in his eyes. Gone before I could really place it. He lay back and turned his head away. "Good night, princess," he said flatly. "I will rejoin you and the others in the morning. Inform Goodfellow that we should be ready to depart at dawn."

He put an arm over his eyes, dismissing me. I swallowed my churning emotions, backed out, and left the room, dark doubts swirling around my head.

In the hallway I met Puck, leaning against the wall with his arms crossed. "So, how is the handsome princeling?" he mocked, shoving away from the wall. "Will he survive his ordeal to fight another day?"

"He's okay," I muttered as Puck fell into step beside me. "He's got a nasty-looking burn where the horse kicked him, and I think his ribs were broken, but he wouldn't say for sure."

"Forgive me if my heart doesn't bleed for him," Puck replied, rolling his eyes. "I don't know how you got him to help, princess, but I wouldn't trust him further than I could throw him. Deals with the Winter Court are bad news. What did you promise him?"

"Nothing," I said, not meeting his eyes. I could feel his disbelieving stare, and went on the offensive to distract him.

And by the way, what's your deal with him, Puck? He said you stabbed him in the back once. What's up with that?"

"That…" Puck hesitated, and I could see I'd hit a sore spot. "That was a mistake," he went on in a quiet voice. "I didn't mean for that to happen." He shook himself, and the self-doubt dropped away, replaced by his irritating smirk. "Anyway, it doesn't matter. I'm not the bad guy here, princess."

"No," I admitted. "You're not. But I'm going to need both of you to help get Ethan back. Especially now. Especially since this Iron King wants me so bad. Do you know anything about him?"

Puck sobered. "I've never heard of him before," he murmured as we entered the dining hall. A long table stood in the center of the room, with a magnificent ice sculpture as a centerpiece. Grimalkin crouched on the table with his head in a bowl, eating something that smelled strongly of fish. He glanced up as we entered, licking his jaws with a bright pink tongue.

"Heard of who before?"

"King Machina." I pulled up a chair and sat down, resting my chin in my hands. "That horse thing—Ironhorse—called him the ruler of the iron fey."

"Hmm. A troubling name to be sure." Grimalkin put his head back in the bowl, chewing loudly. Puck sat down beside me.

"It doesn't seem possible," he muttered, mirroring my pose with his chin in his hands. "Iron fey? It's blasphemous! It goes against everything we know." He touched his fingers to his brow, narrowing his eyes. "And yet, Ironhorse was most definitely fey. I could sense that. If there are more like him and those gremlin things, Oberon must be informed immediately. If this King Machina brings his iron fey against us, he could destroy the courts before we knew what hit us."

"But you know nothing about him," Grimalkin said, his voice echoing inside the bowl. "You have no idea where he is, what his motives are, how many iron fey are actually out there. What would you tell Oberon now? Especially since you have…ahem…fallen out of favor by disobeying him."

"He's right," I said. "We should find out more about this Machina before we tell the courts. What if they decide to confront him now? He might fight back, or he might go into hiding." My stomach twisted as I thought of Oberon sending his armies to destroy the Iron King. The Seelie monarch wouldn't care about the life of a single human child, and he would certainly try to keep me as far from Machina and the Iron Fey as he could. "Oberon can't know about this," I decided. "Not yet. I can't risk losing Ethan."

"Meghan—"

"No telling the courts," I said firmly, looking him in the eye. "That's final."

Puck sighed and threw me a grudging smirk. "Fine, princess," he said, raising his hands. "We'll do it your way."

Grimalkin snickered into the bowl.

"So, how do we find this Machina, anyway?" I asked, voicing the question that had bothered me all evening. "The only trod to his kingdom that we know of is buried under a ton of ice. Where do we start looking for him? He could be anywhere."

Grimalkin raised his head. "I might know somebody who could help us," he purred, slitting his eyes. "An oracle of sorts, living within your world. Very old, older even than Puck. Older than Oberon. Almost as old as cats. If anyone could tell you where this Iron King might be, she could."

My heart leaped. If this oracle could tell me about the Iron King, maybe she would know where my dad was, as well. It couldn't hurt to ask.

"I thought she died," Puck said. "If it's the same oracle I'm thinking of, she vanished ages ago."

Grimalkin yawned and licked his whiskers. "Not dead," he replied. "Hardly dead. But she changed her name and appearance so many times, even the oldest fey would hardly remember her. She likes to keep a low profile, you know."

Puck frowned, knitting his brows together. "Then how is it *you* remember her?" he demanded, sounding indignant.

"I am a cat," purred Grimalkin.

I didn't sleep well that night. The numerous quilts didn't quite protect me from the incessant chill; it crept into whatever cracks it could find, stealing away the heat with frozen fingers. Also, Grimalkin slept on top of me under the blankets, his furry body a blessed warmth, but he kept digging his claws into my skin. Near dawn, after being poked awake yet again, I rose, wrapped a quilt around my shoulders, and went looking for Puck.

Instead, I found Ash in the dining hall, practicing sword drills by the gray light of dawn. His lean, honed body glided over the tiles, sword sweeping gracefully through the air, eyes closed in concentration. I stood in the doorway and watched for several minutes, unable to tear my gaze away. It was a dance, beautiful and hypnotic. I lost track of the time I stood watching him, and would have happily stayed there all morning, when he opened his eyes and saw me.

I squeaked and straightened guiltily. "Don't mind me," I said as he relaxed his stance. "I didn't mean to interrupt. Please, continue."

"I'm finished, anyway." Sheathing his sword, he regarded me solemnly. "Did you need something?"

I realized I was staring and blushed, turning my gaze away. "Um, no. That is... I'm glad you're feeling better."

He gave me a weird little smile. "I have to be on top of my game if I'm going to kill things for you, right?"

I was saved a reply as Puck strolled in, humming, carrying a bowl of strange golden fruit, each about the size of a golf ball. "Mornin', princess," he said with his mouth full, plunking the bowl on the table. "Look what I found."

Ash blinked. "Are you raiding the cellars now, Goodfellow?"

"Me? Stealing?" Puck flashed a devious grin and popped another fruit into his mouth. "In the house of my ancient enemy? What gave you that idea?" He plucked another fruit and tossed it to me with a wink. It was warm and soft, and had the texture of an overripe pear.

Grimalkin leaped onto the table and sniffed. "Summerpod," he stated, wrapping his tail around himself. "I did not think they grew in the Winter territories." He turned to me with a serious expression. "Better not eat too many of those," he warned. "They make faery wine out of that. Your human side will not handle it well."

"Oh, let her try one," Puck snorted, rolling his eyes. "She's been in Faery long enough, eating our food. It won't turn her into a rat or anything."

"Where are we going?" Ash questioned, sounding bored with us all. "Did you manage to come up with a plan to find the Iron King, or are we going to paint targets on our backs and wander in circles until he notices?"

Tentatively, I bit into the fruit, and a cloying, heady sweetness flooded my mouth, along with an instant burst of warmth. I swallowed, and it filled my whole body, driving away the cold. Suddenly the quilt was suffocatingly hot; I draped it over one of the chairs and gulped the rest of the fruit in one bite.

"You're awfully eager to help," Puck drawled, leaning back

against the table. "And here I was getting ready for a duel first thing in the morning. Why the change of heart, prince?"

The effects of the summerpod were fading; cold prickled my arms, somehow worse than before, and my cheeks tingled. Ignoring Grimalkin's warning glare, I snatched another fruit and popped it into my mouth like Puck had done. Wonderful, delicious warmth surged into me, and I sighed in pleasure.

Ash's outline blurred at the edges as he faced Puck. "Your princess and I made a bargain," he said. "I agreed to help her find the Iron King, though I won't bore you with the details. While I will uphold my end of the contract, it did not involve you in any way. I only promised to help *her*."

"Which means we're still free to duel each other anytime we want."

"Exactly."

The room swayed slightly. I plunked into a chair and grabbed another summerpod from the bowl, shoving the whole thing in my mouth. Again, I felt that wonderful rush of heat and headiness. Somewhere far away, Puck and Ash were holding a dangerous conversation, but I couldn't bring myself to care. Hooking the edge of the bowl, I pulled the whole thing to me and grabbed an entire handful.

"Well, why wait?" Puck sounded eager. "We could step outside right now, Your Highness, and get this over with."

Grimalkin sighed loudly, interrupting the conversation. Both faeries turned and glared at him. "This is all quite fascinating," Grimalkin said, his voice slurring in my ears, "but instead of posing and scratching the ground like rutting peacocks, perhaps you should look to the girl."

Both boys glanced at me, and Puck's eyes got huge. "Princess!" he yelped, springing over and tugging the bowl from my grasping fingers. "You're not supposed to... Not all of them.... How many of those did you eat?"

"How very like you, Puck." Ash's voice came from a great distance, and the room started to spin. "Offer them a taste of faery wine, and act surprised when they're consumed by it."

That struck me as hilarious, and I broke into hysterical giggles. And once I began, I couldn't stop. I laughed until I was gasping for breath, tears streaming down my face. *This is wrong*, a tiny voice in the back of my mind warned. *Something is wrong with me.* But I couldn't bring myself to care. My feet itched and my skin crawled. I needed to move, to do something. I tried standing up, wanting to spin and dance, but the room tilted violently and I fell, still shrieking with laughter.

Somebody caught me, scooping me off my feet and into their arms. I smelled frost and winter, and heard an exasperated sigh from somewhere above my head.

"What are you doing, Ash?" I heard someone ask. A familiar voice, though I couldn't think of his name, or why he sounded so suspicious.

"I'm taking her back to her room." The person above me sounded wonderfully calm and deep. I sighed and settled into his arms. "She'll have to sleep off the effects of the fruit. We'll likely be here another day because of your idiocy."

The other voice said something garbled and unintelligible. I was suddenly too sleepy and light-headed to care. Relaxing against the mysterious person's chest, I fell into a heady sleep.

I stood in a dark room, surrounded by machinery. Steel cables as thick as my arm dangled overhead, house-size computers lined the walls, blinking with millions of flashing lights, and thousands of broken televisions, ancient PCs, out-of-date game consoles, and VHS players lay in drifts and heaps throughout the room. Wires covered everything, writhing and slithering along the walls, over the mountains of forgotten technology, dropping in tangled clumps from the ceiling.

A loud thrumming filled the area, making the floor vibrate and my teeth buzz.

"Meggie."

The strangled whisper came from behind me. I turned to see a small shape dangling from the wires. They coiled around his arms, chest, and legs, holding him spread-eagled near the ceiling. With horror, I saw some of the wires stabbing *into* him, plugged into his face, neck, and forehead like electrical outlets. He dangled weakly, blue eyes beseeching mine.

"Meggie," Ethan whispered, as something huge and monstrous rose up behind him. "Save me."

I bolted upright, screaming, the image of Ethan dangling from the wires burned into my mind. Grimalkin leaped away with a yowl, sharp claws stabbing into my chest as he fled. I barely felt them. Flinging aside the bedcovers, I raced for the door.

A dark shape rose from a chair against the wall, intercepting me as I tried to bolt through. It caught my upper arms, holding me still as I struggled with it. All I could see was Ethan's face, contorted in agony, dying in front of me.

"Let go!" I cried, jerking my arm free and trying to shove past my opponent. "Ethan is out there! I have to save him! Let me go!"

"You don't even know where he is." A hand caught my flailing wrist and pinned it to his chest. Silver eyes glared into mine as he shook me, once. "Listen to me! If you go charging out there without a plan, you'll kill us all and your brother will die. Is that what you want?"

I sagged against him. "No," I whispered, all the fight going out of me. Tears welled, and I shook with the effort of holding them back. I couldn't be weak. If I was going to have any hope of saving my brother, I couldn't stand in a corner and cry. I had to be strong.

With a shaky breath, I straightened and wiped my eyes. "Sorry," I whispered, embarrassed. "I'm okay now. No more freaking out, I promise."

Ash still held my hand. Gently, I tried pulling back, but he wasn't letting go. I glanced up and found his face inches from mine, his eyes searingly bright in the shadows of the room.

Time froze around us. My heart stumbled a bit, then picked up, louder and faster than before. Ash's expression was blank; nothing showed on his face or in his eyes, but his body had gone very still. I knew I was blushing like a fire engine. His fingers came up and gently brushed a tear from my cheek, sending a tingle through my skin. I shivered, frightened by the pressure mounting between us, needing to break the tension.

I licked my lips and whispered, "Is this where you say you'll kill me?"

One corner of his lip curled. "If you like," he murmured, a flicker of amusement finally crossing his face. "Though it's gotten far too interesting for that."

Footsteps sounded outside in the hall, and Ash moved away, dropping my hand. He crossed his arms and leaned against the wall as Puck entered, Grimalkin loping lazily behind him.

I took a deep, furtive breath and hoped my burning face was lost in the shadows. Puck shot Ash a suspicious glare before looking at me. A sheepish grin crossed his lips.

"Er, how're you feeling, princess?" he asked, lacing both hands behind his head, a sure sign that he was nervous. "Those summerpod fruits pack quite a punch, don't they? Hey, at least it wasn't bristlewort. You would've spent the rest of the evening as a hedgehog."

I sighed, knowing that was as close to an apology as I would get. "I'm fine," I told him, rolling my eyes. "When do we leave?"

Puck blinked, but Ash answered as if nothing had happened. "Tonight," he said, coming away from the wall, stretching like a panther. "We've wasted enough time here. I assume the cait sith knows the way to this oracle?"

Grimalkin yawned, showing off fangs and a bright pink tongue. "Obviously."

"How far is it?" I asked him.

The cat looked from me to Ash and purred knowingly. "The oracle lives in the human world," he said, "in a large city that sits below sea level. Every year, people dress in costume and throw an enormous fiasco. They dance and eat and toss beads at others for removing their clothing."

"New Orleans," I said, frowning. "You're talking about New Orleans." I groaned, thinking about what it would take to get there. New Orleans was the closest city to our tiny little hick town, but it was still a long drive. I knew, because I'd fantasized about driving to the near-mythical city when I finally got my license. "That's hundreds of miles away!" I protested. "How are we going to get there—or were we planning to hitchhike?"

"Human, the Nevernever touches all borders of the human world." Grimalkin shook his head, sounding impatient. "It has no physical boundaries—you could get to Bora Bora from here if you knew the right trod. Stop thinking in human terms. I am sure the prince knows a path to the city."

"Oh, sure he does," Puck broke in. "Or a path right into the center of the Unseelie Court. Not that I'd mind crashing Mab's party, but I'd like for it to be on my own terms."

"He won't lead us into a trap," I snapped at Puck, who blinked at me. "He promised to help us find the Iron King.

He'd be breaking his word if he handed us over to Mab. Right, Ash?"

Ash looked uncomfortable but nodded.

"Right," I repeated, forcing a bravado I didn't feel. I hoped Ash wouldn't betray us, but, as I'd learned, deals with faeries tended to bite you in the ass. I shook off my hesitation and turned to the prince. "So," I demanded, trying to sound confident, "where can we find this trod to New Orleans?"

"The frost giant ruins," Ash replied, looking thoughtful. "Very close to Mab's court." At Puck's glare, he shrugged and offered a tiny, rueful smirk. "She goes to Mardi Gras every year."

I pictured the Queen of the Unseelie Court flashing a couple of drunken partygoers, and giggled uncontrollably. All three shot me a strange look. "Sorry," I muttered. "Still kind of giddy, I guess. Shall we go, then?"

Puck grinned. "Just let me borrow some supplies."

Later, the four of us walked down a narrow, ice-slick trail, the Chillsorrow manor growing smaller and smaller behind us. Sometime during the night, the gnomes had disappeared; the house was empty when we left, as if it had been that way for a hundred years. I wore a long robe of gray fur that tinkled musically when I walked, like tiny wind chimes. Puck had given it to me when we were clear of the manor, under the disapproving glare of Ash, and I didn't dare ask him where he got it. But it kept me perfectly warm and comfortable as we traveled through Mab's cold, frozen domain.

As we walked, I began to realize that the icy landscape of the Unseelie territory was just as beautiful—and dangerous— as Oberon's domain. Icicles dangled from the trees, sparkling like diamonds in the light. Occasionally, a skeleton lay beneath them, spears of ice between its bones. Crystal flowers bloomed along the road, petals as hard and delicate as glass, thorns angling toward me as I approached. Once I thought I saw a white bear watching us from atop a hill, a tiny figure perched on its back, but a tree passed in front of my vision and they were gone.

Ash and Puck didn't say a word to each other as we traveled, which was probably a good thing. The last thing I wanted was another duel to the death. The prince kept a steady, silent march ahead of us, rarely looking back, while Puck entertained me with jokes and useless chatter. I think he was attempting to keep my spirits up, to make me forget about Machina and my brother, and I was grateful for the distraction. Grimalkin vanished periodically, bounding off into the trees, only to reappear minutes or hours later with no explanation of where he'd been.

Later that afternoon, we reached a range of jagged, ice-covered peaks, and the trek turned sharply uphill. The path grew slick and treacherous, and I had to watch where I put my feet. A frigid wind swirled down the mountains, numbing fingers and toes and causing my cheeks to lose all feeling. Puck had fallen back on the trail; he kept casting suspicious looks over his shoulder, as if he feared an ambush from behind. I glanced back at him again, and in that moment, my feet hit a patch of ice and slid out from under me. I flailed, losing my balance on the narrow trail, trying desperately to stay upright and not go tumbling back down the mountain.

Something grabbed my wrist, pulling me forward. I collapsed against a solid chest, my fingers digging into the fabric to keep myself upright. As the adrenaline surge faded and my heartbeat returned to normal, I glanced up and found Ash's face inches from mine, so close I could see my reflection in his silvery eyes.

His nearness made my senses spin, and I couldn't look away. This close, his face was carefully guarded, but I felt the rapid thud of his heart beneath my palm. My own heartbeat picked up in response. He held me a moment longer, just long enough to make my stomach lurch wildly, then stepped away, leaving me breathless in the middle of the trail.

I looked back and found Puck glaring at me. Embarrassed and feeling strangely guilty, I dusted off my clothes and straightened my hair with an indignant huff before following Ash up the mountain.

Puck didn't speak to me after that.

By late evening, it had begun to snow, big, soft flakes drifting lazily from the sky. They literally sang as they fell past my ears, tiny voices dancing on the wind.

Ash stopped in the middle of the path, looking back at us. Flakes dusted his hair and clothes, swirling around him as if alive. "The Unseelie Court isn't far ahead," he said, ignoring the eddies that spun around him. "We should break from the road. Mab has others besides me looking for you, as well."

As he finished, the snow whirled madly around us, shrieking and tearing at our clothes. My fur coat clanged as the blizzard pelted me with snow, burning my cheeks and blinding me. I couldn't breathe; my limbs were frozen stiff to my sides. As the whirlwind calmed, I found myself encased in ice from the neck down, unable to move. Puck was similarly frozen, except his whole head was covered in crystal glass, his features frozen in shock.

Ash was unharmed, watching us blankly, the snow flurries dancing around him. His eyes were cold in the fading light.

"Dammit, Ash!" I yelled, struggling to free myself. I couldn't even wiggle a finger. "I thought we had a deal."

"A deal?" whispered another voice. The whirlwind of snow solidified, merging into a tall woman with long white hair and blue-tinged skin. A white gown draped her elegant body, and her black lips curled into a smile.

"A deal?" she repeated, turning to Ash with a mock horrified look. "Do tell. Ash, darling, I believe you've been hiding things from us."

18

THE VOODOO MUSEUM

"Narissa," Ash murmured. He sounded disinterested, bored even, though I saw his fingers twitch toward his sword. "To what do I owe the pleasure of this visit?"

The snow faery regarded me like a spider watching an insect in its web, before turning pupil-less black eyes on Ash. "Did I hear her right, darling?" she purred, drifting over the ground toward the prince. "Did you actually make a bargain with the half-breed? As I recall, our queen ordered us to bring the daughter of Oberon to her. Are you fraternizing with the enemy now?"

"Don't be ridiculous." Ash's voice was flat as he leveled a sneer in my direction. "I would never betray my queen. She wants Oberon's daughter, I will bring her Oberon's daughter. And I was in the middle of doing so, until you showed up and interrupted my progress."

Narissa looked unconvinced. "A pretty speech," she crooned, running a finger down Ash's cheek, leaving a trail of frost. "But what of the girl's companion? I believe you swore to kill Robin Goodfellow, Ash darling, and yet you bring him into the heart of our territory. If the queen knew he was here—"

"She would allow me to deal with him on my terms," Ash interrupted, narrowing his eyes. The anger on his face was real now. "I've brought Puck along because I want to kill him slowly, take my time with him. After I've delivered the half-breed, I'll have centuries to exact my vengeance on Robin Goodfellow. And *no one* will deny me that pleasure when it comes."

Narissa floated back. "Of course not, darling," she placated. "But perhaps I should take the half-breed on to court from here. You know how impatient the queen can be, and it really isn't fitting for the prince to be the escort." She smiled and drifted toward me. "I'll just take this burden off your hands."

Ash's sword rasped free, stopping the faery in her tracks. "Take another step and it will be your last."

"How dare you threaten me!" Narissa whirled back, snow flurrying around her. "I offer to help, and this is my reward! Your brother will hear of this."

"I'm sure he will." Ash smiled coldly and didn't lower his sword. "And you can tell Rowan that if he wants to gain Mab's favor, he should capture the half-breed himself, not send you to steal her from me. While you're at it, you can inform Queen Mab that I *will* deliver Oberon's daughter to her, I give my word on that.

"Now," he continued, making a shooing motion with his blade, "it's time for you to leave."

Narissa glared at him a moment longer, her hair billowing around her face. Then she smiled. "Very well, darling. I shall enjoy watching Rowan tear you limb from limb. Until we meet again." She twirled in place, her body dissipating into snow and wind, and blew away into the trees.

Ash sighed, shaking his head. "We need to move fast,"

he muttered, striding over to me. "Narissa will tell Rowan where we are, and he'll come speeding over to claim you for himself. Hold still."

He raised his sword hilt and brought it smashing down on the ice. The frozen shell cracked and began to chip in places. He sliced down again, and the cracks widened.

"D-don't worry about m-me," I said through chattering teeth. "Help P-Puck. He'll suffocate in th-there!"

"My bargain isn't with Goodfellow," Ash muttered, not looking up from his task. "I don't make a habit of aiding mortal enemies. Besides, he'll be fine. He's survived far worse than being frozen solid. Unfortunately."

I glared at him. "Are you really h-helping us?" I demanded as more bits of the ice shell began to crack. "What you said to Narissa—"

"I told her nothing that wasn't true," Ash interrupted, staring back at me. "I will not betray my queen. When this is over, I will deliver Oberon's half-blood daughter to her, as I promised." He broke eye contact and placed his hand over the ice, where the cracking was the greatest. "I'll just do it a little later than she expects. Close your eyes."

I did, and felt the ice column vibrate. The thrumming grew louder and stronger until, with the sound of breaking glass, the ice shattered into a million pieces and I was free.

I sagged to the ground, shaking uncontrollably. My robe was coated in ice, the chiming fur silenced. Ash knelt down to help me up, but I drew away from him.

"I'm not going anywhere," I growled, "until you get Puck out."

He sighed irritably but rose and walked over to the second frozen mound, putting his hand on it. This time, the ice shattered violently, flying in all directions like crystal shrapnel. Several pieces lodged in a nearby tree trunk, glittering ice

daggers sunk deep into the bark. I cringed at the vicious explosion. If he had done that to me, I would've been shredded.

Puck staggered forward, his face bloody, his clothing in tat-
ters. He swayed on his feet, eyes glazed over, and started to fall.
I yelped his name and raced over as he collapsed into my arms.

And disappeared. His body vanished the moment I caught
him, and I was left staring at a frayed leaf, spiraling to the
ground. Beside me, Ash snorted and shook his head.

"Did you hear everything you wanted, Goodfellow?" he
called to the empty air.

"I did," came Puck's disembodied voice, floating out of the
trees, "but I'm not sure I believe my ears."

He dropped from the branches of a pine, landing with a
thump in the snow. When he straightened, his green eyes
blazed with anger. Not directed at Ash, but at me.

"*That's* what you promised him, princess?" he shouted,
throwing up his hands. "That was your bargain? You would
offer yourself to the Unseelie Court?" He turned and punched
a tree, sending twigs and icicles to the ground. "Of all the *stupid* ideas! What is wrong with you?"

I shrank back. This was the first time I'd seen him angry.
Not just Puck, but Robbie, too. He never got mad, viewing
everything as a colossal joke. Now he looked ready to tear
my head off.

"We needed help," I said, watching in horror as his eyes
glowed and his hair writhed like flames atop his head. "We
have to get out of Unseelie territory and into Machina's realm."

"*I* would have gotten you there!" Puck roared. "Me! You
don't need his help! Don't you trust me to keep you safe? I
would've given everything for you. Why didn't you think
I'd be enough?"

I was struck speechless. Puck sounded *hurt,* glaring at me
like I'd just stabbed him in the back. I didn't know what to

say. I didn't dare look at Ash, but I sensed he was vastly amused by this whole display.

As we stared at each other, Grimalkin slid out of the brush, a patch of smoke gliding over the snow. His eyes bore that half-lidded, amused look as he glanced at the fuming Puck, then back to me. "It gets more entertaining every day," he purred with his feline grin.

I wasn't in the mood for his sarcasm. "Do you have anything helpful to say, Grim?" I snapped, watching his eyes slit even more.

The cat yawned and sat down to lick himself. "Actually, yes," he murmured, bending to his flanks. "I do have something you might be interested in." He continued washing his tail for several heartbeats, while I fought the urge to grab that tail and swing him around my head like a bolo. Finally, he stretched and looked up, blinking lazily.

"I believe," he purred, stretching it out, "I have found the trod you are looking for."

We followed Grimalkin to the base of an ancient ruined castle, where shattered pillars and broken gargoyles lay scattered about the courtyard. Bones littered the area as well, poking up through the snow, making me nervous. Puck trailed behind, not speaking to any of us, wrapped in angry silence. I made a promise to talk to him later when he'd cooled down, but for now, I was anxious to get out of Unseelie territory.

"There," Grimalkin said, nodding to a large stone pillar broken in two. One half rested on the other, forming an arch between them.

There was also a body lying in front of it. A body that was at least twelve feet tall, covered in hides and furs, with blue-white skin and a tangled white beard. It lay sprawled on its back with its face turned away, one meaty hand clutching a stone club.

Ash grimaced. "That's right," he muttered as we ducked behind a low stone wall. "Mab leaves her pet giant here to guard the place. Cold Tom doesn't listen to anyone but the queen."

I glared at the cat, who looked unconcerned. "You could have mentioned something, Grim. Did you forget that small but ever-so-important detail? Or did you just not see the twelve-foot giant in the middle of the floor?"

Puck, his animosity forgotten, or suppressed, peeked out from behind a boulder. "Looks like its Tom's nappy time," he said. "Maybe we can sneak around him."

Grimalkin regarded each of us in turn and blinked slowly. "In times like these, I am even more grateful that I am a cat." He sighed, and trotted toward the huge body.

"Grim! Stop!" I hissed after him. "What are you doing?"

The cat ignored me. My heart caught in my throat as he sauntered up to the giant, looking like a fuzzy mouse compared to Tom's bulk. Gazing up at the body, he twitched his tail, crouched, and leaped onto the giant's chest.

I stopped breathing, but the giant didn't move. Perhaps Grimalkin was too light for him to even notice. The cat turned and sat down, curling his tail around his feet and watching us bemusedly.

"Dead," he called to us. "Quite dead, in fact. You can stop cringing in abject terror if you like. I swear, how you survive with noses like that, I will never know. I could smell his stink a mile away."

"He's dead?" Ash immediately walked forward, brow furrowing. "Strange. Cold Tom was one of the strongest in his clan. How did he die?"

Grimalkin yawned. "Perhaps he ate something that disagreed with him."

I edged forward cautiously. Maybe I'd watched too many horror flicks, but I almost expected the "dead" giant to open his eyes and take a swing at us. "What does it matter?" I called to Ash, still keeping a careful eye on the body. "If it's dead, then we can get out of here without having to fight the thing."

"You know nothing," Ash replied. His gaze swept over the corpse, eyes narrowed. "This giant was strong, one of the strongest. Something killed him, within our territory. I want to know what could've taken Cold Tom down like this."

I was close to the giant's head now, close enough to see the blank, bulging eyes, the gray tongue lolling partway out of his mouth. Blue veins stood out around his eye sockets and in his neck. Whatever killed him, it wasn't quick.

Then a metal spider crawled out of his mouth.

I shrieked and leaped back. Puck and Ash rushed to my side as the huge arachnid skittered away, over Tom's face and up a wall. Ash drew his sword, but Puck gave a shout and hurled a rock at it. The stone hit the spider dead on; with a flash of sparks the bug plummeted to the ground, landing with a metallic clink on the flagstones.

We approached cautiously, Ash with his sword drawn, Puck with a good-size rock. But the insect thing lay broken and motionless on the ground, almost smashed in two. Up close, it looked less spidery and more like those face-hugger things from *Aliens,* except it was made of metal. Gingerly, I picked it up by its whiplike tail.

"What *is* that?" Ash muttered. For once, the unflappable prince sounded almost...terrified. "Another of Machina's iron fey?"

Puck gave an exaggerated shudder. "Bugs," he said, wrinkling his nose. "I hate bugs on normal days. Giant metal spider-looking bugs can go right to hell and die."

Something clicked in my head, and suddenly, I understood. "It *is* a bug," I whispered. The boys gave me puzzled frowns, and I plunged on. "Ironhorse, gremlins, bugs—it's starting to make sense to me now." I whirled on Puck, who blinked and stepped back. "Puck, didn't you tell me once that the fey were born from the dreams of mortals?"

"Yeah?" Puck said, not getting it.

"Well, what if these things—" I jiggled the metal insect "—are born from different dreams? Dreams of technology, and progress? Dreams of science? What if the pursuit of ideas that once seemed impossible—flight, steam engines, the internet—gave birth to a whole different species of faery? Mankind has made huge leaps in technology over the past hundred years. And with each success, we've kept reaching—dreaming—for more. These iron fey could be the result."

Puck blanched, and Ash looked incredibly disturbed. "If that's true," he murmured, his gray eyes darkening like thunderclouds, "then all fey could be in danger. Not just the Seelie and Unseelie Courts. The Nevernever itself would be affected, the entire fey world."

Puck nodded, looking more serious than I'd ever seen. "This is a war," he said, locking gazes with Ash. "If the Iron King is killing the guardians of the trods, he must be planning to invade. We have to find Machina and destroy him. Perhaps he's the heart of these iron fey. If we kill him, his followers could scatter."

"I agree." Ash sheathed his sword, giving the bug a revolted look. "We will bring Meghan to the Iron Court and rescue her brother by killing the ruler of the iron fey."

"Bravo," said Grimalkin, peering down from Cold Tom's chest. "The Winter prince and Oberon's jester agreeing on something. The world must be ending."

We all glared at him. The cat sneezed a laugh and hopped down from the body, gazing up at the bug in my hand. He wrinkled his nose.

"Interesting," he mused. "That thing stinks of iron and

steel, and yet it does not burn you. I suppose being half-human has perks, after all."

"What do you mean?" I asked.

"Mmm. Toss it to Ash, would you?"

"No!" Ash stepped back, his hand going to his sword. Grimalkin smiled.

"You see? Even the mighty Winter prince cannot stand the touch of iron. You, on the other hand, can handle it with no ill effects. Now do you see why the courts are scrambling to find you? Think of what Mab could do if she had you under her control."

I dropped the bug with a shudder. "Is that why Mab wants me?" I asked Ash, who still stood a few feet away. "As a weapon?"

"Ridiculous, isn't it?" Grimalkin purred. "She cannot even use glamour. She would be a horrible assassin."

"I don't know why Mab wants you," Ash said slowly, meeting my eyes. "I don't question the orders of my queen. I only obey."

"It doesn't matter now," Puck broke in, stabbing a glare at the Winter prince. "First, we have to find Machina and take him out. Then we'll decide matters from there." His voice hinted that the matters he spoke of would be decided with a fight.

Ash looked like he wanted to say something else, but he nodded. Grimalkin yawned noisily and trotted toward the gate.

"Human, do not leave the bug here when we leave," he called without looking back. "It might corrupt the land around it. You can dump it in your world and it will not make any difference."

Tail waving, he trotted beneath the pillar and disappeared. Pinching the bug between thumb and forefinger, I stuffed it into my backpack. With Ash and Puck flanking me like wary guard dogs, I stepped under the pillars and everything went white.

★ ★ ★

As the brightness faded, I gazed around, first in confusion, then in horror. I stood in the middle of an open mouth, with blunt teeth lining either side and a red tongue below my feet. I squawked in terror and leaped out, tripping over the bottom lip and sprawling flat on my stomach.

Twisting around, I saw Ash and Puck step through the gaping maw of a cartoonish blue whale. Sitting atop the whale statue, smiling and pointing off into the distance, was Pinocchio, his wooden features frozen in plaster and fiberglass.

"'Scuse me, lady!" A little girl in pink overalls stepped over me to rush into the whale's mouth, followed by her two friends. Ash and Puck stepped aside, and the kids paid them no attention as they screamed and cavorted inside the whale's jaws.

"Interesting place," Puck mused as he pulled me to my feet. I didn't answer, too busy gaping at our surroundings. It seemed we had stepped into the middle of a fantasyland. A giant pink shoe sat a few yards away, and a bright blue castle lay beyond, with kids swarming over both of them. Between park benches and shady trees, a pirate ship hosted a mob of miniature swashbucklers, and a magnificent green dragon reared on its hind legs, breathing plastic fire. The flame shooting from its mouth was an actual slide. I watched a small boy clamber up the steps of the dragon's back and zip down the slide, hollering with delight, and smiled sadly.

Ethan would love this place, I thought, watching the boy dart off toward a pumpkin coach. *Maybe, when this is all over, I'll bring him here.*

"Let us go," Grimalkin said, leaping onto a giant pink mushroom. The cat's tail bristled, and his eyes darted about. "The oracle is not far, but we should hurry."

"Why so nervous, Grim?" Puck drawled, gazing around the park. "I think we should stay for a bit, soak up the atmosphere." He grinned and waved at a small girl peeking at him from behind a cottage, and she ducked out of sight.

"Too many kids here," Grimalkin said, glancing nervously over his shoulder. "Too much imagination. They can see us, you know. As we really are. And unlike the hob over there, I do not relish the attention."

I followed his gaze and saw a short faery playing on the shoe with several children. He had curly brown hair, a battered trench coat, and furry ears poking from the sides of his head. He laughed and chased the kids around him, and the parents sitting on the benches didn't seem to notice.

A boy of about three saw us and approached, his eyes on Grimalkin. "Kitty, kitty," he crooned, holding out both hands. Grimalkin flattened his ears and hissed, baring his teeth, and the boy recoiled. "Beat it, kid," he spat, and the boy burst into tears, running toward a couple on a bench. They frowned at their son's wailing about a mean kitty, and glanced up at us.

"Right, time to go," Puck said, striding away. We followed, with Grimalkin taking the lead. We left Storyland, as it was called on a sign by the exit, through a gate guarded by Humpty Dumpty and Little Bo Peep, and walked through a park filled with truly giant oak trees draped in moss and vines. I caught faces peering at us from the trunks, women with beady black eyes. Puck blew kisses at a few of them, and Ash bowed his head respectfully as we passed. Even Grimalkin nodded to the faces in the trees, making me wonder why they were so important.

After nearly an hour of walking, we reached the city streets.

I paused and gazed around, wishing we had more time to explore. I'd always wanted to go to New Orleans, particularly during Mardi Gras, though I knew Mom would never permit it. Even now, New Orleans pulsed with life and activity. Rustic shops and buildings lined the street, many stacked two or three stories atop one another, with railings and verandas overlooking the sidewalk. Strains of jazz music drifted into the street, and the spicy smell of Cajun food made my stomach growl.

"Gawk later." Grimalkin poked me in the shin with a claw. "We are not here to sightsee. We have to get to the French Quarter. One of you, find us some transportation."

"Where exactly are we going?" Ash questioned as Puck flagged down a carriage pulled by a sleepy-looking red mule. The mule snorted and pinned his ears as we piled inside, but the driver smiled and nodded. Grimalkin leaped onto the front seat.

"The Historic Voodoo Museum," he told the driver, who didn't look at all fazed by a talking cat. "And step on it."

Voodoo Museum? I wasn't sure what to expect when the carriage pulled up to a shabby-looking building in the French Quarter. A pair of simple black doors stood beneath the overhang, and a humble wooden sign proclaimed it the New Orleans Historic Voodoo Museum. Dusk had fallen, and the sign in the grimy window read Closed. Grimalkin nodded to Puck, who muttered a few words under his breath and tapped on the door. It opened with a soft creak, and we stepped inside.

The inside was musty and warm. I tripped over a bump in the carpet and stumbled into Ash, who steadied me with a sigh. Puck closed the door behind us, plunging the room into shadow. I groped for the wall, but Ash spoke a quick word, and a globe of blue fire appeared over his head, illuminating the darkness.

The pale light washed over a grisly collection of horror. A skeleton in a top hat stood along the far wall beside a mannequin with an alligator head. Skulls of humans and animals decorated the room, along with grinning masks and numerous wooden dolls. Glass cases bore jars of snakes and frogs floating in amber liquid, teeth, pestles, drums, turtle shells, and other oddities.

"This way," came Grimalkin's voice, unnaturally loud in the looming silence. We trailed him down a dark hall, where portraits of men and women stared at us from the walls. I felt eyes following me as I ducked into a room cluttered with more grisly paraphernalia and a round table in the center covered with a black tablecloth. Four chairs stood around it, as if someone were expecting us.

As we approached the table, one of the desiccated faces in the corner stirred and floated away from the wall. I gasped and leaped behind Puck as a skeletal woman with tangled white hair shambled toward us, her eyes hollow pits in a withered face.

"Hello, children," the hag whispered, her voice like sand hissing through a pipe. "Come to visit old Anna, have you? Puck is here, and Grimalkin, as well. What a pleasure." She gestured to the table, and the nails on her knobby hands glinted like steel. "Please, have a seat."

We sat down around the table as the hag came to stand before us. She smelled of dust and decay, of old newspapers that had been left in the attic for years. She smiled at me, revealing yellow, needlelike teeth.

"I smell need," she rasped, sinking into a chair. "Need, and desire. You, child." She crooked a finger at me. "You have come seeking knowledge. You search for something that must be found, yes?"

"Yes," I whispered.

The hag nodded her withered head. "Ask, then, child of two worlds. But remember…" She fixed me with a hollow glare. "All knowledge must be paid for. I will give you the answers you seek, but I desire something in return. Will you accept the price?"

Defeat crushed me. More faery bargains. More prices to pay. I was so much in debt already, I would never see the end of it. "I don't have much left to give," I told her. She laughed, a sibilant hissing sound.

"There is always something, dear child. So far, only your freedom has been claimed by another." She sniffed, as a dog might when catching a scent. "You still have your youth, your talents, your voice. Your future child. All these are of interest to me."

"You're not getting my future child," I said automatically.

"Really?" The oracle tapped her fingers together. "You will not give it up, even though it will bring you nothing but grief?"

"Enough." Ash's strong voice broke through the darkness. "We're not here to debate the what-ifs of the future. Name your price, oracle, and let the girl decide if she wants to pay it."

The oracle sniffed and settled back. "A memory," she stated.

"A what?"

"A memory," the hag said again. "One that you recall with great affection. The happiest memory of your childhood. I've precious few of my own, you see."

"Really?" I asked. "That's it? You just want one of my memories, and we have a deal?"

"Meghan—" Puck broke in "—don't take this so lightly. Your memories are a part of you. Losing one of your memories is like losing a piece of your soul."

That sounded a bit more ominous. *Still,* I thought, *one memory is a lot easier to pay than my voice, or my firstborn child. And it's not like I'll miss it, especially if I can't remember.* I thought about the happiest moments in my life: birthday parties, my first bike, Beau as a puppy. None of them seemed important enough to keep. "All right," I told the oracle, and took a seat across from her. "You're on. You get one memory of mine, one, and then you tell me what I want to know. Deal?"

The hag bared her teeth in a smile. "Yesssssssss."

She rose up over the table, framing my face with both her claws. I shivered and closed my eyes as her nails gently scratched my cheeks.

"This might feel a bit…unpleasant," the oracle hissed, and I gasped as she sank her claws into my mind, ripping it open like a paper sack. I felt her shuffling through my head, sorting through memories like photographs, examining them before tossing them aside. Discarded images fluttered around me: memories, emotions, and old wounds rose up again, fresh and painful. I wanted to pull back, to make it stop, but I couldn't move. Finally, the oracle paused, reaching toward a bright spot of happiness, and in horror I saw what she was going for.

No! I wanted to scream. *No, not that one! Leave it alone, please!*

"Yesssssss," the oracle hissed, sinking her claws into the memory. "I will take this one. Now it is mine."

There was a ripping sensation, and a bolt of pain through my head. I stiffened, my jaw locking around a shriek, and slumped in my chair, feeling like my head had been split open.

I sat up, wincing at the throbbing in my skull. The oracle watched me over the tablecloth, a pleased smile on her face. Puck was murmuring something that I couldn't make out, and Ash regarded me with a look of pity. I felt tired, drained, and empty for some reason, like there was a gaping hole deep inside me.

Hesitantly, I probed my memories, wondering which one the oracle took. After a moment, I realized how absurd that was.

"It is done," the oracle murmured. She lay her hands, palms up, on the table between us. "And now I will uphold my end of the bargain. Place your hands in mine, child, and ask."

Swallowing my revulsion, I put my palms gently over hers, shivering as those long nails curled around my fingers. The hag closed her pitted eyes. "Three questions," she rasped, her voice seeming to come from a great distance away. "That is the standard bargain. Three questions will I answer, and I am done. Choose wisely."

I took a deep breath, glanced at Puck and Ash, and whispered: "Where can I find my brother?"

Silence for a moment. The hag's eyes opened, and I jumped. They were no longer hollow, but burned with flame, as black and depthless as the void. Her mouth opened, stretching impossibly wide, as she breathed:

Within the iron mountain
a stolen child waits.
A king no longer on his throne
shall guide you past the gates.

"Oh, fabulous," Puck muttered, sitting back in his chair and rolling his eyes. "I love riddles. And they rhyme so nicely. Ask her where we can find the Iron King."

I nodded. "Where is Machina, the Iron King?"

The oracle sighed, voices erupting from her throat to whisper:

In Blight's heart
a tower sings
upon whose thrones
sit Iron Kings.

"Blight." Puck nodded, arching his eyebrows. "And singing towers. Well, this gets better and better. I'm sure glad we decided to come here. Prince, can you think of anything you want to ask our most obliging oracle?"

Ash, deep in thought with his chin in his hands, raised his head. His eyes narrowed. "Ask her how we can kill him," he demanded.

I squirmed, uncomfortable with the thought of having to kill. I only wanted to rescue Ethan. I didn't know how this turned into a holy war. "Ash—"

"Just do it."

I swallowed and turned back to the oracle. "How do we kill the Iron King?" I whispered reluctantly. The oracle's mouth opened.

The King of Iron cannot be slain
by mortal man or fey.
Seek out the Keepers of the trees.
Their hearts will show the way.

No sooner were the last words out of her mouth than the oracle collapsed on the table. For a moment she lay there, a desiccated old woman, and then she just…disintegrated. Dust flew everywhere, stinging my eyes and throat. I turned away, coughing and hacking, and when I could breathe again, the oracle was gone. Only a few floating dust motes showed she had been there at all.

"I believe," Grimalkin said, peering over the table rim, "that our audience is over."

"So where to now?" I asked as we left the Voodoo Museum, stepping into the dimly lit streets of the French Quarter. "The oracle didn't give us much to go on."

"On the contrary," Grimalkin said, looking back at me, "she gave us a great deal. One, we know your brother is with Machina. That was a given, but confirmation is always beneficial. Two, we know Machina is supposedly invincible, and his lair is in the middle of a blighted land. And, most important, three, we know there is someone who knows how to kill him."

"Yeah, but who?" I rubbed a hand over my eyes. I was so tired—tired of searching, tired of running in circles with no answers to anything. I wanted it all to end.

"Really, human, were you not listening?" Grimalkin sighed, exasperated again, but I didn't care. "It was not even much of a riddle, really. What about you two?" he asked, looking to the boys. "Did our mighty protectors glean any bits of knowledge, or was I the only one paying attention?"

Ash didn't reply, too busy staring down the street, eyes narrowed. Puck shrugged. "Seek out the Keepers of the trees," he muttered. "That's easy enough. I assume we should go back to the park."

"Very good, Goodfellow."

"I try."

"I'm so lost," I groaned, sitting down on the curb. "Why are we going back to the park? We just came from there. There are other trees in New Orleans."

"Because, princess—"

"Explain later." Ash appeared beside me. His voice was low and harsh. "We need to go. Now."

"Why?" I asked, just as the streetlamps—and every artificial light on the block—sputtered and went out.

Faery lights glowed overhead as both Ash and Puck called them into existence. Footsteps echoed in the shadows, getting closer, coming from all directions. Grimalkin muttered something and disappeared. Puck and Ash stepped back to flank me, their eyes scanning the darkness.

Beyond the ring of light, dark shapes shuffled toward us. As they came into the light, the faery fire washed over the faces of humans—normal men and women—their features blank as they lurched forward. Most of them carried weapons: iron pipes and metal baseball bats and knives. Every zombie movie I'd ever seen sprang to mind, and I pressed close to Ash, feeling the muscles coil under his skin.

"Humans," Ash muttered, his hand dropping to his sword. "What are they doing? They shouldn't be able to see us."

A dark chuckle rose from the ranks shambling toward us, and the mob abruptly stopped. They moved aside as a woman floated between them, hands on her slender hips. She wore a business suit of poison green, three-inch heels, and green lipstick that glowed with radioactive brightness. Her hair appeared to be made of wires, thin network cables of various color: greens, blacks, and reds.

"Here you are at last." Her voice buzzed, like millions of bees given speech. "I'm shocked that Ironhorse had such a problem with you, but then again, he's so *old*. Past his usefulness, I'd say. You will not have such an easy time with me."

"Who are you?" growled Ash. Puck moved beside him, and together they formed a living shield in front of me. The lady giggled, like a mosquito humming in your ear, and held out a green-nailed hand.

"I am Virus, second of King Machina's lieutenants." She blew me a kiss that made my skin crawl. "Pleased to meet you, Meghan Chase."

"What have you done to these people?" I demanded.

"Oh, don't worry about them." Virus twirled in place, smiling. "They've just caught a little bug. These little bugs, to be exact." She held up her hand, and a tiny insect swarm flew out of her sleeve to hover over her palm, like sparkling silver dust. "Cute little things, aren't they? Quite harmless, but they allow me to get inside a brain and rewrite its programming. Allow me to demonstrate." She gestured to the nearest human, and the man dropped to all fours and started to bark. Virus tittered, clapping her hands. "See? Now he thinks he's a dog."

"Brilliant," Puck said. "Can you make him crow like a rooster, too?"

Ash and I glared at him. He blinked. "What?"

I started, a memory dropping into place, and spun back on Virus. "You…you're the one who set the chimera loose on Elysium!"

"Why, yes, that was my work." Virus looked pleased, though her face fell a moment later. "Although, as an experiment, it didn't quite work out as I'd hoped. The normal fey don't react well to my bugs. That whole aversion-to-iron thing, you know. It drove the stupid beast mad, and probably would have killed it, if it hadn't been sliced to pieces. Mortals, though!" She pirouetted in the air, flinging out her arms, as if to embrace the crowd. "They make wonderful drones. So devoted to their computers and technology, they were slaves to it long before I came along."

"Let them go," I told her.

Virus regarded me with glittering green eyes. "I don't think so, dearie." She snapped her fingers, and the mob shambled forward again, arms reaching. "Bring me the girl," she ordered as the circle tightened around us. "Kill the rest."

Ash drew his sword.

"No!" I cried, grabbing his arm. "Don't hurt them. They're just ordinary humans. They don't know what they're doing."

Ash shot me a wild glare over his shoulder. "Then what do you want me to do?"

"I suggest we run," Puck offered, taking something from his pocket. He tossed it at the crowd, and it exploded into a log, pinning two startled zombie men to the ground, creating a hole in the ring surrounding us.

"Let's go!" Puck yelled, and we didn't need encouraging. We leaped over the thrashing bodies, dodging the pipes they swung at us, and tore down the street.

19

THE DRYAD OF CITY PARK

Pounding footsteps told us we were being followed. A twirling pipe flew over my shoulder, smashing the window of a shop. I yelped and almost fell, but Ash grabbed my hand and hauled me upright.

"This is ridiculous," I heard him growl, pulling me along. "Running from a mob, a human mob. I could take them out with one sweep of my hand."

"Perhaps you didn't see the copious amounts of iron they're carrying," Puck said, wincing as a knife hurled past him, skidding into the street. "Of course, if you want to make a suicide stand, I certainly won't stop you. Though, I'd be disappointed you wouldn't be there for our last duel."

"Scared, Goodfellow?"

"In your dreams, princeling."

I couldn't believe they were bantering while we were running for our lives. I wanted to tell them to knock it off, when a pipe hurled through the air, striking Puck in the shoulder. He gasped and staggered, barely catching himself in time, and I cried out in fear.

Buzzing laughter echoed behind us. I turned my head to see Virus floating above the crowd, her bugs swirling around her like a diamond blizzard. "You can run, little faery boys, but you can't hide," she called. "There are humans everywhere, and all can be my puppets. If you stop now and hand over the girl, I'll even let you choose how you want to die."

Ash snarled. Pushing me on, he spun and hurled a spray of ice shards at the woman overhead. She gasped, and a zombie leaped into the air to block the attack, the shards tearing through his chest. He collapsed, twitching, and Virus hissed like a furious wasp.

"Oh, nice going, prince," Puck called as the zombies lurched forward with angry cries. "Way to piss her off."

"You killed him!" I stared at Ash, horrified. "You just killed a person, and it wasn't even his fault!"

"There are casualties in every war," Ash replied coldly, pulling me around a corner. "He would have killed us if he could. One less soldier to worry about."

"This isn't a war!" I yelled at him. "And it's different when the humans don't even know what's happening. They're only after us because some crazy faery is screwing with their minds!"

"Either way, we'd still be dead."

"No more killing," I snarled, wishing we could stop so I could look at him straight. "Do you hear me, Ash? Find another way to stop them. You don't have to kill."

He glared at me out of the corner of his eye, then sighed with irritation. "As you wish, princess. Though you might regret it before the night is out."

We burst into a brightly lit square with a marble fountain in the center. People wandered down the sidewalks, and I relaxed a bit. Surely, Virus wouldn't attack us here, in front of all these eyewitnesses. Faeries could blend in or go invisible, but humans, especially mobs of humans, had no such power.

Ash slowed, catching my hand and drawing me beside him. "Walk," he murmured, tugging my arm to slow me down. "Don't run, it'll attract their attention."

The crowd chasing us broke apart at the edge of the street, wandering around as if they had always meant to do so. My heart pounded, but I forced myself to walk, holding on to Ash's hand as if we were out for a stroll.

Virus floated into the square, her bugs swarming out in all directions, and my nervousness increased. I spotted a policeman leaning beside his squad car and broke away from Ash, sprinting up to him.

Virus's laughter cut through the night. "I see you," she called, just as I reached the officer.

"Excuse me, sir!" I gasped as the policeman turned to me. "Could you help me? There's a gang chasing—"

I stumbled back in horror. The officer regarded me blankly, his jaw hanging slack, his eyes empty of reason. He lunged and grabbed my arm, and I yelped, kicking him in the shin. It didn't faze him, and he grabbed my other wrist.

The pedestrians in the square lurched toward us with renewed vigor. I snarled a curse and lashed out at the policeman, driving my knee into his groin. He winced and struck me across the face, making my head spin. The mob closed in, clawing at my hair and clothes.

And Ash was there, smashing his hilt into the policeman's jaw, knocking him back. Puck grabbed me and leaped over the police car, dragging me over the hood. We broke free of the mob and ran, Virus's laughter following us into the street.

"There!" Grimalkin appeared beside us, his tail fluffed out and his eyes wild. "Dead ahead! A carriage. Use it, quickly."

I looked across the street and saw an unattended horse and

open-top buggy, waiting on the curb to pick up passengers. It wasn't a getaway car, but it was better than nothing. We crossed the street and ran toward the carriage.

A gunshot rang out behind us.

Puck jerked weirdly and fell, collapsing to the pavement with a howl of agony. I screamed, and Ash immediately hauled him upright, forcing him to move. They staggered across the street, Ash dragging Puck with him, as another shot shattered the night. The horse whinnied and half reared at the noise, rolling its eyes. I grabbed its bridle before the beast fled in terror. Behind me, walking toward us with that zombielike shuffle, I saw the police officer, one arm extended, pointing his gun at us.

Ash shouldered Puck into the carriage and jumped into the driver's seat, Grimalkin bounding up beside him. I scrambled inside and crouched beside Puck, sprawled on the floor of the carriage, gasping. Horrified, I watched dark blood blossom around his ribs, seeping over the floorboards.

"Hold on!" Ash yelled, and brought the reins down on the horse's flanks with a loud "Hiya!" The horse leaped forward with a squeal. We galloped through a red light, barely dodging a honking taxi. Cars blared, people shouted and cursed, and the sounds of pursuit faded behind us.

"Ash!" I cried a few minutes later. "Puck's not moving!"

Preoccupied with driving the carriage, Ash barely looked back, but Grimalkin leaped to the floor and trotted up to the body. Puck's face was the color of eggshells, his skin cool and clammy. I'd tried to stanch the bleeding using a sleeve of his hoodie, but there was so much blood. My best friend was dying, and I couldn't do anything to help.

"He needs a doctor," I called up to Ash. "We need to find a hospital—"

"No," Grimalkin interrupted. "Think, human! No faery

would survive a hospital. With all those sharp metal instruments, he would be dead before the night was out."

"Then what can we do?" I cried, on the verge of hysteria.

Grimalkin jumped up beside Ash again. "The park," he said calmly. "We take him to the park. The dryads should be able to help him."

"*Should?* What if they can't?"

"Then, human, I would start praying for a miracle."

Ash didn't stop at the edge of the park, but instead drove the carriage over the curb and into the grass beneath the trees. Worried for Puck, I didn't notice we'd stopped until the prince knelt beside me, swung Puck onto a shoulder, and dropped down. Numbly, I followed.

We'd stopped under the boughs of two enormous oaks, their gnarled branches completely shutting out the night sky. Ash carried Puck beneath the twisted giants and eased him down to the grass.

And we waited.

Two figures stepped out of the tree trunks, materializing into view. They were both slender women, with moss-green hair and skin like polished mahogany. Beetle-black eyes peered out as the dryads stepped forward, the smell of fresh earth and bark thick in the air. Grimalkin and Ash nodded respectfully, but I was too worried to catch the movement in time.

"We know why you have come," one dryad said, her voice the sigh of wind through the leaves. "The breeze carries whispers to us, news of faraway places. We know of your plight with the Iron King. We have been waiting for you, child of two worlds."

"Please," I asked, stepping forward, "can you help Puck? He was shot on the way here. I'll bargain with you, give you anything you want, if you can save him."

Out of the corner of my eye, I saw Ash shoot me a dark glare, but I ignored it.

"We will not bargain with you, child," the second dryad murmured, and I felt a sinking despair. "It is not our way. We are not like the sidhe or the cait sith, seeking endless ways to empower themselves. We simply are."

"As a favor, then," I pleaded, refusing to give up. "Please, he'll die if you don't help him."

"Death is a part of life." The dryad regarded me with pitiless black eyes. "All things fade eventually, even one as long-lived as Puck. People will forget his stories, forget he ever was, and he will cease to be. It is the way of things."

I fought the urge to scream. The dryads wouldn't help; they'd just doomed Puck to die. Clenching my fists, I glared at the tree women, wanting to shake them, throttle them until they agreed to help. I felt a rush of…something…and the trees above me groaned and shook, showering us with leaves. Ash and Grimalkin took a step back, and the dryads exchanged glances.

"She is strong," one whispered.

"Her power sleeps," the other replied. "The trees hear her, the earth answers her call."

"Perhaps it will be enough."

They nodded again, and one of them lifted Puck around the waist, dragging him toward her tree. They both melted into the bark and disappeared. I jerked in alarm.

"What are you doing?"

"Do not worry," the remaining dryad said, turning back to me. "We cannot heal him, but we can halt the damage. Puck will sleep until he is well enough to rejoin you. Whether that takes a night or several years will be entirely up to him."

She tilted her head at me, shedding moss. "You and your companions may stay here tonight. It is safe. Within these boundaries, the iron fey will not venture. Our power over tree and land keeps them out. Rest, and we will call for you when it is time."

With that, she melted back into the tree, leaving us alone, with one less companion than when we started out.

I wanted to sleep. I wanted to lie down and black out, and wake up to a world where best friends were never shot and little brothers never kidnapped. I wanted everything to be over and my life to go back to normal.

But, as exhausted as I was, I couldn't sleep. I wandered the park in a daze, numb to everything. Ash was off speaking with the resident park fey, and Grimalkin had disappeared, so I was alone. In the scattered moonlight, faeries danced and sang and laughed, calling out to me from a distance. Satyrs whistled tunes on their pipes, piskies buzzed through the air on gossamer wings, and willowy dryads danced through the trees, their slender bodies waving like grass in the wind. I ignored them all.

At the edge of a pond, under the drooping limbs of another giant oak, I sank down, pulled my knees to my chest, and sobbed.

Mermaids broke the surface of the pond to stare at me, and a ring of piskies gathered round, tiny lights hovering in confusion. I barely saw them. The constant worry for Ethan, the fear of losing Puck, and the ill-fated promise to Ash were too much for me. I cried until I was gasping for breath, hiccuping so hard my lungs ached.

But, of course, the fey couldn't let me be miserable in peace. As my tears slowed, I became aware I wasn't alone. A herd of satyrs surrounded me, their eyes bright in the gloom.

"Pretty flower," one of them said, stepping forward. He had a tan face, a goatee, and horns curling through his thick black hair. His voice was low and soft, and had a faint Creole accent. "Why so sad, lovely one? Come with me, and we will make you laugh again."

I shivered and rose shakily to my feet. "No, thank y— No. I'm fine. I just want to be alone for a while."

"Alone is a terrible thing to be," the satyr said, moving closer. He smiled, charming and attractive. Glamour shimmered around him, and I saw his mortal guise for a split second: a handsome college boy, out walking with his friends. "Why don't we get some coffee, and you can tell me all about it?"

He sounded so sincere, I almost believed him. Then I caught the glint of raw lust in his eyes, in the eyes of his friends, and my stomach contracted in fear.

"I really have to go," I said, backing away. They followed me, their gazes hungry and intense. I smelled something strong in the air and realized it was musk. "Please, please leave me alone."

"You'll thank us afterward," the satyr promised, and lunged.

I ran.

The herd pursued me, whooping and shouting promises: that I would enjoy it, that I needed to loosen up a bit. They were much faster, and the lead goat grabbed me from behind, arms around my waist. I screamed as he lifted me off my feet, kicking and flailing. The other satyrs closed in, grabbing and pawing, tearing at my clothes.

A rush of power, the same I'd felt earlier, and suddenly the oak above us moved. With a deafening creak, a gnarled branch as thick as my waist swung down and struck the lead satyr in the head. He dropped me and staggered back, and the limb swung back to hit him again in the stomach, knocking him sprawling. The other satyrs backed away.

Goat-boy got his feet under him and stood, glaring at me.

"I see you like it a little rough," he wheezed, brushing himself off. Shaking his head, he ran a tongue over his lips and stepped forward. "That's okay, we can do rough."

"So can I." A dark shape glided out of the trees, a portion of shadow come to life. The satyrs blinked and hastily stepped back as Ash strode into the middle of the herd. Looming up behind me, he slid an arm around my shoulders and pulled me to his chest. My heart sped up, and my stomach did a backflip. "This one," Ash growled, "is off-limits."

"Prince Ash?" gasped the lead satyr, as the rest of the herd bowed their heads. He paled and held up his hands. "Sorry, Your Highness, I didn't know she was yours. My apologies. No harm done, okay?"

"No one touches her," Ash said, his voice coated with frost. "Touch her, and I'll freeze your testicles and put them in a jar. Understand?"

The satyrs cringed. Stammering apologies to both Ash and me, they bowed and scurried away. Ash shot a glare at two piskies hovering nearby to watch, and they sped into the trees with high-pitched giggles. Silence fell, and we were alone.

"Are you all right?" Ash asked, releasing me. "Did they hurt you?"

I was shaking. That exhilarating rush of power was gone; now I felt completely drained. "No," I whispered, moving away. "I'm all right." I might've cried, but I had no more tears left in me. My knees trembled and I stumbled, putting a hand against a tree to steady myself.

Ash moved closer. Catching my wrist, he gently pulled me to him and wrapped his arms around me, holding me tight. I was startled, but only for a moment. Sniffling, I closed my eyes and buried my face in his chest, letting all the fear and anger seep away under his touch. I heard his rapid heartbeat, and felt the chill prickling my skin through his shirt. Strangely, it wasn't uncomfortable at all.

We stood like that for a long moment. Ash didn't speak, didn't ask questions, didn't do anything but hold me. I sighed and relaxed into him, and for a little while, everything was okay. Ethan and Puck still lingered in the back of my mind, but for now, this was good. This was enough.

Then I made a stupid mistake and looked up at him.

His eyes met mine, and for a moment, his face was open and vulnerable in the moonlight. I caught a hint of wonder there as we stared at each other. Slowly, he leaned forward. I caught my breath, a tiny gasp escaping.

He stiffened, and his expression shuttered closed, eyes going hard and frosty.

Pushing me away, he stepped back, and my heart sank. Ash looked into the trees, the shadows, the pond, anywhere but at me. Wanting to reclaim that lost moment, I took a step toward him, but he slid away.

"This is getting old," he said in a voice that matched his eyes. He crossed his arms and moved back, putting even more distance between us. "I'm not here to play nursemaid, princess. Perhaps you shouldn't go wandering about on your own. I wouldn't want you damaged before you ever reached the Unseelie Court."

My cheeks burned, and I clenched my fists. The memory of being humiliated in the cafeteria, so long ago, rose to my mind to taunt me. "That's all I am to you, isn't it?" I challenged. "Your chance to gain favor from your queen. That's all you care about."

"Yes," he replied calmly, infuriating me even more. "I've never pretended anything else. You knew my motivations from the beginning."

Angry tears stung my eyes. I thought I was all cried out, but I was wrong. "Bastard," I hissed. "Puck was right about you."

He smiled coldly. "Maybe you should ask Puck why I've vowed to kill him someday," he said, eyes glinting. "See if he has the courage to tell you that bit of history between us." He smirked and crossed his arms. "That is, if he ever wakes up."

I opened my mouth to reply, but with a rustle of leaves, two dryads melted out of a nearby trunk. Ash faded into the darkness as they approached, leaving me with my angry words unsaid. I fisted my hands, wanting to smack the arrogance right off his perfect face. I turned and kicked a log instead.

The dryads bowed to me, unconcerned with my mild temper tantrum.

"Meghan Chase, the Elder will see you now."

I followed them to the base of a single oak tree, its branches so draped in moss, it looked like it was hung with moldy curtains. Ash and Grimalkin were already there, though Ash didn't even look my way as I approached. I glared at him, but he continued to ignore me. With the cat on one side and the Winter prince flanking the other, I stepped beneath the boughs of the huge oak and waited.

The bark rippled, and an ancient woman stepped out of the tree. Her skin flaked, like wrinkled bark, and her long hair was the brownish-green of old moss. She was stooped and bent, covered in a robe of lichens that shivered with thousands of insects and spiders. Her face resembled a walnut, lined and wrinkled, and when she moved, her joints creaked like branches in the wind. But her beady eyes were sharp and clear as she looked me over and beckoned with one gnarled, twiggy hand.

"Come closer, child," she whispered, her voice rustling like dry leaves. I swallowed and moved forward, until I could see the insects boring into her skin, smell the earthy scent of her. "Yes, you are the daughter of Oberon, the one whom the wind whispers about. I know why you are here. You seek the one called the Iron King, yes? You wish to find the entrance into his realm."

"Yes," I murmured. "I'm looking for my brother. Machina kidnapped him, and I'm going to get him back."

"As you are, you will not be able to save him," the Elder told me, and my stomach dropped to my toes. "The Iron King waits for you in his lair of steel. He knows you are coming, and you will not be able to stop him. No weapon forged by mortal or fey can harm the Iron King. He fears nothing."

Ash stepped forward, bowing his head respectfully. "Elder," he murmured, "we were told you might know the secret to slaying the Iron King."

The ancient dryad regarded him solemnly. "Yes, young prince," she whispered. "You heard true. There is a way to kill Machina and end his reign. You need a special weapon, one that cannot be forged with tools, something as natural as a flower growing in the sunlight."

Ash leaned forward eagerly. "Where can we find this weapon?"

The Elder Dryad sighed, and seemed to shrink in on herself. "Here," she murmured, looking back at the great oak, her voice tinged with sadness. "The weapon you require is Witchwood, from the heart of the most ancient of trees, as deadly to Machina as iron is to normal fey. A living wood containing the spirit of nature and the power of the natural earth—a bane to the faeries of progress and technology. Without it, you cannot hope to defeat him and save the human child."

Ash fell silent, his face grim. Bewildered, I looked to him, then back at the Elder Dryad. "You'll give it to us, won't you?" I asked. "If it's the only way to save Ethan—"

"Human," Grimalkin murmured from the grass, "you do not know what you are asking. Witchwood is the heart of the Elder's tree. Without it, the oak will die, and so will the dryad connected to it."

Dismayed, I looked at the Elder Dryad, whose lips curled in a faint smile. "It's true," she whispered. "Without its heart, the tree will slowly wither and die. And yet, I knew what you came for, Meghan Chase. I planned to offer it from the beginning."

"No," I said automatically. "I don't want it. Not like this. There has to be another way."

"There is no other way, child." The Elder shook her head at me. "And if you do not defeat the Iron King, we will perish all the same. His influence grows. The stronger he becomes, the more the Nevernever fades. Eventually we will all wither and die in a wasteland of logic and science."

"But I can't kill him," I protested. "I'm not a warrior. I just want Ethan back, that's all."

"You won't have to worry about that." The dryad nodded to Ash, standing silently nearby. "The Winter prince can fight for you, I imagine. He smells of blood and sorrow. I will happily grant the Witchwood to him."

"Please." I looked at her, pleading, wanting her to understand. Puck had already possibly given his life for my quest; I didn't want another's death on my hands. "I don't want you to do this. It's too much. You shouldn't have to die for me."

"I give my life for all fey," the dryad replied solemnly. "You will simply be my instrument of salvation. Besides, death comes for us all, in the end. I have lived a long life, longer than most. I have no regrets."

She smiled at me, an old, grandmotherly smile, and faded back into her oak. Ash, Grim, and the other dryads stood silently, their expressions somber and grave. A moment later, the Elder reemerged, clutching something in her withered hands—a long, straight stick, so pale it was almost white, with reddish veins running down its length. When she stepped up and offered it to me, seconds passed before I could take it. It was warm and smooth in my hands, pulsing with a life of its own, and I almost dropped it in the grass.

The Elder placed a withered, knobby hand on my arm. "One more thing, child," she added as I struggled with holding the living wood. "You are powerful, much more so than you realize. Oberon's blood flows through your veins, and the Nevernever itself responds to your whims. Your talent still sleeps within you, but it is beginning to stir. How you use it will shape the future of the courts, the fey, your own destiny, everything.

"Now," she continued, sounding weaker than before, "go and rescue your brother. The trod to Machina's realm is an abandoned factory down by the wharfs. A guide will lead you there tomorrow. Kill the Iron King and bring peace to both our worlds."

"What if I can't?" I whispered. "What if the Iron King truly is invincible?"

"Then we will all die," said the Elder Dryad, and faded back into her oak. The other dryads left, leaving me alone with a cat, a prince, and a stick. I sighed and looked down at the wood in my hands.

"No pressure or anything," I muttered.

20

IRON DRAGONS AND PACKRATS

We left at dawn. Time enough for me to catch maybe two hours of sleep on the lumpy ground, and say my last goodbyes to Puck. He was still sleeping, deep within the tree, when I woke up in the still hours before sunrise. The dryad attached to the oak told me he still lived, but she didn't have any idea when he would wake.

I stood beside the oak for several minutes, my hand against the bark, trying to feel his heartbeat through the wood. I missed him. Ash and Grimalkin might be allies, but they were not friends. They wanted to use me for their own ends. Only Puck truly cared, and now he was gone.

"Princess." Ash appeared behind me, his voice surprisingly gentle. "We should go. We can't afford to wait for him, not if it could be months before he wakes up. We don't have that time."

"I know." I pressed my palm into the bark, feeling the rough edges scrape my skin. *Wake up quickly,* I told him, wondering if he dreamed, if he could feel my touch through the tree. *Wake up quickly, and find me. I'll be waiting.*

I turned to Ash, who was dressed for battle, with his sword

at his waist and a bow slung across his back. Looking at him made my skin tingle.

"Do you have it?" I asked, to hide the burning in my cheeks.

He nodded, and held up a gleaming white arrow with red veins curling around it. He'd asked for the Witchwood the previous night, claiming he could turn it into a suitable weapon, and I gave it to him without hesitation. Now I stared at the dart, feeling my apprehension grow. It seemed like such a small, fragile thing to take down the supposedly invincible King of the Iron Fey.

"Can I hold it?" I asked, and Ash immediately placed the arrow in my palm, his fingers lingering on mine. The wood throbbed in my hand, a rhythmic *pulse-pulse,* like a heartbeat; I shuddered and held it out, waiting for him to take it back.

"Hold on to it for me," Ash said softly, his gaze never leaving mine. "This is your quest. You decide when I'm supposed to use it."

I blushed and opened my backpack, shoving the dart inside. The shaft of the arrow stuck out of the pack, and I closed the zippers around it, securing it in place before swinging the thing over my shoulders. The bag was heavier now; last night, I'd raided a park fountain and scraped up enough change to buy food and bottled water for the rest of the journey. The clerk at the nearby gas station seemed a bit annoyed at having to count handfuls of dimes and quarters at one in the morning, but I didn't want to start the final leg of our journey empty-handed. I hoped Ash and Grim liked beef jerky, trail mix, and Skittles.

"You'll only get one shot," I murmured. Ash smiled without humor.

"Then I'll have to make it count."

He sounded so confident. I wondered if he was ever afraid, or had second thoughts about what he had to do. Holding a grudge seemed foolish now, since he was about to follow me into mortal danger. "Look, I'm sorry about last night," I offered. "I didn't mean to be a psycho. I was just worried about Ethan. And with Puck getting shot and everything—"

"Don't worry about it, Meghan."

I blinked, my stomach fluttering. That was the first time he'd called me by name. "Ash, I—"

"I have been thinking," Grimalkin announced, leaping onto a rock. I glared and bit down a sigh, cursing his timing. The cat plowed on without notice. "Perhaps we should rethink our strategy," he said, looking at each of us. "It occurs to me that charging headlong into Machina's realm is a singularly bad idea."

"What do you mean?"

"Well." The cat sat down and licked his back toes. "Given that he keeps sending his officers after us, I would guess that he probably knows we are coming. Why did he kidnap your brother in the first place? He must have known you would come after him."

"Overconfident?" I guessed. Grimalkin shook his head.

"No. Something is missing. Or maybe we are just not seeing it. The Iron King would have no use for a child. Unless..." The cat looked up at us, narrowing his eyes. "I am leaving."

"What? Why?"

"I have a theory." Grimalkin stood, waving his tail. "I think I might know another way into Machina's realm. You are welcome to join me."

"A theory?" Ash crossed his arms. "We can't break plan on a hunch, Cait Sith."

"Even if the way you are going leads straight into a trap?"

I shook my head. "We have to risk it. We're so close, Grim. We can't turn back now." I knelt to face Grimalkin eye to eye. "Come with us. We need you. You've always pointed us in the right direction."

"I am not a fighter, human." Grimalkin shook his head and blinked. "You have the prince for that. I accompanied you to show you the way to your brother, and for my own amusement. But I know my limitations." He looked at Ash and pinned his ears. "I would be no help to you in there. Not the way you are going. So, it is time we settled our debts and parted ways."

That's right. I still owed the cat a favor. Uneasiness stirred. I hoped the cat wouldn't ask for my voice, or my future kid. I still didn't know what went on in that devious little head of his. "Right." I sighed, trying to keep my voice from shaking. Ash moved to stand behind me, a quiet, confident presence. "A deal's a deal. What do you want, Grim?"

Grimalkin's gaze bore into me. He sat up straight, flicking his tail. "My price is this," he stated. "I want to be able to call on you, once, at a time of my choosing, no questions asked. That is my debt."

Relief washed through me. That didn't sound so bad. Ash, however, made a thoughtful noise and crossed his arms.

"A summoning?" The prince sounded puzzled. "Odd for you, Cait Sith. What do you hope to accomplish with her?"

Grimalkin ignored him. "When I call," he continued, staring at me, "you must come straightaway without pause. And you must help me in any way you are able. Those are the terms of our contract. You are bound to me until they are fulfilled."

"All right." I nodded. "I can live with that. But if you call, how will I know where to find you?"

Grimalkin sneezed a laugh. "Do not worry about that, human. You will know. But for now, I must leave you." He stood, nodding once to me, then to Ash. "Until we meet again."

Then he slipped into the grass, his bottlebrush tail held straight up, and disappeared.

I smiled sadly. "And then there were two."

Ash moved closer and touched my arm, a brief, featherlight caress. I glanced at him and he offered that tiny, endearing smile, one of apology and encouragement, and a silent promise that he would not leave me. I gave him a shaky grin and resisted the urge to lean into him, wanting to feel his arms around me once more.

A piskie spiraled down from the branches, hovering a few inches from my face. Blue-skinned, with dandelion hair and gossamer wings, she stuck out her tongue at me and zipped to Ash, alighting on his shoulder. Ash cocked his head as the piskie whispered something in his ear. One corner of his mouth turned up; he glanced at me and shook his head. The piskie giggled and spun into the air again. I scowled, wondering what they were saying about me, then decided I didn't care.

"This is Seedlit," Ash said as the piskie spiraled through the air like a drunken hummingbird. "She'll lead us to the wharfs, and then to the factory. Beyond that, we're on our own."

I nodded, my heart hammering in my ears. This was it, the last leg of the journey. At the end was Machina and Ethan, or death. I smirked with rash bravado and raised my chin. "All right, Tinker Bell," I told the piskie, who gave an indignant buzz. "Lead on."

We followed the bobbing light toward the banks of the river, where the cold, slow waters of the Mississippi churned under a slate-gray sky. We didn't speak much. Ash walked beside me, our shoulders almost touching. After several silent minutes, I brushed his hand. He curled his fingers around mine, and we walked like that until we reached the factory.

A corrugated-steel building squatted behind a chain-link fence, a dark smudge against the sky. Seedlit jabbered something to Ash, who nodded gravely, before she zipped away out of sight. She had brought us as far as she could go; now we were on our own.

As we approached the gate, Ash hung back a little, a pained look on his face.

"What's the matter?"

He grimaced. "Nothing. Just..." He nodded to the fence. "Too much iron. I can feel it from here."

"Does it hurt?"

"No." He shook his head. "I'd have to touch it for that. But it's draining." He looked uncomfortable admitting it. "It makes it difficult to use glamour."

I shook the gate experimentally. It wouldn't budge. Heavy chains were wrapped around the entrance, padlocked together, and barbed wire coiled along the top of the fence.

"Give me your sword," I told Ash. He blinked at me.

"What?"

"Give me your sword," I repeated. "We have to get in, and you don't like touching iron, right? Let me have it, and I'll take care of it."

He looked dubious but pulled his blade and offered it to me, hilt up. I took the weapon gingerly. The hilt was painfully cold, the blade throwing off a frozen blue aura. I raised it over my head and brought it slashing down on the chain binding the gate. The links snapped like they were made of glass, shattering with a metallic ringing sound. Pleased, I grabbed the chain to yank it free, but the metal burned like fire and I dropped it with a cry.

Ash was beside me, reclaiming his sword as I shook my singed fingers, dancing about in pain. After sheathing the weapon, he snatched my flailing hand and turned it palm up. A line of red slashed across my fingers, numb and tingly to the touch.

"I thought I was immune to iron." I sniffed. Ash sighed.

"You are," he murmured, moving me away from the fence and its glamour-draining qualities. His expression teetered between amusement and exasperation. "However, grabbing superchilled metal is still very unpleasant for Summer fey, no matter who you are."

"Oh."

He shook his head, examining the wound again. "It's not frostbitten," he muttered. "It'll blister, but you should be fine. You might only lose a couple fingers."

I glanced at him sharply, but he was smirking. For a moment, I was speechless. Good God, the Ice Prince was making jokes now; the world *must* be ending. "That's not funny," I hissed, swatting at him with my other hand. He dodged easily, the amusement still on his face.

"You're a lot like her," he mused, so softly I barely heard him. And before I could say anything, he turned, drew his sword, and swept the chains off the gate. It swung open with a creak, and Ash scanned the compound warily.

"Stay close to me," he muttered, and we eased our way inside.

Large mounds of scrap metal lay piled about the yard as we walked through, the sharp edges glinting in the faint rays of dawn. Ash winced each time we passed one, keeping a wary eye on it, as if it would leap up and attack him. Strange creatures scampered about the metal drifts, tiny men with rat-like features and naked tails. When they nibbled on a piece of metal, it rusted away under their teeth. They didn't bother us, though Ash shuddered whenever he saw one, and his hand never left his sword.

The iron doors had more chains around them, but the ice blade cut through them easily. Stepping inside, I gazed around slowly, my eyes adjusting to the dim light. It looked like an ordinary warehouse, empty and dark, though I heard skittering noises in the corners. More mountains of scrap metal littered the gloom, some larger than I was tall.

Where's the trod? I wondered, stepping farther inside. Metal grates covered the floor, pressing through my sneakers. Ash hesitated, hanging back in the doorway.

Steam drifted over the ground, coiling around my legs. Against the far wall, I saw that one of the grates had been pried up, leaving a square, gaping hole. Smoke boiled out of the opening. *There!*

I started toward the hole. From the doorway, Ash called for me to stop. Before my nerves could jangle a warning, a pile of scrap metal shifted. Then, with a screech that set my teeth on edge, the mound uncurled, sending sparks into the air as it dragged along the floor. From the jumbled mess, a long neck rose up, made of iron, wire, and broken glass. A reptilian head glared down at me, shards of metal bristling from its skull. Then the entire mound lurched up, shifting into a huge lizard of iron and steel, with curved metal talons and a jagged, spiked tail.

The dragon roared, a deafening metallic screech that made my eyes want to pop out of my skull. It lunged, and I scrambled behind another mound, praying this one wasn't a dragon, too. The dragon hissed and followed, steam erupting from its gaping jaws, steel talons clanking over the floor.

A volley of ice darts flew through the air, striking the dragon in the head and shattering harmlessly off its skull. It screamed and reared up, glaring at Ash, who stood at the far end of the room with his sword drawn. Lashing its tail, the dragon charged, sparks flying from its claws as it bore down on Ash. My heart jumped to my throat.

Ash closed his eyes for a moment, then knelt and drove his sword point down into the floor. There was a flash of blue light, and ice spread rapidly from the tip, covering the ground and coating everything in crystal. My breath hung in the air, and icicles formed on the overhead beams. I shivered violently in the sudden chill as the scrap metal frosted over, radiating absolute cold.

Ash leaped aside as the dragon reached him, moving as easily on ice as normal ground. Unable to stop itself, the dragon slammed into the wall, bits of metal flying everywhere. It hissed and struggled to rise, sliding on the slick floor, tail thrashing. Ash jumped forward and blew out a long whistle, sending an icy whirlwind spinning through the air. The dragon shrieked as the blizzard whipped around it, coating it with frost and snow. A hoary rime caked its metal body, its struggles growing weaker as ice weighed it down.

Ash stopped, panting heavily. He staggered away from the frozen dragon and leaned back against a post, closing his eyes. I half ran, half stumbled over, slipping on the ice, until I reached him.

"Are you all right?"

"Never again," he muttered, almost to himself. His eyes were still closed, and I wasn't sure he knew I was there. "I will *not* watch that happen again. I won't...lose another...like that."

"Ash?" I whispered, touching his arm.

His eyes opened and his gaze dropped to mine. "Meghan," he murmured, seeming a bit confused that I was still there. He blinked and shook his head. "Why didn't you run? I tried to buy you some time. You should've gone ahead."

"Are you crazy? I couldn't leave you to that thing. Now, come on." I took his hand, tugging him off the post while glancing nervously at the frozen dragon. "Let's get out of here. I think that thing just blinked at us."

His fingers tightened on mine and pulled me forward. Startled and overbalanced, I looked up at him, and then he was kissing me.

I froze in shock, but only for a moment. Wrapping my arms

around his neck, I rose on my tiptoes to meet him, kissing him back with a hunger that surprised us both. He crushed me close, and I ran my hands through his silky hair, sliding it through my fingers. His lips were cool on mine, and my mouth tingled. And for a moment, there was no Ethan, no Puck, no Iron King. Only this.

He pulled back, slightly out of breath. My blood raced, and I leaned my head on his shoulder, feeling the steely muscles through his back. I felt him tremble.

"This isn't good," he murmured, his voice curiously shaken. But he still didn't release me. I closed my eyes and listened to his rapid heartbeat.

"I know," I whispered back.

"The Courts would kill us if they found out."

"Yeah."

"Mab would accuse me of treason. Oberon would believe I'm turning you against him. They'd both see grounds for banishment, or execution."

"I'm sorry."

He sighed, burying his face in my hair. His breath was cool on my neck, and I shivered. Neither of us said anything for what seemed a long time.

"We'll think of something," I ventured.

He nodded wordlessly and pulled away, but stumbled as he took a step back. I caught his arm again.

"Are you all right?"

"I'll be fine." He released my elbow. "Too much iron. The spell took a lot out of me."

"Ash—"

A piercing crack interrupted us. The dragon freed a fore-paw and smashed it to the floor. More cracks appeared as it struggled to rise, shedding ice. Ash grabbed my hand and ran.

With an enraged shriek, the dragon shattered its ice prison, sending shards flying. We pelted across the room, hearing the dragon give chase, its claws digging into the icy ground. The hole with its missing grate loomed ahead, and we flung ourselves toward it, leaping through the steam and plummeting into the unknown. The dragon's frustrated bellow rang overhead, as clouds of steam enveloped us, and everything went white.

I didn't remember landing, though I was aware of Ash holding my hand as the steam cleared around us. Eyes widening, we both stared around in horror.

A twisted landscape stretched out before us, barren and dark, the sky a sickly yellow-gray. Mountains of rubble dominated the land: ancient computers, rusty cars, televisions, dial phones, radios, all piled into huge mounds that loomed over everything. Some of the piles were alight, burning with a thick, choking smog. A hot wind howled through the wasteland, stirring dust into glittering eddies, spinning the wheel of an ancient bicycle lying on a trash heap. Scraps of aluminum, old cans, and foam cups rolled over the ground, and a sharp, coppery smell hung in the air, clogging the back of my throat. The trees here were sickly things, bent and withered. A few bore lightbulbs and batteries that hung like glittering fruit.

"This is the Nevernever," Ash muttered. His voice was grim. "Somewhere in the Deep Tangle, if I had to guess. No wonder the wyldwood is dying."

"*This* is the Nevernever?" I asked, gazing around in shock. I remembered the frigid, pristine beauty of Tir Na Nog, the blinding colors of the Summer Court. "No way. How could it get like this?"

"Machina," Ash replied. "The territories take on the aspects of their rulers. I'm guessing his realm is very small right now, but if it expands, it'll swallow the wyldwood and eventually destroy the Nevernever."

I thought I hated Faeryland, and everything in it, but that was before Ash. This was his home. If the Nevernever died, he would die, too. So would Puck and Grim, and everyone else I met on my strange journey here. "We have to stop it," I exclaimed, gazing around the dead landscape. Smog tickled my throat, making me want to cough. "We can't let this spread."

Ash smiled, cold and frightening. "That's why we're here."

Slowly, we made our way through the mountains of junk, keeping a wary eye on any that might come to life and attack. Out of the corner of my eye I caught movement and spun toward it, fearful of another dragon disguised as harmless debris. It wasn't a dragon this time, but several small, hunchbacked creatures waddling to and fro between the mounds. They looked like withered gnomes, bent over by the huge amount of stuff piled on their backs, like giant hermit crabs. When they found an item they liked—a broken toy, the spokes of a bicycle—they attached it to the collection on their backs and shuffled to the next mound. Some of their humps were large and quite impressive, in a sad kind of way.

A few of the creatures saw us and came waddling up, beady eyes bright and curious. Ash went for his sword, but I laid a hand on his arm. I sensed these beings weren't dangerous, and perhaps they could point us in the right direction.

"Hello," I greeted softly as they surrounded us, snuffling like eager dogs. "We don't want any trouble. We're just a little lost."

They cocked their heads but didn't say anything. A few pressed closer, and several long fingers reached out to poke my backpack, tugging on the bright material. Not maliciously, but curious, like seagulls pecking at a button. Two of them crowded Ash, pawing at his sword sheath. He shifted uneasily and stepped away.

"I need to find King Machina," I said. "Can you show us where he lives?"

But the creatures weren't paying attention, too busy pawing at my backpack, jabbering among themselves. One gave
it an experimental yank that nearly toppled me off my feet.

In a flash of blue light, Ash drew his sword. The creatures
scuttled back, their eyes wide and fixated to the glowing blade.
A few twitched their fingers, like they wanted to touch it, but
knew better than to approach.

"Come on," Ash muttered, pointing his sword at any gnome
that edged forward. "They're not going to help us. Let's get
out of here."

"Wait." I grabbed his sleeve as he turned. "I've got an idea."

Taking off my pack, I unzipped the side pocket, reached
inside, and pulled out the broken phone from so long ago.
Stepping forward, I raised it high, seeing the gnomes follow
it with wide, unbroken stares.

"A deal," I called into the silence. They watched me without blinking. "Do you see this?" I said, waving the phone back
and forth. They followed it, like dogs eyeing a cookie. "I'll
give it to you, but in return, you take me to the Iron King."

The gnomes turned and jabbered to one another, occasionally peeking back to make sure I was still there. Finally,
one of them stepped forward. A whole tricycle teetered at the
top of his hump. He fixed me with an unblinking stare, and
beckoned me to follow.

We trailed the odd little creatures—whom I secretly dubbed
the pack rats—through the wasteland of junk, drawing curious stares from the other residents living there. I saw more of
the ratlike men whose teeth rusted metal, a few scrawny dogs
wandering about, and swarms of iron bugs crawling over everything. Once, in the distance, I caught a terrifying glimpse
of another dragon, unfurling from a mound of trash. Thankfully, it only shifted into a more comfortable sleeping position
and returned to its perfect disguise as a pile of debris.

At last, the mountains of garbage fell away, and the lead pack rat pointed a long finger down a barren plain. Across a cracked, gray plateau, spiderwebbed with lava and millions of blinking lights, a railroad stretched away into the distance. Hulking machines, like enormous iron beetles, sat beside it, snorting steam. And silhouetted against the sky, a jagged black tower stabbed up from the earth, wreathed in smog and billowing smoke.

Machina's fortress.

Ash drew in a quiet breath. I stared at the imposing tower, my stomach contracting with fear, until a tug on my backpack snapped me out of my daze. The pack rat stood there, an expectant look on his face, fingers twitching.

"Oh, yeah." Fishing out the phone, I handed it to him solemnly. "A deal's a deal. Hope you enjoy it."

The pack rat chittered with joy. Clutching the device to his chest, he scuttled off like an enormous crab, vanishing back into the wasteland of junk. I heard excited jabbering, and imagined him showing off his trophy for all to see. Then the voices faded and we were alone.

Ash turned to me, and I was struck with how awful he looked. His skin was ashen; there were shadows under his eyes, and his hair was damp with sweat.

"Will you be all right?" I whispered. One corner of his mouth curled up.

"We'll see, won't we?"

I reached for his hand, wrapped my fingers around his, and squeezed. He put my hand to his face and closed his eyes, as if drawing strength from my touch. Together, we descended into the heart of Machina's realm.

21

KNIGHTS OF THE IRON CROWN

"Don't look now," Ash muttered after hours of walking, "but we're being followed."

I craned my head over my shoulder. We were following the railroad—walking beside it, instead of directly on the iron tracks—toward the looming fortress, and hadn't encountered a single creature, faery or otherwise, on the journey. Streetlamps grew out of the ground, lighting the way, and iron behemoths, reminding me of vehicles in a steam-punk anime, crouched along the tracks, hissing smoke. Through the writhing steam, it was difficult to see more than a few yards away.

But then, a small, familiar creature scuttled across the tracks, vanishing into the smoke. I caught a glimpse of a tricycle poking up from a mound of junk and frowned. "Why are the pack rats following us?"

"Pack rats?" Ash smirked at me.

"Yeah, you know, they collect shiny stuff, hoard it in their dens? Pack rats? Oh, never mind." I mock glared at him, too worried to be irritated. Ash never complained, but I could see the iron everywhere was taking a toll on him. "Do you want to stop somewhere and rest?"

"No." He pressed a palm to one eye, as if trying to squelch a headache. "It won't make any difference."

The twisted landscape went on. We passed pools of molten lava, bubbling and shimmering with heat. Smokestacks loomed overhead, belching great spouts of black pollution that writhed into the yellow-gray sky. Lightning arched and crackled across blinking metal towers, and the air hummed with electricity. Pipes crisscrossed the ground, leaking steam from joints and valves, and black wires slashed the sky overhead. The tang of iron, rust, and smog clogged my throat and burned my nose.

Ash spoke very little, stumbling on with grim determination. My worry for him was a constant knot in my stomach. I was doing this to him; it was my contract that bound him to help, even though it was slowly killing him. But we couldn't turn back, and I could only watch, helpless, as Ash struggled to continue. His breath rasped painfully in his throat, and he grew paler by the hour. Fear clawed my insides. I was terrified he would die and leave me alone in this dark, twisted place.

A day passed, and the iron tower loomed black and menacing overhead, though it was still far in the distance. The sickly yellow-gray of the sky darkened, and the hazy outline of a moon shimmered behind the clouds. I stopped, looking up at the sky. No stars. None at all. The artificial lights reflected off the haze, making the night nearly as bright as the day.

Ash began coughing, putting a hand against a crumbling wall to steady himself. I slipped my arms around him, holding him steady as he leaned into me. The harsh explosions made my heart constrict. "We should rest," I muttered, gazing around for a place to camp. A huge cement tube lay half buried in the dirt at the bottom of the tracks, covered in graffiti, and I motioned him toward it. "Come on."

He didn't argue this time, but followed me down the slope and into the cement shelter. It wasn't tall enough for us to stand up straight, and the floor was sprinkled with chips of colored glass. Not the best of campsites, but at least it wasn't iron. I kicked away a broken bottle and sat down carefully, shrugging off my backpack.

Pulling the sword from his belt, Ash sank down opposite me with a barely concealed groan. The Witchwood arrow throbbed as I unzipped the pack and reached around it for the food and bottled water.

Ripping open a bag of jerky, I offered some to Ash. He shook his head, his eyes weary and dull.

"You should eat something," I chided, gnawing on the dried meat. I wasn't particularly hungry myself, too tired, hot, and worried to have an appetite, but I wanted something in my stomach. "I have trail mix or candy if you want something else. Here." I waggled a bag of peanut mix at him. He eyed it dubiously, and I frowned. "I'm sorry, but they don't sell faery food at mini-marts. Eat."

Mutely, he accepted the bag and poured out a handful of peanuts and raisins. I gazed into the distance, where the looming black tower stabbed into the clouds. "How long do you think until we reach it?" I murmured, just to get him talking again.

Ash tossed the whole handful back, chewed, and swallowed without interest. "I'd guess a day at most," he replied, setting down the bag. "Beyond that…" He sighed, and his eyes darkened. "I doubt I'd be of much use anymore."

My stomach convulsed with dread. I couldn't lose him now. I'd lost so much already; it seemed especially cruel that Ash might not reach the end of our adventure. I needed him as I'd never needed anyone before. *I'll protect you,* I thought, surprising myself. *You'll get through this, I promise. Just don't die on me, Ash.*

Ash met my gaze, as if he could tell what I was thinking, his gray eyes solemn in the shadows of the pipe. I wondered if my emotions were giving away my thoughts, if Ash could read the glamour aura that surrounded me. For a moment, he hesitated, as if fighting a battle within himself. Then with a resigned sigh, he smiled faintly and held out his hand. I took it, and he pulled me close, settling me in front of him and wrapping his arms around my stomach. I leaned back against his chest and listened to his beating heart. With every thump, it told me that this was real, that Ash was here, and alive, and still with me.

The wind picked up, smelling of ozone and some other weird, chemical scent. A drop of rain hit the edge of the pipe, and a tiny wisp of smoke curled into the air. Except for his slow breathing, Ash was perfectly still, as if he feared that any sudden movement would scare me away. I reached down and traced idle patterns on his arm, marveling at the cool, smooth skin under my fingers, like living ice. I felt him shiver, heard his ragged intake of breath.

"Ash?"

"Hmm?"

I licked my lips. "Why did you vow to kill Puck?"

He jerked. I felt his eyes on the back of my neck and bit the inside of my cheek, wishing I could take it back, wondering what made me ask in the first place. "Never mind," I told him, waving a hand. "Forget it. You don't have to tell me. I was just wondering—"

Who you really are. What Puck has done to make you hate him. I want to understand. I feel I don't know either of you.

A few more drops of rain hit the ground, hissing in the silence. I chewed my jerky strips and stared out into the rain, hyperaware of Ash's body, of his arms around my waist. I heard him shift to a more comfortable position and sigh.

"It was a long time ago," he murmured, his voice almost lost in the rising wind, "before you were even born. Winter and Summer had been at peace for several seasons. There were always minor skirmishes between the courts, but for the longest time in centuries, we actually left each other alone.

"Near the end of summer," he went on, a bit of pain creeping into his voice, "things began to change. The fey don't deal well with boredom, and some of the more impatient members started mischief with Summer again. I should've known there would be trouble, but that season, I wasn't thinking of politics. The entire court was bored and restless, but I…" His voice broke, only for a moment, before continuing. "I was with my lady, Ariella Tularyn."

I felt the breath sucked out of me. His lady. Ash had been involved, once. And, judging from the veiled hurt in his voice, he'd loved her a lot. I stiffened, suddenly too aware of my breath, of his arms around my waist. Ash didn't seem to notice.

"We were hunting in the wyldwood," he went on, resting his chin atop my head. "Following the rumor of a golden fox that had been seen in the area. There were three of us that day, hunting together. Ariella, myself, and…and Robin Goodfellow."

"Puck?"

Ash shifted uncomfortably. Thunder growled in the distance, shooting threads of green lightning across the sky. "Yes," he muttered, as if it pained him to say it. "Puck. Puck was…he was a friend, once. I wasn't ashamed to call him that. Back then, the three of us would often meet one another in the wyldwood, away from the condemnation of the courts. We didn't care about the rules. Back then, Puck and Ariella were my closest companions. I trusted them completely."

"What happened?"

Ash's voice was soft with memory as he continued. "We were hunting," he explained again, "following our quarry into a territory none of us had seen. The wyldwood is huge, and some parts are constantly shifting, so it can be dangerous, even for us. We tracked the golden fox for three days, through unfamiliar woods and forest, making bets on whose arrow would finally take it down. Puck boasted that Winter would surely lose to Summer, and Ariella and I made the same boast in reverse. All the while, the forest around us grew dark and wild. Our horses were fey steeds whose hooves didn't touch the ground, but they were growing increasingly nervous. We should have listened to them, but we didn't, stubborn pride leading us on like fools.

"Finally, on the fourth day, we came to a rise that plunged down into a vast hollow. On the other side, trotting along the ridge, was the golden fox. The hollow separating us wasn't deep, but it was wide and filled with tangled shadows and undergrowth, making it difficult to see what was down there.

"Ariella wanted to go around, even though it would take us longer. Puck disagreed, insisting we would lose our quarry unless we rode straight through. We argued. I sided with Ariella—though I didn't see the reason for her apprehension, if she wasn't willing to go forward, I wasn't going to make her.

"Puck, however, had other ideas. As I turned my horse around, he let out a whoop, slapped Ariella's horse on the rump, and kicked his own steed forward. They plunged over the edge, racing down the slope, with Puck yelling at me to catch up if I could. I had no choice but to follow."

Ash fell silent, his eyes dark and haunted. He gazed off into the distance, until I couldn't take it anymore. "What happened?" I whispered.

He gave a bitter laugh. "Ariella was right, of course. Puck had led us straight into a wyvern nest."

I felt stupid for asking but… "What's a wyvern?"

"It's cousin to a dragon," Ash replied. "Not as intelligent, but still extremely dangerous. And highly territorial. The thing rose up out of nowhere, all scales and teeth and wings, lashing at us with its poisoned stinger. It was enormous, an ancient drake, vicious and powerful. We fought our way free, the three of us, side by side. We'd been together so long we knew one another's fighting styles, and used them to take down the enemy. It was Ariella who landed the killing blow. But, as it was dying, the wyvern whipped its tail out one last time, striking her in the chest. Wyvern poison is extremely potent, and we were miles from any healers. We…we tried to save her, but…"

He paused, taking a shaky breath. I squeezed his arm to console him.

"She died in my arms," he finished, making an audible effort to compose himself. "She died with my name on her lips, begging me to save her. As I held her, watched the life fade from her eyes, I could only think one thing—that Puck had caused this. If it wasn't for him, she would still be alive."

"I'm so sorry, Ash."

Ash nodded once. His voice turned steely. "I swore, on that day, to avenge Ariella's death, to kill Robin Goodfellow, or die trying. We've clashed several times since, but Goodfellow always manages to slip away, or throw me some trick that ends our duels. I cannot rest while he lives. I promised Ariella that I would continue hunting Robin Goodfellow until one of us lies dead."

"Puck told me it was a mistake. He didn't mean for that to happen." The words were sour in my mouth. It didn't feel right, defending him. Ash had lost someone he loved because of Puck's actions, a prank that finally went too far.

"It doesn't matter." Ash shifted away from me, his voice

cold. "My vow is binding. I cannot rest until I've completed my oath."

I didn't know what to say, so I stared into the rain, miserable and torn in two. Ash and Puck, two enemies locked in a struggle that would end only when one of them killed the other. How could you stand between two people like that, knowing that one day, one of them would succeed? I knew faery oaths were binding, and Ash had good reason to hate Puck, but I still felt trapped. I couldn't stop this, but I didn't want either of them to die.

Ash sighed and leaned forward again, brushing my hand, tracing the skin with his fingertips. "I'm sorry," he murmured. A shiver went up my arm. "I wish you didn't have to be involved. There is no way to unmake a vow, once it has been spoken. But know this—were I aware then that I would meet you, perhaps my oath would not have been so hasty."

My throat closed up. I wanted to say something, but at that moment, a sharp blast of wind blew a few drops of rain into the tube. Water splashed over my jeans, and I yelped as something burned my skin.

We examined my leg. Tiny holes marred my jeans where the drops had hit, the material seared away, the skin underneath red and burned. It throbbed as if I'd jabbed needles into my flesh.

"What the heck?" I muttered, glaring into the storm. It looked like ordinary rain—gray, misty, somewhat depressing. Almost compulsively, I stuck my hand toward the opening, where water dripped over the edge of the tube.

Ash grabbed my wrist, snatching it back. "Yes, it will burn your hand as well as your leg," he said in a bland voice. "And here I thought you learned your lesson with the chains."

Embarrassed, I dropped my hand and scooted farther into the tube, away from the rim and the acid rain dripping from it. "Guess I'm staying up all night," I muttered, crossing my arms. "Wouldn't want to doze off and find half my face melted off when I wake up."

Ash pulled me back against him, brushing my hair from my neck. His mouth skimmed my shoulder, up my neck, sending butterflies swarming through my insides. "If you want to rest, then do so," he murmured against my skin. "The rain will not touch you, I promise."

"What about you?"

"I wasn't planning to sleep." He made a casual gesture at a trickle of rainwater seeping into the tube, and the water turned to ice. "I fear I wouldn't be able to wake up."

My worry spiked. "Ash—"

His lips brushed my ear. "Sleep, Meghan Chase," he whispered, and suddenly I couldn't keep my eyes open. Half my consciousness still struggled as darkness pulled me under and I sank into his waiting arms.

When I awoke, the rain had stopped and everything had dried, though the ground still steamed. There was no visible sun through the choking clouds, but the air still blistered with heat. I grabbed my backpack and crawled out of the pipe, looking around for Ash. He sat against the outside of the tube, head back, sword resting on his knees. Seeing him, I felt a rush of anger and fear. He'd enchanted me last night, spelled me to sleep without my consent. Which meant he'd probably used glamour, though his own body was getting weaker and weaker. Fuming and afraid, I stomped up to him and put my hands on his hips. Gray eyes cracked open and regarded me blearily.

"Don't do that again." I'd intended to yell at him, but his vulnerability made me pause. He blinked but had the grace not to ask what I was talking about.

"My apologies," he murmured, bowing his head. "I thought at least one of us could benefit from a few hours' sleep."

God, he looked awful. His cheeks were hollow, dark circles crouched under his eyes, and his skin was almost translucent. I needed to find Ethan and get us all out of here, before Ash turned into a walking skeleton and collapsed dead at my feet.

Ash looked past me to the tower, seeming to draw strength from it. "Not far now," he murmured, as if it were a mantra that kept him going. I held out my hand, and he let me pull him to his feet.

We started following the tracks again.

The smokestacks and metal towers slowly fell away behind us as we continued across Machina's realm. The land grew flat and barren, and steam billowed out of cracks in the ground, coiling around us like wraiths. Colossal machines, with enormous iron wheels and armored shells, lay beside the tracks. They looked like a cross between modern-day tanks and the mecha vehicles of anime. They were old and rusty, and reminded me strangely of Ironhorse.

Ash grunted suddenly and fell, his legs buckling underneath him. I grabbed his arm as he pulled himself upright, panting. He felt so thin.

"Should we stop and rest?" I asked.

"No," he gritted out. "Keep going. We have to—"

Suddenly he straightened, his hand going to his sword.

Ahead of us, the steam cleared, parting enough to reveal a hulking figure standing on the tracks. A horse made of iron and snorting flame, steel hooves pawing the ground. His glowing eyes watched us balefully.

"Ironhorse!" I gasped, wondering, for a surreal moment, if my earlier thoughts had summoned him here.

"THOUGHT YOU GOT RID OF ME, DID YOU?" Ironhorse boomed, his voice reverberating off the machines around us. "IT WILL TAKE MORE THAN A CAVE-IN TO KILL ME. I MADE THE MISTAKE OF UNDERESTIMATING YOU BEFORE. THAT WON'T HAPPEN AGAIN."

Movement surged around us as hundreds of gremlins crawled into view, hissing and crackling. They swarmed over the machines like spiders, laughing and chittering, and scuttled along the ground. In seconds, they had us surrounded, a living black carpet. Ash drew his sword, and the gremlins hissed at him nastily.

Two figures appeared through the steam on either side of us. They marched forward in unison, and the gremlins parted to let them through. Warriors in full battle armor, with helmets and masks covering their faces, stepped into the circle. Their insectlike suits looked like something from a science-fiction movie, somehow ancient and modern at the same time. Their breastplates bore the insignia of a barbed-wire crown. Drawing their swords, they stepped forward.

"Meghan, get back," Ash muttered, squaring off against the armored pair coming at him.

"Are you crazy? You can't fight like this—"

"Go!"

Reluctantly, I backed away, but was suddenly grabbed from behind. I yelped and kicked, but was dragged to the edge of the circle, where the gremlins jabbered at me. I twisted around and saw that my captor was a third warrior.

"Meghan!" Ash tried to follow, but the first two knights blocked his way, the sickly light glinting off their iron blades. Glaring at them, Ash flourished his sword and sank into a battle stance.

They lunged at him, swords sweeping down in a blur, coming both low and high. Ash leaped over the first and parried the second, knocking it away with a flurry of ice and sparks. He landed, spun to his left to block the savage back strike, and ducked as the second blade hissed overhead. Whirling around, his sword lashed out, slicing across one armored chest with a grinding screech. The knight staggered back, the image of the wire crown cut through and coated with frost.

They broke away for a moment, facing each other, swords at the ready. Ash was panting, his eyes narrowed in concentration. He didn't look good, and my stomach tightened in fear. The other knights slowly began to circle him, coming at him from different sides like stalking wolves. But before they could get into position, Ash snarled and lunged.

For a moment, the knight he engaged was driven back by the ferocity of the attack. Ash hammered into him relentlessly, his blade slipping through his enemy's guard to smash at his armor. Sparks flew, and the knight stumbled, almost falling. Ash's blade swept up and struck a vicious blow to the side of his head, ripping the helmet clean off.

I gasped. The face beneath the helmet was Ash, or at least a long-lost brother. Same gray eyes, same ebony hair, same pointed ears. The face was a little older, and a scar slashed its way down his cheek, but the similarities were almost perfect.

The real Ash hesitated, just as stunned as I, and that cost him dearly. The second knight rushed up behind him, his sword slashing down, and Ash whirled—too late. His blade caught his opponent's sword, but the blow knocked the weapon from his hands. At the same time, his companion backhanded Ash with his metal gauntlet, striking him behind the ear. Ash crumpled to the ground on his back, and two iron swords were pressed against his throat.

"No!" I tried to run to him, but the third warrior held me and twisted my arms behind my back. Manacles were snapped around my wrists. The two knights kicked Ash onto his stomach and wrenched his arms behind him, binding him similarly. I heard him gasp as the metal touched his flesh, and his doppelgänger jerked him savagely to his feet.

They shoved us toward Ironhorse, who waited for us in the middle of the tracks, swishing his tail. His iron mask gave nothing away.

"GOOD," he snorted. "KING MACHINA WILL BE PLEASED." His red eyes fastened on Ash, who was barely able to stand, and he pinned back his ears. "DISPOSE OF THEIR WEAPONS," he ordered disdainfully.

Ash's face was twisted in agony. Sweat trickled down his brow, and he clenched his teeth. He watched the iron knight take his sword to the edge of the tracks and toss it into a ditch. There was a soft splash as the blade hit the oily water and sank from view. A second knight did the same with the bow. I held my breath, praying they wouldn't see the most important weapon of all.

"THE ARROW, TOO."

My heart sank and despair rose up in me. Ash's doppelgänger approached, yanked the Witchwood arrow from my backpack, and tossed it into the ditch with the rest of the weapons. My heart plummeted even further, and the tiny sliver of hope shriveled into a ball and died. That was it, then. Game over. We had failed.

Ironhorse looked us both over and snorted steam. "NO FUNNY BUSINESS FROM YOU, PRINCESS," he warned, blowing smoke at me. "OR MY KNIGHTS WILL WRAP SO MUCH IRON AROUND THE WINTER PRINCE THAT HIS SKIN WILL PEEL OFF HIS BONES." He coughed flame, singeing my eyebrows, and swung his head toward the waiting fortress. "LET'S GO. KING MACHINA AWAITS."

22

ASH'S FINAL STAND

It was a torturous, nightmare march toward Machina's tower. A length of chain had been wrapped around my waist, attaching me to Ironhorse, who walked briskly down the tracks without pausing or looking back. Beside me, Ash wore another, and I knew it was hurting him. He kept stumbling, barely managing to keep his feet as we followed Ironhorse down the railroad tracks. Gremlins cavorted around us, poking and pinching and laughing at our torment. The knights walked to either side and refused to let Ash step off the iron tracks, shoving him back if he tried. Once, he fell, and was dragged several yards before he finally got his feet under him again. Angry red burns crisscrossed his face where his skin had touched the metal tracks, and I ached for him.

The sky clouded over, changing from yellow-gray to an ominous reddish-black in a matter of moments. Ironhorse stopped and craned his neck, flaring his nostrils.

"DAMN," he muttered, stomping a hoof. "IT'S GOING TO RAIN SOON."

My stomach turned at the thought of the acid rain. Lightning flashed, filling the air with a sharp tang.

"QUICKLY, BEFORE THE STORM HITS." The horse stepped off the tracks, breaking into a trot as thunder growled overhead. My legs burned as I broke into an awkward sprint behind him, every muscle screaming in protest, but it was either keep up or be dragged. Ash stumbled and fell, and this time he did not get up.

A drop of rain spattered against my leg, and a searing pain lanced through me. I gasped. More drops fell, hissing as they struck the ground. The air reeked of chemicals, and I heard a few gremlins screech as the raindrops hit them, as well.

A silvery curtain of rain crept toward us. It caught up to a few of the slower gremlins, engulfing them. They screamed and writhed, sparks leaping off their bodies, until they gave a final twitch and were still. The rain came on.

Panicked, I looked up to see Ironhorse leading us into a mine shaft. We ducked under the roof just as the storm swept over us, catching a few more gremlins, who squealed and danced around in agony, holes burned through their skin. The rest of the gremlins jeered and laughed. I turned away before I was sick.

Ash lay motionless on the ground, covered in dust and blood from where he'd been dragged. Steam curled off his body where the raindrops had hit. He groaned and tried to get up, but didn't quite make it off his back. Snickering, a few gremlins started poking him, climbing onto his chest to jab at his face. He flinched and turned away, but this only encouraged them further.

"Stop it!" I lunged and kicked a gremlin with all my might, launching it away from Ash like a football. The others turned on me, and I lashed out at them all, kicking and stomping. Hissing, they swarmed up my pant legs, pulling my hair and raking me with their claws. One sank its razor-sharp teeth into my shoulder, and I screamed.

"ENOUGH!" Ironhorse's shout made the ceiling tremble. Dirt showered us, and the gremlins skittered back. Blood ran down my skin from a dozen tiny wounds, and my shoulder throbbed where the gremlin had bitten it. Ironhorse glared at me, swishing his tail against his flanks, then tossed his head at the knights.

"TAKE THEM INTO THE TUNNELS," he ordered with a hint of exasperation. "MAKE SURE THEY DO NOT ESCAPE. IF THE STORM DOES NOT ABATE, WE MIGHT BE HERE AWHILE."

The chains binding us to Ironhorse were released. Two knights pulled Ash to his feet and half dragged him away down a tunnel. The last knight, the one with Ash's face, took me by the arm and led me after his brothers.

We paused at a junction where several tunnels merged. Wooden tracks led off into the darkness, and rickety cars half-filled with ore sat off to the sides. Thick wooden beams held up the ceiling, standing along the tracks every few feet. A few lanterns had been nailed into the wood, though most were broken and dark. In the flickering torchlight, glimmering veins of iron snaked across the walls.

We continued down a tunnel that dead-ended in a small room, where two wooden posts stood side by side in the middle of the room. A few crates and an abandoned pickax lay stacked in a corner. The knights pushed Ash against one post, unlocked a cuff, and reattached it behind the beam, securing him in place. The flesh under the metal band was red and burned, and he jerked when they snapped it around his wrist again. I bit my lip in sympathy.

The knight who'd first caught me straightened and patted Ash on the cheek, chuckling as Ash flinched away from the steel gauntlet. "Feels good, don't it, worm?" he said, and I started in surprise. This was the first time I'd heard one of them speak. "You oldbloods are completely weak, aren't you? It's high time you moved over. You're obsolete now, ancient. Your time is done."

Ash raised his head and stared the other faery in the eye. "Bold words for someone who stood aside and wrestled a girl while his brothers fought for him."

The knight backhanded him. I cried out in fury and started forward, but the knight behind me grabbed my arm. "Leave him alone, Quintus," he said in a calm voice.

Quintus sneered. "Feeling sorry for him, Tertius? Maybe some brotherly affection for your twin here?"

"We're not supposed to speak to the oldbloods," Tertius replied in the same cool tone. "You know that. Or should I inform Ironhorse?"

Quintus spat on the ground. "You were always weak, Tertius," he snarled. "Too softhearted to be made of iron. You're a disgrace to the brotherhood." He spun on a heel and marched up the tunnel, the last knight following behind. Their boots rang loudly on the stone floor, then faded into silence.

"Jerk," I muttered as the remaining knight maneuvered me against the post. "Your name's Tertius, right?"

He unlocked a shackle and wound the chain around the beam, not looking at me. "Yes."

"Help us," I pleaded. "You're not like them, I can feel it. Please, I have to rescue my brother and get him out of here. I'll make a deal with you, if that's what it takes. Please, help us."

For a moment, he met my eyes. I was struck again by how much he resembled Ash. His eyes were gunmetal-gray instead of silver, and the scar made him look older, but he had that same intense, honorable face. He paused, and for a moment, I dared to hope. But then he snapped the cuff around my wrist and stepped away, his eyes darkening to black.

"I'm a Knight of the Iron Crown," he said, his voice as hard as steel. "I will not betray my brothers, or my king."

He turned and walked away without looking back.

In the flickering darkness of the tunnel, I heard Ash's raspy breathing, the shift of gravel as he sank into a sitting position. "Ash?" I called softly, my voice echoing down the shafts. "You all right?"

Silence for a moment. When Ash finally spoke, his voice was so low I could barely hear it. "Sorry, princess," he murmured, almost to himself. "Looks like I won't be able to uphold our contract after all."

"Don't give up," I told him, feeling like a hypocrite as I struggled with my own despair. "We'll get out of this somehow. We just have to keep our heads." A thought came to me, and I lowered my voice. "Can't you freeze the chains until they shatter, like you did in the factory?"

A low, humorless chuckle. "Right now, it's taking everything I have not to pass out," Ash muttered, sounding pained. "If you have any of that power the Elder Dryad was talking about, now would be the time to use it."

I nodded. What did we have to lose? Closing my eyes, I concentrated on feeling the glamour around us, trying to remember what Grimalkin had taught me.

Nothing. Except for a flicker of raw determination from Ash, there were no emotions to draw from, no hopes or dreams or anything. Everything here was dead, devoid of life, passionless. The iron fey were too machinelike—cold, logical, and calculating—and their world reflected that.

Refusing to give up, I pushed deeper, trying to get past

the banal surface. This had been the Nevernever once. There had to be something left untouched by Machina's influence.

I felt a pulse of life, somewhere deep below. A lone tree, poisoned and dying, but still clinging to life. Its branches were slowly turning to metal, but the roots, and the heart of the tree, were not yet corrupted. It stirred to my presence, a tiny piece of the Nevernever in the void of nothingness. But before I could do anything, shuffling footsteps broke my concentration, and the link faded away.

I opened my eyes. The light in the tunnel had gone out, leaving us in pitch blackness. I heard creatures moving toward us, surrounding us, and I couldn't see a thing. My mind jumped to all sorts of terrifying conclusions: giant rats, huge cockroaches, massive underground spiders. I almost fainted when something patted my arm, but then I heard the low babble of familiar voices.

A yellowish beam clicked on in the darkness: a flashlight. It illuminated the curious, wrinkled faces of a half-dozen pack rats, blinking in the sudden light. Surprised, I stared at them as they chittered at me in their odd language. Several surrounded Ash, pulling at his sleeves.

"What are you doing here?" I whispered. They jabbered nonsense and tugged on my clothes, as if trying to drag me away. "Are you trying to help?"

The pack rat with the tricycle stepped forward. He pointed at me, then at the back of the room. In the flashlight beam, I saw the mouth of another tunnel, nearly invisible in the shadows. It was only partly formed, as if the miners had started digging only to abandon it. A way out? My heart leaped. The pack rat jibbered impatiently and beckoned me forward.

"I can't," I told him, rattling my chain. "I can't move."

He chattered at the rest of them, and they shuffled forward.

One by one, they reached behind them, to the lumps of trash on their backs, and began pulling things out.

"What are they doing?" Ash muttered.

I couldn't begin to answer. One of the pack rats produced an electric drill, showing it to the leader, who shook his head. Another pulled out a butterfly knife, but the leader declined that, too, as well as a lighter, a hammer, and a round alarm clock. Then one of the smaller pack rats chittered excitedly and stepped forward, holding something long and metallic.

A pair of bolt cutters.

The lead pack rat jabbered and pointed. But at the same time, I heard the clank of steel boots coming down the tunnel, and the scuttling of thousands of claws on rock. My stomach twisted. The knights were coming back, and so were the gremlins.

"Hurry!" I urged, as the pack rat waddled over and began sawing at the chain. Lights appeared in the distance, bobbing along the ground; gremlins with lanterns or flashlights. Laughter drifted into the room, and my stomach churned. *Hurry!* I thought, furious with the pack rat's slow progress. *We're not going to make it! They'll be here any second!*

I felt the snap of links as they parted, and I was free.

Grabbing the bolt cutters, I raced over to Ash. The lights moved closer and closer, and the hissing of gremlins could be heard down the tunnel. I inserted the chain between the metal jaws and squeezed the handles, but the tool was rusty and hard to use. Snarling curses, I gripped the handles and pushed.

"Leave me," Ash muttered as I strained to close the jaws. "I won't be able to help, and I'll only slow you down. Just go."

"I'm not leaving you," I panted, gritting my teeth and pushing with all my might.

"Meghan..."

"I'm not leaving you!" I snapped, fighting angry tears. Stupid chain! Why wouldn't it break already? I threw my whole weight against it, sawing with a fury born of fear.

"Remember when I told you about your weakness?" Ash murmured, craning his head to look at me. Though his eyes were hard, glazed over with pain, his voice was gentle. "You have to make that choice now. What is most important to you?"

"Shut up!" Tears blinded me, and I blinked them away. "You can't ask me to make that decision. You're important to me, too, dammit. I'm not leaving you behind, so just shut up."

The first wave of gremlins entered the tunnel and shrieked in alarm when they saw me. With a snarl of fear and terror, I gave the bolt cutters a final jerk, and the chain finally snapped. Ash pulled himself to his feet as the gremlins howled with outrage and surged forward.

We ran for the hidden tunnel, following the pack rats as they scuttled through. The corridor was low and narrow; I had to duck my head to avoid the ceiling, and the walls scraped my arms as we fled. Behind us, gremlins poured through the opening like ants, skittering along the walls and ceiling, hissing as they pursued.

Ash suddenly stopped. Turning to face the horde, he raised a pickax like a baseball bat, bracing himself against the wall. I gave a start; he must've snatched it from the crates, right before we reached the tunnel. The broken chains, still dangling from his wrists, trembled as his arms shook. The gremlins halted a few yards away, their eyes bright as they analyzed this new threat. As one they began edging forward.

"Ash!" I called. "What are you doing? Come on!"

"Meghan." Ash's voice, despite the pain below the surface, was calm. "I hope you find your brother. If you see Puck again, tell him I regret having to step out of our duel."

"Ash, no! Don't do this!"

I felt him smile. "You made me feel alive again," he murmured.

Screeching, the gremlins attacked.

Ash smashed two of them senseless with the pickax, ducked as another leaped at his head, and was overwhelmed. They swarmed over him, clinging to his legs and arms, biting and clawing. He staggered and dropped to a knee, and they skittered up his back, until I could no longer see him through the writhing mass of gremlins. Still, Ash fought on; with a snarl, he surged back to his feet, sending several gremlins flying only to have a dozen more take their place.

"Meghan, go!" His voice was a hoarse rasp as he slammed a gremlin into the wall. *"Now!"*

Choking on tears, I turned and fled. I followed the beckoning pack rats until the tunnel split and branched off in several directions. A pack rat pulled something from his lump and waved it at the leader. I gasped when I saw that it was a stick of dynamite. The leader snarled something, and another pack rat scuttled forward with a lighter.

I couldn't help but look back, just in time to see Ash finally pulled under the sea of gremlins and lost from view. The gremlins screeched in triumph and flowed toward us.

The fuse sputtered to life. The lead pack rat hissed at me and pointed to the tunnels, where the rest of them were vanishing. Tears flowing down my cheeks, I followed, and the pack rat holding the dynamite flung it toward the oncoming gremlins.

The *boom* shook the ceiling. Dirt and rocks rained down on me, filling the air with grit. I coughed and sagged against the wall, waiting for the chaos to die down. When everything was still, I looked up to see that the entrance to the tunnel had caved in. The pack rats were moaning softly. One of their own hadn't made it through in time.

Sagging down the wall, I pulled my knees to my chest and joined them in their grieving, feeling I'd left my heart in the tunnel where Ash had fallen.

23

THE IRON KING

For several minutes, I sat there, too numb to even cry. I couldn't believe that Ash was really dead. I kept staring at the caved-in wall, half expecting him to somehow, miraculously, push through the rubble, bruised and bloody, but alive.

How long I sat there, I don't know. But eventually, the lead pack rat tugged gently on my sleeve. His eyes, solemn and sad, met mine, before he turned away and beckoned me to follow. With one final look at the cave-in behind us, I trailed them into the tunnels.

We walked for hours, and gradually, the tunnels turned into natural caverns, dripping with water and stalactites. The pack rats loaned me a flashlight, and as I shined it about the caves, I saw that the floor was littered with strange items, a fender here, a toy robot there. It seemed we were heading deep into the pack rats' nest, for the farther we went, the more junk lay strewn about.

At last, we entered a cathedral-like cave, where the ceiling soared up into blackness, and the walls were piled with mountains of trash, resembling the Wasteland in miniature.

In the center of the room, sitting on a throne made entirely of junk, was an old, old man. His skin was gray, and I don't mean pale or ashen, but metallic-gray, mercury-gray. His white hair flowed past his feet, nearly touching the floor, as if he hadn't moved from his chair in centuries. The pack rats shuffled around him, holding up various items, placing them at his feet. I saw my phone among them. The old man smiled as the pack rats chittered and milled around him like eager dogs, then his pale green eyes looked up at me.

He blinked several times, as if he couldn't trust what he was seeing. I held my breath. Was this Machina? Had the pack rats brought me straight to the Iron King? For an all-powerful ruler, I didn't expect him to be so...old.

"Well," he wheezed at last, "my subjects have brought me many curious things over the years, but I do believe this is the most unusual. Who are you, girl? Why are you here?"

"I... My name is Meghan, sir. Meghan Chase. I'm looking for my brother."

"Your brother?" The old man looked at the pack rats, aghast. "I don't recall you bringing home a child. What has gotten into you?"

The pack rats chittered, shaking their heads. The old man frowned at them as they jabbered and bounced around, then looked back at me. "My subjects tell me they have not encountered anyone except you and your friend out in the Wasteland. Why do you think your brother would be here?"

"I..." I stopped, gazing around at the dingy cavern, the pack rats, the frail old man. This couldn't be right. "I'm sorry," I continued, feeling stupid and confused, "but...are you Machina, the Iron King?"

"Ah." The old man settled back, lacing his hands together. "Now I understand. Machina has your brother, yes? And you are on your way to rescue him."

"Yes." I relaxed, breathing a sigh of relief. "Then, I guess you're not the Iron King?"

"Oh, I wouldn't say that." The old man smiled, and my guard went back up. He chuckled. "Worry not, child. I mean you no harm. But you would do well to abandon your plan to rescue your brother. Machina is too strong. No weapon can hurt him. You'd be throwing your life away."

I remembered the Witchwood arrow, lying at the bottom of a ditch, and my heart constricted. "I know," I whispered. "But I have to try. I've come this far. I'm not giving up now."

"If Machina has stolen your brother, he must be waiting for you," the old man said, leaning forward. "He wants you for something. I can feel the power in you, my girl, but it will not be enough. The Iron King is a master of manipulation. He will use you to further his own schemes, and you will not be able to resist. Go home, girl. Forget what you have lost and go home."

"Forget?" I thought of my friends, who had sacrificed everything to see me this far. Puck. The Elder Dryad. Ash. "No," I murmured, a lump forming in my throat. "I can never forget. Even if it's hopeless, I have to go on. I owe everyone that much."

"Foolish girl," the old man growled. "I know more about Machina than anyone—his ways, his power, the way his mind works—and yet you still will not hear me. Very well. Rush to your doom, like everyone who came before you. You will see, as I did, far too late. Machina cannot be defeated. I only wish I'd listened to my councilors when they told me as much."

"*You* tried to defeat him?" I stared, trying to imagine the frail old man fighting anyone and failing. "When? Why?"

"Because," the old man explained patiently, "I was once the Iron King.

"My name is Ferrum," the old man explained into my

shocked silence. "As you no doubt noticed, I am old. Older than that whelp Machina, older than all of the iron fey. I was the first, you see, born of the forges, when mankind first began to experiment with iron. I rose from their imagination, from their ambition to conquer the world with a metal that could slice through bronze like paper. I was there when the world started to shift, when humans took their first steps out of the Dark Ages into civilization.

"For many years, I thought I was alone. But mankind is never satisfied—he is always reaching, always trying for something better. Others came, others like me, risen from these dreams of a new world. They accepted me as their king, and for centuries, we remained hidden, isolated from the rest of the fey. I realized, beyond a doubt, that if the courts knew of our existence, they would unite to destroy us.

"Then, with the invention of computers, the gremlins came, and the bugs. Given life by the fear of monsters lurking in machines, these were more chaotic than the other fey, violent and destructive. They spread to every part of the world. As technology became a driving force in every country, powerful new fey rose into existence. Virus. Glitch. And Machina, the most powerful of all. He was not content to sit and hide. His plan was conquest, to spread throughout the Nevernever like a virus, destroying all who opposed him. He was my First— my most powerful lieutenant—and we clashed on several occasions. My advisers told me to banish him, to imprison him, even to kill him. They were afraid of him, and rightly so, but I was blind to the danger.

"Of course, it was only a matter of time before Machina turned on me. Gathering an army of like-minded fey to his side, he attacked the fortress from within, slaughtering all who were loyal to me. My forces fought back, but we were old and obsolete, no match for Machina's cruel army.

"In the end, I sat on my throne and watched him approach, knowing I was going to die. But, as Machina threw me to the floor, he laughed and said he would not kill me. He would let me fade away a bit at a time, becoming obscure and forgotten, until no one remembered my name or who I was. And, as he settled back upon my throne, I felt my power slip away and flow into Machina, acknowledging him as the new Iron King.

"So, now I live here." Ferrum gestured to the cavern and the pack rats milling about. "In a forgotten cave, sitting on a throne made of garbage, king of the mighty trash collectors. A noble title, is it not?" His lips twisted into a bitter smile. "These creatures are very loyal, bringing me offerings that I cannot use, making me ruler of this junk heap. They have accepted me as their king, but what good is that? They cannot give me back my throne, and yet they are the only ones that keep me from fading away. I cannot die, but I can hardly bear to live, knowing what I've lost. What was stolen from me. And Machina is the one who designed it all!"

He slumped on his throne and buried his face in his hands. The pack rats shuffled forward, patting him, making worried chittering sounds. Watching him, I felt a surge of sympathy and disgust.

"I've lost things, too," I said, over the sound of his quiet sobbing. "Machina has stolen a lot from me. But I'm not going to sit on a chair and wait for him. I'll confront him, invincible or not, and somehow I'll take back what's mine. Or I'll die trying. Either way, I'm not giving up."

He stared at me through his fingers, his frail form shaking with tears. He sniffed and lowered his hands, his face sullen and dark.

"Go, then," Ferrum whispered, shooing me away. "I cannot sway you. Perhaps a single unarmed girl will succeed where an entire army has failed." He laughed then, bitter and petulant, and I felt a flicker of annoyance. "Good luck to you, foolish one. If you will not listen to me, you are welcome here no longer. My subjects will take you under his fortress, through the secret tunnels that honeycomb the land. It's the quickest way to rush to your destruction. Now, go. I am through with you."

I didn't bow. I didn't thank him for his help. I only turned and followed the pack rats out of the cave, feeling the hateful glare of the deposed king on my back.

More tunnels. The brief respite with the last Iron King wasn't enough to stave off my exhaustion. We rested infrequently, and I caught what little sleep I could. The pack rats gave me some strange mushrooms to chew on, tiny white things that glowed in the dark and tasted like mold, but allowed me to see in pitch blackness as if it were twilight. This was a good thing, because my flashlight eventually flickered and died, and no one offered fresh batteries.

I lost track of time. All the caverns and tunnels seemed to meld together into one giant, impossible maze. I knew that, even if I did get into Machina's fortress and rescue Ethan, I wouldn't be getting out the same way.

The tunnel fell away, and suddenly I stood on a stone bridge across a vast precipice, jagged rocks spearing up from the bottom. Around me, on the walls and ceiling, hanging precariously close to the bridge, massive iron gears turned and creaked, making the ground vibrate. The closest gears were easily three times my height; some were even larger. It was like being inside a giant clock, and the noise was deafening.

We must be under Machina's fortress, I thought, gazing around in awe. *Wonder what those huge gears are for?*

There was a tug on my arm, and I turned to see the lead pack rat point across the bridge, his jabbering lost in the grinding noise of the room. I understood. They had taken me as far as they could go. Now the last part of the trek would be on my own.

I nodded to show I understood and started forward, when he grabbed my hand. Holding my wrist, he beckoned to his pack rats, chattering at them. Two waddled forward, reaching back for some item on their humps.

"It's okay," I told them. "I don't need any—"

My voice died away. The first pack rat drew out a long sheath with a familiar hilt, gleaming blue-black in the darkness. I caught my breath. "Is that...?"

He handed it over solemnly. Grasping the hilt, I pulled the blade free, washing the chamber in pale blue light. Steam writhed on the edge of Ash's blade, and a lump caught in my throat.

Oh, Ash.

I sheathed the blade and fastened it around my waist, grimly tightening the belt. "I appreciate this," I told the pack rats, unsure if they understood. They chattered at me and still didn't move, and the leader pointed at the second, smaller pack rat who'd approached. He blinked and reached back, drawing forward a slightly battered bow and—

For the second time, my heart stopped. The pack rat held up the Witchwood arrow, slimy and covered with oil, but otherwise intact. I took it reverently, my mind spinning. They could have given it to Ferrum, but they hadn't, saving it for me all this time. The arrow pulsed in my hands, still alive and deadly.

I didn't think. I dropped to my knees and hugged the pack rats, both the leader and the small one. They squeaked in surprise. Their lumps poked my skin, making it impossible to get my arms around them completely, but I didn't care. When I rose, I thought the leader was blushing, though it was difficult to see in the darkness, and the small one grinned from ear to ear.

"Thank you," I said, putting as much sincerity into my voice as I could. "Really, 'thank you' isn't enough, but it's all I have. You guys are amazing."

They jabbered at me and patted my hands. I wished I knew what they were saying. Then, with a sharp bark from the leader, they turned and faded into the tunnels. The small one looked back once, his eyes bright in the gloom, and then they were gone.

I straightened, tucking the arrow into my belt much as Ash had done. Gripping the bow, and with Ash's sword hanging from my waist, I stepped beneath Machina's tower.

I followed the walkway, which turned from stone to iron grating, through the giant maze of clockwork, setting my teeth against the grinding of metal on metal. I found a twisting iron staircase and followed it up to a trapdoor, which opened with a ringing bang. I winced and peeked out cautiously.

Nothing. The room I stared into was empty, save for the enormous boiler ovens that glowed red and filled the air with hissing steam.

"All right," I muttered, climbing out of the floor. My face and shirt were already drenched with sweat from the shimmering heat. "I'm inside. Where to now, I wonder?"

Up.

The thought came unbidden, and yet I knew it was right. Machina, and Ethan, would be at the top of the tower.

Clanking footsteps caught my attention, and I ducked behind one of the boilers, ignoring the searing heat radiating from the metal. Several figures entered the room, short and stocky and dressed in bulky canvas suits like firemen. They wore breathing apparatus that covered their entire faces, a pair of tubes snaking from the mouth to some kind of tank on their back. They stomped among the boilers, pinging on them with wrenches, checking the numerous pipes and valves. A large ring of keys dangled from each of their belts, jingling as they moved. As I scrambled back to an isolated corner, an idea floated to mind.

I followed them, staying hidden in the steam and shadows, observing how they worked. The workers didn't converse or speak to one another, being too caught up in their own work, which suited me fine. One broke off from the rest of the group, which paid him no attention as he wandered off into the steam. I trailed him down a hallway made of pipes, watching as he bent to check a hissing crack in the metal, and snuck up behind him.

Drawing Ash's sword, I waited until he turned around before stepping up and pressing the point of the blade against his chest. The worker jumped and scuttled backward, but the network of pipes trapped him between me and the exit. I stepped forward and angled the blade at his throat.

"Don't move," I snarled as fiercely as I could. He nodded and held up his gloved hands. My heart pounded, but I rushed on, poking at him with the blade. "Do exactly as I say and I won't kill you, all right? Take off your suit."

He obeyed, shedding his outer clothes and taking off the mask, revealing a sweaty little man with a thick black beard. A dwarf, and an ordinary-looking one at that; no steel skin, no cables coming out of his head, nothing to mark him as an iron fey. He glared at me with coal-black eyes, his arms rippling with muscle, and broke into a sneer.

"Come at last, have you?" He spat on the ground near a pipe, where it sizzled noisily. "We were all wondering what route you'd end up taking. Well, if you're going to kill me, girl, get it over with."

"I'm not here to kill anyone," I said carefully, keeping the sword trained on him as I'd seen Ash do. "I'm only here for my brother."

The dwarf snorted. "He's upstairs in the throne room with Machina. Top west tower. Good luck getting to him."

I narrowed my eyes. "You're being awfully helpful. Why should I believe you?"

"Bah, we don't care about Machina or your whiny brother, girl." The dwarf hawked and spat on a pipe, where it bubbled like acid. "Our job is to keep this place running, not play court with a bunch of snotty aristocrats. Machina's business is his own, and I'll ask you to keep me out of it."

"So, you're not going to stop me?"

"Do you have lead in your ears? I don't care what you do, girl! So kill me or leave me the hell alone, would you? I won't get in your way, if you don't get in mine."

"All right." I lowered the sword. "But I'll need your suit."

"Fine, take it." The dwarf kicked it toward me with a steel-toed boot. "We've got several. Now, can I get back to work, or do you have more inane demands to keep me from my job?"

I hesitated. I didn't want to hurt him, but I couldn't leave him running loose. No matter what he said, he could tell the other workers, and I was pretty sure I couldn't fight off all of them. I looked around and saw another trapdoor, like the one I'd come up from a few feet away.

I pointed at it with the sword. "Open that and get down there."

"Into the Cogworks?"

"Leave your boots. And your keys."

He glowered, and I raised my sword, ready to slash if he lunged at me. But the dwarf growled a curse, stalked over to the metal grate, and shoved a key into the lock. Pushing it open with a bang, he wrenched off his boots and stomped down the twisting staircase, making it ring with every step.

With the dwarf glaring up at me, I shut the door and locked it, ignoring the guilt that gnawed my insides.

I dressed in the dwarf's suit, which was hot and heavy and reeked of sweat. I gagged as I slipped it on. It was too short, but between the suit's bagginess and my skinny frame, I made it work. My calves stuck out of the pant legs, but I shoved my sneakers into the dwarf's boots and it wasn't so noticeable. At least, I hoped it wasn't. I heaved the tank onto my back, finding it surprisingly light, and put on the mask. Cool, sweet air hit my face, and I sighed in relief.

Now the only problem was the sword and the bow. I figured the workmen of the tower didn't stomp around with weapons, so I found a piece of canvas and wrapped them up in it, tucking it under my arm. The Witchwood arrow was still secured to my belt inside the suit.

Heart pounding, I returned to the boiler room, where the other dwarfs were shuffling out in a broken line. Taking a deep breath to calm my twisting stomach, I joined them, keeping my head down and not making eye contact. No one paid any attention to me, and I followed them up a long flight of stairs, until we reached the main tower.

Machina's fortress was huge, metallic, and sharp. Thorned creepers crawled over the ramparts, their barbs made of metal. Jagged shards jutted away from the walls for no apparent reason. Everything was harsh lines and sharp edges, even the fey that lived here. Besides the ever-present gremlins, I saw more armored knights, hounds made of clockwork, and creatures that looked like metallic praying mantises, their bladed arms and silvery antennae glinting in the dim light.

The dwarfs scattered as they left the staircase, breaking away in little groups of twos and threes. I drifted away from the rapidly diminishing crowd and followed the wall, trying to look as if I had a purpose. Gremlins scuttled along the walls, chasing one another and tormenting the other fey. Computer mice with tiny ears, feet, and blinking red eyes scurried away as I approached. Once, a gremlin landed on one, eliciting a high-pitched squeak, before stuffing the tiny creature into its mouth and crunching the sparks. It grinned at me, the mouse's tail hanging between its pointed teeth, and scuttled off again. Wrinkling my nose, I continued walking.

At last I discovered a staircase, spiraling up hundreds of feet along the tower walls. Gazing up at the infinite number of stairs, I felt a pull in my stomach. This was the one. Ethan was up there. And Machina.

I felt a pain in my heart, as if there was something...someone else I should remember. But the memory skipped away, out of reach. With my heart fluttering around my ribs like a crazed bat, I started the last leg of my journey.

There were small, narrow windows every twenty steps up the stairs. I peered out once and saw the open sky, with strange glittering birds soaring on the wind. At the top of the stairs stood an iron door, bearing the insignia of a barbed crown. I quickly shed the dwarf's clothing, relieved to be out of the bulky, smelly garments. Taking off the bow, I carefully fit the Witchwood arrow to the string. When the arrow was nocked, it began to throb even faster, as if its heartbeat raced in excitement.

And, standing at the last door in the Iron King's tower, I hesitated. Could I really do this, kill a living creature? I wasn't a warrior like Ash or a brilliant trickster like Puck. I wasn't smart like Grim, and I certainly didn't have the power of my father, Oberon. I was just me, Meghan Chase, an ordinary high school student. Nothing special.

No. The voice in my head was mine, and it wasn't. *You're more than that. You're the daughter of Oberon and Melissa Chase.*

You're the key to preventing a faery war. Friend of Puck; sister to Ethan; beloved of Ash: you are much more than you think. You have everything you need. All that is left is to step forward.

Step forward. I could do that. Taking a deep breath, I pushed the door open.

I stood at the entrance of an enormous garden, the door creaking as it swung away from me. The smooth iron walls surrounding me were topped with jagged spines, silhouetted black against the open sky. Trees lined a stony path, but they were all made of metal, their branches twisted and sharp. Birds watched me from the steel limbs. When they fluttered their wings, it sounded like knives scraping against one another.

In the center of the garden, where all the paths converged, a fountain stood. Made not of marble or plaster, but of different-size gearheads, turning sluggishly with the water's flow. I squinted and looked closer. On the bottom cog, lying on his back as the gear slowly spun him around, was a figure.

It was Ash.

I didn't scream his name. I didn't run to him, though every fiber in my body was telling me to do so. Forcing myself to be calm, I looked around the garden, wary of traps and sudden ambushes. But there weren't many places for attackers to hide; except for the metal trees and a few thorny vines, the garden seemed empty.

Only when I'd made sure I was alone did I sprint across the stony ground to the fountain.

Don't be dead. Please, don't be dead. My heart plummeted when I saw him. He'd been chained to the cog, wrapped in metal links, spinning round and round in an endless circle. One leg dangled over the edge; the other was folded beneath him. His shirt had been ripped to shreds, the skin a shocking contrast of pale flesh and vivid red claw marks. The flesh where the chains touched him was raw and crimson. He didn't appear to be breathing.

Hands trembling, I drew the sword. The first slash shattered most of the links, the second cracked the gearhead nearly in two. The chains slid away, and the cog squealed as it ground to a halt. I dropped the blade and pulled Ash off the fountain, his body limp and cold in my arms.

"Ash." I cradled him in my lap, beyond tears, beyond anything but an awful, yawning emptiness. "Ash, come on." I shook him a little. "Don't do this to me. Open your eyes. Wake up. Please…"

His body was limp, unresponsive. I bit my lip hard enough to taste blood, and buried my face in his neck. "I'm sorry," I whispered, and now I did start to cry. Tears ran from my closed eyelids and down his clammy skin. "I'm so sorry. I wish you hadn't come. I wish I never agreed to that stupid contract. This is my fault, all of it. Puck and the dryad and Grim, and now you—" It was getting hard to speak, my voice was so choked with tears. "I'm sorry," I murmured again, for lack of anything else to say. "Sorry, so sorry—"

Something fluttered under my cheek. Blinking, I pulled back and looked at his face. The skin was still pale, but I caught a flicker of movement beneath his eyelids. Heart pounding, I lowered my head and brushed a kiss to his mouth. His lips parted, and a broken sigh escaped him.

I breathed his name in relief. His eyes opened and flickered to mine, confused, as if he wasn't sure if he was dreaming or not. He moved his lips, but it was a few tries before anything came out.

"Meghan?"

"Yes," I whispered immediately. "I'm here."

His hand came up, fingers resting on my cheek, trailing down my skin. "I…dreamed you…would come," he murmured, before his eyes cleared a bit and his face darkened. "You shouldn't...be here," he gasped, digging his fingers into my arm. "This...a trap."

And then, I heard it—horrible, dark laughter, rising up from the wall behind us. The gears in the fountain shivered, then began to turn backward. With a loud clanking and grinding, the wall behind us sank into the ground, revealing another part of the garden. Metal trees lined the path to an enormous iron throne, spiking into the sky. A squadron of armored knights stood at the foot of the throne with weapons drawn, pointed at me. Another squad entered through the door and slammed it shut, trapping us between them.

Standing at the top of his throne, surveying us all with a look of grim satisfaction, was Machina, the Iron King.

24

MACHINA

The figure on the throne threw me a smile as sharp as razors. "Meghan Chase," he murmured, his scintillating voice echoing over the garden. "Welcome. I've been expecting you."

I gently laid Ash down, ignoring his protests, and stepped forward, shielding him behind me. My heart pounded. I didn't know what I expected the Iron King to look like, but it wasn't this. The figure on the throne stood tall and elegant, with flowing silver hair and the pointed ears of the fey nobility. He faintly resembled Oberon, refined and graceful, yet incredibly powerful. Unlike Oberon and the finery of the Summer Court, the Iron King wore a stark black coat that flapped in the wind. Energy crackled around him, like thunder with no sound, and I caught flashes of lightning in his slanted black eyes. His face was beautiful and arrogant, all sharp planes and angles; I felt I could cut myself on his cheek if I got too close. And yet, when he smiled, it lit up the whole room. A strange, silvery cloak lay across his shoulders, wriggling slightly as if it were alive.

I snatched the bow and arrow off the ground, bringing it

to bear on the Iron King. This might be the only chance I got. The Witchwood pulsed in my hands as I drew back the string, aiming the tip at Machina's chest. The knights shouted in alarm and started forward, but they were too late. I released the string with a yell of triumph, seeing it speed right on target, toward the heart of the Iron King.

And Machina's cloak came alive.

Silvery cables unraveled with lightning speed, springing from his shoulders and spine. They spread around Machina like a halo of metal wings, wickedly barbed on one end, needle points glinting in the light. They whipped forward to protect the Iron King, knocking the Witchwood away, sending it flying in another direction. I watched the arrow strike a metal tree and snap in two, fluttering to the ground in pieces. Someone screamed in rage and horror, and I realized it was me.

The guards rushed us, their swords raised, and I watched them come with a certain detachment. I was aware of Ash, trying to get to his feet to protect me, and knew it was too late. The arrow had failed, and we were about to die.

"Stop."

Machina's voice wasn't loud. He didn't scream or bellow the order, but every knight jerked to a halt as if pulled by invisible string. The Iron King floated down from his throne, the cables writhing slowly behind him like hungry snakes. His feet touched the floor, and he smiled at me, completely unconcerned with the fact that I had just tried to kill him.

"Leave," he told the knights without taking his eyes from me. Several of them jerked their heads up in surprise.

"My king?" stammered one, and I recognized his voice. Quintus, one of the knights who'd been with Ironhorse in the mines. I wondered if Tertius was here, too.

"The lady is uncomfortable with your presence," Machina went on, not looking away from me. "I do not wish her to be uncomfortable. Go. I will take care of her, and the Winter prince."

"But, sire—"

Machina didn't move. One of his cables whipped out, almost too fast to see, punching through the knight's armor and out his back. The cable lifted Quintus high in the air and threw him into the wall. Quintus clanged against the metal and slumped motionless to the ground, a jagged hole through his breastplate. Dark, oily blood pooled beneath him.

"Leave," Machina repeated softly, and the knights scrambled to obey. They filed out through the door and slammed it shut, and we were alone with the Iron King.

Machina regarded me with depthless black eyes. "You are as beautiful as I imagined," he said, walking forward, his cables coiling behind him. "Beautiful, fiery, determined." He stopped a few yards away, the cables settling back into that living cloak. "Perfect."

With a final glance at Ash, still slumped next to the fountain, I stepped forward. "I'm here for my brother," I said, relieved that my voice didn't tremble. "Please, let him go. Let me take him home."

Machina regarded me silently, then gestured behind him. A loud clanking began, and something rose out of the ground beside his throne, as if it was borne on an elevator. A large, wrought-iron birdcage came into view. Inside...

"Ethan!" I started forward, but Machina's cables whipped out, blocking my path. Ethan gripped the bars of the cage, peering out with frightened blue eyes. His voice rang shrilly over the courtyard.

"Meggie!"

Behind me, Ash growled a curse and tried to stand. I turned on Machina furiously. "Let him go! He's only a little kid! What do you want with him, anyway?"

"My dear, you misunderstand me." Machina's cables waved threateningly, moving me back. "I did not take your brother because I wanted him. I did it because I knew it would bring you here."

"Why?" I demanded, whirling on him. "Why kidnap Ethan? Why not just take me instead? Why drag him into all this?"

Machina smiled. "You were well protected, Meghan Chase. Robin Goodfellow is a formidable bodyguard, and I could not risk taking you without drawing attention to myself and my realm. Fortunately, your brother had no such protection. Better to draw you here, of your own volition, than risk the wrath of Oberon and the Seelie Court. Besides..." Machina's eyes narrowed to black slits, though he still smiled at me. "I needed to test you, make certain you were truly the one. If you could not reach my tower on your own, you were not worthy."

"Worthy of what?" Suddenly, I was very tired. Tired and desperate to save my brother, take him away from this madness before it consumed him. I couldn't win; Machina had us at checkmate, but I would get Ethan home, at least. "What do you want, Machina?" I asked wearily, feeling the Iron King step closer. "Whatever it is, just let me take Ethan back to our world. You said you wanted me. Here I am. But let me take my brother home."

"Of course," Machina soothed. "But first, let us make a deal."

I froze, everything going still inside me. A deal with the Iron King, in exchange for my brother's life. I wondered what he would ask for. Somehow, I knew it would cost me either way.

"Meghan, don't," Ash growled, pulling himself up by the fountain, ignoring the burns to his hands. Machina ignored him.

"What kind of deal?" I asked softly.

The Iron King stepped closer. His cables caressed my face and arms, making me shiver. "I have watched you," he murmured, "waiting for the day you would finally open your eyes and see us. Waiting for the day you would come to me. Your father would have blinded you to this world forever. He is afraid of your power, afraid of your potential—a half-fey who is immune to iron, yet has the blood of the Summer King in her veins. *So* much potential." His gaze lingered on Ash, finally on his feet, and dismissed him just as quickly. "Mab realized your power, which is why she wants you so much. Which is why she sent her best to capture you. But even she cannot offer what I can."

Machina closed the last few steps between us and took my hand. His touch was cool, and I felt power humming through him, like currents of electricity. "I want you to be my queen, Meghan Chase. I offer you my kingdom, my subjects, myself. I want you to rule at my side. The oldbloods are obsolete. Their time is done. It is time for a new order to rise up, stronger and better than the ancient ones. Only say yes, and you will live forever, Queen of the Fey. Your brother can go home. I'll even let you keep your prince if you wish, though I fear he may not adapt well to our kingdom. Regardless, you belong here, at my side. Isn't that what you've always wanted? To belong?"

I hesitated. To rule with Machina, to become a queen. No one would tease or mock me anymore, I would have scores of creatures ready to jump at my bidding, and I would finally be the one on top. I would finally be the most loved. But then I saw the trees, twisted and metallic, and remembered the terrible, barren wasteland in the wyldwood. Machina would corrupt the entire Nevernever. All the plants would die, or become twisted versions of themselves. Oberon, Grimalkin,

Puck: they would fade away with the rest of the Nevernever, until only gremlins, bugs, and the iron fey remained.

I swallowed. And, even though I already knew the answer, I asked, "What if I refuse?"

Machina's expression didn't falter. "Then your prince will die. And your brother will die. Or, perhaps, I will make him one of my playthings, half human, half machine. The eradication of the oldbloods will begin with or without you, Meghan Chase. I am giving you the choice of leading it or being consumed by it."

My desperation grew. Machina reached up and stroked my face, running his fingers down my cheek. "Is it really so terrible to rule, my love?" he asked, tilting my chin up to look at him. "Throughout millennia, both humans and fey have done it. Weeded out the weak to make room for the strong. The oldbloods and the iron fey cannot exist together, you know this. Oberon and Mab would destroy us if they knew about us. How is that any different?" He brushed a kiss over my lips, featherlight and vibrating with energy. "Come. One word, that is all you have to say. One word to send your brother home, to save the prince that you love. Look." He waved a hand, and a great iron archway rose out of the ground. On the other side, I could see my house, shimmering through the portal, before it faded from view. I gasped, and Machina smiled. "I will send him home now, if you only say yes. One word, and you will be my queen, forever."

I took a breath. "I—"

And Ash was there. How he could even stand, let alone move, was a mystery. But he shoved me aside, his face feral, as Machina's eyebrows rose in surprise. The cables flared, stabbing toward Ash as the prince lunged forward and slammed his blade into Machina's chest.

Machina staggered back, his face contorted with agony.

Lightning crackled around the blade in his chest. His cables thrashed wildly, striking Ash and hurling him into a metal tree with a sickening crunch. Ash collapsed against the trunk as Machina straightened, giving him a look of white rage.

Reaching down, the Iron King grasped the hilt and pulled, sliding the blade out of his chest. Lightning sizzled, melting the ice around the hole, and thin wires wove themselves around the wound, knitting it together. Machina tossed the sword away and looked at me, his black eyes sparking with fury.

"I am losing patience with you, my dear." One of his cables shot forward, coiling around Ash's throat and lifting him off his feet. Ash choked and struggled weakly as Machina dangled him several feet overhead. Ethan wailed in his cage. "Rule with me, or let them die. Make your choice."

I sank to my knees as my legs buckled, trembling. The stone floor was cold against my palms. *What can I do?* I thought desperately. *How can I choose? Either way, people will die. I can't allow that. I won't.*

The ground pulsed under my hands. I closed my eyes and let my consciousness flow into the earth, searching for that spark of life. I felt the trees in Machina's court, their branches lifeless and dead, but their roots and hearts uncorrupted. *Just like last time.* I gave them a nudge and felt them respond, writhing to meet me, pushing up through the dirt, like the trees of the Summer Court had for Oberon with the chimera.

Like father, like daughter.

I took a deep breath, and *pulled.*

The ground rumbled, and suddenly, live roots broke through the surface, pushing up through the pavement, snapping and coiling about. Machina gave a shout of alarm, and the roots flew to meet him, wrapping around his body, entangling the cables. He roared and lashed out, lightning streaking from his hands, blasting away the wood. Roots and iron cables twined around one another like maddened snakes, swirling in a hypnotic dance of fury.

Ash dropped from the cables, hitting the ground by a metal tree, winded and dazed but still trying to get to his feet, staggering after his weapon. I saw a strip of pale wood beneath the trunk—one half of the snapped Witchwood arrow—and lunged after it.

A cable wrapped around my leg, jerking me off my feet. I twisted around to see Machina glaring at me, his arm outstretched as he fought the web of roots. The cable tightened around my leg and dragged me toward him. I screamed and clawed at the ground, tearing my nails and bloodying my fingers, but I couldn't stop. The furious face of the Iron King loomed closer.

Ash's blade slashed down once more, cutting into the cable, severing it. More cables whipped toward him, but the Winter prince stood his ground, sword flashing as iron tentacles writhed around us.

"Go," he snarled, slashing the end of a cable out of the air. "I'll hold them back. Go!"

I leaped to my feet, rushing for the trunk and the arrow beneath. My hand closed over the wood and I spun back, only to see a cable slice through Ash's defenses and slam into his shoulder, staking him to the ground. Ash howled, swinging his sword weakly, but another cable knocked it from his grasp.

I charged the Iron King, dodging cables and snaking roots. For a moment, his attention was riveted on Ash, but then his gaze snapped to me, lightning flashing in the depths of his eyes. Shrieking a battle cry, I lunged.

Just as I reached him, something slammed into my back, driving the breath from me. I couldn't move, and realized that one of the cables had stabbed me from behind. Strangely, there was no pain.

Machina drew me to him as roots and cables waged their war overhead. Everything else faded away, and there was just us.

"I would have made you a queen," he muttered, reaching a hand to me. The roots circling his torso, pinning his other arm, tightened around him, but he didn't seem to notice. "I would have given you everything. Why reject such an offer?"

My hand tightened on the Witchwood, feeling a faint beat of life still within. "Because," I whispered, raising my arm, "I already have everything I need."

I drove my arm forward, sinking the arrow into his chest.

Machina's lips gaped in a soundless scream. He arched his head back, still screaming, and green shoots erupted from his mouth, spreading down his neck. A strange pulse of energy, like an electrical jolt, coursed through my body, making my muscles spasm. The cable flung me away; I hit the ground and bit back a shriek as pain lanced up my spine. Clawing myself upright, I looked around, grabbed the sword, and rushed to Ethan's cage. One stroke of the ice blade smashed the door open, and I hugged my brother to me, feeling him sob into my hair.

"Meghan!" Ash staggered toward me, holding his shoulder, dark blood streaming down his skin. Behind him, the door burst open, and dozens of knights poured inside. For a moment, they froze in shock, staring at their king in the center of the garden.

Machina still writhed in his prison, but weakly. Branches grew from his chest, his cables turning into vines that bloomed with tiny white flowers. As we watched, he split apart, as the trunk of a brand-new oak burst from his chest, rising into the air. Branches rushed skyward as the tree unfurled, spreading its canopy over everything, until only a giant oak stood where the Iron King had been, shivering in the breeze.

"Wow," I whispered into the silence.

The knights turned on us with a roar. They rushed forward, but suddenly, the ground trembled. Rumblings filled the air as the iron throne began to collapse, shedding jagged shrapnel like scales. A tremor shook the ground, causing everyone to stagger.

Then, a huge chunk of the garden cracked and fell away, taking several knights with it into oblivion. More cracks appeared as the courtyard began to come apart. The knights howled and scattered, and screams rose into the air.

"The whole tower's coming down!" Ash yelled, dodging a falling beam. "We have to get out of here, now!"

I ran to the iron archway, stumbling as more cracks slashed across the ground, and ducked through, only to reappear on the other side. Nothing happened. Despair rose up, and I gazed around wildly.

"Human," said a familiar voice, and Grimalkin appeared, twitching his tail. I gaped at him, hardly believing my eyes. "This way. Hurry."

"I thought you weren't coming," I gasped, following him across the garden to where two metal trees grew together, the trunks forming an archway between them. Grimalkin looked back at me and snorted.

"Trust you to take the hardest route possible," he said, lashing his tail. "If you had only listened to me, I would have shown you an easier way. Now, hurry. This air is making me sick."

A deafening roar shook the ground, and the garden crumbled away altogether. Clutching Ethan tightly, I dived between the trunks, Ash right on my heels. I felt the tingle of magic as we passed through the barrier, and realized I was falling, before everything went completely black.

I awoke slowly, a hard tile floor cold against my cheek. Wincing, I sat up, testing my body for any lingering pain. I was vaguely aware that there should be some; I remembered Machina stabbing me through the back with his iron cables, felt the blaze of agony as he ripped them from my flesh—but there was no pain. In fact, I felt better than I had in a long time, my senses buzzing with energy as I gazed around. I lay in a long, dim room filled with desks and computers. The school computer lab!

With a jerk, I sat up and looked around for my brother, wondering, for one heart-stopping instant, if everything had been a horrible dream. A moment later, I relaxed. Ethan lay under a nearby desk, his face peaceful, his breath slow and deep. I brushed a stray curl from his forehead and smiled, then got to my feet.

Ash was nowhere to be seen, but Grimalkin lay on a desk beneath a dingy window, purring in the sunlight coming through the glass. Careful not to disturb Ethan, I rose and joined him.

"There you are." The cat yawned, cracking open one golden eye to stare at me. "I was beginning to think you would sleep forever. You snore, you know."

I ignored that comment, hopping up on the desk beside him. "Where's Ash?"

"Gone." Grimalkin sat up and stretched, wrapping his tail around himself. "He took off earlier, before you woke up. He said he had some things to take care of. Told me to tell you not to wait for him."

"Oh." I let that sink in, not knowing what to feel. I could've been upset, angry, resentful that he left so suddenly, but all I felt was tired. And a little sad. "He was hurt pretty bad, Grim. Will he be all right?"

Grimalkin yawned, obviously unconcerned. I wasn't re-assured, but Ash was strong: strong enough to make it all the way to the heart of the Iron Kingdom and back. A lesser faery would've died. He almost did die. Had he been draw-ing glamour from me, in that desolate place? Or was it some-thing else that enabled him to survive? I wondered if I'd ever get the chance to ask him.

After a moment, I turned to gaze around the room, mar-veling that the trod to the Iron Kingdom had been so close. Did one of the computers hide the path to Machina's realm? Had we come flying out of a monitor, or had we just blipped into existence, like the gremlins?

"So." I turned back to the cat. "You found us the path home. Congratulations. What do I owe you for this one? An-other favor or life debt? My firstborn child?"

"No." Grimalkin's eyes slitted in amusement. "We will let this one go. This once."

We sat in silence for a bit, enjoying the sunlight, content just to be alive. Still, as I watched Ethan, sleeping under the desk, a strange heaviness filled me, as if I was missing something. As if I'd forgotten something vitally important, back in Faery.

"So," Grimalkin mused, licking his front paw, "what will you do now?"

I shrugged. "I don't know. Take Ethan home, I guess. Go back to school. Try to get on with my life." I thought of Puck, and a lump rose to my throat. School wouldn't be the same without him. I hoped he was all right, and that I would see him again. I thought of Ash, and wondered if the prince of the Unseelie Court would consent to dinner and a movie. I almost laughed at the ridiculousness of the idea.

"Hope springs eternal," the cat muttered.

"Yeah." I sighed, and we fell silent again.

"What I have been wondering," Grimalkin went on, "is how Machina kidnapped your brother in the first place. He used a changeling, yes, but that wasn't an iron faery. How did he make the switch, if it was not one of his own?"

I thought about it and frowned. "Somebody must've helped him," I guessed.

Grimalkin nodded. "I would imagine so. Which means Machina had normal fey working for him as well, and now that he is gone, they will be none too happy with you."

I shivered, feeling hope for a normal life slipping rapidly away. I imagined knives on the floor, my hair tied to the bedpost, missing items, and irate faeries lurking in my closet or under my bed, ready to pounce. I'd never be able to sleep again, that much was certain. I wondered how I would protect my family.

A groan came from the sleeping form in the corner. Ethan was waking up.

"Go on, then," Grimalkin purred as I rose. "Take him home."

I wanted to say thank-you, but there was no way I was

putting myself even more in the cat's debt. Instead, I went to gather Ethan, and we started across the room, weaving around desks and dark, silent computers. At the door, which was thankfully unlocked, I looked back to the window and the shaft of sunlight, but Grimalkin was no longer there.

The school halls were empty and dark. Puzzled, I made my way down the dingy corridors, clutching Ethan's hand and wondering where everyone was. Perhaps it was the weekend, but that didn't explain the dusty floors and lockers, the feeling of complete emptiness as we passed one locked classroom after another. Even on Saturdays, there would be at least one extracurricular class going on. It felt like the school had been empty for weeks.

The front doors were closed and locked, so I had to open a window. After hoisting Ethan up, I wiggled out after him, dropping to the pavement and gazing around. No cars stood in the parking lot, even though it was the middle of the day. The place looked completely deserted.

Ethan gazed around in silence, round blue eyes taking everything in. There was a wariness to him that seemed terribly out of place, like he was older now but his body remained the same. It worried me, and I gently squeezed his hand.

"We'll be home soon, okay?" I whispered as we started across the parking lot. "Just one short bus ride, and you can see Mom again, and Luke. Are you excited?"

He regarded me solemnly and nodded once. He didn't smile.

We left the school campus, following the sidewalk until we reached the nearest bus stop. Around us, cars sped by, weaving in and out of late-afternoon traffic, and people milled around us. Some older ladies smiled and waved to Ethan, but he paid them no attention. My concern for him knotted my stomach. I tried cheering him up, asking questions, telling him little stories about my adventures, but he just stared at me with those mournful blue eyes and didn't say a word.

So we stood on the corner, waiting for the bus to come, watching the people surge around us. I saw faeries, slipping through the crowds, entering the little shops lining the street, following humans like stalking wolves. A fey boy with leathery black wings grinned and waved to Ethan from an alley across the street. Ethan shivered, and his fingers tightened on mine.

"Meghan?"

I turned at the sound of my name. A girl had come out of the coffee shop behind us, and was staring at me in amazement and disbelief. I frowned, shifting uncomfortably. She looked familiar, with her long dark hair and cheerleader-thin waist, but I couldn't remember where I knew her from. Was she a classmate? If so, I think I would have recognized her. She would have been very pretty, if it wasn't for the huge, distorted nose marring her otherwise perfect face.

And then it hit me.

"Angie," I whispered, feeling the shock punch me in the stomach. I remembered then: the cheerleader's mocking laughter, Puck muttering something under his breath, Angie's horrified screams. Her nose was flat and shiny, with two large nostrils that looked very much like a pig's. Was this faery vengeance? An awful sense of guilt gnawed at my insides, and I tore my gaze from her face. "What do you want?"

"Oh my God, it *is* you!" Angie gaped at me, nostrils flaring. I saw Ethan staring unabashed at her nose. "Everyone thought you were dead! There have been police and detectives looking for you. They said you ran away. Where have you been?"

I blinked at her. This was new. Angie had never spoken to me before, except to mock me in front of her friends. "I...

How long have I been gone?" I stammered, not knowing what else to say.

"More than three months now," she replied, and I stared at her. *Three months?* My trek to the Nevernever hadn't taken that long, had it? A week or two, at most. But I remembered how my watch stopped while in the wyldwood, and a sick feeling rose to my stomach. Time flowed differently in Faery. No wonder the school was locked and empty; it was summer vacation by now. I really had been gone three months.

Angie was still staring at me curiously, and I floundered for a reply that wouldn't sound insane. Before I could think of anything, a trio of blondes heading for the coffee shop stopped and gaped at us.

"Oh my God!" one of them screeched. "It's the swamp girl! She's back!" Shrill laughter rang out, echoing over the sidewalk, causing several people to stop and stare. "Hey, we heard you got knocked up and your folks shipped you off to some military school. Is that true?"

"Oh my God!" one of her friends yelled, pointing to Ethan. "Look at that! She's already had her kid!" They collapsed into hysterical giggles, shooting me subtle looks to see my reaction. I gazed at them calmly and smiled. *Sorry to disappoint you,* I thought, seeing their brows knit with confusion. *But after facing homicidal goblins, redcaps, gremlins, knights, and evil faeries, you just aren't that scary anymore.*

But then, to my surprise, Angie scowled and took a step forward. "Knock it off," she snapped, as I recognized the blond trio from her old cheerleading squad. "She just got back to town. Give her a break already."

They shot her evil glares. "I'm sorry, Pigface, were you talking to us?" one asked sweetly. "I don't believe I was speaking to you at all. Why don't you go home with the little swamp bitch? I'm sure she can find a place for you on the farm."

"She can't understand you," another piped up. "You have to speak her language. Like this." She broke into a chorus of oinks and squeals, and the other two took up the cry. The street echoed with high-pitched grunts, and Angie's face flushed crimson.

I stood there, stunned. It was so weird, seeing the most popular girl in school standing in my shoes. I should've been happy; the perfect cheerleader was finally getting a taste of her own medicine. But my instincts also said this treatment wasn't new. It started the day Puck had pulled his cruel joke, and all I felt was empathy. If he were here, I would twist his arm until he changed her back.

If he were here…

I quickly pushed those thoughts away. If I kept thinking about him, I would start to cry, and that was the *last* thing I wanted to do in front of the cheerleaders. For a second, I thought Angie herself would burst into tears and flee. But, after a moment, she took a deep breath and turned to me, rolling her eyes.

"Let's get out of here," she whispered, jerking her head toward a nearby parking lot. "Have you been home yet? I can drive you, if you want."

"Um…" Shocked again, I glanced down at Ethan. He gazed up at me, his face wan and tired. Despite my hesitation, I wanted to get him home as soon as possible. Though I still had my doubts, Angie certainly seemed different now. Briefly, I wondered if it was great adversity that made a person stronger. "Sure."

She asked a lot of questions on the drive home: where I had been, what made me leave, was it really a pregnancy that drove me off. I answered as vaguely as I could, leaving out the parts with the homicidal faeries, of course. Ethan curled up beside me and fell asleep, and soon his faint snores were the only sounds besides the hum of the engine.

Angie finally pulled up alongside a familiar gravel road, and my stomach twisted nervously as I opened the door, pulling Ethan out with me. The sun had gone down, and an owl hooted somewhere overhead. In the distance, a porch light glimmered like a beacon in the twilight.

"I appreciate the ride," I told Angie, slamming the car door. She nodded, and I made myself say those two little words. "Thank you." Guilt stabbed me again as I looked at her face. "I'm sorry about…you know."

She shrugged. "Don't worry about it. I'm going to a plastic surgeon in a couple weeks. He should take care of it." She went to put the car in gear, but stopped, turning back to me. "You know," she said, frowning, "I don't even remember how it got like this. Sometimes, I think I've always been this way, you know? But then, people look at me weird, like they can't figure it out. Like they're scared, because I'm so different." She blinked at me, shadows under her eyes. Her nose seemed to leap off her face. "But you know what that's like, don't you?"

I nodded breathlessly. Angie blinked again, like she was seeing me for the first time. "Well, then…" Slightly embarrassed, she waved to Ethan and gave me a brisk nod. "See you around."

"Bye." I watched her pull away, her taillights growing smaller and smaller, until they rounded a corner and disappeared. The night suddenly seemed dark and still.

Ethan took my hand, and I looked down at him in concern. He still wasn't talking. My brother had always been a quiet kid, but this complete, brooding silence was disturbing. I hoped he wasn't too traumatized by his ordeal.

"Home, kiddo." I sighed, looking up the long, long driveway. "Think you can make it?"

"Meggie?"

Relieved, I looked down at him. "Yeah?"

"Are you one of Them now?"

I sucked in a breath, feeling as if he had punched me. "What?"

"You look different." Ethan fingered his ear, gazing up at mine. "Like the bad king. Like one of Them." He sniffled. "Are you going to live with Them now?"

"Of course not. I don't belong with Them." I squeezed his hand. "I'll live with you and Mom and Luke, just like always."

"The dark person talked to me. He said I'd forget about Them in a year or two, that I won't be able to see Them anymore. Does that mean I'll forget you, too?"

I knelt and looked him in the eye. "I don't know, Ethan. But, you know what? It doesn't matter. Whatever happens, we're still a family, right?"

He nodded solemnly, far too old for his age. Together, we continued walking.

The outline of our house grew larger as we approached. It looked familiar and strange all at once. I could see Luke's beat-up truck in the driveway, and Mom's floral curtains waving in the windows. My bedroom was dark and still, but a night-light shone out of Ethan's room, flickering orange. It made my stomach churn, to think what slept up there. A single light shone in the bottom window, and I picked up my pace.

Mom was asleep on the couch when I opened the door. The television was on, and she held a box of tissues in her lap, one twisted up in her fingers. She stirred when I shut the door behind me, but before I could say anything, Ethan wailed, "Mommy!" and flung himself into her lap.

"What?" Mom jerked awake, startled by the shaking child

in her arms. "Ethan? What are you doing downstairs? Did you have a nightmare?"

She glanced up at me then, and her face went pale. I tried for a smile, but my lips wouldn't work right, and the lump in my throat made it hard to speak. She rose, still holding on to Ethan, and we fell into each other. I sobbed into her neck, and she held me tightly, her own tears staining my cheek.

"Meghan." At last, she pulled back and looked at me, a spark of anger warring with the relief in her eyes. "Where have you been?" she demanded with a little shake. "We've had the police looking for you, detectives, the whole town. No one could find any trace of you, and I've been worried sick. Where have you *been* for three months?"

"Where's Luke?" I asked, not really knowing why. Maybe I felt that he didn't need to hear this, that this was between me and Mom alone. I wondered if Luke had even noticed that I was gone. Mom frowned, as if she knew what I was thinking.

"He's upstairs, asleep," she replied, pulling back. "I should wake him up, tell him you've come home. Every night for the past three months, he's taken his truck down the back roads, looking for you. Sometimes he doesn't come home until morning."

Stunned, I blinked back tears. Mom gave me a stern look, the one I got right before I was grounded. "You wait right here until I get him, and then, young lady, you can tell us where you've been while we've been going crazy. Ethan, honey, let's put you to bed."

"Wait," I said as she turned away, Ethan still clinging to her robe. "I'll come with you. Ethan, too. I think everyone should hear this."

She hesitated, looking down at Ethan, but finally nodded. We turned to leave together, when a noise on the stairs froze us in our tracks.

The changeling stood there, his eyes narrowed, his lips peeled back in a snarl. He wore Ethan's bunny pajamas, and his small fists were clenched in rage. The real Ethan whimpered and pressed into Mom's side, hiding his face. Mom gasped, her hand going to her mouth, as the changeling hissed at me.

"Damn you!" it shrieked, stamping a foot into the ground. "Stupid, stupid girl! Why'd you have to bring him back? I hate you! I hate you! I—"

Smoke erupted from its feet, and the changeling wailed. Twisting in on itself, it disappeared into the smoke, shouting curses as it grew smaller and smaller, and finally vanished altogether.

I allowed myself a small smirk of triumph.

Mom lowered her hand. When she turned to me again, I saw understanding in her eyes, and a terrible, terrible fear. "I see," she whispered, glancing at Ethan. She trembled, and her face was ashen. She knew. She knew all about Them.

I stared at her. Questions rose to mind, too jumbled and tangled to make out. Mom seemed different now, frail and frightened, not the mother I knew at all. "Why didn't you tell me?" I whispered.

Mom sat on the couch, pulling Ethan up with her. He snuggled into her side like he was never going to let go. "Meghan, I... That was years ago, when I met...him...your father. I barely remember it—it seemed more like a dream than anything." She didn't look at me as she spoke, lost in her own world. I perched on the edge of the armchair as she continued in a faint voice.

"For months, I convinced myself that it hadn't happened. It didn't seem real, what we did, the things he showed me. It was just one time, and I never saw him again. When I discovered I was pregnant, I was a little nervous, but Paul was so happy. The doctors had told us we would never have children."

Paul. My mind stirred uneasily at that name. It felt like I should recognize it. Then Mom's words sank in and it hit me: Paul had been my father, or at least married to my mom. I didn't remember him, not in the slightest. I had no idea who he was, what he looked like. He must've died when I was very young.

The thought made me sad, and angry. Here was another father that Mom had tried to hide from me.

"Then you were born," Mom continued, still in that distant, faraway voice, "and strange things started happening. I'd often find you out of your crib, on the floor or even outside, though you couldn't walk yet. Doors would open and close on their own. Items went missing, only to show up in the oddest places. Paul thought the house was haunted, but I knew *They* were lurking about. I could feel Them, even though I couldn't see Them. It terrified me. I was afraid They were after you, and I couldn't even tell my husband what was going on.

"We decided to move, and for a while, things were normal. You grew into an ordinary, happy child, and I thought everything was behind us. Then..." Mom's voice trembled, and tears filled her eyes. "Then there was that incident in the park, and I knew They had found us again. Afterward, after everything had died down, we came here, and I met Luke. You know the rest."

I frowned. I remembered the park, with its tall trees and little green pond, but I couldn't recall what "incident" Mom was talking about. Before I could ask, Mom leaned forward and gripped my hand.

"I wanted to tell you for so long," she whispered, her eyes wide and teary. "But I was afraid. Not that you wouldn't believe me, but that you *would*. I wanted you to have a normal life, not to live in fear of Them, to wake up every morning dreading that They had found you."

"Didn't really work, did it?" My voice came out hoarse and

raspy. Anger simmered, and I glared at her. "Not only did *They* come for me, but Ethan got pulled in, as well. What are we going to do now, Mom? Run away, just like the last two times? You saw how well that worked."

She leaned back, hugging Ethan protectively. "I... I don't know," she stammered, wiping her eyes, and I immediately felt guilty. Mom had gone through the same things I had. "We'll think of something. Right now, I'm just glad you're safe. Both of you."

She gave me a tentative smile, and I returned it, though I knew this wasn't over. We couldn't stick our heads in the sand and pretend the fey weren't out there. Machina might be gone, but the Iron Kingdom would continue to grow, poisoning the Nevernever, little by little. There was no way to stop progress or technology. Somehow, I knew we couldn't escape them. Running away just didn't work—they were too stubborn and persistent. They could hold a grudge forever. Sooner or later, we would have to face the fey once more.

Of course, sooner came more quickly than I expected.

"Ethan," Mom said after a while, once the adrenaline had worn off and the house was still, "why don't you run upstairs and wake Daddy? He'll want to know that Meghan is home. Then you can sleep between us if you want."

Ethan nodded, but at that moment, the front door creaked open, and a cold breeze shivered across the room. The moonlight beyond the door shimmered, consolidating into something solid and real.

Ash stepped over the threshold.

Mom didn't look up, but Ethan and I jumped as my heart began to thud loudly in my chest. Ash looked different now, the cuts and burns healed, his hair falling softly around his face. He wore simple dark pants and a white shirt, and his sword hung at his side. Still dangerous. Still inhuman and deadly. Still the most beautiful being I'd ever seen. His mercury eyes found mine, and he inclined his head.

"It's time," he murmured.

For a moment, I stared at him, not understanding. Then it hit me all at once. *Oh, God. The contract. He's here to take me to the Winter Court.*

"Meghan?" Mom looked from me to the door, not seeing the Winter prince silhouetted against the frame. But her face was tight; she knew *something* was there. "What's happening? Who's there?"

I can't go now, I raged silently. *I just got home! I want to be normal; I want to go to school and learn to drive and go to prom next year. I want to forget faeries ever existed.*

But I gave my word. And Ash had upheld his end of the bargain, though he almost died for it.

Ash waited quietly, his eyes never leaving mine. I nodded at him and turned back to my family.

"Mom," I whispered, sitting on the couch, "I... I have to go. I made a promise to someone that I would stay with Them for a while. Please don't worry or be sad. I'll be back, I swear. But this is something I gotta do, or else They might come looking for you or Ethan again."

"Meghan, no." Mom gripped my hand, squeezing hard. "We can do something. There has to be a way to...keep Them back. We can move again, all of us. We—"

"Mom." And I let my glamour fade away, revealing my true self to her. It wasn't difficult this time, to manipulate the glamour surrounding me. Like the roots in Machina's domain, it came so naturally I wondered how I ever thought it hard. Mom's eyes widened, and she jerked her hand back, pulling Ethan close. "I'm one of Them now," I whispered. "I can't run from this. You should know that. I have to go."

Mom didn't answer. She kept staring at me with a mix of sorrow, guilt, and horror. I sighed and rose to my feet, letting the glamour settle on me again. It felt like the weight of the entire world.

"Ready?" Ash murmured, and I paused, glancing up toward my room. Did I want to take anything with me? I had my clothes, my music, little personal items collected in my sixteen years.

No. I didn't need them. That person was gone, if she had been real in the first place. I needed to figure out who I really was, before I came back. If I came back. Glancing at Mom, still frozen on the couch, I wondered if this would ever be home again.

"Meggie?" Ethan slid off the couch and padded up to me. I knelt, and he hugged me around the neck with all the strength a four-year-old could muster.

"I won't forget," he whispered, and I swallowed the lump in my throat. Standing up, I ruffled his hair and turned to Ash, still waiting silently at the door.

"You have everything?" he asked as I approached. I nodded.

"Everything I need," I murmured back. "Let's go."

He bowed, not to me, but to Mom and Ethan, and walked out. Ethan sniffled loudly and waved, trying hard not to cry. And I smiled, seeing their emotions as clearly as a beautiful painting: blue sorrow, emerald hope, scarlet love. We were connected, all of us. Nothing, fey, god, or immortal, could sever that.

I waved to Ethan, nodded forgiveness at Mom, and shut the door, following Ash into the silver moonlight.

★ ★ ★ ★ ★

ACKNOWLEDGMENTS

The road to publication is a long and arduous one, and I have many people to thank for seeing me through to the end. My parents, for encouraging me to go for my dreams instead of getting a real job. My sister, Kimiko, and my brother-in law, Mike, for their willingness to read those horrible first drafts. My mentor, Julianne Lee, and the wonderful authors, teachers, and students at Green River Writers of Louisville, KY. My fabulous agent, Laurie McLean, for giving me a chance, and my editor, Natashya Wilson, for making the dream happen. My writing group, for all the weekends we've spent together, bleeding on one another's manuscripts, shredding one another's characters, and beating dead horses.

But mostly, I want to thank my amazing husband, Nick, who has been my writing partner, cheerleader, editor, sounding board, proofreader, voice of reason, and always willing to talk story, plot, and character whenever I got myself stuck. I couldn't have done it without him.

KEEPING PROMISES

In the shadows of the cave, I watched the Hunter approach. Silhouetted black against the snow, it stalked closer, eyes a yellow flame in the shadows, breath coiling around it like wraiths. Ice-blue light glinted off wet teeth and a thick shaggy pelt, darker than midnight. Ash stood between the Hunter and me, sword unsheathed, his eyes never leaving the massive creature that had tracked us for days, and now, had finally caught up.

"Meghan Chase." Its voice was a growl, deeper than thunder, more primitive than the wildest forests. The ancient golden eyes were fixed solely on me. "I've finally found you."

My name is Meghan Chase.

If there are three things I've learned in my time among the fey, they are this: don't eat anything you're offered in Faeryland, don't go swimming in quiet little ponds and never, ever, make a bargain with anyone.

Okay, sometimes, you have no choice. Sometimes, you've been backed into a corner and you have to make a deal. Like when your little brother has been kidnapped, and you have to convince a prince of the Unseelie Court to help you rescue him instead of dragging you back to his queen. Or, you're lost, and you have to bribe a smart-mouthed, talking cat to guide you through the forest. Or you need to get through a certain door, but the gatekeeper won't let you through without a price. The fey love their bargains, and you have to listen to the terms *very* carefully, or you're going to get screwed. If you do end up in a contract with a faery, remember this: there's no way you can back out, not without disastrous consequences. And faeries *always* come to collect.

Which is how, forty-eight hours ago, I found myself walking across my front yard in the middle of the night, my house growing smaller and smaller in the background.

I didn't look back. If I looked back, I might lose my nerve. At the edge of the woods, a dark prince and a pair of glowing, blue-eyed steeds waited for me.

Prince Ash, third son of the Winter Court, regarded me gravely as I approached, his silver eyes reflecting the light of the moon. Tall and pale, with raven-black hair and the unattainable elegance of the fey, he looked both beautiful and dangerous, and my heart beat faster in anticipation or fear, I couldn't tell. As I stepped into the shadows of the trees, Ash held out a pale, long-fingered hand, and I placed my own in his.

His fingers curled over mine, and he drew me close, hands resting lightly on my waist. I lay my head against his chest and closed my eyes, listening to his beating heart, breathing in the frosty scent of him.

"You have to do this, don't you?" I whispered, my fingers clutched in the fabric of his white shirt. Ash made a soft noise that might've been a sigh.

"Yes." His voice, low and deep, was barely above a murmur.

I pulled back to look at him, seeing myself reflected in those silver eyes. When I'd first met him, those eyes were blank and cold, like the face of a mirror. Ash had been the enemy, once. He was the youngest son of Mab, queen of Winter and the ancient rival of my father, Oberon, the king of the Summer Court. That's right. I'm half-fey—a faery princess, no less—and I didn't even know it until recently, when my human brother was kidnapped by faeries and taken into the Nevernever. When I found out, I convinced my best friend, Robbie Goodfell—who turned out to be Oberon's servant, Puck—to take me into Faeryland to get him back. But being a faery princess in the Nevernever proved to be extremely dangerous. For one, the Winter Queen sent Ash to capture me, to use me as leverage against Oberon.

That's when I made the bargain with the Winter prince that would change my life: help me rescue Ethan, and I'll go with you to the Winter Court.

So, here I was. Ethan was home safe. Ash had kept his side of the bargain. It was my turn to uphold my end and travel with him to the court of my father's ancient enemies. There was only one problem.

Summer and Winter were not supposed to fall in love.

I held his gaze, watching his expression. Though I had once viewed it as frozen solid, his demeanor had thawed somewhat during our time in the Nevernever. Now, looking at him, I imagined a glassy lake: still and calm, but only on the surface.

"How long will I have to stay there?" I asked.

He shook his head slowly, and I could feel his reluctance. "I don't know, Meghan. The queen doesn't disclose her plans to me. I didn't dare ask why she wanted you." He reached up and caught a strand of my pale blond hair, running it through his fingers. "I was only supposed to bring you back," he murmured, and his voice dropped even lower. "I swore I would bring you back."

I nodded. Once a faery promises something, he's obligated to carry it through, which is why making a deal is so tricky. Ash couldn't break his vow even if he wanted to.

I understood that, but... "I want to do something before we go," I said, watching for his reaction. Ash raised an eyebrow, but otherwise his expression stayed the same. I took a deep breath. "I want to see Puck."

The Winter prince sighed. "I suppose you would," he muttered, releasing me and stepping back, his expression thoughtful. "And, truth be told, I'm curious myself. I wouldn't want Goodfellow dying before we ever resolved our duel. That would be unfortunate."

I winced. Puck and Ash were ancient enemies and had already engaged each other in several vicious, life-threatening duels before I was even in the picture. Ash had sworn to kill Puck, and Puck took great pleasure in goading the dangerous ice prince whenever he had the chance. It was only because I'd insisted they cooperate that they had agreed to an extremely shaky truce. One that wouldn't last long, no matter how much I intervened.

One of the horses snorted and pawed the ground, and Ash turned to put a hand on its neck. "All right, we'll check on him," he said without turning around. "But, after that, I *have* to take you to Tir Na Nog. No more delays, understand? The queen won't be happy with me for taking this long."

I nodded. "Yes. Thank y— I mean... I appreciate it, Ash."

He smiled faintly and offered a hand again, this time to help me into the saddle. I gingerly picked up the reins and envied Ash, who swung easily aboard the second horse like he'd done it a thousand times.

"All right," he said in a faintly resigned voice, staring up at the moon. "First things first. We have to find a trod to New Orleans."

★ ★ ★

Trods are faery paths between the real world and the Nevernever, gateways straight into Faeryland. They can be anywhere, any doorway: an old bathroom stall, the gate to a cemetery, a child's closet door. You can go anywhere in the world if you know the right trod, but getting through them is another matter, as sometimes they're guarded by nasty creatures the fey leave behind to discourage unwanted guests.

Nothing guarded the enormous rotting barn that sat in the middle of the swampy bayou, so covered in moss it looked like a shaggy green carpet was draped over the roof. Mushrooms grew from the walls in bulbous clumps, huge spotted things that, if you looked closely enough, sheltered several tiny winged figures beneath them. They blinked at us as we went by, huge multifaceted eyes peering out from under the mushroom caps, and then took to the air in a flurry of iridescent wings. I jumped, but Ash and the horses ignored them as we stepped beneath the sagging frame and everything went white.

I blinked and looked around as the world came into focus again.

An eerie gray forest surrounded us, mist creeping over the ground like a living thing, coiling around the horses' legs. The trees were massive, soaring to mind-boggling heights, interlocking branches blocking out the sky. Everything was dark and faded, like all color had been washed out, a forest trapped in perpetual twilight.

"The wyldwood." I sighed. Well, here I was in Faeryland once again. My time in the real world didn't seem nearly long enough. "I suppose from here we have to find a trod to New Orleans?"

"Yes." Ash pulled his horse around to look at me. "The trod we want is about a day's ride north. We'll be going through the wyldwood, so stay close. There are still those in the Winter Court who are after you."

Before I could reply, my horse let out a terrifying whinny and reared, slashing the air with its forelegs. I grabbed for the mane, but it slipped through my fingers, and I tumbled backward out of the saddle, hitting the ground behind the horse, snapping bushes underneath. Snorting in terror, the fey steed charged off toward the trees, leaped over a fallen branch and vanished into the mist.

Groaning, I sat up, testing my body for pain. My shoulder throbbed where I'd landed on it, and I was shaking, but nothing seemed broken.

Ash's mount was also throwing a fit, squealing and tossing its head, but the Winter prince was able to keep his seat and bring it back under control. Swinging out of the saddle, he tied the horse's reins to an overhead branch and knelt beside me.

"Are you all right?" His fingers probed my arm, surprisingly gentle. "Anything broken?"

"I don't think so," I muttered, rubbing my bruised shoulder. "That lovely patch of bramble broke my fall." Now that the adrenaline had worn off, dozens of stinging scratches began to make themselves known. Scowling, I glared in the direction my mount had disappeared. "You know, that's the second time I've been thrown off a faery horse. And another time one tried to eat me. I don't think horses like me very much."

"No." Abruptly serious, Ash stood, offering a hand to pull me to my feet. "It wasn't you. Something spooked them." He gazed around slowly, hand dropping to the sword at his waist. Around us, the wyldwood was still and dark, as if the inhabitants were afraid to move.

I looked behind us, where the trunks of two trees had grown into each other, forming an archway. The space between the trunks, where the trod lay, was cloaked in shadow, and it seemed to me that the shadows were creeping closer.

A cold wind hissed through the trunks, rattling branches and tossing leaves, and I shivered.

With a frantic rushing sound a flock of tiny winged fey burst from the trod, swirling around us in panic and spiraling into the mist. I yelped, shielding my face, and Ash's horse screamed again, the sound piercing the ominous quiet. Ash took my hand and pulled me away from the trod, hurrying back to his mount. He lifted me to sit just behind the saddle, then grabbed the reins and climbed up in front.

"Hold on tight," he warned, and a thrill shot through me as I slipped my arms around his waist, feeling the hard muscles through his shirt. Ash dug in his heels with a shout, and the horse shot forward, snapping my head back. I squeezed Ash tightly and buried my face in his back as the faery horse streaked through the wyldwood, leaving the trod far behind.

We stopped infrequently, and when we did, it was only to let me and the horse rest for a few minutes. As evening fell, Ash pulled several food items from the horse's pack and gave them to me; bread and dried meat and cheese, ordinary human food. Apparently, he remembered my last experiment with eating faery food, which hadn't turned out so well. I nibbled the dry bread, gnawed on the jerky and hoped he wouldn't mention the Summerpod incident and the embarrassment that followed.

Ash didn't eat anything. He remained wary and alert, and never truly relaxed the entire journey. The horse, too, was jumpy and restless, and it panicked at every shadow, every rustle or falling leaf. Something was following us; I felt it every time we stopped, a dark, shadowy presence drawing ever closer.

As we rode on through the night, the eternal twilight of the wyldwood finally dimmed and a pale yellow moon rose into the sky. Ash and the fey horse both had seemingly unlimited endurance, more so than me, anyway. Riding a horse for hours and hours is not easy, and the stress of being chased by an unknown enemy was taking its toll. I struggled to stay awake, dozing against the prince's back, leaning dangerously off the sides until a jolt or sharp word from Ash snapped me upright.

I was dozing off once more, fighting to keep my eyes open, when Ash suddenly pulled the horse to a stop and dismounted. Blinking, I looked around dazedly, seeing nothing but trees and shadows. "Are we there yet?"

"No." Ash glared at me in exasperation. "But you keep threatening to fall off the horse, and I can't keep reaching back to make sure you're still on." He motioned to the front of the saddle. "We're switching places. Move forward."

I eased into the saddle and Ash swung up behind me, wrapping an arm securely around my waist, making my pulse beat faster.

"Hold on," he murmured as the horse started forward again. "We're almost to the trod. Once we're in the mortal realm, you can rest. We should be safe there."

"What's following us?" I whispered, making the horse's ears twitch back. Ash didn't reply for a moment.

"I don't know," he muttered, sounding reluctant to admit it. "Whatever it is, it's persistent. We've been keeping a pretty steady pace and haven't lost it yet."

"*Why* is it following us? What does it want?"

"Most likely, it's something or someone from the Winter Court." Ash's grip around my waist tightened. "It doesn't matter. If it wants you, it'll have to get past me first."

My stomach prickled, and my heart did a weird little flop. In that moment, I felt safe. Ash wouldn't let anything happen to me. Settling back against him, I closed my eyes and let myself drift.

I must have dozed off, for the next thing I knew Ash was

shaking me gently. "Meghan, wake up," he murmured, his cool breath fanning my neck. "We're here."

Yawning, I looked at the small glade ahead of us. Without the cover of the trees, I could see the sky, dotted with stars. The dell was clear, except for one massive gnarled oak in the very center. Roots snaked out over the ground, huge thick things that prevented anything bigger than a fern to flourish. The trunk was wide and twisted, like three or four trees had been squashed together into one. But even with the oak's size and dominating presence, I could see that it was dying. Its branches drooped, or had snapped off and were scattered about the base of the tree. Most of its broad, veined leaves were dead and brittle; the rest were a sickly yellow-brown. The glade, too, looked withered and sick, as if the tree was leeching life from the forest around it.

"It wasn't like this before," Ash said behind me. I gazed at the dying tree and felt an incomprehensible sadness, as if I were seeing an old friend about to die. Shaking it off, I looked around for a doorway or gate, but the tree was the only thing here.

"Will it still work?" I wondered as he urged the horse into the clearing, toward the ancient tree. "The trod, I mean. Will it open?"

"We'll see." Ash dismounted and led the horse up to the trunk. When it stopped, I slid out of the saddle and joined him.

"So, how does the trod work?" I asked, peering at the trunk for a door of some kind. Doors in trees were not unusual in the Nevernever. In fact, during my first time to Faeryland, I'd spent the night in a wood sprite's tree, somehow shrinking down to the size of a bug to fit through his door. "I don't see a gate. How do you get it to open?"

"Easy," Ash replied. "For this trod, just ask."

Ignoring my scowl, he faced the trunk and put a hand on the rough bark. "This is Ash," he said clearly, "third son of the Unseelie Court, requesting passage to the mortal realm and the clearing of the Elder."

"Please," I added.

For a moment, nothing happened. Then, with a loud groaning and creaking, one of the massive roots snaked out of the ground, shedding dirt and twigs. Rising into the air, it formed an archway between itself and the earth, and the space between shimmered with magic.

"There's your trod," Ash murmured, as my heart beat faster in my chest. Puck was through that gateway. If he was still alive.

Clutching Ash's hand, almost pulling him along in my impatience, I ducked through the arch.

I tripped over a root on the other side and stumbled forward, barely catching myself. Straightening, I gazed around the moonlit grove of New Orleans City Park, recognizing the huge mossy oaks from our last visit. The air was humid, warm and peaceful. Crickets buzzed, leaves rustled and moonlight shimmered off the nearby lake. Nothing had changed. It had been this peaceful the last time we were here, though my world had been falling apart.

Ash touched my arm and nodded at a tree, where a willowy girl with moss-green skin watched us from the shadow of an oak, her dark eyes wide and startled.

"Meghan Chase?" The dryad swayed toward us, moving like a wind-blown branch. "What are you doing here?" I blinked at the fear in her voice. "You must not stay!" she hissed as she drew close. "It is not safe. There is something dangerous following you."

"We know," Ash said beside me, calm and unflustered as always. The dryad blinked and shifted her gaze to him. "But we came through the Elder gate, so hopefully she won't let whatever is hunting us into this world."

Elder gate? I glanced behind me, and my stomach twisted so hard I felt nauseous.

It was the Elder Dryad's tree, the great oak that once stood tall and proud, looming over the others. Now, like its twin in the clearing, it was dying. Its branches were bare of leaves, the shaggy moss that covered it brown and dead.

A lump rose to my throat. I remembered the Elder Dryad from our first visit here: an old, grandmotherly fey with a soft voice and kind eyes who had given the very heart of her tree to make sure I could rescue my brother...and kill the faery who'd kidnapped him. The Elder had known she would die if she helped me. But she'd given us the weapon we needed to take down the enemy fey and get Ethan back.

The dryad girl stepped beside me, gazing at the dying oak. "She lives still," she murmured, her voice like the whisper of leaves. "Dying, yes. Too weak to leave her tree, she sleeps now, dreaming of her youth. But not gone, not yet. It will take a long time for her to fade completely."

"I'm so sorry," I whispered.

"No, Meghan Chase." The dryad shook her head with a faint rustling sound, and a shiny beetle crawled across her face to burrow into her hair. "She knew. She knew all along what was going to happen. The wind tells us these things. Just as it tells us you are in terrible danger now." She fixed me with piercing black eyes. "You should not be here," she said. "It is very close. Why have you come?"

My skin prickled, but I shook off the feeling of trepidation and held her gaze. "I'm here for Puck. I need to see him."

The dryad's expression softened. "Ah. Yes, of course. I will take you to him, but I fear you will be disappointed."

"It doesn't matter." I felt cold, even in the warm summer night. "I just want to see him."

The dryad nodded and shuffled back, swaying in the breeze. "This way."

2

THE HEART OF THE OAK

Puck, or the infamous Robin Goodfellow, as he was known in *A Midsummer Night's Dream,* had another name, once. A human name, belonging to a lanky, red-haired boy, who had been the neighbor of a shy farm girl in the Louisiana bayou. Robbie Goodfell, as he'd called himself back then, had been my classmate, confidant and best friend. Always looking out for me, like an older brother. Goofy, sarcastic and some-what overprotective, Robbie was…different. When he wasn't around, people barely remembered him, who he was, what he looked like. It was like he simply faded from their memo-ries, despite the fact that whenever anything went wrong in school—mice in desks, superglue on chairs, an alligator in the bathrooms one day—Robbie was somehow involved. No one ever suspected him, but I always knew.

Still, it had come as a shock when I'd discovered who he really was: King Oberon's servant, charged with keeping an eye on me in the mortal world. To keep me safe from those who would harm a half-human daughter of Oberon. But also, to keep me blind to the world of Faery, unaware of my true nature and all the danger that came with it.

When Ethan was kidnapped and taken into the Never-never, Robbie's plans to keep me blind and ignorant unraveled. Defying Oberon's direct orders, he agreed to help me rescue my brother, but his loyalty came at a huge cost. During a battle with an Iron faery, a brand-new species of fey born from technology and progress, he was shot and very nearly killed. Ash and I brought him here, to City Park, and the dryads took him into one of their trees to sleep and heal from his wounds. Suspended in stasis, he slept while the dryads kept him alive, but they didn't know when he would wake up. If he woke up at all. We had to leave him behind when we left to rescue Ethan, and the guilt of that decision had haunted me ever since.

I pressed my palm against the mossy trunk, wondering if I could feel his heartbeat within the tree, a vibration, a sigh. Something, *anything,* that would tell me he was still there. But I felt nothing except sap, moss and the rough edges of the bark. Puck, if he still lived, was beyond my reach.

"Are you sure he's in there?" I asked the dryad, not taking my eyes from the trunk. I didn't know what to expect: his head to pop out of the wood and grin at me, perhaps? But I felt that if I took my eyes away for a second, I would miss something.

The dryad girl nodded. "Yes. He lives still. Nothing has changed. Robin Goodfellow sleeps his dreamless slumber, waiting for the day he will rejoin the world."

"When will that be?" I asked, running my fingers down the trunk.

"We do not know. Perhaps days. Perhaps centuries. Perhaps he does not want to wake up." The dryad placed her hand on the trunk and closed her eyes. "He is resting comfortably, in no pain. There is nothing you can do for him but wait and be patient."

Unsatisfied with her answer, I pressed my palm against the tree and closed my eyes. Summer glamour swirled around me, the magic of my father, Oberon, and the Summer Court, the glamour of heat and earth and living things. I prodded the tree gently, feeling the sun-warmed leaves and the life running through their emerald veins. I felt thousands of tiny insects swarming over and burrowing into the trunk, the rapid heartbeat of birds, dreaming in the branches.

I pressed deeper, past the surface, past the softer, still-growing wood, deep into the heart of the tree.

And there he was. I couldn't physically see him, of course, but I could sense him, feel his presence in front of me, a bright spot of life against the heartwood. I felt the wood cradling his thin, lanky frame, protecting it, and heard the faintest *thump-thump* of a beating heart.

I drifted closer, wishing I could touch him, brush my insubstantial fingers over his cheek, push back unruly red bangs. He didn't stir. If I didn't hear his heartbeat, vibrating faintly through the tree, I would've thought he was dead.

I'm so sorry, Puck, I whispered, or maybe I just thought it, deep inside the giant oak. *I wish you were here with me now. I'm scared, and I don't know what's going to happen. I really need you to come back.*

If he heard me, he didn't show it. There was no flicker of life, no twitch of his presence responding to my voice. His heartbeat continued, calm and steady, echoing through the wood. My best friend was far from me, beyond my reach, and I couldn't bring him back.

Depressed, feeling strangely sick, I pulled out of the tree, returning to my own body. As the sounds of the world returned, I found myself fighting back tears. So close. So close to Puck, and still so far away.

Ash's expression was grave as I met his eyes; he knew what I'd done and could guess the outcome.

"He's still alive," he told me. "That's all you can hope for." I sniffed, turning away, and Ash sighed. "Don't worry too much about him, Meghan. Robin Goodfellow has always been extraordinarily difficult to kill." His voice hovered between irritation and amusement, as if he spoke from experience. "I can almost guarantee Goodfellow will pop up one day when you least expect it, just be patient."

"Patience," said an amused voice somewhere over my head, "has never been the girl's strong suit."

Startled, I looked up, into the branches of the oak. A pair of familiar golden eyes peered down at me, attached to nothing else, and my heart leaped.

"Grimalkin?"

The eyes blinked slowly, and the body of a large gray cat appeared, crouched on one of the lower branches. It was Grimalkin, the faery cat I met on my last journey to Faery. Grim had helped me out a few times in the past…but his help always came with a price. The cat loved collecting favors and did nothing for free, but I was still happy to see him, even if I still owed him a debt or two from our last adventure.

"What are you doing here, Grim?" I asked as the feline yawned and stretched, arching his fluffy tail over his back. True to form, Grimalkin finished stretching, sat down and gave his fur several licks before deigning to reply.

"I had business with the Elder Dryad," he replied in a bored voice. "I needed to know if she'd heard anything about the whereabouts of a certain individual." Grim scratched behind an ear, examined his back toes and gave them a lick. "Then I heard that you were on your way here, so I thought I would wait, to see if it was true. You have always proved most entertaining."

"But…the Elder Dryad is asleep," I said, frowning. "They told me she's too weak to even come out of her tree."

"What is your point, human?"

"Never mind." I shook my head. Grimalkin was exasperating and secretive, and I learned long ago he wouldn't share anything until he was ready. "It's still good to see you, Grim. Wish we could stay and talk awhile, but we're in sort of a hurry right now."

"Mmm, yes. Your ill-contrived deal with the Winter prince." Grimalkin's eyes shifted to Ash and back to me, blinking slowly. "Hasty and reckless, just like a human." He sniffed, staring straight at Ash, now. "But… I would have thought that you knew better, Prince."

Before I could ask what he meant by *that,* I felt a hand on my arm and turned to meet Ash's solemn gaze. "We should go," he murmured, and though his voice was firm, his expression was apologetic. "If something is chasing us, we should try to make it to Tir Na Nog as soon as we can. It won't be able to follow us, then. And I can protect you better in my own territory than the wyldwood or the mortal realm."

"One moment." Grimalkin yawned and sidled down from the tree, landing noiselessly on the roots. "If you are leaving now, I believe I will come with you. At least part of the way."

"Really?" I stared at him, surprised. "You're going to Tir Na Nog? Why?"

"I told you before. I am looking for someone."

"Who?"

"You ask a wearying amount of questions, human." Grimalkin hopped down from the roots and trotted off, tail in the air. Several yards away, he glanced back over his shoulder, twitching an ear. "Well? Are you coming or not? If you say there is something after you, it would make sense not to be here when it comes to call, yes?"

Ash and I shared a bemused look and trailed after him.

The Elder Gate loomed before us, tall and imposing even though the tree was dying. As we approached, the entire trunk suddenly shifted with a groan. A face pushed its way out of the bark, old and wrinkled, part of the tree come to life. The Elder Dryad opened her eyes, squinting as though it was difficult to focus, and her gaze fastened on me.

"Nooooooooo," she breathed, barely a whisper in the darkness. "You must not go back this way. *He* waits for you on the other side. He will…" Her voice trailed off, and her face sank back into the wood, vanishing from sight. "Run," was the last thing I heard.

I shivered all the way down to my toes. Ash immediately took my hand and drew me away, striding in the opposite direction, his body tense like a coiled wire. Grimalkin slipped after us, a gray ghost in the shadows, the fur on his tail standing on end. It would've been funny if I didn't feel eyes on the back of my neck, old, savage and patient, watching us flee into the night.

Ash paused beneath the limbs of another oak, put his fingers to his lips and let out a piercing whistle. Moments later, the fey horse trotted out of the shadows, snorting and tossing its head, skidding to a stop before us.

"Where are we going now?" I asked, as Ash helped me into the saddle.

"We can't use the Elder Gate to get back," the prince replied, swinging up behind me. "We'll have to find another way into the Nevernever. And quickly." He gathered the reins in one hand and snaked an arm around my waist. "I know of another trod that will take us close to Tir Na Nog, but it's in a part of the city that's…dangerous for Summer fey."

"You are speaking of the Dungeon, are you not?" Grimalkin said, appearing suddenly in my lap, curled up like he belonged. I blinked in surprise. "Are you sure you want to take the girl there?"

"Not much choice, now." Tightening his grip on my waist, Ash kicked the horse forward, and we galloped into the streets of New Orleans.

I'd forgotten what it was like to be a half faery in the real world, or at least in the company of a powerful, full-blooded fey. The horse trotted down brightly lit streets, weaving through cars and alleyways and people, and no one saw us. No one even glanced our way. Regular humans couldn't see the faery world, though it was all around them. Like the two goblins sifting through a spilled Dumpster in an alley, gnawing on bones and other things I didn't want to dwell on. Or the dragonfly-winged sylph perched atop a telephone pole, watching the streets with the intensity of an eagle observing her territory. We nearly ran into a group of dwarves leaving one of the many pubs on Bourbon Street. The short, bearded men shouted drunken curses as the horse swerved, barely missing them, and galloped away down the sidewalk.

We were deep in the French Quarter when Ash stopped in front of a wall of stone buildings, old wooden shutters and doors lining the sidewalk. An orange sign swinging above a thick black door read The Dungeon. Ash pushed open the door, revealing a long, extremely narrow alleyway, and turned to me.

"This is Unseelie territory," he murmured close to my ear. "There's a rough crowd that frequents this place. Don't talk to anyone, and stay close to me."

I nodded and peered down the closed-in space, which was barely wide enough to walk through. "What about the horse?"

Ash removed the horse's pack and pulled off its bridle, tossing it into the shadows. "It'll find its own way home," he murmured, swinging the pack over one shoulder. "Let's go."

We slipped down the narrow corridor, Ash in front, Grim trailing behind. The alley ended in a small courtyard, where a scraggly waterfall trickled into a moat at the front of the building. We crossed the footbridge, where a heavy door, painted black and looking like the entrance to a medieval castle, was set into the wall on the other side.

But before we could open the door, there was a low growl, and something huge and green rose from the shadows along the wall. It shambled forward, crimson eyes glaring down from the monstrous, toothy face of a female troll. I squeaked and took a step back, as the huge creature lurched in front of the door, blocking our way.

"I smell me a Summer whelp," the troll growled. Up close, she towered over us, with swamp-green skin and long, taloned fingers. Beady red eyes glared down at me from her impressive height. "You're either really brave or really stupid, whelp. Lost a bet with a phouka or something? No Summer fey allowed in here, so get lost."

"She's with me," Ash said, his voice low and cool as he eased me behind him. "And you're going to step aside now. We need to use the hidden trod."

"Prince Ash." The troll took a step back but didn't move aside completely. "Your Highness, of course I would let you in, but..." She glanced over Ash's shoulder at me. "The boss says absolutely no Summer blood in here unless we're going to drink it."

"We're just passing through," Ash replied, still in that same calm, cool voice. "We'll be gone before anyone notices us."

"Your Highness, I can't," the troll protested, sounding more and more unsure. She glanced back over her shoulder, lowering her voice. "I could lose my job if I let her through."

Very casually, Ash dropped his hand to the hilt of his sword. "You could lose your head if you don't."

The troll's nostrils flared. She glanced at me again, then back at the Winter prince, claws flexing at her side. Ash didn't move, though the air around him grew colder, until the troll's breath hung in the air before her face.

Sensing her dire predicament, the huge faery finally backed off. "Of course, Your Highness," she muttered, and pointed at me with a curved black claw. "But if she gets stuffed into a bottle and served as the next drink special, don't say I didn't warn you."

"I'll keep that in mind," said Ash, and led me into the Dungeon.

The Dungeon, for all its eerie decor, turned out to be nothing more than a bar and nightclub, though it definitely catered to the more macabre crowd. The walls were brick, the lights dim and red, casting everything in crimson, and skulls hung on the walls over the bar. Music pounded the ceiling from an overhead room, AC/DC screaming out the lyrics to "Back in Black."

There were a couple human patrons at the bar and standing throughout the room with drinks in hand, but I saw only the inhuman ones. The room was quite small, crowded even without the fey, but the Unseelie moved through and around the humans like shadows. Goblins, phouka and redcaps, and a lone ogre in the corner, drinking a whole pitcher of a dark purple liquid. Unseen and invisible, the Unseelie fey milled through the throng of humans, spitting in their drinks, tripping the drunker ones, stealing items from purses and wallets.

I shivered and drew back, but Ash took my hand firmly.

"Stay close," he murmured again. "This isn't as bad as upstairs, but we'll still have to be careful."

"What's upstairs?"

"Skulls, cages and the dance floor. Not something you want to see, trust me."

Ash kept a tight hold on my hand as we navigated through the crowd, moving toward the back of the room. Grimalkin had disappeared—normal for him—so it was just us receiving the cold, hungry glares from every corner of the room. A red-cap—a short, evil faery with sharklike teeth and a cap dipped in his victim's blood—reached for me as we passed his corner, snagging my shirt. I tried to dodge, but the space was tight and narrow, and the clawed fingers latched on to my sleeve.

Ash turned. There was a flash of blue light, and a half second later the redcap froze, a glowing blue sword at his throat.

"Don't. Try. Anything." Ash's voice was colder than the chill coming off his blade. The redcap's Adam's apple bobbed, and he very slowly pulled back his claws. The rest of the Unseelie fey had frozen as well and were staring at us with glowing, hostile eyes.

"Meghan, go." Ash kept his threatening gaze on the rest of the crowd, daring anyone to get up. No one moved. I slipped past him and the redcap, who was keeping very still, and moved toward the back of the room.

"This way, human." Grimalkin appeared at the edge of a hallway, his eyes coming into focus before the rest of his body. "The trod to the wyldwood is through here."

I looked at the door a few feet from the cat and frowned. "The *bathroom*?"

Grimalkin yawned. "It is a doorway like any other, in a place that reeks of glamour and emotion, albeit on the darker end of the spectrum. I would not be so picky, human. Especially since that redcap motley has taken quite an interest in you."

I looked back to see that the redcap had been joined by three of his friends, and all four faeries were staring at us and muttering among themselves. Ash joined us in the corridor, his icy blade still unsheathed, tendrils of mist writhing off it to mingle with the smoke.

"Hurry," he growled at us, moving close to shield me from the stares of the redcaps. "I don't like the attention we're getting. Cat, have you opened the trod?"

"Give me a moment, Prince." Grimalkin sighed and sauntered toward the bathroom door near the end of the hall.

"Wait, aren't you their prince?" I wondered. "They're Unseelie, too, right? Can't you just order them to leave us alone?"

Ash gave a low, humorless chuckle. "I'm *a* prince," he replied, still keeping an eye on the redcaps, who in turn were keeping an eye on us. "But I'm not the only one. My brothers are looking for you, as well. Rowan has eyes and ears everywhere, I'm sure. He's much more ruthless than I am. Those redcaps could work for him, or they could be spies for Mab herself. Either way, they're going to inform *someone* of our passing the moment we leave this place. I can guarantee it."

"Sounds like a great family," I muttered.

Ash snorted. "You have no idea."

"Done," said Grimalkin from the end of the hallway. "Let us go."

"Go," Ash said, motioning me forward. "I'll make sure nothing follows us."

I walked to the door and pushed it open, half expecting to see a tiny bathroom with a dirty mirror and a couple toilet stalls. Instead, a cold breeze blew into the hallway, smelling of frost and bark and crushed leaves, and the gray, misty forest of the Nevernever stretched away through the door.

Grimalkin slipped through first, becoming nearly invisible in the fog. I followed, stepping through the doorway that became a split tree trunk on the other side. Ash ducked through and shut the door firmly behind us, where it faded into nothingness as soon as he let it go, leaving the mortal world behind.

It was colder in this part of the wyldwood. Frost coated the ground and the branches of the trees, and the mist clung to my skin with clammy fingers. I couldn't see more than a few yards in any direction. Everything was overly quiet and still, as if the forest itself was holding its breath.

"Tir Na Nog is close," Ash said, his voice muffled by the clinging fog. His breath did not puff or hang in the air like mine did. Trembling, I rubbed my arms to get warm. "We should move quickly. I want to get to Winter as fast as possible."

I was tired. My legs were cramped, both from riding and walking, my head hurt and the cold was sapping the last of my willpower. And I knew from personal experience that it would only get colder the closer we got to Tir Na Nog.

Thankfully, Grimalkin noticed my reluctance. "The human is about to fall over from exhaustion," he stated bluntly, twitching his tail. "She will only slow us down if we push her much farther. Perhaps we should look for a place to rest."

"Soon," Ash said, and turned to me. "Just a little farther, Meghan. Can you do that? We'll stop as soon as we cross the border into Tir Na Nog."

I nodded wearily. Ash took my hand, and with Grimalkin leading the way, we walked into the curling mist.

Minutes later, the howl rang out behind us.

3

THE LIVING COLD

Ash stopped, every muscle in his body coiling tight, as the echo of that eerie cry faded into the mist.

"Impossible," he murmured, his voice frighteningly calm. "It's on our trail again. How? How could it find us so quickly?"

Grimalkin suddenly let out a long, low growl, which shocked me and caused goose bumps to crawl up my arms. The cat had never done that before. "It is the Hunter," Grimalkin said, as his fur began to rise along his back and shoulders. "The Eldest Hunter, the First." He glanced at us, teeth bared, looking feral and wild. "You must flee, quickly! If he has your trail he will be coming fast. Run, now!"

We ran.

The woods flashed by us, dark and indistinct, shadowy shapes in the mist. I didn't know if we were running in circles or straight into the Hunter's jaws. Grimalkin had disappeared. Direction was lost in the coiling mist. I only hoped that Ash knew where he was going as we fled through the eerie whiteness.

The howl came again, closer this time, more excited. I dared a backward glance, but could see nothing beyond the swirling fog and shadows. But I could *feel* whatever it was, getting closer. It could see us now, fleeing before it, the back of my neck a tempting target. I stifled my panic and kept running, clinging to Ash's hand as we wove through the forest.

The trees fell away, the fog cleared a bit and suddenly a great chasm opened before us, wide and gaping like the maw of a giant beast. Ash jerked me to a stop three feet from the edge, and a shower of pebbles went clattering down the jagged sides, vanishing into the river of mist far below. The crack in the earth ran along the edge of the wyldwood for as far as I could see in either direction, separating us from the safety of the other side.

Beyond the chasm, a snow-covered landscape stretched away before us, icy and pristine. Trees were frozen, covered in ice, every twig outlined in sparkling crystal. The ground beneath looked like a blanket of clouds, white and fluffy. Snowdrifts glittered in the sun like millions of tiny diamonds. Tir Na Nog, the land of Winter, home to Mab and the Unseelie Court.

"This way." Ash tugged my hand and pulled me along the chasm, where the mist from the wyldwood rolled off the edge and down the cliff sides like a slow-moving waterfall. "If we can get to the bridge, I can stop him."

Panting, I followed the edge of the gorge and gasped in relief. About a hundred yards away, an arched bridge, made completely of ice, sparkled enticingly in the sun. Behind us, the woods were deathly quiet, but I could feel a presence, huge and dangerous, drawing ever closer. The Hunter was silent now, no howls or deep throaty bays; it was moving in for the kill.

We reached the bridge, and Ash pushed me forward onto the icy surface. There were no guards or handrails, just a narrow arch over a terrifying drop. Stomach clenching, I started across, trying not to look down. Because the bridge was ice, it was perfectly clear; I felt I was walking out over nothing, seeing the dizzying fall right beneath my feet.

My foot slipped, and my heart slammed against my ribs, pounding wildly as I flailed. Right behind me, Ash grabbed my arm tightly, and somehow we made it to the other side.

As soon as we were off, the Winter prince drew his sword. Sunlight flashed along the blade as he raised it and brought it slashing down on the narrow bridge. The bridge cracked, icy shards glittering as they spiraled into the air, and he raised the sword for another blow.

Across the chasm, something dark and monstrous broke out of the trees, fog swirling around it. Through the mist and shadows, I couldn't see it clearly, but it was huge, black and terrifying, with burning, yellow-green eyes. When it saw what Ash was doing, it roared, making the air tremble, then bounded for the bridge.

Ash brought his sword down again, then once more, and with a deafening crack, the ice bridge shattered. Our end slid away and dropped into oblivion, taking with it the entire arch, which clashed and screeched its way down the side of the cliff. The shadow on the other side slid to a halt, green eyes blazing with fury as it stalked up and down the edge for a moment, panting. Then, with a snarl that showed a flash of huge white teeth, it turned and slipped back into the misty wyldwood, vanishing from sight.

I shuddered with relief and sank down into the snow, gasping, feeling as if my lungs and legs and whole body were on fire. But as the adrenaline wore off, I realized how frigidly cold it was on this side of the chasm. The icy wind cut through my bones and stabbed into me like a knife.

Ash knelt beside me and gently pulled me close, wrapping me in his arms. I leaned into him, felt his heart racing and shivered against his chest. He was silent, resting his forehead against mine, saying nothing. Just there.

"Come on," he murmured after a few moments. "Let's find a place to rest."

"What about the Hunter?"

He rose, pulling me to my feet. "The Ice Maw runs for miles in either direction," he said, nodding at the chasm behind us, "until it meets the Wyrmtooth Mountains in the north and the Broken Glass Sea in the south. The Hunter won't find a way across for a long time. Besides," he added, narrowing his eyes, "this is *my* realm. I doubt it will attack us here."

"Do not be too sure of that, Prince," said Grimalkin, popping into view on what was left of the shattered bridge. "The Hunter is older than you—much older. He does not care whose realm he is in when tracking his prey. If he is after you, you will see him again."

I sneezed, causing the cat to pin his ears. Ash took my elbow and drew me away from the chasm, positioning himself so that he blocked the wind howling up from the gap. "We'll worry about that if he ever gets across," the prince stated calmly as I hugged myself to conserve heat. "But night is coming, and so is the cold. We have to get Meghan inside."

"Before she turns into an icicle? I suppose." Grimalkin hopped off the shattered post, landing lightly in the snow. "The only shelter I know of is old Liaden's place in the frozen wood. Surely you are not taking the girl there?" He blinked under Ash's steady gaze. "You are. Well, this will be interesting. Follow me, then." He trotted away, making light paw prints in the snow, a fuzzy cloud gliding over the whiteness.

"Who's Liaden?" I asked Ash.

An icy gale howled up from the chasm before he could answer, slicing into me and tossing drifts of snow into the air. "Later," Ash said brusquely, giving me a slight push. "Follow Grimalkin. Go."

We trailed the paw prints into the woods. Icicles hung from frozen trees, some longer than my arms and as sharp as a spear. Every so often one would snap off and plummet to the ground with the tinkle of breaking glass. The cold here was a living thing, clawing at my exposed skin, stabbing my lungs when I breathed. I was soon shivering violently through my jeans and T-shirt, teeth chattering, thinking longingly of sweaters and hot baths and burrowing under a thick feather quilt until spring.

The woods grew darker, the trees closer together, and the temperature dropped even more. By now I was losing feeling in my fingers and toes, the cold making me sluggish. I felt as if icy hands were grabbing my feet, dragging me down, urging me to curl up in a ball and hibernate until it was warm again.

A flash of color in the trees caught my eye. On the branch above me, a small bird perched on a twig, bright red against the snow. Its eyes were closed, and it was fluffed out against the cold, looking like a feathery red ball. And it was completely encased in ice, covered head-to-toe in crystallized water, so clear that I could see every detail through the shell.

The sight should have chilled me, but I was so cold all I felt was the spreading numbness. My legs belonged to someone else, and I couldn't even feel my feet anymore. I tripped over a branch and fell, sprawling in a snowbank, ice crystals stinging my eyes.

I was suddenly very tired. My eyelids felt heavy, and all I wanted to do was lay my head down and sleep, like a bear through the winter. It was an appealing thought.

"Meghan!"

Ash's voice cut through the layers of apathy, as the Winter prince knelt in the snow. "Meghan, get up," he said, his voice urgent. "You can't lie here. You'll freeze over and die if you don't move. Get up."

I tried, but it seemed a Herculean effort to even raise my head when all I wanted to do was sleep. I muttered something about how tired I was, but the words froze in the back of my throat, and I only grunted.

"The cold has her." Grimalkin's voice seemed to come from

far away. "She is already icing over. If you do not get her up now, she will die."

My eyelids were slipping shut, even though I tried keeping them open. If they closed, they would freeze and stay shut forever. I tried using my fingers to pry them open by force, but a layer of ice now covered my hands and I couldn't feel them anymore.

Give in, the cold whispered in my ear. *Give in, sleep. You'll never feel pain again.*

My eyelids flickered, and Ash made a noise that was almost a growl. "Dammit, Meghan," he snarled, grabbing both my arms. "I am not going to lose you this close to home. Get *up!*"

He rose, pulling me to my feet and, before I could even register what was going on, pressed his lips to mine.

The numbness shattered. Surprise flooded in, as my heart leaped and my stomach twisted itself into a knot. I laced my arms around his neck and kissed him back, feeling his arms around me, crushing us together, breathing in the sharp, frosty scent of him.

When we finally pulled back, I was breathing hard, and his heart raced under my fingers. I was also shivering again, and this time I welcomed the cold. Ash sighed and touched his forehead to mine.

"Let's get you out of the cold."

Grimalkin had vanished again, perhaps annoyed with our display of emotion, but his delicate paw prints cut plainly through the snow. We followed them until the trail finally ended at a small, dilapidated cabin beneath two rotting trees. I wouldn't think anyone lived there, but smoke curled from the chimney and a dim orange light glowed through the windows, so someone must've been home.

I was eager to get inside, out of the biting chill, but Ash took my hand, forcing me to look at him.

"You're in Unseelie territory now, remember that," he

warned. "Whatever you see in that room, don't stare, and don't make any comments about her baby. Understand?"

I nodded, willing to agree to anything if I could just be warm again. Ash released me, stepped onto the creaking, snow-covered porch and knocked firmly on the door.

A woman opened it, peering out with tired, bloodshot eyes. A gray robe and cowl draped her body like old curtains, and her face, though fairly young, was lined and weary.

"Prince Ash?" she said, her voice breathy and frail. "This is a surprise. What can I do for you, Your Highness?"

"We wish to spend the night here," Ash stated quietly. "Myself and my companion. We won't bother you, and we intend to be gone by morning. Will you let us in?"

The woman blinked. "Of course," she murmured, opening the door wide. "Please, come inside. Make yourselves comfortable, poor children. I'm Dame Liaden."

That's when I saw her baby, cradled lovingly in her other arm, and bit my lip to stifle a gasp. The wrinkled, ghastly creature in a stained white blanket was the most hideous child I'd ever seen. Its deformed head was too large for its body, its tiny limbs were shriveled and dead, and its skin had an unhealthy blue tinge, like it had been drowned or left out in the cold. The child kicked weakly and let out a feeble, unearthly cry.

It was like watching a train wreck. I couldn't tear my eyes away...until Ash nudged me sharply in the ribs. "Nice to meet you," I said automatically, and followed him over the threshold into the room. Inside, a fire crackled in the hearth, and the warmth seeped into my frozen limbs, making me sigh in relief.

There was no crib anywhere in the cabin, and the woman didn't put her infant down once, moving about the room clutching her baby as if she feared something would snatch it away.

"The girl can take the bed under the window," Liaden said, wrapping the baby in another ratty, once-white blanket. "I fear I must go out now, but please make yourselves at home. There is tea and milk in the cupboards, and extra blankets in the closet. But midnight draws close, and we must depart. Farewell."

Holding her infant close to her chest, she opened the door, letting in a blast of painfully cold air, and slipped out into the night. The door clicked behind her, and we were alone.

"Where is she going?" I asked, moving closer to the fireplace. My fingers were finally getting some feeling back, and were all tingly now. Ash didn't look at me.

"You don't want to know."

"Ash..."

He sighed. "She's going to wash her baby in the blood of a human infant to make her own child whole and healthy again. If only for a little while."

I recoiled. "That's horrible!"

"You asked."

I shuddered and rubbed my upper arms, looking out the cabin's grimy window. Moonlight sparkled through the glass, and the land beyond was frozen solid. This was Unseelie territory, like Ash had said. I was far from home and family and the safety of a normal life.

Closing my eyes, I started to shake. What would happen to me once I reached the Winter Court? Would Mab throw me in a dungeon, or maybe feed me to her goblins? What would a centuries-old faery queen do to the daughter of her ancient rival? Whatever it was, I couldn't imagine it would be good for me. Fear twisted my gut.

I felt Ash move behind me, so close that I could feel his breath on the back of my neck. He didn't touch me, but his presence, quiet and strong, calmed me somewhat. Though the logical part of my mind told me he might be the one I should fear the most.

"So, how will this work?" I asked casually, trying to keep the accusation from my voice. It crept out, anyway. "Am I a prisoner of the Winter Court? A guest? Will Mab toss me in a cell, or is she planning something much more interesting?"

He hesitated, and I could hear the reluctance in his voice when he finally spoke. "I don't know what she intends to do," he said softly. "Mab doesn't share her plans with me, or anyone."

"It's going to be dangerous for me there, isn't it? I'm Oberon's daughter. Everyone will hate me." I remembered the redcap's hungry gaze and rubbed my arms. "Or want to eat me."

His hands lightly grasped my shoulders, making my skin tingle and my heart flutter in my chest. "I will protect you," he murmured, and his voice went even lower, as if talking to himself. "Somehow."

Grimalkin appeared abruptly, leaping onto a stool by the fire, making me jump and Ash withdraw his hands. I mourned the loss of his touch. "Get some rest," the Winter prince said, moving away. "If nothing else happens, we should reach the Winter Court by tomorrow night."

Gingerly, I lay down on the bed beneath the window, trying not to imagine the last thing that used the mattress. Ash claimed a chair by the fire, turning it so he faced the door, and drew his sword into his lap. Surprisingly, the bed was warm and comfortable, and I drifted off to the outline of Ash's profile keeping watch by the fire.

I must've woken sometime in the night, or perhaps I dreamed, for I remember opening my eyes to see Ash and Grimalkin standing before the hearth, talking quietly. Their voices were too low to hear, but the look on Ash's face was scary in its bleakness. He raked a hand through his hair and said something to Grimalkin, who nodded slowly and replied. I blinked, or maybe drifted off again, because when I opened my eyes again Grimalkin was gone. Ash stood with his hands braced on the mantel and his shoulders hunched, staring into the flames, and didn't move for a long time.

"Get up."

The cold voice was the first thing I heard the next morning, cutting through layers of sleep and grogginess, bringing me fully awake. Ash loomed over me, his posture stiff, regarding me with empty silver eyes.

"We're leaving," he said in a flat voice, and tossed something on the bed, where it landed in a cloud of dust. A thick, hooded cloak, gray and dusty, as if all color had been leached out of it. "Found that in the closet," Ash continued, turning away. "It should keep you from freezing. But we need to go, now. The sooner we reach the Winter Court the better."

"Where's Grim?" I asked, struggling upright, reeling from his sudden change in mood. Ash opened the door, letting in a blast of frigid air.

"Gone. Left early this morning. Hurry up." He waited, still holding the door, as I swirled the cloak around my shoulders. When I drew up the hood, the prince nodded briskly. "Let's go."

"Is something coming?" I asked, jogging after him through

the snow, my breath puffing in the air. Everything was covered in a new layer of ice. "Is the Hunter getting close again?"

"No." He didn't look at me. "Not that I can tell."

I swallowed, drawing alongside him. His face was blank, and he stared straight ahead, as if I wasn't there at all. "Did I...do something wrong?"

He hesitated this time, then sighed. "No," he said in a softer voice. "You did nothing wrong."

"Then why are you being like this? Ash? Hey!" He'd lengthened his stride, starting to outpace me, but I lunged forward and grabbed his sleeve, bringing us both to a halt.

"Let go." Ash's voice held the subtle hint of warning. I shook off my fear and stubbornly planted my feet.

"Or what? You'll kill me? Haven't you already made that threat?"

"Don't tempt me." But his voice had lost its coldness—now it just sounded tired. He sighed, raking his free hand through his hair. "It's not important. Just...something Grimalkin said. Something I already knew."

"What?"

He turned, and for just a moment, his expression was anguished. "Meghan..."

In the distance, a howl echoed over the trees.

I jerked, and Ash straightened, his gaze sharpening. "The Hunter," he muttered. "Again. How could it catch up so quickly?"

The howl came again, and I shivered, drawing closer to Ash. "What *is* it?"

The prince's eyes narrowed. "I don't know. But this stops now. Come on!"

Ash kept a tight hold on my hand as we sprinted through the snow. I thought of the bridge and the impossible chasm that Hunter had, somehow, cleared, and hoped this plan would work out better. It didn't seem likely that we would outrun whatever tireless beast was behind us.

The forest thinned, and jagged cliffs rose up on either side of us, sparkling in the sun. Huge blue-and-green crystals jutted out from the sides, sending fractured prisms of light over the snow. Ash led me through a narrow canyon, sheer cliff walls pressing in on either side until it opened up in a snowy clearing surrounded by mountains.

The howl rang out again, echoing eerily through the gully we had just come through. Whatever it was, it was closing fast.

"This way." Ash tugged on my hand and pulled me toward the far side of the clearing. Between two pine trees, a dark blot in the cliff face marked the entrance to a cave, icicles dangling from the opening like teeth.

"Go," Ash said, pushing me forward. "Get inside, hurry."

I scrambled through the opening, being careful not to stab myself on the icicles, and straightened, looking around. The cave was huge, a vast, ice-covered cavern, sunlight slanting in through the holes in the roof far, far above us. The ceiling sparkled, every square inch covered with sharp, gleaming icicles, some longer than I was tall. A breeze howled through the cave, and the icicles tinkled like wind chimes, filling the cavern with song.

"Ash," I said as the Winter prince came through the opening, shaking snow from his hair. "What—"

"Shh." Ash put a finger against my lips, shaking his head in warning. He pointed to the skeletons scattered about the cave, half-buried in snow. The bones of some large animal lay sprawled on the ground nearby, a fallen icicle jutting through its ribs. I winced and nodded my understanding.

And then something black and monstrous exploded through the cave mouth, snapping at my face.

Ash jerked me backward, his hand snaking around my

mouth to stifle my shriek, as the snap of teeth echoed inches from my head. If Ash's hand hadn't been pressed hard against my lips, I would've screamed again as two burning, yellow-green eyes peered at me from the face in the door.

It was a wolf, a huge black wolf the size of a grizzly bear, only longer and leaner and a thousand times more frightening. This wasn't the majestic creature you saw on the nature channels, loping through the snowy wilderness with its pack. This was the rabid beast in every horror movie about wolves: dark shaggy fur, slavering muzzle, glowing, pupil-less eyes. Its lips were curled back to reveal shiny fangs longer then my hand, and ribbons of drool dripped from its jaws, crystallizing in the snow. Only its head fit through the opening, but it turned its muzzle in my direction, and I swore it grinned at me.

"Meghan Chase. I finally found you."

Ash pulled me back farther, toward the far end of the cave, as the enormous wolf thrashed and wriggled in the doorway, somehow, impossibly, sliding through. My heart thudded as the creature rose to its full height inside the cave. He seemed to fill the chamber. Ash shoved me behind him, pressing me against the wall beneath a rocky overhang, and drew his sword. The wolf chuckled, the deep tone making my skin crawl, and bared his teeth in a savage grin.

"Think you're going to hurt me with that little thing?" His guttural voice echoed through the cavern, and icicles clinked above him, swaying dangerously. "Do you know who I am, boy?" He lowered his head, peeling his lips back. "I am *Wolf.* I am older than you, older than Mab, older than the most ancient faery to walk this realm. I was in stories long before the humans knew my name, and even then they feared me." He took one step forward, his huge paw sinking into the snow. "I am the wolf at the door, the creature that stalked the girl in the red hood to Grandma's house. I am the wolf who becomes a man, and the man who is a beast inside. My stories outnumber all the tales ever told, and you cannot kill me."

"I know who you are." Ash's voice shook slightly, which chilled me even more. That Ash, fearless, unshakable Ash, was afraid of this thing filled me with dread. "But you're here for the Summer princess, and I have my own vow to bring her back to my court. So I can't let you take her." He brandished his sword, the faery glamour of Winter swirling around him. "You'll have to go through me first."

The Wolf smiled. "As you wish."

He lunged with a roar, jaws gaping wide, tongue lolling between dripping fangs. Insanely fast, he covered the area in a single bound and leaped at us, a dark blur in the air. I shrank back as the Wolf charged but Ash whirled, glamour snapping around him, and slammed his sword hilt into the wall.

A deafening crack echoed throughout the cavern, like a gunshot. The ceiling trembled, icicles clicking wildly and then, like a million china plates being smashed at once, collapsed in a deadly gleaming rain. The Wolf paused for an instant, looking up...and was buried under a ton of pointed crystal shards.

I turned away, covering my eyes as a single high-pitched yelp rose over the clatter of smashing ice. The snow cleared, the cacophony died away and there was silence.

I started to peek through my fingers, but Ash grabbed my hand, blocking my view. "Don't look," he warned softly, and I saw a spatter of red behind him, seeping through the snow, making my stomach curl. "Let's get out of here."

Deliberately not looking at the dark mass in the center of the room, we fled the cave, scrambling through the hole back into the clearing. Snow was falling, light wispy flakes that danced on the breeze. I took a shaky breath, and the cold burned my lungs, reminding me I was still alive. I glanced at Ash, who was staring back at the cave mouth.

"The Wolf," he murmured, almost to himself. "The Big Bad Wolf. Few ever live to tell of seeing him." He shook his head in wonder, glancing back at me. "I wonder why he was after you? Who sent him, that he would track us this far?"

"Mab?" I guessed. Ash snorted and his lips curled in a smirk.

"Mab wants you alive," he said, walking away from the cave mouth, back toward the gully. I pulled my hood up and hurried after him, jogging through the snow. "You're no use to her dead. She was very specific about that. Besides, she wouldn't put me at risk like that." He paused, frowning slightly. "I think."

He sounded terribly unsure. I felt a pang of sympathy, that Ash didn't know if his queen, his own mother, would send the Wolf after us, not caring if it hurt him. I closed the last few paces and reached out to touch his arm.

The Wolf's giant, bloody head lunged between us with a roar, knocking me back, sending me sprawling. Lightning quick, Ash drew his sword, a second too late. The monster's jaws clamped shut on his arm, and the Wolf hurled him away. I screamed.

"I told you, you can't kill me!" the Wolf snarled, stalking toward Ash, who had rolled to his feet with his sword in front of him. The thick, shaggy pelt was covered in blood. It dripped in a steady rain to the ground, raising faint puffs of steam where it struck the snow. Icicles stuck out of his body like a hundred jagged spears. Despite that, he moved smoothly, easily, as if he felt no pain.

"Foolish boy," the Wolf growled, circling Ash, leaving a crimson trail behind him. "You will not win this. I am immortal."

"Meghan, run," Ash ordered, his eyes never leaving the

Wolf. His own blood dripped from his sword arm to stain the ground. "The Winter Court isn't far from here. You'll be protected—tell whomever you meet that Ash sent you. Run, now."

"I'm not leaving!"

"Go!"

The Wolf shook himself, sending blood, foam and icicles flying. "I will deal with you momentarily, Princess," he growled, lowering himself into a crouch. Muscles bunched under his shaggy pelt, and the icicles gleamed as they stuck out of his thigh and bony ribs. "Are you ready, boy? Here I come!"

He leaped. Ash brought up his sword. And I charged the Wolf.

The Wolf hit Ash with the full weight of his body behind him, driving them both into the snow, ignoring the sword that slashed into his shoulder. His massive paws slammed into Ash's chest and arms, pinning the sword beneath them. They hit the ground with the Wolf on top, those huge jaws gaping wide to bite off Ash's head.

I slammed into the Wolf with every bit of strength I had, aiming for one of those gleaming ice spears, driving my shoulder into it. The sharp edge sliced into me, cutting my skin through the cloak, but I felt the spear jam farther into the Wolf's ribs. The huge creature let out a startled, painful yelp and swung around, pinning me with a blazing yellow glare.

"Foolish girl! What are you doing? I'm trying to help you!"

Shocked, I stared at him, panting. Still pinned beneath the Wolf, Ash tried to get up, but two giant paws held him down. "What are you talking about?" I demanded. "Let Ash go, if you say you're helping me."

The beast shook his head. "I was sent to rescue you and kill this one," he replied, shifting his weight to better lean on Ash, who gritted his teeth in pain. "You are a prisoner no more, Princess. Just let me finish him off and you can return to the Summer Court."

"No!" I lunged forward as the Wolf turned back, opening his jaws. "Don't kill him! I'm not a prisoner. We made a deal, a contract—I would go to the Winter Court in return for his help. He's not keeping me here by force. I *chose* this."

The Wolf blinked slowly. "You made a contract," he repeated.

"Yes."

"A contract with this one."

"Yes!"

"Then…your father was mistaken."

"Oberon?" I stared at him, aghast. "Oberon ordered you to do this?"

The Wolf snorted. "No one orders me," he growled, baring his fangs. "The Summer Lord thought you had been captured. He asked me to find you, kill your captor and free you to return to the Summer Court. He thought the hunt might be difficult, so deep within Winter's territory, and I could not pass up the challenge." The Wolf paused, scrutinizing me with intense yellow eyes, a flicker of irritation crossing his face. "However, if you have made a deal with the Winter prince, that changes things. The agreement with Oberon was to rescue you from your captor, and you do not have a captor. Therefore…" He snarled in annoyance and reluctantly stepped back, freeing Ash from beneath his paws. "I must honor the contract and let you go."

He glared at us as he moved aside, the Hunter so close to his prey only to have it ripped from his jaws. I stepped between him and Ash, just in case the Wolf changed his mind, and helped the prince to his feet. Ash's sword arm bled freely, and the other was wrapped around his ribs, as if the Wolf's weight had crushed them. Sheathing his blade, he faced our pursuer and gave a slight bow.

The Wolf nodded. "You're very lucky," he told Ash. "Today." Backing off, he shook himself once more and glared at us with grudging respect. "It was a good chase. Pray we do not meet again, for you will not even see me coming."

Throwing back his head, the Wolf howled, wild and chilling, making the hairs on my neck stand up. Bounding into the trees, his huge dark form vanished instantly, swallowed up by snow and shadows, and we were alone.

I looked at Ash in concern. "Are you all right? Can you walk?"

He took a step and winced, sinking to one knee. "Give me a moment."

"Come on." I slipped an arm under his shoulder and carefully eased him upright. The clearing looked like a war zone: trampled snow, crushed vegetation and blood everywhere. It could attract Unseelie predators and, though I was sure none were as scary as the Big Bad Wolf, Ash was in no shape to fight them off. "We're going back to the cave."

He didn't argue, and together we limped across the clearing to the ice cave, ducking inside. The floor was a mess of shattered icicles, making passage difficult and treacherous, but we found a clear space near the back of the room. Ash sank down against the wall, and I tore a strip off the hem of my cloak.

He was silent as I wrapped the makeshift bandage around his arm, but I could feel his eyes on me as I tied it off. Releasing his arm, I looked up to meet his silvery gaze. Ash blinked slowly, giving me that look that meant he was trying to figure me out.

"Why didn't you run?" he asked softly. "If you didn't stop the Wolf, you wouldn't have to come back to Tir Na Nog. You would have been free."

I frowned at him.

"I agreed to that contract, same as you," I said, and watched his brow furrow, as if puzzled by choices that made no sense to him. Angry now, I glared at the prince. "What, you think just because I'm human I would back out? I knew what I was getting into, and I am going to uphold my end of the bargain, no matter what happens. And if you think I would leave you to that monster just so I wouldn't have to meet Mab, then you don't know me at all."

"It's *because* you're human," Ash continued in that same quiet voice, holding my gaze, "that you missed a tactical opportunity. A Winter fey in your position wouldn't have saved me. They wouldn't let their emotions get in the way. Emotions can make you weak, make you question the obvious. If you're going to survive in the Unseelie Court, you have to start thinking like them."

"Well, I'm *not* like them." I rose and took a step back, trying to ignore the feelings of hurt, the stupid angry tears pressing at the corners of my eyes. "I'm not a Winter faery—I'm human, with human feelings and emotions. I can't just shut them off like you can. Though the next time you're about to get eaten or killed, I guess you don't want me saving your life."

I whirled to stalk away, but Ash rose with blinding speed and gripped my upper arms. I stiffened, locking my knees and keeping my back straight, but struggling with him would have been useless. Even wounded and bleeding as he was, he was much stronger than me.

"I'm not ungrateful," he murmured against my ear, making my stomach flutter despite itself. "I just want you to understand. The Winter Court preys on the weak. It's their nature. They will try to tear you apart, physically and emotionally, and I won't always be there to protect you."

I shivered, anger melting away as my own doubts and fears

came rushing back. Ash sighed, and I felt his forehead touch the back of my hair, his breath fanning my neck. "I don't want to do this," he admitted in a low, anguished voice. "I don't want to see what they'll try to do to you. A Summer faery in the Winter Court doesn't stand much of a chance. But I vowed that I would bring you back, and I'm bound to that promise." He raised his head, squeezing my shoulders in an almost painful grip as his voice dropped a few octaves, turning grim and cold. "So, you have to be stronger than they are. You can't let down your guard, no matter what. They will lead you on, with games and pretty words, and they will take pleasure in your misery. Don't let them get to you. And don't trust anyone." He paused, and his voice went even lower. "Not even me."

"I'll always trust you," I whispered without thinking, and his hands tightened, turning me to face him almost savagely.

"No," he said, narrowing his eyes. "You won't. I'm your enemy, Meghan. Never forget that. If Mab tells me to kill you in front of the entire court, it's my duty to obey. If she orders Rowan or Sage to carve you up slowly, making sure you suffer every second of it, I'm expected to stand there and let them do it. Do you understand? I'm a prince of the Unseelie—cold, ruthless and unmerciful. My feelings for you don't matter in the Winter Court. Summer and Winter will always be on opposite sides, and nothing will change that."

I knew I should be afraid of him. He was an Unseelie prince after all, and had basically admitted he would kill me if Mab ordered him to. But he also admitted to having feelings for me—feelings that didn't matter, true, but it still made my stomach squirm when I heard it. And maybe I was being naive, but I couldn't believe Ash would willingly hurt me, even in the Winter Court. Not with the way he was looking at me now, his silver eyes conflicted and angry.

He stared at me a moment longer, then sighed. "You didn't hear a word I said, did you?" he murmured, closing his eyes.

"I'm not afraid," I told him, which was a lie; I was terrified of Mab and the Unseelie Court that waited at the end of this journey. But if Ash was there, I would be all right.

"You are infuriatingly stubborn," Ash muttered, raking a hand through his hair. "I don't know how I'm going to protect you when you have no concept of self-preservation."

I stepped close to him, placing a hand on his chest, feeling his heart beat under his shirt. "I trust you," I said, rising up so our faces were inches apart, trailing my fingers down his stomach. "I know you'll find a way."

His breath hitched, and he regarded me hungrily. "You're playing with fire, you know that?"

"That's weird, considering you're an ice prin—" I didn't get any further, as Ash leaned in and kissed me. I looped my arms around his neck as his snaked around my waist, and for a few moments, the cold couldn't touch me.

We spent the night in the cave, both to give Ash a chance to heal from his wounds and to give us one more night of rest before entering Tir Na Nog. It didn't take long for Ash to recover. The fey heal insanely fast, especially if they are within their own territories, and by the time darkness fell his bite wounds were almost gone. As the temperature dropped, he started a fire, solely for my benefit, and we sat around the flames sharing the last of the food, lost in our own thoughts.

Outside, the snow continued to fall, piling outside the entrance and in the center of the room through the holes in the ceiling. It sparkled in the icy moonlight, like flakes of diamonds drifting from the sky, tempting me to stand in the center of the light and catch them on my tongue.

Ash was silent through most of the evening. He'd broken

the kiss earlier, pulling away with a guilty, agonized look, and mumbled something about making camp. Since then, he'd given me short, one-word answers whenever I tried talking to him, and avoided eye contact whenever possible.

He sat across from me now, chin on his hands, brooding into the fire. Part of me wanted to walk up to him and hug him from behind, and part of me wanted to hurl a snowball at his perfect face to get some kind of reaction.

I opted for a less suicidal route. "Hey," I said, poking at the flames with a stick, making them cough sparks. "Earth to Ash. What are you thinking about?"

He didn't move, and for a second I thought he would reply with his favorite one-word answer of the night: *nothing*. But after a moment he sighed and his eyes flickered, very briefly, to mine.

"Home," he said quietly. "I'm thinking of home. Of the court."

"Do you miss it?"

Another pause, and he shook his head slowly. "No."

"But it's your home."

"It's the place I was born. That's all." He sighed and gazed into the fire. "I don't go back often, and I rarely stay at court for any length of time."

I thought of Mom, and Ethan, and our tiny farmhouse out in the bayou, and a lump rose to my throat. "That must be lonely," I murmured. "Don't you get homesick once in a while?"

Ash regarded me across the flames, understanding and sympathy dawning in his gaze. "My family," he said in a solemn voice, "is not like yours."

He rose gracefully, abruptly, as if the subject had become tiring. "Get some sleep," he said, and the chill was back in his voice. "Tomorrow we reach the Winter Court. Queen Mab will be anxious to meet you."

My gut twisted. I curled up inside my cloak, as close to the fire as I dared, and let my mind go blank. I was certain that Ash's last words would prevent me from getting any sleep, but I was more exhausted than I realized and soon drifted into oblivion.

That night, for the first time, I dreamed of the Iron King.

The scene was eerily familiar. I stood atop a great iron tower, a hot wind stinging my face, smelling of ozone and chemicals. Before me, a huge metal throne rose into the mottled yellow sky, black iron spikes raking the clouds. Behind me, Ash's cold, pale body was sprawled against the edge of a fountain, blood oozing slowly into the water.

Machina the Iron King stood at the top of his metal throne, long silver hair whipping in the wind. His back was to me, the numerous iron cables extending from his shoulders and spine surrounding him like glittering wings.

I took a step forward, squinting up at the silhouette on the throne. "Machina!" I called, my voice sounding weak and small in the wind. "Where's my brother?"

The Iron King raised his head slightly, but didn't turn around. "Your brother?"

"Yes, my brother. Ethan. You stole him and brought him here." I kept walking, ignoring the wind that tore at my hair and clothes. Thunder boomed overhead, and the mottled yellow clouds turned black and crimson. "You wanted to lure me here," I continued, reaching the base of the throne. "You wanted me to become your queen in exchange for Ethan. Well, here I am. Now let my brother go."

Machina turned. Only it wasn't the Iron King's sharp, intelligent face that stared down at me.

It was my own.

★ ★ ★

I jerked awake, my heart hammering against my ribs, cold sweat trickling down my back. The fire had gone out, and the ice cave lay dark and empty, though the sky showing through the holes was already light. Snow lay in huge glimmering piles where it had drifted in through the roof, and several new icicles were already forming on the ceiling, growing back like teeth. Ash was nowhere to be seen.

Still trembling from the nightmare, I rolled away from the dead campfire and stood, shaking snow clumps from my hair. Pulling my cloak tighter around myself, I went searching for Ash.

I didn't have to look far. He stood outside in the clearing, snow flurries drifting around him, his sword glowing blue against the white. From the sweeping footprints in the snow, I knew he'd been practicing sword drills, but now he stood motionless, his back to me, gazing toward the entrance of the gully.

I pulled up my hood and walked out, tromping through the deep snow until I stood beside him. He acknowledged me with a flick of his eyes, but otherwise didn't move, his gaze riveted to the edge of the canyon.

"They're coming," he murmured.

A group of horses appeared then, seeming to materialize out of the falling snow, pure white and blue-eyed, trotting a few inches above the ground. Atop them sat Winter knights in icy blue-and-black armor, their gazes cold beneath their snarling wolf helms.

Ash stepped forward, very subtly moving in front of me as the knights swept up, horses snorting small geysers from flared nostrils. "Prince Ash," one knight said formally, bowing in the saddle. "Her majesty the queen has been informed of your return and has sent us to escort you and the…human to the palace."

I bristled at the way he said *human*, the way his lip curled like I was some kind of disgusting insect, but Ash didn't seem terribly fazed by their arrival.

"I don't need an escort," he said in a bored voice. "Return to the palace and tell Queen Mab I will arrive shortly. I'm perfectly capable of handling the human by myself."

I cringed at his tone. He was back to being Prince Ash, third son of the Unseelie Court, dangerous, cold and heartless. The knights didn't seem at all surprised, which somehow made me even more apprehensive. This cold, hostile prince was the Ash they were used to.

"I'm afraid the queen insists, Your Highness," the first one replied, unapologetic. "By order of Queen Mab, you and the Summer girl will come with us to the Winter Court. She is rather impatient for your arrival."

Ash sighed.

"Very well," he muttered, not even looking at me as he swung into an empty saddle. Before I could protest, another knight reached down and pulled me up in front of him. "Let's get this over with."

We rode for several silent hours. The knights did not speak to me, Ash or each other, and the horse's hooves made no sound as they galloped over the snow. Ash didn't even look in my direction; his face remained blank and cold throughout the ride.

Completely ignored, I was left to my own thoughts, which were dark and growing more disturbing the farther we went. I missed home. I was terrified of meeting Queen Mab. And Ash had turned into someone cold and unfamiliar. I replayed our last kiss in my mind, clinging to it like a life vest in a raging sea. Had I imagined his feelings for me, misread his intentions? What if everything he'd said was just a ploy, a scheme to get me to Tir Na Nog and the queen?

No, I couldn't believe that. The emotion on his face that night was real. I had to believe that he cared, I had to believe in him, or I would go crazy.

Night was falling and a huge frozen moon was peeking over the tops of the trees when we came to a vast, icy lake. Jagged ice floes crinkled against one another near the shoreline, and fog writhed along the surface of the water. A long wooden dock stretched toward the middle of the lake, vanishing into the hanging mist.

As I wondered how close we were to the Winter Court, the knights abruptly steered their horses onto the rickety dock and rode single file, the dark waters of the lake lapping the posts beneath us. I squinted and peered through the fog, wondering if the Winter Court was on an island in the center.

The mist cleared away for just a moment, and I saw the edge of the dock, dropping away into dark, murky lake water. The horses broke into a trot, then a full gallop, snorting eagerly, as the end of the dock rushed at us with terrifying speed.

I closed my eyes…and the horses leaped.

We hit the water with a loud splash and sank quickly into the icy depths. The horse didn't even try to resurface, and the knight's grip was firm, so I couldn't kick away. I held my breath and fought down panic as we dropped deeper and deeper into the frigid waters.

Then, suddenly, we resurfaced, bursting out with the same noisy splash, sending water flying. Gasping, I rubbed my eyes and looked around, confused and disoriented. I didn't recall the horse swimming back up. Where were we, anyway?

My gaze focused, my breath caught and I forgot about everything else.

A massive underground city loomed before me, lit up with

millions of tiny lights, gleaming yellow, blue and green like a blanket of stars. From where we floated in the black waters of the lake, I could see large stone buildings, streets winding upward in a spiral pattern and ice covering everything. The cavern above soared into darkness, farther than I could see, and the twinkling lights made the entire city glow with hazy etherealness.

At the top of a hill, casting its shadow over everything, an enormous, ice-covered palace stood proudly against the black. I shivered, and the knight behind me spoke for the first time.

"Welcome to Tir Na Nog."

I glanced at Ash and finally caught his gaze. For a moment, the Unseelie prince looked torn, balanced between emotion and duty, his eyes begging forgiveness. But a half second later he turned away, and his face shut into that blank mask once more.

We rode through the snow-laced streets toward the palace, and the denizens of the Unseelie Court watched us pass with glowing, inhuman eyes. We stopped at the palace doors, where a pair of monstrous ogres glared menacingly, drool dripping from their tusks, but let us through without a word.

Even within the palace, the rooms and hallways were coated with frost and translucent, crystal ice in various colors; it was possibly colder inside than it was outside. More Unseelie roamed the corridors: goblins, hags, redcaps, all watching me with hungry, evil grins. But since I was flanked by a group of stone-faced knights and one lethally calm Winter prince, none dared do more than leer at me.

The knights escorted us to a pair of soaring double doors carved with the images of frozen trees. If you looked closely, you could almost see faces peering at you through the branches, but if you blinked or glanced away they would be gone. A chill wafted from between the cracks, colder than I thought possible, even in this palace of ice. It brushed across my skin and tiny needles of cold stabbed into me. I shivered and stepped back.

The knights, I realized, were now standing at attention along the corridor, gazing straight ahead, paying us no attention. As I rubbed my stinging arms, Ash stepped close, not touching me, but close enough to make my heart beat faster. With his back to the knights, he put a hand on the door and paused, as if gathering his resolve.

"This is the throne room," he murmured in a low voice. "Queen Mab is on the other side. Are you ready?"

I wasn't, really, but nodded, anyway. "Let's do this," I whispered, and Ash pushed open the door.

A blast of that same cold, stinging air hit my face as we went through, nearly taking my breath away. The room beyond was painfully cold; ice columns held up the ceiling, and the floor was slick and frozen. In the center of the room, surrounded by pale, aloof Winter gentry and pet goblins, the queen of the Unseelie Court waited for us.

Queen Mab sat atop her throne of ice, regal, beautiful and terrifying. Her skin was paler than snow, her blue-black hair coiled elegantly atop her head, held in place with icy needles. She wore a cloak of white fur and held a crystal goblet in one delicate, long-fingered hand. Her eyes, black and as depthless as space, rose slowly, capturing me in a piercing stare. Above the furred ruff, bloodred lips curled into a slow smile.

"Meghan Chase," Queen Mab purred. "Welcome to the Winter Court. Please, make yourself comfortable. I'm afraid you could be here for a long, long time."

★ ★ ★ ★ ★

Thank you for coming on this journey into the Nevernever.
We hope you enjoyed your stay!
Look for special editions of the first four books in
The Iron Fey series, with bonus material and exclusives.
Next up, book 2, The Iron Daughter!

Meanwhile…we are proud to present an
exclusive excerpt from the first original hardcover novel
in The Iron Fey…

The Iron Raven

Turn the page to meet the infamous prankster
of the Summer Court as you've never seen him before…
Welcome back to the land of Faery,
where anything can happen…and always does.

Only from Julie Kagawa and Inkyard Press!

I love the Goblin Market.

I mean, don't get me wrong, the Market is super sketchy and dangerous. Make the wrong deal and you'll find yourself cursed or enslaved for a thousand years. Or under contract to give away your firstborn kid—not that I have any. Or in possession of a thing that wasn't *quite* what you were expecting, due to the fact that it tries to eat your face off every now and again. You can find anything in the Goblin Market. Need a potion that will make someone fall in love with you? Child's play; there's a vendor on every corner that will sell you one. Want to buy a lamp with a genie inside that will grant you three wishes? The Goblin Market has you covered. What they neglect to mention is that the love potion you bought will make your target psychotically obsessed with you, and the genie will grant your wishes in the most twisted and sadistic way possible, because that's what they do. And this is after you've bargained away your soul, or your voice, or your best friend. The prices at the Goblin Market are high—mostly too high—for anyone to pay without massive regrets.

So yeah, the Goblin Market equals dangerous. Dangerous, risky…and tempting. Because that's the allure, isn't it? What's life without a little danger? And Robin Goodfellow never backs down from a challenge.

It was midnight as I strolled through the weed-covered gates of the abandoned amusement park, the grounds silver and black under the light of the full moon. Beyond the fence, I could see the rusted hull of the Ferris wheel silhouetted against the sky, looming over the trees. Straight ahead, an ancient carousel sat silently in the dirt, its once bright horses flaking and chipped, paint and plaster scattered around the platform. An old popcorn booth rested close by, the glass shattered, all the kernels long nibbled away by rats or crows or roaches. Pulling up the hood of my green hoodie, I headed into the park.

Crowds of fey milled through the aisles, faeries of every shape, size, and court, from Summer to Winter to the wyldwood, as the Goblin Market was neutral ground and everyone was welcome as long as they could pay. The vendors at the various booths came in every shape and size, as well. A green, pointy-eared goblin stood beside a table selling dice sets of carved bone. A few tents down, a Summer gentry brushed at her collection of cloaks, all made of leaves, feathers, or spiderweb. The smell of grilled meat filled the air, coming from a spit with an entire boar spinning slowly over the flames, a lanky gray troll turning the handle. Its beady red eyes caught sight of me and widened, the troll's sinewy body straightening in alarm. With a grin, I ducked my head and melted into the crowd. As fun as pissing off a troll could be, the aftermath would probably cut my visit to the Goblin Market short, and I wasn't quite ready to leave.

The ground under my boots became packed and hard as I walked down the center fairway, colorful booths and tents lining either side. I hesitated at a table selling beads that would turn into mice if they got wet, my brain spinning with hilarious ideas, but I shook my head with a frown. *Stop it, Goodfellow. You're already in hot water with Titania*, I reminded myself. *Making her tub explode with rodents while she's taking a bath would get the hounds and the knights and those creepy spriggan assassins sent after you. It's* probably *not worth it.*

Pause.

Nah, it would be totally worth it.

"Robin Goodfellow?"

I winced at the sound of my name, then turned to the one who had spoken it. Across the aisle, a crinkle-faced gnome whose white hair looked like she'd licked her finger and stuck it in a socket peered at me over a long, low table. The counter before her was lined with green, longnecked bottles that, even from several paces away, let off a heady sweet smell that could make a lesser faery slightly dizzy.

I grinned and stepped up to the table, putting my fingers to my lips. "Shh, Marla. Don't say my name too loudly. I'm incognito tonight."

"Incognito." The ancient gnome scowled, making her eyes nearly disappear into the folds of her face. "In a heap of trouble, more likely. What are you doing here, you terrible thing? And get away from my bottles. The last thing I need is for my wine to *somehow* make its way into the livestock tents. I can just see the nobles' carriages veering into ditches and trees because their horses are all suddenly very drunk."

"What?" I blinked at her, wide-eyed. "That happened at only one Elysium, and no one could prove what went wrong. Though come on, admit that watching Mab's carriage walk in circles the whole way out was hilarious."

"I will admit no such thing," the wine vendor snapped, and jabbed a withered finger in my direction. "Only that you are an incorrigible troublemaker and always up to no good. I don't know why Lord Oberon hasn't banished you permanently."

"Well, he keeps trying." I shrugged, grinning at her. "But it never sticks. I guess I'm just too charming. I've been banished from the Nevernever...what, three times, now? Or, was it four? Eh, it doesn't matter. Eventually, he always orders me to come back. Funny how that happens." It happened because I was far too useful to keep away for long, and Oberon knew it. The gnome shot me a dark look, and I gave a dreamy, over-exaggerated smile. "Though between us, I think Titania secretly misses me too much."

Marla snorted. "If the Summer Queen heard you say that, there'd be lightning storms for a month," she muttered, then straightened in alarm. "Wait, you were looking at Ugfrig's wares a moment ago," she exclaimed. "Don't tell me you were contemplating the mouse beads."

"Well..."

A snuffle interrupted us. I looked down to see a small brown-and-white dog gazing up at me, stub tail wagging. It was cute, in a scraggly, ankle biter kind of way. But I could see the copper gears, cogs, and pistons poking through its fur that marked it as a creature of the Iron Realm. A clockwork hound. Or terrier, I supposed. The pair of flight goggles on its head glittered in the moonlight as the dog gazed up at me and whined.

I smiled. "Hey, pooch," I greeted. "Where did you come from?" It gave a small, hopeful yap, wagging its tail, and I shrugged. "I don't have any gears you can munch on, sorry."

Marla gazed over the edge of the table and recoiled like I was talking to a giant cockroach. "Abomination!" she spat, and the clockwork terrier cringed at the sound of her voice. "Get out of here, monster! Shoo!"

The small creature fled, gears and pistons squeaking as it

scurried away, vanishing around a booth and out of sight. I frowned.

"Well, it's a good thing you scared it off. It looked terribly vicious."

"It was of the Iron Realm," the gnome muttered, wrinkling her nose. "It belongs to the Iron faery that has set up shop in the Goblin Market. Horrible creature. They shouldn't be allowed."

"Wait, there's an Iron faery here? In the Market?" I was surprised. Though there was no law that barred the Iron fey from the Goblin Market, in those early days, most of the traditional fey would not have welcomed their presence. Recently, however, it had been officially decreed that the Goblin Market was open to *all* fey, including the faeries of the Iron Realm. This was mostly at the Iron Queen's insistence, because the faeries of Summer and Winter welcomed change about as well as an old cat welcomed a new puppy. But this was the first I'd heard of one setting up shop.

"Where is this Iron faery?" I asked.

The gnome gave a disapproving sniff. "In a tent on the far edge of the Market," she replied, stabbing a finger in that direction. "Beneath the old Ferris wheel. At least it has the good sense to keep away from the rest of us." She eyed me in a critical manner. "I guess I shouldn't be surprised that someone like you would want to associate with those abominations."

"Nope, that's me. I love hanging around abominations." I grinned at her sour expression, though truthfully, I was surprised at the venom coming from the tiny gnome. Though the Iron fey still faced fear and distrust from the rest of the Nevernever, most residents of Faery had accepted they were here to stay. "But uh, you are aware that we've been at peace with the Iron Realm for years now, right? And that they've done nothing to threaten or aggravate the other courts? And that their queen is kind of a good friend of mine?"

She snorted. "I don't mind the Iron Queen," she stated. "Or the rest of them, as long as they stay within their own borders. But I don't want to have to worry about iron poisoning when I'm in the Goblin Market." Marla shook a finger at me. "The next time you see the Iron Queen, you should tell her to keep her subjects within her own territory, not allow them to wander where they please, terrorizing normal fey."

"Well, this has been a riveting conversation, but I'm afraid I must go." I stepped back from the counter, smoothly avoiding a collision with a dwarf, who grumbled at me under his beard. Tugging my hood up farther, I glanced at Marla over the bottles of wine and offered my best disarming smile. "I'm off to find this Iron vendor and send him your well wishes."

She sighed, shaking her head. "This will fall on deaf ears I'm sure, but be careful, Robin. You might be in the good graces of the Iron Queen, but none of those things can be trusted."

"Careful?" I grinned. "I'm Robin Goodfellow. When am I not careful?"

She rolled her eyes, and I left, melting back into the crowds of the Goblin Market.

Well, that was weird. I wonder what's up? Did a gremlin spit in her wine or something? I wasn't naive. I knew there were those in the Nevernever that still hated and feared Meghan's subjects; I just didn't expect to run into such blatant hostility here. In the Market, you left all grudges, feuds, and personal vendettas behind. It was how a Summer sidhe and a Winter gentry could browse side by side without killing each other. Or why a halfling could walk past a motley of redcaps without fear of having his limbs ripped off. One did not tamper with the sanctity of the Market, especially since many of the vendors sold some of the most dangerous, rare, and questionable items in the entire world of Faery. Make trouble here, and the least that could happen was being banned for life. Not even I would risk pissing off the Goblin Market.

I made my way through scattered booths and tents, ignoring the vendors that called to me. Finally, the crowds thinned, the booths and tents falling away, until I stood beneath the rusted hulk of the Ferris wheel, which groaned softly as the wind blew through the metal frame. Straight ahead stood a strange setup that was part carnival stall, part wagon, part junkyard. The booth sat on four rusty wheels and looked like it had been slapped together with corrugated metal and duct tape. Boxes, crates, and flimsy metal shelves surrounded it, blinking with strands of Christmas lights, and a neon pink sign flashed OPEN against the wall of the booth. Another sign, this one made of wood and iron, had been jammed into the ground near the entrance. "Cricket's Collectables," it read in bold copper letters. "Trinkets, gadgets, oddities."

A low growl echoed from the shadows as I approached the booth, and a pair of clockwork hounds, these much bigger than the brown-and-white terrier from earlier, slid from between crates and boxes to stare at me. They looked like rottweilers, the gears and cogs in their fur spinning lazily as they came forward.

"Oh, hey, guys." I stopped, raising a hand to the dogs, who eyed me with flat, unfriendly gazes. "I come in peace. I'm not going to snitch your stuff." They continued to shoot me baleful looks, and I offered a weak smile. "Um… I'll trade you safe passage for a squeaky bone."

"Ooh, a customer." The door of the stall opened, and a figure emerged, the small brown-and-white dog at her heels. The two clockwork hounds immediately turned and trotted back into the shadows, becoming one with the piles of junk surrounding the stall.

"Howdy, stranger." The figure strode toward me, beaming a bright, toothy smile. She was small and willowy, with long pointed ears and bright copper hair that seemed metallic in nature. She wore a brown leather corset, leather gloves, and knee-high leather boots, all trimmed in gold, iron, and copper gears. Her skin was circuit-board green, and the pair of leather-and-gold goggles perched on her head were almost identical to the dog's.

Yep, this was definably an Iron faery. Just the amount of metal studs and loops in her long ears would be enough to give a normal faery heart palpitations.

"Welcome, welcome!" the Iron faery said. "What can Cricket find for you this fine evening? Have you come to browse my wares or are you looking for something in particular? Waaaaaaait a second," she added before I could answer, and shiny black eyes peered at me beneath the goggles. "I've seen you before. You're Robin Goodfellow, aren't you?"

I grinned. "Guilty as charged."

"Oh, wow." The faery grinned back with excitement. "I hear the stories they tell. You're famous! Is it true you stormed Ferrum's moving fortress with Queen Meghan and helped her defeat the False King? And went to the End of the World with the prince consort? And ventured into the Between to fight the entire army of Forgotten by yourself?"

"All true." I smiled. "Well, most of it, more or less." She sighed dreamily, and I gestured to the booth behind us. "But what about you? Can't imagine you get many customers, even in the Goblin Market."

"Not yet," Cricket admitted cheerfully. "But setting up shop in the Iron Realm sounded so boring. There's huge potential to be had in the Goblin Market! Just think of the profit that will come from being the first Iron faery to run a successful trade alongside the other courts."

"Right," I said. "But there is that small, nagging problem of regular fey being deathly allergic to iron. Kinda hard to sell someone a product that melts their fingers off."

Cricket shrugged. "All great treasures come with a certain amount of risk," she said. "And not all of my wares are from the Iron Realm. Some come from the mortal realm, from the places I've seen and traveled to." She waved an airy hand. "Besides, I'm confident that the regular fey will find a way to deal with their iron intolerance. They'll adapt and evolve, I'm sure of it. It might take a while, but hey, I've got time. Eventually, Cricket's Collectables will be a household name through all of Faery!"

"Yeah…sure," I said, because I didn't want to dampen her enthusiasm. "Well…good luck with that."

She gave me an appraising look. "And what about you? Do you need anything special tonight, Robin Goodfellow? A pocket watch with a heartbeat? A mechanical bird that sings? A handkerchief embroidered with the fur of a silver-metal fox?"

"Um…"

A deep, low growl cut through our conversation. Both clockwork hounds had stepped forward again, only this time, their hackles were raised and their iron teeth were bared to the gums as they came toward me. Cricket turned on them with a frown.

"Ballpeen! Springtrap! That's not nice. I'm with a customer."

"Excuse me."

The quiet voice echoed behind us, and my stomach lurched. Even before we turned around, I knew who it was.